PICTURES AT 11

PICTURES

AT 11

NORMAN SPINRAD

BANTAM BOOKS
NEW YORK   TORONTO   LONDON   SYDNEY   AUCKLAND

PICTURES AT 11

A Bantam Book / December 1994

BOOK DESIGN BY GLEN M. EDELSTEIN

Library of Congress Cataloging-in-Publication Data
Spinrad, Norman.
    Pictures at 11 / Norman Spinrad.
      p.   cm.
    ISBN 0-553-37384-6
    I. Title.   II. Title: Pictures at eleven.
  PS3569.P55P5 1994
  813'.54—dc20   94-11550
                          CIP

Published simultaneously in the United States and Canada

Bantam Books are published by Bantam Books, a division of Bantam
Doubleday Dell Publishing Group, Inc. Its trademark, consisting of
the words "Bantam Books" and the portrayal of a rooster, is
Registered in U.S. Patent and Trademark Office and in other
countries. Marca Registrada. Bantam Books, 1540 Broadway, New
York, New York 10036.

For Angela and Karlheinz Steinmüller
Wir haben Kameraden. . . .

DAY 1

4:45 P.M.

THE BLAZER'S AIR-CONDITIONING sealed Toby Inman away from the ninety-five-degree June heat and saturation smog but did nothing to shield him from the surly boredom of the stop-and-go traffic, so as he inched along east on Sunset toward the station, Toby—like several million of his fellow Angelenos —found himself wishing he really *could* take the subway to work.

Even though his schedule put him inbound against the outbound flow and in theory outside the rush hour too, even though his commute from Van Nuys to East Hollywood was a tool around the block by Los Angeles standards, it *still* took him half an hour minimum to get to work no matter what clever route he tried through L.A.'s more or less permanent gridlock.

The subway, pushed through by an unholy coalition of ecological dreamers, Congressional pork-barrel barons, and Los Angeles real-estate mavens, and built at hideous taxpayers' expense, had a line that in theory would whip him from the Valley to Hollywood in half the time without all this hassle.

In practice, of course, he would have to drive from the house to the nearest subway station, or have Claire drive him, and then either hike for twenty minutes or take a crawl through the Hollywood traffic on a bus at the other end.

Someday, perhaps, it would all go according to the fantasy. The city would somehow magically rearrange itself into a series of high-rise megamalls clustered around subway stations with nothing but parkland in between, cars would become redundant, the smog would clear, the drought would break, the coyotes would retreat back up into the hills, and the San Fernando Valley would become a verdant paradise of orange groves.

For sure. And I'll be the prime-time anchor for major network news or numero uno at CNN, and Claire will be on the wagon, and the kids will be straight-A students, and Jesus H. Christ himself will be the mayor.

Toby pulled into the KLAX parking lot, drove around the side to the staff area, and parked the Blazer snug against the tire-stop with his very own name stenciled on the concrete in fading white-wash.

What a poor boy's dream-come-true *that* had been the first time he did it three years ago!

Poor boy? Methinks you kick a bit too much shit, my son!

Actually, Toby had grown up in relative middle-class comfort in a suburb of Atlanta and had gotten through LSU on a little partial scholarship, a big parental loan, and nothing worse than the usual student odd jobs. With his clean blond good looks, his mellifluous middle-American accent with only a soft breath of Dixie, he had segued from DJing on college radio to an FM DJ job in Athens fresh out of college, to FM newsreader, AM newsreader, tank-town UHF TV, to WBLAR in Columbus, to WBLAR evening news anchor, without what could honestly be called an undue amount of sweat.

True, Columbus, Georgia, was hardly a major market. True that it had seemed like a hick town to Toby when he first arrived to take his first job in VHF TV, and true too that the locals had a thing against city slickers from Atlanta.

But it was also true that even the low reporter on the WBLAR airtime totem pole was instant celebrity in a town the size of Columbus, and a professional hunk like Toby had himself a high old time with the local ladies before finally allowing himself to be caught by Claire Bayley, fairly recent college homecoming queen and general belle of the local ball.

By that time, Toby was anchoring the morning news, and not that long after Ellis was born, he moved up to features at six and eleven, and when Billy was two, old Horace Stone retired, and they made Toby the evening anchor.

Columbus might not have exactly been Atlanta, but it wasn't a bad little town at all, not when you were the cock of the local media walk, and your wife was a grande dame in what passed for local society. Of course Toby had no intention of staying in a place like Columbus forever, but life was good, and he was young, and his career was proceeding more or less nominally. A couple more years in Columbus, and he'd get picked up by a network affiliate in a somewhat bigger market and start moving up the chain to places like Birmingham, New Orleans, maybe even Atlanta, and eventually, who knows, CNN might need a boy like him for a national beat, and. . . .

No, Toby wasn't exactly some poor shit-kicker when the big call from Eddie Franker came. He was a real celebrity, a young man moving up at a measured pace, a major media catfish in this minor media pond. He had more or less expected to move onwards and upwards long about now. . . .

Still, he hadn't imagined it would be so far so fast.

Main evening news anchor in a small southern city to main evening news anchor in *Los Angeles* in a single bound! A 25 percent pay raise! A fat relocation bonus! Prime-time exposure in *Hollywood*! Surely a major network position could only be a year or two away!

If not exactly a poor boy's dream-come-true, it sure had been a small-town news anchor's dream of a major career move come true, or so it had seemed at the time.

At the time . . .

At the time, Claire had been all for it, and even the boys were caught up in the fantasy. Disneyland! Movie stars! Roger Rabbit! The Dodgers!

Franker had flown them all out from Atlanta business class, put them up in a by-the-week furnished apartment, found them a three-bedroom house in northern Van Nuys to rent, and in fact the biggest decision they had to make was the cars.

Back in Columbus, they had a four-year-old Dodge minivan as the main family vehicle and a three-year-old white Firebird convertible in which to arrive wherever as Prince and/or Princess of the city. This would obviously not do for Hollywood, the name by which they thought of all of Los Angeles at the time, besides which they could hardly drive both cars solo from Georgia to California.

So they hired a nanny for the boys, flew back, unloaded the

Dodge at a distressed price, closed things down in Columbus, and drove the Firebird back to L.A., a romantic seven days on the road that improved their love life but did little for the transmission and rear end.

Most of the relocation bonus went into fixing up the Firebird and buying the Blazer. There had been much discussion of what to buy during the cross-country drive, with Claire entertaining fantasies of humongous Mercedeses and Toby dreaming of Porsches and Ferraris, but in the real world they needed a solid four-seater with plenty of cargo space. Such German and Italian fantasies were out of reach anyway; two young boys would destroy the upholstery, besides which Toby had his qualms about the political correctness of purchasing foreign iron.

So they finally settled on this four-wheel-drive Blazer, and did it up brown, or rather chrome and royal blue, loading it with everything from air-conditioning, CD-stereo, car phone, and leather upholstery to custom pinstriping, fog lights, long-distance lights, outsized mag wheels, and smoked-glass windows.

It might not have been a Porsche or a Ferrari, but the first time Toby pulled this downhome dreamboat into the KLAX lot and parked it in his very own space with the lettering still fresh and shiny had been a perfect Hollywood version of a Hollywood dream-come-true.

Toby sighed, turned off the engine, pocketed the keys, braced himself for the shock, opened the door, and stepped out of the protection of the air-conditioning and into the naked atmosphere of Planet Los Angeles.

As a son of the South, Toby had grown up accustomed to sultry climes, and indeed, degree for degree, Los Angeles's dry desert heat would have been much more bearable than the same temperature in Georgia, let alone the steambath of a New Orleans summer, were it not for the smog.

But that was like saying that Chernobyl would be an okay place to live if only it wasn't still radioactive. Old-time Angelenos claimed that the smog had been worse back in the 1960s, before various clean-air acts had cleaned up cars' exhausts, but Toby found that mercifully hard to imagine.

You could *see* this shit even up close. The air had a strange kind of dull gray sparkiness to it, and everything inside it looked a bit washed of color, like a TV monitor with the gain set too low. Toby couldn't exactly taste it, maybe, but he could feel it drying his eyeballs and sandpapering the back of his throat even on the short walk across the parking lot from his air-conditioned car to the air-conditioned building.

Yet this was only Hollywood. You could take Mulholland Drive along the crest of the Santa Monica Mountains, and look down north into the Valley or south toward Torrance and Long Beach where the cityscape disappeared beneath crud that was visibly *brown*. On a really bad day, there were patches over certain stretches of freeway that shone a sickly luminous *green*.

And this was only June. According to the old-timers, meaning anyone who had been in L.A. more than ten years, this wasn't even supposed to be the smog season; it used to be the end of the so-called rainy season.

Heather Blake had done one of her minifeatures on the smog and the disappearance of Southern California rainy seasons last Thursday. According to the chrome-dome from USC, all the good done by the air-quality laws in the past two or three decades had been overwhelmed by the population increase, human and automotive, more and more cars on the road that spent more and more dirty time idling in the gridlock traffic, plus the greenhouse warming, and the ozone erosion, and something about the snowfall in the Sierras and. . . .

Toby shrugged. The bottom line was that the endless drought went on, the coyotes got more desperate, and the smog had been like this for about nine or ten months a year for as long as Toby had been here.

Like everything else about the Hollywood myth, even the fabled Southern Californian climate dissolved on the ground into the grubby reality of Los Angeles.

Including the KLAX building itself. What a letdown it had been at first sight! Toby had pictured a gleaming tower of black glass set in a vast white plaza festooned with palm trees. Only when he drove past Universal City a day later and saw the Black Tower did he realize that he had picked up his notion of a big-time television station on Sunset Boulevard in Hollywood from a TV image of this studio headquarters in the Valley.

KLAX was indeed located on Sunset Boulevard in Hollywood,

but in *East Hollywood* where the property values were more afford-able, the palm trees bedraggled and moribund, and the neighbors ran to the likes of obscure Asian car dealerships, discount depart-ment stores, porn movie houses, and Thai pizza parlors.

The building itself was older and certainly seedier than the WBLAR building in Columbus—five stories of dirty pink stucco occupying about a quarter of a block.

There was a tall pipe-frame structure beside it holding the sta-tion logo shakily aloft and pretending to be a broadcast tower, an-other seedy piece of Hollywood illusion. Actually, nothing was broadcast from down here in the lowlands. The satellite dishes on the roof linked the station to the StarNet transponders, and a micro-wave antenna atop the phony broadcast tower beamed the local signal to the broadcast complex up in the hills used by most of the independents.

Toby ambled quickly around to the main front entrance. The building wasn't much, but after all, when you thought about it, a local independent TV station in Los Angeles really needed no more floor space than the same sort of operation in Bumfuck, Mississippi.

Toby's mood improved as soon as he stepped inside. Claire's increasingly booze-sodden boredom, the boys' school problems and isolated friendlessness, the necessity of driving them everywhere, the necessity of driving everywhere period, the endless traffic, the blind-ing heat, the choking smog, the damn coyotes—that was all *Los Angeles,* that was *out there.*

This was *in here,* this was The Station, and once you were in-side, it didn't matter all that much whether it was WBLAR in Co-lumbus or KLAX in Los Angeles.

A sealed air-conditioned environment with no windows except for the offices. Cool. Windless. Optimum humidity. A little public lobby with only the emergency fire exit connecting it to the rest of the building. A receptionist in a glassed-off booth controlling access to the working interior. A bored security guard reading a dirty comic book in there with her.

Columbus or L.A., not all that different. Different accents from the off-air staff. Somewhat different graffiti in the toilet. Same corkboard bulletin boards. Same crummy coffee.

"Afternoon, Mr. Inman."

"Afternoon, Dawnie."

Same sort of greeting from the same sort of receptionist as she buzzed you inside, and probably the same sort of fantasy inside her head if you were the main news anchor, though Toby hadn't checked that out as yet, and probably wouldn't.

As the anchor-man hunk back in Columbus, married or not, Toby could have pretty much scored at will. But maybe because it *had* been so readily available, because he *was* the cock of the walk, and because he was already married to the belle of the burg, he had remained disgustingly and happily faithful.

In L.A., though, where there were hundreds of male faces more recognizable than his own and legions of wannabe actors who were hunkier, and where Claire was devolving into a bored Valley hausfrau under the pressure of unaccustomed anonymity and the ubiquitous presence of endless would-be starlets at least as good-looking as she was, and where Toby's level of celebrity was reduced to the ability to maybe walk into some bar and eventually be dimly recognized as some nameless face off the tube by one of same—well, after a few drinks, a quickie in a convenient nearby motel with the hourly meter running was no longer always above him.

But while an uncomplicated piece of ass once in a while to keep your pecker up might be no worse than slightly sleazy, screwing around with station staff if you were an anchor, here, no less than in Columbus, was, moral questions aside, major stupid.

Nine times out of ten, they had fantasies of some kind of *affair* in their heads, and once it got through to them that all *you* were interested in was a quickie once in a while or a one-shot, they did tend to get vindictive, they did lose all motivation to be discreet, and, whatever his problems at home, Toby Inman wanted no such high-school intrigues in the workplace.

Toby stopped for a piss in the first-floor men's room, then made his way to the green room to have his makeup applied.

KLAX, like any such independent in a major market these days, was a shoestring operation trying to survive on a minuscule market share. Mostly, the station ran moldy syndicate packages of network reruns dating back to *Gilligan's Island, I Dream of Jeannie,* and of course the ever-popular *Star Trek: The Geriatric Generation,* ancient horror movies and westerns, syndicated soaps on their third run, old cartoons for the kiddies, taped wrestling, and things cheaper and worse when they were to be had.

Meaning that the only programming of its own that the station did was a cooking show, a few talk shows, the occasional feature, and live news at seven A.M., noon, six P.M., and eleven. Meaning that there were only two live broadcasting studios, both on the first floor, one for the standing newsroom set and the other for everything else, with the control room between them and the shared green room, such as it was, located across the corridor.

Some smartass had actually had the walls of the room painted a perky lime green long before Toby had arrived at KLAX, though by now years of smoke and greaseburger fumes had browned them to the usual grim institutional shade. The ceiling was grayish-white fiberboard, the carpeting the expected dusty brown, and the furniture was the usual collection of ancient mismatched sofas and armchairs and old motel tables with the veneer peeling along the edges.

The usual clanky refrigerator sat next to the usual rickety table holding the coffee machine and hot-water urn. An air-feed monitor flanked by speakers was hung high on the wall facing the door, the sound controllable by a rheostat mounted on the wall at shoulder level. Some prehistoric western was currently being broadcast, and the sound, as usual, was off.

At KLAX, though, the green room's limited area was crowded by an untidy old desk laden with paints and powders and two chairs facing a mirror, for the management was so cheap that it doubled as the makeup studio. Melanie James, who apparently had been at the station for centuries, doubled, or rather quadrupled as relief receptionist, tape librarian, bookkeeper, and makeup artist. She was applying the final touches to Heather Blake, the evening weathergirl, a gilding of the lily that to Toby's eyes seemed entirely redundant.

If anyone could have persuaded Toby to break his sensible resolution to keep his prick in his pants around the station, it was Heather, and the same applied to anyone else of the requisite gender and sexual orientation.

Heather Blake was a formidable piece of ass even by Hollywood standards. Built like the proverbial brick shithouse, with long yellow cornsilk hair and peaches-and-cream complexion that were apparently quite natural, bright-blue-eyed and swishy-tailed with a radiant young smile that could melt glass, Heather was perfect casting as the midwestern blond bombshell.

But she was also the most relentlessly professional weathergirl in the business. Certainly the most *serious* weathergirl that Toby had ever encountered. She *understood* the scripts she was reading. She wrote them herself. She studied meteorology and climatology. Toby had seen her interpret raw weather-sat pix straight from the download. She had persuaded Franker (not even the old fart could deny Heather) to let her do the occasional "mini-doc" spot.

"Hi, Heather."

"Hi, Toby."

Heather was intelligent, friendly, prompt, professional, helpful, distant without being an ice goddess, and after a year and a half of working with her, that was really about all that Toby knew about her. Sometimes he had the feeling that "KLAX Weatherwoman Heather Blake" was a part someone else was playing.

Even now, Heather was trying to read some script or weather report or something while Melanie applied a final dot of powder to her forehead. Intense! Tantalizing, yet somehow intimidating and off-putting, and Toby had a feeling that was exactly the effect she intended.

By the time Melanie had finished applying his makeup, it was 5:36, and time, by Toby's lights, to wander over to the set and prep himself for the 6:00 P.M. broadcast.

It was a pretty standard cut-rate newsroom set, with nothing much—or to tell the truth, nothing at all—in the way of bells and whistles to distinguish it from five hundred or a thousand other such newsroom sets across the country from Los Angeles to New York, Eureka to Bridgeport.

The anchor sat in the focus of a big crescent-shaped desk, or rather a fiberboard mock-up of same, walnut with black trim in this case, with the station logo beneath him for establishing shots. The weathergirl sat to his left and the sportsreader to his right. The background was a blue matte; all background visuals were mixed in the control room.

The control room itself was two-faced, with one window looking out into studio B and one into this one, and a single mixing console and director's position. The miking was fixed to the set positions, the microphones hidden behind the desk fairings. There were only two cameras, another cost-cutting measure; after all, as Franker pointed out to the displeasure of the directors, only one camera could be live at any given moment, and any halfway competent hack should be able to anticipate his next shot with a simple setup like this.

At least the three main air personalities didn't have to share the same teleprompter; *that* cheesy KLAX was not. They all had their own—old see-through models on pedestals rather than state-of-the-art heads-up displays to be sure—but at least not primitive desktop monitors that made it impossible to maintain eye contact with the camera.

There was a printout of the script on the desk in front of Toby's chair. As far as the director was concerned, this was a prop designed to convey the impression that he was a hardworking reporter who dug it out and wrote it up himself to anyone who still believed in the tooth fairy. But Toby Inman actually *used* it.

He had seen newsreaders walk on the set three minutes before airtime and read the whole thing cold off the prompter, but Toby believed in reading through the whole script beforehand.

You never knew. You didn't want to tie your tongue up around unfamiliar syllables in some foreign language. You didn't want to screw up the emphasis in a sentence or a paragraph because you didn't know what you were going to say next until you read it. If you took the time to read the script through before airtime, you could think these things through, you could even ponder the content of what you were going to read on the air, develop an attitude toward the material, convey a bit of emotional sincerity, establish a rapport with your audience.

KLAX might be a struggling independent with horrendous ratings, but this *was,* after all, Los Angeles, and *anyone* might be watching. Besides which, Toby Inman was no aging has-been on the way down going through the motions; he had gone from FM DJ in Athens to prime-time independent major-market anchor in his first decade. This was not going to be the high point of his career, the last stop.

He was still young, he was telegenic, he hadn't given up; he was still a rising TV newsman, and he believed in being professional.

6:13 P.M.

GLANCING AT THE STUDIO air-feed monitor, Carl Mendoza noted with zero surprise that they were doing it again. The same stock footage of the same six gaunt and scraggly coyotes snarling at the camera to defend their favorite supermarket dumpster that they always used as the visual for the current coyote attack story.

". . . and in Silverlake, five-year-old Elvira Garcia escaped serious injury thanks to the timely intervention of her mother, Sandra, but her Yorkshire terrier Wanda was carried off and apparently devoured by yet another marauding pack of coyotes, though no remains have yet been discovered. KLAX's Terry Gill has details from the scene of the attack. . . ."

Cut to Terry Gill's taped interview with Mom, a heavyset middle-aged woman still clutching some kind of cute designer assault rifle as she poses awkwardly for the camera in front of a sprawling hillside bungalow dangerously shrouded in tinder-dry chaparral.

". . . when I heard the screams and the yapping, I *knew* what was happening, we've had a lot of problems around here, so I grabbed my piece right away, but by the time I got outside, they were halfway up the hillside with poor Wanda, I got off a few bursts, but I don't know if I hit anything. . . ."

Carl tuned out the interview and Inman's subsequent babble—serial killer apprehended, record dope bust in Venice, latest instapoll gives Seawater Referendum 5 percent edge, Elvis impersonator sights UFO over Griffith Park, pictures at eleven—as he usually did at this stage in the broadcast, with two minutes to go before his own slot, and concentrated on getting the pronunciation of the kid's name right.

Nguyen Zyzmanski . . . Caramba, what a mouthful! A no-hitter by some goddamn slope-Polack rookie, would you believe it, could you pronounce it, and Carl had a feeling he had better learn, 'cause the kid had a Ryan-class fastball and a major-league knuckler, and he had walked only two in the process of writing it in the record books.

Why couldn't the star of today's sportscast have a nice easy All-American name, like, say, *Carl Mendoza*?

Bad thought, cholo! Do try to remember that all that's as dead as your arm.

Carl had never had a knuckler, but as an eighteen-year-old straight out of high school, his fastball had been clocked at ninety-two that first season in the California League, sure he was wild, but he was averaging 9.8 Ks a game and was learning the split-finger when he was drafted, had hopes of jumping straight to Triple A.

Nam had ended all that, though he hadn't given up on the dream until he had kicked around for three years afterward in the minors without ever getting his ERA below four. It hadn't seemed like such a bad wound at the time, just enough shrapnel in his right arm to buy him a ticket back to The World.

Just enough to take the edge off his fastball, make his pitching arm ache after about three innings, make it painfully impossible to throw a curve. If he had been a power-hitting first baseman, say, he still could have made it, or at least as a DH in the AL. But as a pitcher—forget it, kid.

Not that forgetting it was easy. But at least he hadn't ended up like one of those bitter professional Namvet losers you still saw cached out around the fringes of downtown, blown-out derelicts still blaming everything in their fucked-up lives on the war. Not Carl's way. As a pitcher, he had learned to play it one inning at a time, one out at a time, one pitch at a time, don't let the base runners get to you, be here *now*.

Even in Nam.

So there he was, handed the ball with the bases loaded, and nobody out, and the meat of the order coming up. Show 'em what you got, kid.

So he did.

He went LURP. Why? For the mad machismo of it all? To see if he could cut it? He was a nineteen-year-old frustrated ballplayer with his brains in his cojones, so quién sabe. . . .

He found that he liked it, bad-ass missions deep behind the lines, Company stuff under grunt contract. He liked the competitive edge of the game, not unlike baseball played with M-16s and grenades instead of a ball and a bat to a nineteen-year-old temporarily ex-hotshot minor-league fireballer. You could even move up to the big time if you racked up the stats. And in fact there was a CIA scout named Coleman looking him over on the mission when he took the hit.

Coleman had even offered him a cup of coffee with the Agency in the hospital afterward, but Carl still dreamed of beating the odds and making the majors. After he got cut off his last minor-league roster, he had drifted around odd-jobbing, drinking, and doping for a year before he finally got it together enough to approach Coleman and ask for a tryout, still about as politically conscious as an earthworm.

They put him through the CIA version of spring training, brushed up his Spanish, then optioned him to Guatemala, definitely the bushes, as part of some team supposedly assigned to train the locals in counterinsurgency tactics.

The whole thing turned out to be a front for the middle part of some coke-for-arms deal with sleazoid colonels in the early stages of inventing Manuel Noriega, and worse things clearly waiting, an unpleasantly fast education in the depths of Agency cynicism, not exactly the kind of scene that could keep an ex-ballplayer from the barrio rooting for the team he found himself playing on. Nor was the manager exactly entranced with his attitude when he chose to make it apparent, and they graciously let him go on the voluntary retirement list before they were forced to ax him.

More drifting around in downward spirals, factory jobs, a six-month failed marriage, security guard crap at a bank, then at an FM radio station in Bakersfield, where one of his ex-minor-league managers was reading the scores and got him started in the business. And now here he finally was, back in L.A., doing the sports for KLAX, not the majors for sure, but it paid enough, and free tickets to everything besides.

It was as good a job as he could get; he was over forty, and face it, he was probably about where he would have been after a career in the majors anyway, a retired pitcher doing the ball scores on a local TV station, trying to figure out how to pronounce the name of the latest phenom and pissing and moaning to himself about glory days gone by.

Noy-yen, Ziz-man-ski . . .

Be here now.

"And now, it's time for sports—with KLAX's own . . . *Carl Mendoza!*"

6:20 P.M.

''. . . ON WALL STREET, THE New York Stock Exchange was down fourteen points on moderate volume, and in the broader and secondary markets. . . .''

Heather Blake scanned the printout of tonight's script again as she waited for her slot, not at all pleased with the cuts the producer had made, and not very pleased with Eddie Franker, either.

Quinlan she expected it from; to him she was just a pretentious little bimbo whose pants she had made clear he wasn't going to get into. "Just stick to reading the weather and lookin' good, will ya," was his chronic attitude.

If it wasn't for Eddie, she wouldn't have been able to squeeze in *any* of her mini-docs. The station manager was old enough to be her father, old enough to be her grandfather maybe, and he was married enough and mature enough to accept it. Because his interest in her was strictly fatherly, Eddie could see her clearly enough to take her seriously, to treat her as a colleague, to force reluctant producers to "humor" his pet weathergirl with 120 seconds of something other than reading straight forecasts every once in a while.

But he had refused to stand up to Quinlan for her this time.

"Not this stuff, Heather, sorry."

"But *why,* Eddie? It's a good piece."

Eddie Franker had shrugged, hadn't quite met her eyes, did not look comfortable.

"It's a good little bite, but it's political opinion," he said, "and that's over the line."

"I'm just reporting the findings of reputable scientists."

"*Their* opinions on a political issue that's got nothing to do with the weather. . . ."

"Come on, Eddie, you're telling me that how we deal with the drought's got nothing to do with the weather?"

Eddie sighed. "I'm telling you the facts of life, kid," he said. "Like every other bunch of nitwits with a lot of capital tied up in dry real estate, our esteemed owners are desperately ardent supporters of the Seawater Referendum. There's only two days left to go, it's too close for their comfort, and I've gotten away with keeping our coverage neutral so far. But if I let you or anyone else do stuff like this obviously slanted to hurt Proposition Seventeen, and it should happen to *lose,* whether we really had anything to do with it or not, they will have my ass. Sorry, Heather, that's news in the age of show business."

Well, at least Eddie had been honest about it. At least he had treated her like an intelligent adult instead of a mop of blond hair and a big pair of tits.

Of course, to be fair about it, looking like Miss Teenage Wet Dream had its ups as well as its downs. Heather hadn't been born looking like this, any more than she had been born "Heather Blake," but by the time such things started to matter, say around the second year of junior high school, her formidable mammary architecture had already started sprouting, and pulchritude had already begun to shape destiny.

Heather had in fact been born in Cedar Rapids, Iowa, with the decidedly unglamorous name of Hester Gluck, a source of much discomfort until the juicy burgeoning of adolescence had silenced the callow male barnyard humor forever. Well before high school, the same boys who had so recently tormented her with their chicken jokes were mooning after her slaveringly and fantasizing her future as a movie star.

As the teenage cheerleader high school heartthrob, Hester had used her primo datability to secure free entry to four or five films a week without having to put out for the unsavory.

For Hester Gluck was more than she seemed, the proverbial bimbo with a mind of gold. Even with all that time spent at the movies, she was a straight-A student, and while she did indeed cherish Hollywood dreams, she didn't want to star in movies, she wanted to *make* them.

She read all the serious film journals religiously. She saved up her money and bought an old 16mm Bolex in a hockshop, made her own shorts, and entered them in every obscure festival she could find, racking up cheap trophies, fancy certificates, and credits. The UCLA Film School, not the Hollywood casting couch, was her Ultima Thule.

When she got there though, she found that her looks tended to prevent most of the male student auteurs from taking her entirely seriously as a colleague, even as they made her the fave rave of their term projects as an actress.

It was hardly surprising that she had trouble picking up an entry-level job like assistant director or even script girl after graduation. But she couldn't really blame *that* on male chauvinism or her looks, since most of her class were in the same unemployed pickle. And it was a sort of sweetly ironic justice that in the end all that exposure in all those student films bouncing around town as demos eventually led to a phone call from an agent.

For want of any other offer of gainful employment promising entree into the Industry, she allowed herself to be recruited as an actress and soon found herself doing bit parts in commercials and soaps and rebaptized Heather Blake.

Finding herself at least temporarily stuck in the acting end of the business, Heather decided she had better take acting seriously, but to her way of thinking, that didn't mean hanging out in the right places and screwing advantageous people; it meant taking *acting* seriously, bullshitting and charming herself into the Actors Studio Workshops.

There, instead of connecting up with hot directors and producers slumming for a little intellectual cachet, she was taken under the wing of Nancy Clarke. Nancy was pushing fifty, from which side it was hard to tell. She had had what she called a "semi-unsuccessful career" as a film and TV actress playing ingenues and bimbos, and when at length it had devolved into bit parts as salesladies and the sidekick's mom, she had segued out and into a second and far more mature career as a local stage director.

You've got the right instincts, Nancy told her. Learn the craft. Become a real actress. Stop doing sleazy stuff before you become an aging B-movie starlet whom no one will ever take seriously as anything else. Do the little-theater circuit, make a respectable name for yourself around town, and sooner or later you'll start getting film parts worth having. Working with real talents, not schlockmeisters. Do that for five years, maybe ten, and *then* you'll have the experience and connections to ease into directing.

As a long-range career strategy, this made sense to Heather; she was young enough and had seen enough to know by now that she had to be patient, and it appealed to her desire to maintain a certain intellectual dignity.

But of course she might as well have been speaking Etruscan when she tried to explain such matters to her agent in these terms, and after the third time she turned down a perfectly good day's work in a legitimate soap because she thought the part was tawdry, he dropped her.

Nor was her landlord more sympathetic when it came to her resultant problems with the rent. So when a friend of a friend of a friend of Nancy's got her an audition for weathergirl on KLAX, Heather went for it.

She studied the weathergirls already gracing the local channels, created a character based on what her research told her was wanted, rehearsed it a bit with Nancy, and, easily enough playing the competition better than they could play their own bimboid selves, got the part.

At first, at least, she simply thought of it as no more than the perfect actress's part-time job. It certainly beat waitressing. Four hours a day at the station paid more than enough to cover her monthly nut, leaving her free to pursue her acting studies and go to theatrical auditions for parts that were worthy.

And while playing the airhead sexy weatherreader might not exactly be Chekhov, it *did* have more dignity than doing panty-hose commercials or bit parts as a screaming victim in slasher films.

She was, as Nancy kept reminding her, only twenty-five, and she *was* exposing her face to a large nightly audience without pandering to the slavering masses.

Still, Heather being Heather, she just couldn't help taking weathergirling seriously too, perhaps more seriously than any of the breed ever had before. She read meteorology textbooks. She taught herself weather-sat photo interpretation. She backgrounded herself in climatology and geology. She developed the concept of the 120-second weather mini-doc and sold it to Eddie Franker.

Maybe this *was* only a part-time job to pay the rent, a kind of bit part to keep body and soul together, another career detour. But if you were going to play a part, you played it from the inside, you tried to become the character, and if the part was KLAX Weatherwoman Heather Blake, then you made the most of it that you could, you tried to make her the best goddamn weathergirl that ever poked a pointer at a cold front. . . .

Of course the inherent problem with Method acting was that you tended to submerge yourself in the character, to lose all emotional distance or distinction. When it came to soaps or episodic TV, it could become seriously dangerous to your mental health, another good reason for a serious actress to stay well away from such stuff.

In the present circumstances, it meant that Heather could not quite keep herself from being rather pissed off—at Quinlan for having written out her mini-doc on the stupidity of building a string of offshore nuclear reactors close by a subduction zone, at dear old Eddie Franker for not sticking up for her, at the nameless assholes who owned the station for their irresponsible cupidity.

That was the way a weathergirl who took her job seriously would feel about it, now wasn't it . . . ?

"And now . . . the weather—today and tomorrow—with . . . *Heather Blake!*"

Camera two moved in, the red light went on, Heather flashed a brilliant plastic smile at Toby Inman, then turned it on the audience behind the lens.

"Hi there, Los Angeles," she piped perkily. "Well, unfortunately, the weather tomorrow will be pretty much like the weather today in sunny smoggy Southern California, but you knew that already, now didn't you guys. . . ."

6:25 P.M.

". . . ESTIMATED THAT IT WOULD take at least another two hours to bring the blaze fully under control, while rescue workers continued to risk their lives searching still-smoldering rubble for survivors. . . ."

From his fifth-floor corner office, Eddie Franker, KLAX's station manager, had a commanding view of the Sexray Cinema marquee across the boulevard out one window and the station parking lot out the other, but Eddie, as usual, had one eye on the air-feed monitor across the room, one eye on the latest ratings numbers displayed on his desk terminal's main screen, and both eyes on the screen window displaying the running StarNet balance. And if that added up to four, so, he had been wearing specs for the last thirty years, hadn't he, so what else was new?

Eddie lit his twelfth cigarette of the day, swore to himself as he had every day for the last twenty-five years that he'd start making a serious attempt to quit this weekend, and took another sip of his fifth cup of tepid coffee.

What was going out on the air was Toby Inman voicing KLAX spin over StarNet coverage of a pretty hideous airliner crash in Des Moines. What the numbers said, as usual, was that KLAX was running dead last in the broadcast-channel ratings, indeed behind even half the cable channels that were pounding the independents into the ground, and what the StarNet balance showed was that KLAX was buying twice as much from the video wire as it was managing to sell.

So what else was new?

Eddie knew damn well that it was only nostalgic longing that made him follow the StarNet figures so obsessively. After all, the whole news operation—salaries, production expenses, StarNet buys, StarNet sells, commercial-time income—amounted to no more than 25 percent of the station's cash flow, the lion's share coming from the other 75 percent of the station's programming. Hence, in theory, it should occupy no more than 25 percent of the station manager's attention.

But Eddie Franker had begun his career back in New York as a print reporter, moved up to the editorial end via the rewrite desk, then radio news producing, TV news producing, station manager at network outlets in Dayton, Boulder, and Denver, and finally this dumb dead-end job in L.A., where at least the winters were kinder to his aching old bones and Ellie's arthritis.

Meaning station manager or not, he was still an old newshound at heart, and after all, the news operation was the only part of this job that didn't essentially run on automatic.

The ubiquity of cable hookup in the Los Angeles market and the proliferation of cable channels meant that independent local stations like KLAX had little real reason left to exist. Cable subscribers had access to movies on a minimum of five channels in any given time slot, and the Dodgers, the Lakers, the Kings, the Rams, the Raiders, even the Clippers, were sewed up long term by the competition.

The station was owned by a nebulous holding company called Sierra Communications Incorporated, whose major identifiable shareholders were a big Orange County Toyota dealership, a Valley real-estate developer, a retired actor, and a rich lettuce baron in the

San Joaquin Valley. Eddie had the feeling that they kept the station going as some kind of tax dodge he had no desire to know about, the point being that it skated perpetually along the edge of apparent bankruptcy by keeping expenses minimized.

Except for a few dumb game shows with prizes donated by area merchants for commercial considerations and lame talk shows with subterranean ratings, the news was about all that KLAX originated itself, the rest of the airtime being filled with the cheapest moldy B-movies and old syndicated rerun packages that Eddie could find.

Meaning that most of his job consisted of buying whatever crap he could afford on his miserly budget and selling commercial time at standardized cut rates, with no hope of doing anything to improve the miserable ratings and no real pressure to do so.

His baby—KLAX Action News, as it was laughingly called— was a shoestring operation, to say the least. Inman, Mendoza, and Heather Blake doubled at six and eleven, Kelvin, Wu, and Masterston did the morning broadcasts, and he had budget for four part-time field reporters, entry-level jobs with instant turnover.

A newscopter like the network outlets and the better-heeled local independents? Shit, it had taken him months of blood, sweat, and tears to get the misers to let him buy a second mobile unit, and then they had forced him to get a used one!

Small wonder then that StarNet transactions occupied a far greater portion of Eddie Franker's attention than their impact on the balance sheet warranted. StarNet, at least, was a game that could arouse a ghost of his old professional passion.

StarNet, in its way, was as great a stroke of broadcasting genius as Ted Turner's Cable News Network. It was the independent news operation's white hope, such as it was, in the losing battle to retain audience share against the network stations and CNN itself.

Robby Hildebrandt had started StarNet after the newspaper feature syndicator he had been running folded. He did it on virtually no capital at all, selling shares here and there, raising money from prospective subscribers, and what he had done was obvious in retrospect—he had updated the old idea of the wire service into the age of the TV satellite and the cheap uplink.

StarNet essentially consisted of little more than a small building in Tarrytown, New York, with a few offices, a central routing and billing computer, some dishes on the roof, and leased satellite transponders.

StarNet originated nothing. It picked up news footage from independents like KLAX via satellite uplink and sold it back to the same network of subscriber stations via downlink. StarNet paid the contributing stations for what they uplinked via a formula based on airtime multiplied by total audience, and sold the coverage back to the downlinking outlets using the same formula plus 30 percent.

Meaning automatic profits for StarNet, and the ability of any of its network of independent subscribers to create the illusion of direct coverage of breaking stories anywhere in the country via StarNet uplink of footage from local stringer stations voiced-over by its own anchor.

Also meaning, however, that a station like KLAX had to sell 30 percent more to StarNet than it bought just to break even, which it never had in Eddie Franker's five years as station manager.

But hope springs eternal. Or at least the illusion of same could keep Eddie's ennui at bay. The way the numbers were set up, a local story of sufficient national marketability, and preferably one that stayed at the top of the news for a while, could make KLAX more money in a few days than the whole news operation cost in six months. And while Eddie might be supremely indifferent to the enrichment of Sierra Communications Incorporated, as long as he was still breathing, the primal newshound's fantasy of the Great National Scoop could still keep his tired old juices flowing.

Giant earthquake drops Los Angeles into the Pacific! Alien flying saucer lands in Rose Bowl! Mass escape of ferocious wild animals from L.A. Zoo! Meteor strikes Universal City! Godzilla rampages through downtown Burbank! Brought to you live, by KLAX in Hollywood, pictures at eleven!

". . . meanwhile, at the Southern California Cat Show in Northridge, several thousand devotees of what is known as the Fancy have been pursuing a different sort of purr-fection. KLAX's Allie Christien has the story. . . ."

"What the—"

Without knock or warning, the office door suddenly slammed open, and Gus Jason, this shift's chief of security, staggered inside off balance, a big blond man in a strangely bulky Dodgers jacket prodding him forward roughly with a machine-pistol in the pit of his back.

"Hands on your head, please, and we'll talk about it later! Do it now!"

This from a black woman in camouflage fatigues and flak vest who burst into the room behind the blond man, reached Eddie's desk in four long strides, and stuck another automatic weapon right in his face.

Two more armed men entered the room behind her, slammed the door shut behind them, and stood there barring it.

Biff, bam, pow, boom, boom, like in some fucking comic book!

Eddie didn't have time to even feel the shock, let alone react, before it was done.

A second later though, when it hit him, it came as a heart-thumping blast of primal animal reflex that had him bolting to his feet before he even knew what he was doing.

"Don't give yourself an embolism, Mr. Franker. Calm down. You don't wanna do anything stupid."

Eddie's blood pressure backed off a tad from the redline.

"Take a deep breath, look around, put yourself in the picture."

Eddie did.

About a foot from the tip of his nose and pointed right at it was the short barrel of a boxy machine-pistol—an Uzi, he was pretty sure.

Eddie still found himself having trouble understanding that this was something that was happening to him, not something he had watched a thousand times on the tube.

The kid doing the talking couldn't be more than twenty-three. She one-handed the gun from a sling worn over her shoulder like a Gucci purse strap, and she was duded up for the occasion in some kind of life vest and a military jumpsuit that seemed to have been custom-tailored to her athletic body on Rodeo Drive.

She had a meticulously barbered Afro, or whatever they called them these days. Eddie dimly remembered when it was called a "natural," but he somehow doubted this one was. She had sharp Ethiopian nose and cheekbones, flaring nostrils, clear morning-coffee-colored skin, big brown eyes. She posed there legs akimbo like something straight off the poster for the Hollywood version.

She was beautiful. She was hot shit.

The secret smile behind the theatrical scowl seemed well satisfied to know it.

It didn't do much for Eddie's sense of reality, maybe, but somehow it did make him feel better.

Gus Jason, though, looked pretty awful. His doughy face was ashen, bilious, he looked like he might throw up. The blond man prodded him with his gun, and he staggered a few steps toward Eddie, then stood there uncertainly in the middle of the room while the blond man came up beside the girl with the gun.

He may have once had the flowing blond locks of a surfer, but now they were thinning a bit and receding slightly, making his forehead look bigger, more intellectual; Eddie remembered the early-warning signs all too well. He looked something like forty. He had tough square features that didn't jibe with those Pacific-blue eyes somehow, eyes that gave him the look of an aging surfer reluctantly turned stickup artist.

But that seemed to be an optical illusion. There was something in those eyes that had been around. There was something far too intelligent in there. There was an absence of sleaze. There was also something illusively very wrong about this guy wearing a Dodgers jacket.

Two, well, punks stood in front of the door, Uzis pointed in his general direction.

Leather pants with holes in weird places, T-shirts with some strange symbol hand-painted in red, multiple earrings, black leather jackets festooned with chrome zippers and doodahs, what else could you call 'em?

Both looked to be in their mid-twenties. One was tall and slim, with a pallid pasty complexion and a scraggly and unimpressive mousy brown Mohawk running down the center of his shaved head. The other, shorter, more muscular, with a florid beefy look, had very bad teeth, but a much more impressive punk hair-do, a crest of bright red tufts varnished, or greased, or however they did it, into sharp pointy spikes.

"Okay?" said the girl. "You got it? We're the Green Army Commandos and we've seized control of your station in the name of the peoples of the Earth. We're the good guys. Nobody gets hurt as long as you remember that and act accordingly. Otherwise we could become kinda bad."

She opened her vest to reveal slabs of something sewn into the lining, some sort of little jury-rigged console with a knife-switch, teased the handle with a finger.

"This stuff is plastic explosive, and we're all carrying a couple of kilos," she said, "and this little switchy makes it go boom."

The blond man peeled himself out of his Dodgers jacket, flipped it away like Superman doing his phone-booth act, to reveal the same sort of explosive vest. The punks showed him the charges hidden beneath their jackets too.

"We've also stashed great gobs of this goo in strategic places around this building, enough to blow us, and you, and the whole shitpile to hell and gone if we have to. Horst and I have special detonator switches that trigger their radio remotes. We decide we have to go, everyone and everything goes with us. So don't make us paranoid, okay?"

"Got it," Eddie muttered. "Can I put my hands down now, please? I'm a harmless old fart and my arms are getting tired."

The woman glanced at the man, Horst, who nodded. "Palms down on the desk top, and no sudden moves."

Eddie lowered his arms. "Thank you," he said carefully. "Is it okay if I hear Gus's version? I mean, you gotta admit it's all a bit hard to swallow just on your say-so. . . ."

Horst nodded again, turned, waved Gus forward with the muzzle of his gun, spoke for the first time.

"You will please confirm the truth of what Kelly has been saying," he said.

His grammar was somehow too correct, his pronunciation too generically perfect, for him to have been a native English speaker from anywhere. His voice was crisp and well modulated. He almost sounded like a schoolteacher calling on a student.

Gus Jason didn't seem to notice. "Oh it's true all right, I'm afraid, Mr. Franker," he said in the hangdog voice of an old cop whose professional pride had been severely diminished.

"My guys were dumb as fence posts, and *they* were slick as owlshit. Guy with a pizza delivery shows up at the front entrance, says it's for the cameramen or something. Box is too big to slip through the grill, so George comes out to take it, guy pulls a pistol outa the box, sticks it in his face, disarms him, gets inside, shuts down the switchboard, and four more of 'em come charging in through the front door, seal the front entrance an' catch me comin' outa the john. . . ."

Gus sighed. "Not a fuckin' thing I could do at that point, you unnerstand, Mr. Franker. One of 'em's got me, the other three come up on Johnny from inside the building which he ain't exactly expecting, an' secure the loading dock, a van pulls up, more of 'em come inside, and according to Johnny, they start unloading all this shit. . . ."

"All *what* shit, Gus? Explosives?"

Gus shrugged. "Didn't say," he said. "Look, I'm sorry, Mr. Franker, was nothing I could do, look, I hope you don't, I mean this job. . . ."

"Later, Gus," Eddie said, "if there *is* a later. . . ."

"No need for you to get so heavy about it, Mr. Franker," the girl, Kelly, said. "We're the good guys. Didn't I tell you? We're not out to hurt anyone. And to prove it, we've made ourselves hostages too."

"We are only resorting to these extreme measures because there are no remaining alternatives to direct action," Horst said with a strange earnestness. "We hope that once you understand, you will cooperate of your own free will."

"My men . . . ?" said Gus.

"Have not been harmed. We are not a pacifist group as you would understand it but we have no love of unessential violence. Our object is not to take life but to preserve it. To save the biosphere of the planet itself from the stupidity of our own species."

"Is that all?" Eddie grunted. "Why don't you try something difficult?"

Horst smiled thinly, merely a humorless acknowledgment of the sarcasm. Charming.

"Yes, of course, our strategic goal seems utopian, but we are neither wild absolutist fanatics, nor unfocused theoreticians, the world has seen far too much of both, wouldn't you agree? The tactical goal of this action is limited, well defined, and achievable."

"Huh?"

"What Horst is trying to tell you is that we're not going to hold this station any longer than it takes to accomplish a limited objective," Kelly said. "We are going to defeat Proposition Seventeen."

"And demonstrate the power of direct action!"

"In a cause that anyone not sucking on the titty of the agro-industrial complex can stand up and cheer for!"

Eddie felt the aura of a possible migraine teasing at his gray matter. Without asking permission, without really thinking about what he was doing, he let his hands walk across the desk top to his pack and pull out a cigarette.

Sure, anyone with the brains or moral sensibility of a garden slug—if they had no capital tied up in ending the drought before the value of their desert properties sunk out of sight—might indeed be able to somehow perceive that constructing a string of offshore nuclear desalination plants in an earthquake zone could be considered a tad shortsighted.

But as Eddie had so recently explained to Heather Blake, the owners of KLAX had mucho dinero tied up in just the sort of desert real estate whose value the Seawater Project was designed to enhance.

Who knows, the tightwads might have even sprung for a few miserly bucks on the campaign to pass it. No doubt there was a way to make it tax deductible. Sierra Communications Incorporated was all for the Seawater Referendum.

Indeed, they had not only told Eddie in no uncertain terms that his job would be in jeopardy if the station didn't lay off anything less than supportive of their sacred economic self-interest in the passage of Proposition 17, they had exerted considerable pressure to go further and slant the coverage toward winning it votes.

If these kids were good guys, his bosses were surely among those wearing the black hats.

Did these terrorists, whatever they called themselves, know that? Is that why they made KLAX the target?

Eddie lit up and sucked in a big lungful, which, under the circumstances, seemed less foolhardy than usual.

Is the bear Catholic? Does a Pope shit in the woods?

6:47 P.M.

Onscreen:

A **HEAD-AND-SHOULDERS** shot of Toby Inman in his tan suit, light yellow shirt, forest-green tie, his earnest baby-blues coming right at you.

". . . rejected her husband's accusations and declared that her relationship with country-and-western singer Bobby Joe Martin was strictly professional. . . ."

A shaky full shot on an aged blond former starlet in her well-mummified seventies and dressed for a night out on the town crawling all over a long-haired twenty-five-year-old rhinestone cowboy as they stagger through the paparazzi into a limo.

Toby Inman's voice-over: ". . . when reporters caught up to the couple in Las Vegas. . . ."

Ancient starlet: "I've got more talent in my mouth and throat than Dirk's shown in thirty years of all those stupid movies. . . ."

Cut to Toby Inman, visibly choking back his laughter, but otherwise extroing from the sequence professionally without missing a beat.

"She and Bobby Joe plan to cut a record together, she explained when—"

Inman suddenly stops in midsentence, his eyes bug at something off camera to the left, he starts to bolt to his feet.

"What the fuck—"

The camera pans jerkily to the right, where a young black woman in camouflage fatigues stands behind KLAX Weatherwoman Heather Blake, waving a machine-pistol and shouting something that Heather's mike doesn't pick up. She motions upward and leftward with her gun barrel, Heather stands up, looking very shaken, staggers out of the shot to the left.

The black woman sits down in the weathergirl's seat, pointing the gun to the right as the camera pulls back into a two-shot on her and Toby Inman. The gun is pointed straight at his head and about six inches from it. He looks as if he's about to shit in his pants until he realizes he's on camera, then his eyes become glassy, his lips tight and rigid, and he stares into it like a wax museum anchorman zombie.

"You too," the black woman says, glancing to the left. "Off the set, or I blow his head off!"

A rather sloppy and sudden cut to a shot from another camera, still in the act of pulling back into an unnatural long shot on the whole set, revealing a hint of the overhead lights structure, the other camera, Toby Inman, the black woman, sportscaster Carl Mendoza, on his feet, his hands balled into fists, looking rather menacing.

"For chrissakes, don't do anything stupid, Carl!" Inman shouts.

Everything freezes for a beat, then Mendoza unfreezes, turns, moves out of the shot to the left—

Another sudden choppy cut, to a badly framed, slightly off-center two-shot of Inman and the terrorist.

"Put your hands on the desk, palms down, arms outstretched, and keep them there," she says. Inman, woodenly, does as he is told.

She props her left elbow and her right hand on the tabletop, cradles the machine-pistol across her chest, with the trigger and grip in her right hand and the barrel snugged into the pit of her left arm and elbow, comfortably aimed at Toby Inman for the long haul.

She looks above and slightly to the right of the camera. "Give me a close-up," she says, apparently to the director. Nothing happens for a beat.

"Do it!" moans Inman.

The camera moves in and centers on her. She looks right at it and smiles.

It's a hard smile, but there's something appealing about it too. Her big clear brown eyes come right at you, radiating courage and sincerity. She's got full lips and dramatically flared nostrils, high cheekbones and an almost aquiline nose. No lipstick or makeup, and none needed. Tough, earnest, but very good-looking, very young, quite feminine; if there is such a thing as raw star quality, an instinct for a relationship with the camera, this is it, and she's got it.

"Hi there, fellow Earthlings, I'm Kelly Jordan, Minister of Information of the Green Army Commandos, stay tuned to this channel and I'll explain what just happened and why," she says.

The tone is mellow, the enunciation clear, the accent middle-American overlaid with an elusive something else, the cadence is a bit chirpy, but the total effect is, under the circumstances, weirdly professional.

"But first we're gonna have to wait a few beats for our technical crew to get our local live coverage pumped up to the StarNet satellite and out there to their affiliate stations, so bear with us for a moment, folks, while we verify the uplink. . . ."

She stares at the camera for long beats of silence—or rather, perhaps through it at something beyond, squinting, blinking, finally nodding.

"Okay, for those of you outside of Los Angeles who've just gotten tuned in to this coverage, I'm Kelly Jordan, and KLAX-TV has just been liberated by the Green Army Commandos in the name of the peoples of the Earth," she finally says. "We don't want to do anything bad to anyone. We are noble green warriors of Gaia who wouldn't dream of hurting even the teeniest itsy-bitsy of the biosphere, let alone the highly evolved mammals in this building. We just want to talk. We just want you to hear what we have to say. That's the American Way. That's democracy! They say that's what made this country great."

Her tone becomes a slight parody of the previous motormouth VJ, the sweetness gets pulled off her face, and she's suddenly quite credibly scary.

"Of course, if any undemocratic assholes out there try to shut us up, we are prepared to make their day," she says, flipping open her vest to reveal the flat oblong shapes sewn into its lining, the little metal console with its knife-switch.

"This is about two kilos of fancy plastique from Slovakia, and that is enough to take out this whole studio and everyone in it. We're all wearing these vests, and we've stashed a ton or so more of this stuff all over the building, so you figure out what a boom it makes if it all goes off at once."

The camera zooms in on her hand for a beat as she flicks a finger teasingly at the knife-switch detonator, then back out into the close-up on Kelly Jordan.

"Which it will if I flip this little switch," she says. "Which *I* will if anyone tries to rambo their way in here, or if anyone tries to take this station off the air. KLAX-TV belongs to the peoples of the Earth for the duration, and the Green Army Commandos will defend its liberty to the death—ours, our hostages, anyone too near this building to know what's good for them if we have to."

Kelly Jordan smiles, shrugs, almost winks her way back into a lighter vein, and it almost works. She's almost doing MTV again. Almost.

"That's what's just happened. We've begun the Green Revolution, comrades, we're putting our lives where our mouths are, we've taken direct action to save the Earth."

She mugs at the camera engagingly. "Right, we're extremists," she says. "We're terrorists. We're no better than the Mafia and the IRA. We're bad boys and girls. We're desperate people. We should know better."

She shrugs, she frowns, she waxes fierce. "We are," she says, "and so are you. We do, and *you* should, and that's the why!"

She pauses, relaxes a bit, becomes the sappy green girl next door.

"But you *do* know better, don't you? No more *if* or *maybe* about it, we're killing this planet. We got permanent ozone holes over both poles sucking their way toward us through the atmosphere like runaway vacuum cleaners. We got melting ice caps and islands disappearing and no more live coral to speak of, and the plankton in the ocean thinning, and fish disappearing, and when was the last White Christmas?"

She sneers at the camera, nods. "Yeah, yeah, we know all that, we seen it on the tube," she mocks. "In a hundred years or two the Earth will be uninhabitable. But what can we do? And who cares? By that time we'll all be dead anyway."

A grimace, a nasty little smile.

"Of course here in sunny rainless Southern California, we *do* see the graffiti on the wall already, now don't we? It's worth your life to get a tan, we're running out of water, no matter what we do the smog keeps getting worse, there's brushfires most of the year, and starving coyote packs are coming down out of the hills after our cute little pets and children. . . ."

She's good. She maintains eye contact. The delivery is a little mechanical, as if she's memorized it all and is reading it off a teleprompter inside her head, but the build is there. As she gets more sarcastic, she gains enough presence to maintain it.

"And what do you do? You send a check to Greenpeace or Friends of the Earth. You smear yourself with sunscreen and hold protest rallies. You use scratchy recycled toilet paper and feel like heroes. But mostly, you pop open a six-pack, tube out, and forget about it."

She leans backward, starts to throw up her hands, remembers she's holding the Uzi with them, an awkward moment that throws her off stride, breaks her rhythm.

"You . . . we . . . everyone knows what we've gotta do. Get rid of our gas-burning cars. Stop burning fossil fuels, period. Stop tearing up the rain forests to grow feed-grain for greaseburgers. Shut down our nuclear power plants before any more of them go Chernobyl. Put planetary survival first."

A bit mechanical, perhaps even deliberately, as she reels off the laundry list.

"Blah, blah, blah, and so forth. Change the channel, Maude!"

Kelly Jordan plays a phantom TV remote like an air guitar.

"Only sooner or later, you're not gonna be able to change channels anymore. We'll have killed this planet as dead as the dark side of the moon or the flip side of Venus. Oh yeah, our great-grandchildren will sure remember us fondly in the unlikely event we have any."

She smiles. She looks girlish again. "So we're all desperate people, aren't we?" she says. "We all know what we gotta get done, and soon, or it's curtains for our planet. But no one seems to know how to do it. Or even begin."

She lifts the machine-pistol slightly, not a big gesture, but definitely noticeable; she's *brandishing* it now, and her voice hardens.

"Well the Green Army Commandos may not know how to win the Green Revolution, but we do know how to start it, and when, which is now. No more petitions, no more rallies, no more bullshit. Direct action must be taken to save the planet, an inspirational demonstration is required to prove that it's possible, and we are going to provide it, live, on the air, at eleven P.M. on KLAX-TV!"

She stares resolutely into the camera for a long beat.

And another . . . and another . . . and another that extend

into an eternity of dead air, almost a full minute of it, as Kelly Jordan looks silently into the camera, resolutely, heroically, woodenly, confusedly, glancing to the left, to the right, to the left. . . .

"Uh . . . uh . . . that's it. . . ." she finally says into the live mike.

"What are we supposed to do now?" says a faint off-camera voice.

Kelly Jordan shrugs, looks around distractedly. Another twenty seconds or so of dead air.

Then the camera pans rather abruptly to the right, along the line of the machine-pistol's barrel into a medium close-up on Toby Inman in the process of pulling the shot onto himself with an inward wave of his right hand.

Inman recovers his professional aplomb, stares somewhat grimly into the camera, does the extro.

"Ecoterrorists seize KLAX and hold us hostage. More live coverage at eleven!"

Toby Inman's silent talking head for several embarrassing beats.

KLAX in star-spangled blue letters, four-note station theme, bright masculine voice-over: "KLAX-TV, Los Angeles!"

A panoramic aerial shot of a gorgeous South Sea island beach beneath a stunning ocean sunrise, a building-sized cereal box rising from the waves before it to a reggae fanfare, its illo a primary-color version of the background scene.

Deep, lilting, male Caribbean voice-over:

"Wake up to sunshine! Wake up to music! Wake up to six whole grains, toasted coconut, raisins, hazelnuts, exotic mangoes and passion fruit, and a naughty early-morning kiss of island rum and molasses! Wake up to Caribbea, the good-times granola with a reggae beat!"

7:25 P.M.

SURE IT WAS A scary situation, but Carl Mendoza had known more immediate physical jeopardy, in Guatemala, in Nam, and at least he was able to find the professionalism of the terrorist operation so far reassuring.

Slick and quick, with no unnecessary roughness or verbal posturing. Which was a hell of a lot better than being captured by a bunch of swaggering, loudmouthed, macho amateurs with chilies up their assholes!

For want of anything better to do except sit here in the crowded cafeteria and get paranoid about what was going to happen next, Carl had passed the time trying to count noses, phantom or otherwise.

How many of these Green Army Commandos were there? Near as he could tell so far, it figured to be something less than twenty, maybe a dozen.

So far, he had seen the girl who had done the broadcast, and the Arab and the Japanese-looking guy who had marched Heather and himself at Uzi-point to the third-floor cafeteria and now guarded the only door. Most of the staff had already been corralled up here, including the security guards, who claimed to have seen no more than four of the terrorists but were still too spooked to be sure whether these two had been among them.

Inman had been thrown in here by some kind of Indian after the broadcast, then he and an Anglo woman had fetched the control-room staff and the cameramen. That made five. Quinlan said they had installed one of their own in the control room. Six. Everyone who had been in the building was now here except Eddie Franker, so unless they had snuffed him, which didn't figure, that maybe meant a seventh, though one of the women or the Indio could be doubling. You had two building accesses to cover, the main entrance and the loading dock. Nine.

Yeah, you could pull it off with a force of nine or ten, a bare minimum of seven if you had to. Less than that, and you couldn't control the hostages and keep the building sealed at the same time, much over a dozen, and you'd have a command-and-control problem. . . . Of course you couldn't control these many hostages with a force that size for very long. . . .

"What do you think they're going to do with us, Carl?" Inman whispered theatrically.

It hardly seemed necessary. The so-called station cafeteria consisted of nine tables, a coffee and tea machine, a soft-drink machine, a snack machine, a water cooler, and a machine that dispensed long-dead sandwiches. Without even windows, it was more of a people-fueling station than a real commissary, and with more than three dozen people presently crammed into it, the noise level was such that you could shout and not be overheard two tables away.

Besides which, there were only two guards; they stayed by the door, and they didn't seem to care what anyone did as long as they didn't try to escape. People were allowed to circulate, to get food and drink from the machines across the room from the toilets, to go to the cans themselves, which had no exits out of the cafeteria, to stand in front of the air-feed monitor mounted high on the walls between "Men" and "Women" and watch an old *Simpsons* rerun.

Cool. Professional. No wasted effort.

Carl shrugged. "Depends what they're after," he said in a normal voice. "Depends if they *know* what they're after."

"If they *know* what they're after?" Heather said, stage-whispering to no real purpose like Inman.

The three air personalities, though no more than nodding acquaintances off the set, nevertheless found themselves seated together at a table in front of the food and drink machines in a bubble of the customary isolation from below-the-line staff.

Not the sort of people Carl would have chosen to walk into the jungle with. He had no idea what Inman might do in a physical confrontation; what he had seen so far was ambiguous. Inman had freaked a bit, settled down, then had the cool to end the broadcast. Heather . . . well, Heather Blake was a primo piece of ass who gave off vibes that told him to forget it, and that was all he really knew about her.

But Carl was pretty sure he was stuck with them. The three of them were the USDA Prime when it came to hostage meat. The terrorists, whatever they planned, if they had anything planned at all, were likely to treat them as a unit.

"Save the Earth? Start the Green Revolution?" Carl drawled. "A bunch of vague impossible nonnegotiable demands? I sure hope they've thought out a better endgame than that, or we are in for a long tour in deep shit."

Brilliant, just brilliant, Mendoza, he told himself the moment after he had said it, as Heather Blake's mouth slackened, and Inman squinted at him like a worried catcher with the bases loaded and no one out and his control going.

"What do you mean by that, Carl?" he said, forgetting to whisper now.

"Nothing . . ."

"Come on!"

Carl sighed. "Sometimes guys like this just want to get on the tube to make a statement, is all, and these Green Army Commandos have already had their airtime, and then the problem is. . . ."

"Is what?" said Heather.

Carl shrugged. "Then they don't know what to do next, they haven't thought it out that far."

"They don't have an extro," said Heather. "Like what's-her-name, Kelly, didn't when she was done talking."

Carl looked at her sharply, with a sudden flash of unexpected respect. "Yeah, they get in, they get what they came for, they want to get out clean, but they don't know how."

"And that's when it starts getting dicey for the hostages," Inman said.

Carl shot him a cool-it look, but Heather, the object thereof, didn't freak, didn't wince, didn't do anything but shake her pretty little head.

"You're both wrong," she said flatly. "These people are following their own full shooting script. They know just where the story is going, and this is just the teaser. I know it. I can feel it. Can't you?"

Carl regarded her with no little amazement. He found himself thinking about it. It certainly jibed with what he had seen of the operation so far. No panic. No emotion. No argument in the ranks. No wasted motion. All according to plan. Whatever that might be. . . .

He smiled at her, actually feeling a bit better about the situation and at least one of the people in it with him. Heather, it would seem, was not exactly your little blond airhead.

7:46 P.M.

EDDIE FRANKER PAUSED BY his desk to light up another Winston, take another sip of very dead coffee, then resumed pacing his office in small obsessive circles, wishing his headache would go away, wishing the phone would stop ringing, wishing these lunatics would at least let him start answering it already.

Out the window facing Sunset, he could see that the cops had barricaded the boulevard for two blocks on either side of the station. What a mess that must be making of late rush-hour traffic, what a sweet disposition that must be giving L.A.'s fabled minions of the law!

Out the window facing the parking lot, he could see the LAPD preparing for action in a manner that was a good deal less than reassuring. There were about a dozen squad cars, a riot-squad bus, a SWAT team, the battering ram, and what looked to be one of those robot minitanks. Dozens of cops armed with shotguns and automatic weapons stood around, already looking bored and restless. With the air-conditioning on and the windows sealed, Eddie couldn't hear the rotors of the police helicopters overhead, but knowing the fondness of boys of the Los Angeles Police Department for playing army with their toys, he had no doubt they were there.

Kelly Jordan and Horst whatever-it-was sat on folding chairs in front of his desk cradling their Uzis in their arms, glancing at their watches every few minutes for some reason, but otherwise apparently oblivious to the incessant ringing of the phones, the two punkers having departed for errands Eddie didn't care to think about.

Both of them were obviously too young to have seen the live coverage of the SLA shoot-out as comprehending adults, but Eddie wasn't. The armed terrorists of the Symbionese Liberation Army, kidnappers of Patty Hearst, had been cornered by the Los Angeles Police Department in an L.A. bungalow. The LAPD had used the occasion of the resultant shoot-out to put on a prime-time display of firepower that would have made the average Central American generalissimo green with envy. When the dust and napalm smoke cleared, that was about all that was left of the building and what was in it—smoke, and dust, and smoldering rubble.

No one could accuse the LAPD of being a bunch of liberal pussies, and if you did, they would blow you away. Given sufficient provocation—say, a cross look or an unkind word—they were fully capable of doing the same to KLAX. Or, as they used to say in Vietnam, it would be easy enough for them to convince themselves to destroy the station in order to save it.

"Look, you've at least got to start *talking* to the cops," Eddie pleaded. "Look down there for yourselves. The natives are getting restless."

"No," said Horst, checking his watch yet again. "We will wait a while longer, and then you will put us in contact with those in authority at StarNet."

"*StarNet?* What for?"

"To arrange the television coverage for the special event which will occur at eleven," Horst said.

"Which will be?" Eddie asked nervously, taking another drag.

Horst smiled at him unpleasantly. "Very special indeed," he said.

All at once, with a sudden sinking feeling in his gut, it came to Eddie that maybe these people were stonewalling the LAPD for their own demented reasons. Maybe they *intended* to make some lunatic statement and go out in a blaze of ordnance and explosions on live TV.

It would certainly be easy enough to arrange. A burst of automatic weapons fire out the window at the boys in blue, and the whole shitpile would surely go up. And even if that *wasn't* what the terrorists intended, there was, to say the least, no guarantee that the LAPD wouldn't provide the footage on their own anyway.

"Look, we're gonna *have* to talk to the cops to free up an outgoing line, so—"

"We have no interest in negotiating with the police."

"Jesus, will you just look out there before you say that!" Eddie groaned. "SWAT teams, riot squads, robot minitanks, the works, that's the *LAPD* out there, and they are not famous for their sweet temper. You really think they're gonna sit around patiently for three hours waiting for you to finally pick up the phone? Those guys are planning how to take this building right now."

Horst did not move. But Kelly Jordan went to the window and stared down into what was being assembled in the parking lot.

"We are serious people," Horst said. "We mean what we say. At the first move to take this building, we will blow it to pieces. We have already made that clear."

Eddie threw up his hands. "Look, let me try to explain it in a way you'll maybe understand. The cops, when they're dealing with a hostage situation, they wanna get the terrorists talking, establish a relationship, keep 'em calm so they don't do anything crazy, right?"

"You are saying that we—"

"I'm saying that *you* damn well better think of *the LAPD* as a terrorist organization, 'cause in this situation, that's just what they are. You've got us, they've got you, and those guys are more trigger-happy than you are! You can't stonewall them, you've got to talk to them, involve them in negotiations, even if it's about nothing at all, keep them calm, don't let them get too frustrated, humor them a little. . . ."

Kelly Jordan came away from the window looking somewhat shaken. "Maybe he's right, Horst, this *is* Los Angeles, and the LAPD has been known to blow people away for double-parking, there's a lot of angry meat down there, we can't count on them to be rational, we'd better get talking with them or they might just start shooting. . . ."

"This is a *professional police force*, is it not?"

Kelly Jordan shrugged. "You have to have lived here to believe it. Better just take my word for it. We gotta bullshit them."

"This is not according to the plan."

"And having those cops storm the station before we go on the air again is?"

Their eyes locked for a beat. Something passed between them as Eddie held his breath.

"Very well," Horst finally said. "Mr. Franker, you will answer the phones. You will do the talking. On the speakerphone, so that we can hear. And you will talk *only* to the police."

Eddie nodded. His phone console had five incoming lines, all punchable through the squawk box and pickup mike, and all of the lights were flashing. He sat down behind the desk and began hitting buttons.

Line one was Burton Faye, Sierra Communications' mouth-piece president, and it gave Eddie a certain perverse pleasure to hang up.

Line two was Fred McGuire, KLAX's account executive at StarNet. "Eddie? Great stuff, can you—"

"Can't talk now, Fred, get you later," Eddie babbled as Horst made a cut sign with his gun barrel.

The third line was the police.

"Hello, sir," said a deep, smooth, calm voice, "this is Captain Enrico Calderon of the Los Angeles Police Department Hostage Negotiation Unit. May I ask who I am speaking with?"

"Eddie Franker, the station manager."

"Are you free to brief me on the internal situation?" The guy was practically hypnotic. Eddie glanced at Horst. Horst nodded.

"No one has been harmed. The Green Army Commandos are in total control of the building."

"May I speak with their spokesperson?"

Eddie locked eyes with Horst. Horst shook his head no.

"I'm afraid not."

"Can they hear me?"

Horst gave the assent.

"Yes."

"I would like them to know that I am in general sympathy with their ecological position, though of course neither I nor the department can endorse the methods employed," Calderon said.

Jeez, this guy is good, Eddie thought, we get out of this, maybe I should try and sign him up as an air personality.

"I would also like to point out that their point has already been made, no one has been harmed, and therefore from a humanitarian point of view, their own public-relations point of view, and the eventual degree of leniency or harshness of the judicial system, their best logical course would be to release the hostages now and surrender."

Not a flicker from Horst or Kelly Jordan.

"I couldn't agree with you more, Captain Calderon," Eddie told him wholeheartedly. "But they're not going to do it."

"That possibility has been anticipated. So I have been authorized to negotiate a stabilization of the situation."

"Does that mean you can promise that no attempt to take the building will be made as long as no hostages are harmed?" Eddie asked hopefully.

"I'm afraid that issuing such assurances is contrary to department policy. However, I *am* authorized to state that should we come to believe that hostages *are* being harmed or are in imminent danger, we will be forced to take appropriate action."

Just terrific! Eddie glanced at Horst, at Kelly Jordan. He shrugged an I-told-you-so shrug. No reaction.

"That's not exactly reassuring," Eddie said. "That's making these people kinda nervous." He paused. "At least can you confirm that *you're* not planning anything provocative . . . like trying to drop a SWAT team on the roof . . . or lobbing tear gas through the windows?"

"I can assure you that no such preemptive action will be taken," Calderon said. A beat of silence. "As long as there are no further attempts to broadcast terrorist manifestos, of course. The policy is not to permit this."

Oh shit.

KLAX's local signal went by microwave relay to a shared broadcast tower up in the hills, and it would be easy enough to shut off the station's local transmissions from that end and black out Los Angeles. And an order from the FCC would be enough to keep StarNet from downlinking anything the terrorists uplinked to their satellite.

Unless, of course, StarNet was given a powerful enough incentive to ignore it and sort the legalities out later. . . . The ghost of an idea began to tease at Eddie's bonging brain.

"I will talk with this person now," Horst said, and even though the terrorist was well in range of the speakerphone pickup mike, he grabbed up the handset.

"This is Horst Klingerman, Chairperson of the Green Army Commandos," he shouted angrily. "*We* are in control here! If you interfere in any way with our transmissions, we will destroy this building and everyone in it! We will vaporize it! That is *our* policy!"

Klingerman was raving, but his expression was calm and composed.

He's doing a deliberate dingo act! Eddie realized. And doing it convincingly. This was not exactly clever.

"Jesus Christ, cool it, will you!" Eddie said, punching the hold button. "You can't talk like that to the LAPD! You'd better let me handle it!"

Horst Klingerman whipped his Uzi around to bear straight at Eddie's Adam's apple.

"Do remember who is the hostage," he said.

Eddie held up his hands. "All I'm doing is volunteering my services to our common cause," he said.

"Our common cause?"

"The cause of saving our own asses, the cause of not doing anything to get them blown away," Eddie told him. He held Klingerman's attention with a cigarette-lighting ritual, an old trick that had absolutely nothing to do with nicotine addiction.

"Besides which, I'm a newsman, and this is a big story, and KLAX is *my* goddamn station, why would I want these bastards shutting us down?"

Horst Klingerman kept hold of his weapon, but laid it down on the desk top and looked right at Eddie. "Continue please," he said politely.

"Look, they can shut us off the local broadcast antenna any time they want to," Eddie said, "but we've got a dish on the roof that gives us direct satellite uplink to StarNet. Even if they cut the power to the building, we've got our own emergency generator, so—"

"We know all this," said Klingerman. "It has been taken into account. Warren has already taken control of this system. We will use it to bring live coverage of our eleven o'clock broadcast to every major television station in America."

"*What?*"

"Time to talk a little turkey with the turkeys at StarNet," said Kelly Jordan, looking up from her watch. "Time to get rid of this guy, Horst."

Horst picked up his gun, gestured with it in the general direction of the phone console. "You will politely disconnect the good captain now and put us through to your StarNet contact," he said evenly.

"I don't—"

"Just do it!" Klingerman snapped in a much harder voice.

Shaking a bit physically, his mind whirling, Eddie took Calderon off hold, took a callback number, called Fred McGuire at StarNet. But instead of McGuire, the StarNet switchboard put him straight through to Arlene Berkowski, vice-president of marketing, a personage who had never deigned to speak with the likes of Eddie Franker before.

"That was great stuff, Eddie, may I call you Eddie . . . ?" she said. "Can you tell me what they're gonna do at eleven, I mean we still got over two hours to hype—"

"This is Kelly Jordan," Kelly interrupted, "and I can promise you you won't be disappointed."

"Kelly? Hey, I gotta thank you for giving us that little break to downlink your feed to the affiliates, and the second intro was really a thoughtful touch, I want you to know that we at StarNet appreciate that kind of professional courtesy even from terrorists, uh, I mean—"

"We are happy to hear that," Horst said. "For now you will reciprocate."

"I'll *what*? Who the hell is this? What are you talking about?"

"This is Horst Klingerman, Chairperson of the Green Army Commandos, Miss Berkowski—"

"*Ms.,* please if you don't mind—"

"—you will use your satellite to distribute our eleven o'clock broadcast to the networks, to CNN—"

"*Use our own goddamn satellite to downlink our exclusive on a story like this to the competition?*" Arlene Berkowski shrieked. "Are you out of your mind?"

Then, in another tone of voice: "Franker . . . ? Eddie . . . ? You still there? This is some kind of dumb joke, right?"

Although his mind was entirely blank, Eddie found himself starting to speak, but Horst cut him off with an upraised palm and a hard stare.

"You have this technical capacity," he said. "Do not attempt to deny it."

"I have the technical capacity to fry my brains in a microwave oven too," Berkowski snapped back, "but that doesn't mean I'm gonna be self-destructive enough to do it."

"Turn on your TV set, Arlene," Kelly Jordan said, her eyes on her watch as she moved across the room and turned on the one in Eddie's office. "You do have a TV set, now don't you?"

"I don't see what—"

"Just a little demonstration of *our* technical capacity," Kelly said sweetly. "Tune it in to any station broadcasting the StarNet newsfeed."

She came back to Eddie's desk, picked up his remote, began flicking through channels, stopped when she had KLAX itself, apparently now broadcasting the current StarNet downlink, something about an algae bloom in Long Island Sound.

"We will control the horizontal, we will control the vertical," she burbled. "Five . . . four . . . three . . . two . . . one. . . ."

"What the fuck?" Eddie grunted.

The algae bloom story was abruptly interrupted by a screenful of dancers in brightly colored Indian costumes screeching in what sounded like off-key Hindi. Then a stone-faced talking head in a burnoose babbling Arabic. What appeared to be a Chinese weather report.

"What the hell is going on?" Berkowski's voice shouted over the phone.

"We now return control of your television set to you, the viewing audience," said Kelly Jordan. "But it could only be temporary."

". . . declared the area off-limits to pleasure boats and fishermen. . . ."

A beat after the normal StarNet newsfeed came back on extroing the algae bloom story, Eddie had it figured. You didn't exactly have to be a technical genius.

The satellite dish on the roof was aimable. Warren, whoever he was, could easily enough downlink anything from any number of Chinese or Indian or Arabic satellites, whatever, record it, and then uplink it back to the StarNet transponder.

Arlene Berkowski had it figured too.

"Cute," she said. "And I gotta admit that overriding *our* feed with your pirated garbage is kind of wizard. And maybe it would take our guys a day or so to figure out how to lock you out, but if you think—"

"If you do not do as we say," said Horst, "you will be unable to broadcast anything but what we choose for hours at least, by your own admission."

"And Warren's found this nifty Italian porn channel," said Kelly.

"Look, I suppose I should be reading you kids the riot act," Arlene Berkowski said in tones of world-weary patience, "but the ratings were sweet on your last performance, and we *would* very much like to air the coverage of whatever you're gonna do at eleven on the usual market-exclusive basis, so I will write this pathetic attempt at blackmail off to naivete and break it to you gently. If you do not play ball with us, whatever you do at eleven will be a nonevent."

"Nonevent?" said Horst.

"Will not be broadcast."

"You can't stop us from uplinking it to your satellite, as we have just demonstrated," Horst said. "And our technical expert is confident that he can downlink it to CNN and the major networks via your transponders."

"Maybe he can, and maybe he can't," Berkowski said blithely. "It doesn't matter. Neither the nets nor CNN will air it, because they will know only all too well that we will sue their asses off if they do. Every last dime of commercial time they've sold for two hours around it, plus monster punitive damages. And the FCC will file amicus curae on our side too, better believe it."

"You are forgetting we have the power to destroy this station if you do not accede to our demands," Horst snapped back.

"*You* are forgetting that no one will see it if you persist in trying to push us around," Berkowski told him peevishly. "Not to mention the fact that our temporary little hacking problem will be solved, now won't it?"

Eddie had been listening to this crap with growing apprehension, but now he found it transmuted into a certain exasperation, not a fearless exasperation, maybe, but listening to these amateurs trying to bullshit a professional with *his own life* riding on it was more than he was about to take any longer with his mouth shut.

"Listen, Arlene, hang on a minute, will you?" he snapped, punching the hold button. "We got a little talking to do on this end."

Horst whipped his Uzi around to bear on Eddie's chest, his face contorted, more with surprise than rage, or so it seemed.

"Go ahead, do it, blow me away right now," Eddie told him. "Or you can listen to me for about a minute, and maybe we all get to live through the night."

Horst didn't lower the gun, but his outraged surprise seemed to transmute itself to something almost like amusement.

"So?" he said quite calmly.

"So you've gotten yourself into a stupid pissing match you can't win over next to nothing," Eddie told him. "StarNet's got an independent affiliate in just about every market area in the country. Forget this crap about trying to force them to distribute this story to the competition. Let them have the exclusive."

"Why?" said Horst evenly.

"Why? Because Berkowski isn't bluffing. Even if you can keep control of their satellite long enough to downlink to the nets and CNN, no one but the StarNet affiliates will air it anyway, because StarNet will have every economic incentive to sue anyone who does."

Of course there *is* another reason, Eddie realized, but not one that would carry any weight with these people. Maybe it was madness to care about the station's balance sheet under these circumstances, but this was certainly the scoop of his career, and it went against an old newshound's religion to just *give such an exclusive away*.

"Look," he said instead, "let *me* negotiate with her. I'll calm her down. I'll get you coverage in every market in America. I mean, come on, what are you saying, you're gonna get us all killed just because you don't want the nets and CNN to lose market share?"

"Perhaps you do have a point. . . ." Horst said slowly.

"Besides which, no one east of the Rockies will be awake to watch the live coverage anyway," Eddie motormouthed at him. "You want wider distribution, maybe I can get it for you on the tapes, come on, let me take a shot at it at least, you don't like the deal I make, you can always blow us all up later, right. . . ."

Horst actually smiled at that one, shrugged, gestured toward the phone with the barrel of his gun.

"Arlene . . . ?" Eddie said.

"That you, Franker?" Berkowski grumbled. "I'm not exactly accustomed to sitting around on hold."

"Yeah, it's me, Arlene," Eddie said, "sorry about that, but I've done some fast talking on my end and come up with something you're really gonna like."

"I am?" Berkowski said dubiously.

"The Green Army Commandos have agreed to give StarNet the exclusive after all—"

"They have?"

"—in return for certain considerations."

"Like what?"

"Look, we both know eleven P.M. is a pretty dead time slot outside the West Coast—"

"Tell me about it!"

"—but it gave me an idea, and I've sold it to these people. You keep your exclusive live coverage, but you sell *the tapes* to all comers on a nonexclusive basis."

"Oooh . . ." Arlene Berkowski crooned softly. "Keep talking, *Eddie*."

"This is going to be a big national story tomorrow, and we *will* have the only legal air tape. The StarNet subscribers get their exclusive on the live coverage in their markets, after which you violate no contracts by selling nonexclusive rights to the tape on the open market. KLAX gets seventy-five percent of the take, you get twenty-five percent, what do you say to that, Arlene?"

"I say vice versa."

"Come on, Arlene, we're the ones who're liable to get killed. Sixty-five–thirty-five."

"There could be a lot of legal problems with all of this, Eddie," Berkowski said. "We'll cover all that on our end. Sixty-five–thirty-five, in our favor."

"Down the middle."

"Sixty–forty."

"Deal," Eddie said. "Nice talking to you, Arlene."

"Ooh, fancy footwork," Kelly Jordan said approvingly when he had hung up on her.

"Okay by you, Horst?" Eddie said, eyeing Klingerman. "Is that a deal you can, uh, live with?"

"Except for one final detail," Klingerman said. "No matter what happens, the event *must* be carried live in Los Angeles. Should the police shut down the KLAX transmitter, StarNet must downlink the coverage to another local station."

"Sell *our* coverage of *our own fucking kidnapping* to the competition in *our own market*!" Eddie screamed.

Kelly Jordan laughed. "Don't bust a gut, Mr. Franker," she said. "It ain't gonna happen. Just a little insurance policy. Time for me to have a little powwow with the Parker Center porkers."

Who the hell had been flimflamming whom? Eddie wondered as he handed her the handset and dumped Calderon's number out of the recall memory.

Kelly Jordan sat down on the edge of the desk itself to take the call, vamping it up for the benefit of her little audience.

"Hi there, Captain Calderon, this is Kelly Jordan, Minister of Information of the Green Army Commandos, is that you?"

"Yes, ma'am."

"Well now, Captain, we've been thinking over your words of wisdom, and maybe you're right, so we're willing to consider a hostage release in return for a teeny-tiny concession on your part."

She winked rather disconcertingly at Eddie.

"That is welcome news, Ms. Jordan . . . assuming that your quid pro quo requirements are reasonable."

"Hey, no sweat, Captain, you don't interfere with KLAX's transmission, and we release the hostages at the beginning of the eleven o'clock news, before anything else is broadcast. Is that reasonable enough for you, Captain Calderon?"

Why the hell was she grinning like a Cheshire cat?

"Indeed it is, ma'am."

Why was Klingerman nodding in self-satisfaction?

"Of course, in order to insure that you *do* live up to your end of the bargain, we *will* keep four hostages just a little bit longer—the news team of Toby Inman, Heather Blake, and Carl Mendoza, and the station manager, Edward Franker."

There was a beat of silence. "I'll have to pass your proposal on to my superiors," Calderon said, and he hung up.

But of course their decision was a foregone conclusion, Eddie realized. Release of most of the hostages in return for not doing something that they would have been afraid to do at this stage anyway.

Kelly Jordan hung up the phone, peeled herself off the desk, sat back down on her folding chair beside Klingerman.

"Pretty slick," Eddie said.

These people were sharper than they had seemed, and perhaps more rational. That was somehow both reassuring and scary.

Kelly Jordan smiled at him. "And you're another," she said sweetly.

"You intended to release everyone but the four of us all along anyway, didn't you?"

"Of course," said Klingerman. "It is much easier for a unit of our size to hold four hostages than dozens. And the tactical value is really no different."

"You mind telling me what's going to happen after the hostage release?"

Klingerman looked at Jordan. Jordan shook her head imperceptibly.

"That would ruin the surprise, wouldn't it?" she drawled.

"I tell you one thing," Klingerman said much more intensely. "Our tactical objective is to defeat the Seawater Referendum. And we will achieve it with a single revolutionary act."

Eddie didn't like the sound of that, or the look on his face as he said it, and it must have shown.

"Don't worry, Mr. Franker, we can promise you one thing," Kelly Jordan said with a strange sardonic grimness. "It *is* going to be great television."

10:56 P.M.

"JUST READ THE SCRIPT and pretend it's an ordinary broadcast, and everything will be all right," Kelly Jordan said.

"Right, sure, hey, no problem, just like any other broadcast," Toby Inman babbled nervously.

There was Carl Mendoza on his right and Heather Blake on his left, and the prompter in front of him at eye level, and the two-camera setup, and the control-room window across the studio, and the shooting lights on, and the air monitor running the station-break commercials, just like any other broadcast.

With a few minor variations . . .

Like the two regular cameramen had been replaced by some Arab-looking guy and a nasty-looking punk in black leather jacket, red spiked hair, and chrome fetish gear, both of whom had machine-pistols slung from their shoulders. And there were two more armed terrorists running the control room. And Eddie Franker was on the set, seated on a folding chair off camera, with Jordan and Klingerman standing right behind him covering the air personalities with Uzis. . . .

10:57 P.M.

"**YOU THINK WE'RE GOING** to be all right, Toby?" Heather Blake whispered breathily, playing the terrified ingenue to the hilt.

Toby Inman looked pretty green, maybe more terrified than she was playing, although she was certainly scared.

Not that she could blame him. All she and Carl had to do was sit there off camera like dummies, at least for the moment, but *he* had to go on quite literally under the gun, read the terrorist's script, and look professional.

It was Heather's experience, reinforced by about three quarters of a century of schlocky movies, that the display of fear on the part of a beautiful young blonde was the best antidote to male terror, arousing the protective instinct and challenging the male ego to the point where, whatever they felt, most guys would try to pretend to be heroes, or at least hold themselves together.

It seemed to work. Toby forced a manly smile, gave her a wink, even managed a gallant wisecrack.

"Hey, no sweat, Heather," he said. "Look at it this way—at least we're still in show business!"

10:58 P.M.

IT HAD SOUNDED LIKE good news when Klingerman and Jordan appeared in the cafeteria to announce that they were going to release most of the hostages at eleven, but something about it had made Carl Mendoza nervous even then, a state of mind that the subsequent announcement that they would continue to hold Inman, Heather, Franker, and himself temporarily did little to ease.

But now that he saw what they seemed to be planning and how they had set themselves up to do it, Carl's fear had sharpened and focused.

He was now pretty damn sure that whatever these people were up to, they were in it for a long haul. This force seemed to have been put together not just to take the station but to *run* it.

At least two cameramen. Two guys in the control room who seemed to know what they were doing. Carl had never really gotten too deep into the technical end of things, but he had been around KLAX long enough to realize that you could keep the station on the air, and the entrances guarded, with no more than what the Green Army Commandos were now showing.

Not just armed people, but technically proficient people. They could not just hold the station, they could run it, keep it on the air.

For what purpose?

And how long would the authorities let such a situation continue?

11:00 P.M.

Onscreen:

''THE KLAX ELEVEN O'CLOCK News—with Toby Inman, Heather Blake, and Carl Mendoza!''

Toby Inman looks rather pallid and slightly disheveled perhaps, but otherwise KLAX's familiar anchorman in the standard intro close-up.

"At the top of the news tonight, ourselves, the . . . uh, hostage situation here at KLAX, where an . . . ecological action group called the Green Army Commandos has taken control of the station. After . . . after negotiations with the Los Angeles Police Department, the Green Army Commandos have agreed to release all station personnel except station manager Edward Franker, weatherwoman Heather Blake, sports reporter Carl Mendoza, and, uh, myself, in return for assurances from the mayor's office and the Los Angeles Police Department that this broadcast will be allowed to continue. . . ."

Cut to a somewhat shaky hand-held shot on the front entrance to KLAX, an angle from the side, as one by one, and then in twos and threes, people begin to emerge from the building. The camera pans with the first group of them as they shamble somewhat hesitantly down the short flight of steps, picking up speed, but not quite running, as they troop across the parking lot toward the police cordon.

Toby Inman's voice-over: "Uh, our apologies for any technical problems, folks, but this . . . ah, coverage is being brought to you by the Green Army Commandos' own cameraman using their own equipment. . . ."

More hostages emerge from the building, make their way across the parking lot to the police line. Then just a shot on the empty doorway for a beat.

A man emerges onto the top of the stairs. He's wearing faded blue jeans, dirty black Wellington boots, and a bulky yellow vest that looks vaguely like an uninflated life preserver over a red tartan shirt. The camera moves in slightly raggedly for a head-and-shoulders shot.

The man's face looks awful. The skin is sallow, almost greenish, dappled with eczemalike red blotches, stretched tight against the bone structure. Sickly patches of grayish hair remain here and there on his peeling pate. Feverish angry eyes glower at the camera from deep back in blackened sockets.

A hand, apparently that of the cameraman, reaches out from the foreground of the shot to adjust a minimike clipped to his shirt collar, perhaps just for effect.

"My name is Anthony Ellingwood," he says when the hand has withdrawn. The voice is raspy and hoarse but simmering with barely contained rage.

"I used to be a technician at the Long Beach offshore nuclear desalination plant—"

Toby Inman's voice-over: "Can you hear me, Mr. Ellingwood, this is Toby Inman. . . ."

Ellingwood reaches up reflexively toward the minispeaker in his right ear, drops his hand back, begins toying nervously with something inside his vest.

"Yeah, I can hear you."

Toby Inman's voice-over: "For the viewers out there, that's, uh, the pilot demonstration plant for the Seawater Project, isn't it?"

"Oh yeah, it demonstrates what will happen if the full-scale catastrophe gets built all right."

Cut to a rather messy split-screen shot, Ellingwood on the right half, Toby Inman on the left. The colors of Ellingwood's image are somewhat washed out compared to those of Inman's, his image is slightly unsteady, and the dividing line between the two of them is visibly blue and somewhat wavery.

Toby Inman doesn't look too terrific himself. He's looking right into the camera, but his expression is wooden, and his gaze invariant. It's obvious that he's reading unrehearsed script straight off the teleprompter.

"Uh . . . just to remind you, folks, what we're talking about is what you're . . . ah . . . going to be voting about two days from now in the primary, Proposition Seventeen, the bond issue to finance the Seawater Project, a series of eight nuclear reactors built on schlock, er, *shock*-mounted offshore platforms off the coast between San Diego and Moro Bay to desaltinate . . . ah, *desalinate*, massive amounts of seawater to relieve the drought. . . ."

"Yeah, right, Proposition Seventeen," Ellingwood says, his voice nearly snarling with sarcasm. "The agro-industrial-real-estate complex is losing its precious ass because there's no more water table left in this state to suck, so what else do they do but run yet another flimflam on the same bunch of rubes they sold their desert real-estate pipe dreams to in the first place!"

Anthony Ellingwood has full-screen close-up now, a sickly corpselike figure animated by a fury that sets him vibrating, that turns his eyes into black death-ray lasers.

"Give us a lousy twenty-five billion of the taxpayers' dollars, they say, and we'll save California from the drought! Give us the money, and leave us alone, and we'll rebuild you your Xanadu in the Sahara!"

Toby Inman's voice-over: "But we *do* need the water—"

"Need the water! Of course we need the water! We need the

water because the same avaricious unprincipled pinheads who now say they can end the drought by building cut-rate cookie-cutter nuclear reactors offshore from an earthquake coast created the drought in the first place by convincing forty million assholes like you that you could turn the Sahara into suburbia and the San Joaquin Valley into an oasis and everybody could have their own backyard swimming pools too!"

With purplish veins throbbing across his greenish and flaking pate, spittle spraying from his lips, and eyes bulging down there in their deep caverns, Anthony Ellingwood is something of a horror-movie monster, but the naked surrender to a deep raging hatred is much more terrifying.

Toby Inman's voice-over: "But the platforms will be shock-mounted, won't they? And the reactors will be inside containment shells that break away and float if the platform legs fail—"

"Hydraulic shock absorbers! Breakaway flotation fail-safes! Jesus what bullshit! This is *California*, remember, a great big rock cracking off the continent and already as fault-lined as a bowling ball that King Kong creamed with a sledgehammer!"

Back to the amateurish split-screen shot, with Toby Inman on the left side of the screen, all too obviously staring earnestly through the teleprompter he is reading off instead of at Ellingwood, who appears to glare directly across the wavering blue line that separates their images at his interviewer.

"But Long Beach has been up and running for . . . a year with no problem, right? Even after last October's quake, which, uh, measured, ah, four point two on the Richter scale—"

"Right," says Ellingwood, "just your average California quake, not even enough to beat out a really juicy coyote pack attack for the top of the news on your shitty station! But even that was too much for the miserable cheap-jack piece of shit! A leg slipped but didn't go all the way, but that was enough to crack some of their stupid cut-rate low-weight internal shielding. But hey, the containment capsule held, and only one worker was killed."

Toby Inman's image still isn't looking in quite the right video direction, but there's genuine surprise in his voice now, real emotion, no more teleprompter babble.

"There was no report of death or injury! Not even a radiation leak—"

"Of course there wasn't, you asshole! What are they gonna do, admit the stupid design can't even handle one little quake! That might wake up the voters! That might give them some small idea of what will happen when there are *eight* of these pieces of shit up and running for a really *big* quake to crack open like a box of rotten radioactive eggs!"

"But how do you know all—"

A full-screen close-up on Anthony Ellingwood, his hands balled into bony old man's fists, his sallow skin flushing a pallid red, screaming at the camera in a hoarse cracking voice.

"Because the worker that they killed is me! You're looking at a dead man!"

Suddenly he becomes preternaturally calm. "Do I finally have your attention?" he says in an icy voice, looking right at the camera for a long beat of silence. "I've been trying to speak to you idiots ever since I found out they'd lied to me."

Back to the split-screen shot, but now, thanks to technical corrections in the control room or just blind chance, Toby Inman's image is nose-to-nose with Ellingwood's, and the illusion of eye contact is there.

"Lied to you?"

"Nothing to worry about, Tony, the company doctors told me, just a minor exposure, we wouldn't even be giving you this nice indefinite sick leave at full pay and a free three-week vacation on Maui if it weren't for what the antinuke loonies would make of this minor malf, you know how it is, they could set the press pack coyotes on your scent, set up an ignorant howl loud enough to kill the bond issue and cost all of us our jobs."

"You weren't suspicious when they put you on sick leave?"

"Who me? I was just a dumb tech. I certainly didn't want to say anything to anyone that would help those antinuke jerks take away my job. But if my bosses were paranoid enough to send me to Hawaii and let me loaf around at home afterward at full pay plus bonuses because they thought I might, well, hey, wouldn't you?"

"Some people might consider that a form of hush money, Mr. Ellingwood," Toby Inman points out.

"Of course it was hush money," Ellingwood admits forthrightly. "And as long as I thought I was okay, I took it, why not, they were only paying me to do what I would've done to save my own job anyway. First they told me it was to keep me out of the earthquake story, then they told me it was to keep the anti–Proposition Seventeen antinuke nuts away from me till after the referendum."

"And you believed them?"

"Why not? It was true. That *was* why they were paying me to stay lost. The only thing they lied about was why."

A full-screen close-up on Anthony Ellingwood now, still rather eerily calm on the surface but visibly beginning to return to a boil beneath it.

"If I had gone downhill a little slower, if I hadn't got to feeling worse and worse while those bastards kept telling me I was fine, if I finally hadn't gone to outside doctors, if they could have kept bullshitting me through the election, they would've gotten away with it," he says, his voice rising in pitch, his cadence quickening.

"They thought they were going to get away with it anyway. 'No one will believe you,' they said. 'No one will print or air a word.' They made sure they were right. The papers wouldn't touch it. TV news wouldn't touch it. Your own fucking station wouldn't touch it. Everyone said their lawyers wouldn't let them. The Militant Anti-Nuclear Coalition believed me, but none of you assholes would believe raving green loonies like them! If they hadn't had connections with Kelly Jordan, if the Green Army Commandos hadn't been willing to put themselves on the line . . ."

Ellingwood pauses. There's an awkward silence for a beat or two as if he's waiting for a straight line to react to, and maybe he is, for when Inman delivers it, he seems to be sight-reading his teleprompter again.

"Why, uh, *should* we believe you, Mr. Ellingwood? Isn't it just your, er, word against the Seawater Project authorities, the media, and most of the politicians in this state? And haven't you already admitted to . . . taking payola . . . payoff money . . . ?"

"Seeing is believing, take a good look, and tell me I'm really not rotting away like a walking corpse," Ellingwood says. "Why do you think they switched to hardball to keep me off the tube when it started to get obvious? Why do you think I finally had to find terrorists willing to hijack this television station just to get my hideous face on the air?"

The camera pulls back into a fuller shot as he preens horribly like a runway model of living death. "This is you when one of those babies blows, suckers. Any questions?"

Ellingwood begins to walk slowly down the steps past the camera. "When they try to tell you I didn't get any fatal dose and their design is safe, let them explain why I did *this*!" he screams when he reaches the bottom of the short flight.

He turns and begins backing away slowly from the building across the parking lot, the camera allowing him to dwindle away into the middle distance, become an expressionless blur.

He stops.

The camera zooms in steadily on Anthony Ellingwood as he crosses himself, glances skyward, slips one hand inside his bulky vest. It's holding a flat washed-out medium close-up of Ellingwood's face at the extreme range of its lens by the time he speaks again.

"Don't let these bastards do to this whole state what they've done to me!" he shouts somehow distantly, waving his free fist in the air. "Defeat their fucking Seawater Referendum! Save yourselves! Here's *my* vote against Proposition Seventeen, what about yours?"

The camera reverse-zooms into a full head-to-toe shot on Anthony Ellingwood as he takes a deep breath, closes his eyes—

—a blast of reddish-orange flame fills the screen to the sound of—

—an enormous thunderclap—

—that whites out the mike—

—and dies away into echoes—

—as the camera holds on the greasy dissipating smoke over the blackened spot on the concrete where a man had just stood.

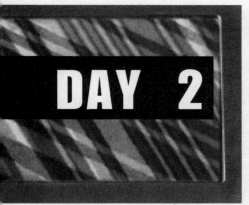

DAY 2

12:19 A.M.

OLD CIGARETTE ADDICT OR not, my heart must be in better shape than it's supposed to be, Eddie Franker thought breathlessly as Horst Klingerman ushered him into his own office at gunpoint.

The ticker had held up without missing a beat through watching Anthony Ellingwood blow himself up, through being marched into the cafeteria with Inman, Heather, and Mendoza after the news hour and being held there incommunicado without knowing what was going to happen next. True, he had felt something blip in there when Klingerman showed up and practically shoved him out into the hallway. But hey, who *wouldn't* have had at least a tiny cardiac conniption at being selected out from the rest of the hostages by an armed terrorist who did not look as if things were quite going according to the best-laid plans of mice and men?

The lungs, on the other hand, admittedly maybe left something to be desired. Klingerman had hustled him up here at a pace that left him gasping. Eddie hadn't even had enough breath to ask what the hell was going on and trot fast enough to keep Klingerman's gun barrel out of the small of his back at the same time. Or maybe, under the circumstances, he just didn't want to know.

Perversely, of course, the first thing he did after Horst slammed the door behind him was scrabble over to his desk, fish one out, and light up before even collapsing into his chair.

He exhaled, groaned, took another deep breath, air this time rather than nicotine. "So?" he managed to croak.

Kelly Jordan, he now noticed, was sitting in front of the desk holding the phone handset above its cradle.

"It's Captain Calderon," she said. "He insists on talking to one of the hostages. Under the circumstances, and considering what we both know about the LAPD, Mr. Franker, I've convinced Horst maybe we better humor him."

Horst Klingerman didn't sit down. "Talk to him," he said nervously as Kelly dropped the handset onto its cradle and pumped the call through the speakerphone. "You will express your extreme disagreement with his position."

"I will?" Eddie grunted.

Kelly Jordan grinned at him in a less-than-reassuring manner. "Hey, no problem," she drawled sarcastically.

"Calderon?" Eddie said. "This is Eddie Franker."

"Are you all right, Mr. Franker?" Calderon asked in a tone of obviously forced neutrality. "Can you confirm that no one in there has been harmed?"

"Yeah, we're all more or less in one piece so far," Eddie told him.

"A condition which may not persist much longer, I warn you, Captain Calderon," Klingerman said menacingly. "Your position is entirely unacceptable to the Green Army Commandos."

"What the hell is going on?" Eddie found himself demanding.

A long beat of silence on the other end of the phone, and when Enrico Calderon spoke again, his voice seemed to have acquired a certain unsettling robotic quality.

"I've been ordered to inform your captors that it has been decided to terminate KLAX's transmissions."

Nice choice of phrasing, Eddie thought sourly.

"And I have reminded the good captain that Kelly and I both have the capacity to detonate all the explosives in this building," Klingerman said, dropping down into a chair in front of the desk, but well within the sphere of the phone pickup mike. "Which we will do the moment KLAX is taken off the air."

"I am aware of the policy you have enunciated, and so are my superiors," Calderon said in an even more constipated voice. "And while I myself find your threat reasonably credible . . . there are those higher on the chain of command who do not."

"Anthony Ellingwood's demonstration of credibility wasn't enough for them?" Klingerman said in a kind of sinister purr as he and Jordan exchanged winks and nod. "They require further proof? Would they like us to shoot one of the hostages and toss the body from the roof?"

"Tell you what, Captain," Kelly Jordan cooed winsomely, "we're so keen to please, *they* get to pick which one."

"Please, ma'am—"

"Don't do anything stupid? Then you don't do anything stupid. Don't up the ante, my man, don't make us tell you something you really don't wanna know."

"Further threats would be counterproductive under the circumstances, ma'am," Calderon's oh-so-polite voice said. When one of L.A.'s finest began to talk like that, it was much worse than the pop-eyed curse of a red-faced New York cop. Eddie had been too terrified to try to put his two cents in, but now he was too terrified not to.

"Listen, Calderon, these people mean what they say," he broke in. "Don't do anything to provoke them!"

"Threats of violence are not being issued by the Los Angeles Police Department at this time," Calderon said in that tone of voice whose music denied the words.

Eddie glanced pleadingly at Klingerman, ran a finger across his throat in a cut sign. Horst shrugged, blinked, nodded.

"Look, Captain, we're going to have to get back to you," Eddie said soothingly. "Just please, please, don't make any decisions we all might regret until we do, okay?"

And without waiting for any answer he didn't want to hear, he hung up. "I might say the same to you, if I wasn't afraid you'd blow me away for it," Eddie told Klingerman with what he hoped was a certain disarming sense of gallows humor.

Klingerman looked at him quite coolly. "Merely a rhetorical stratagem," he said blithely. "I assure you we will use a demonstration of lethal force only as a last resort."

"And we're a long way from out of resorts, don't you worry your little head about it, Mr. Franker," Kelly Jordan said.

"Look," Eddie said, "I'm not sure how far you people will really go, and as you can appreciate, I don't want to find out. But I *do* know what the cops in this town are like, and I know we're all gonna find out if you continue to threaten them like that."

"We have good reason to believe otherwise," Klingerman said.

"Look, what you want right now is to keep this station on the air, right?" Eddie told him. "Well, so do I. First because it's my station, and second because it's my ass."

He squinted at Klingerman speculatively. "You might say we had a mutual class self-interest at the moment," he said. "Mightn't you?"

"I might if I were a Marxist," Klingerman said evenly, giving nothing away.

"Well, I'm not, and if you'll give me five minutes, I'll show you how good old predatory capitalism can get us what we both want and make a fast buck in the process besides." Eddie shrugged. "You don't like what I'm doing, you can terminate the conversation anytime, now can't you?"

Klingerman shrugged back with a mirthless little grin, and Eddie called StarNet without waiting for any other reply. He was through to Arlene Berkowski before he could finish pronouncing her last name to the switchboard.

"Jesus, Eddie, that was—"

"I talk, you listen, Arlene," Eddie motormouthed. "They're gonna shut us off the local transmitter, and they'll be on you about the downlink—"

"—the FCC's been on the horn already—"

"—you talk to—?"

"—had them tell 'em I was in the can—"

"You gotta do me one, Arlene, you gotta stonewall them."

"I can't do that Eddie, I don't have the authority, take the board of directors itself to—"

Eddie found his mind racing along in overdrive. God help him, and maybe he was, but there was a certain crazed exhilaration in all this, a compression of time, an adrenal high, Christ he hadn't felt this young in years.

"It's the wee hours out there, isn't it, Arlene, you must all be real tired, so why doesn't everyone remotely in authority go home and get some sleep?" he said.

A long beat of silence.

"Now that you mention it, we all are pretty beat," Arlene Berkowski drawled in quite another voice. "Why I suppose there's nothing so important the FCC's got to say to us that it won't keep till morning. . . . Or maybe till after lunch, girl's gotta get her beauty sleep, right, and I've put in a lot of overtime tonight. . . ."

"Right, Arlene, nighty-night," Eddie said.

"What *are* you doing?" Kelly Jordan said when he hung up.

"Putting our ducks in a line," Eddie told her. "Live and learn, kid. And hopefully vice versa."

Then he called Calderon back and put as much breathless relief into his voice as he could muster, which, under the circumstances, was quite a bit.

"Look, Calderon, I've done some fast talking, better believe it, and I've persuaded these people to back off a notch if you do. They don't shoot me and drop my dead body in your lap to make their point, and you don't pull the plug on the station without further orders."

"I don't believe I have that authority, Mr. Franker," Calderon said uncertainly.

"Then talk to someone who does before you get me killed!" Eddie snapped. "Or are you prepared to be their fall guy if these maniacs call their bluff? You just tell them you've held off a hostage killing with your fantastic negotiating skills, that the situation has therefore been altered, and you need new orders."

"I suppose that would be . . . prudent . . . under the circumstances," Calderon admitted. "But I must tell you it will probably only delay the inevitable."

"We're in no hurry if you're not," Eddie said dryly and hung up.

12:39 A.M.

"WHAT DO YOU THINK they're doing with Eddie . . . with Mr. Franker?" Heather Blake asked sotto voce.

"Who?" Toby Inman muttered, cocking a glance across the cafeteria at the guards. "These guys or the FCC?"

"Very funny," Carl Mendoza grumbled, shoveling another handful of trail mix into his mouth.

"Not meant to be," Toby said. "You have any idea of how many regs got broken tonight?"

"Guy blows himself to hamburger on the air while you're interviewing him, and you're worried it violates the Carlin rule?"

Toby gave Mendoza an exasperated frown, rolled his eyes upwards, then leftward, trying to signal *Not in front of her, asshole.*

"Point is, Eddie is probably okay, I mean from *these guys,*" Toby said. "Klingerman and Jordan probably have him on the phone trying to talk everyone from the FCC to the cops out of pulling our plug—"

Mendoza toasted him with a cup of Coke from the machine. "Nice turn of phrase there, Toby," he said.

What do you do for an encore after your interviewee commits explosive suicide with forty minutes of live airtime left to kill?

This had not been covered in any media course Toby had taken at LSU, but in the real world, the Green Army Commandos in the control room had pumped the usual stuff from the wires and StarNet up on the prompter, and Klingerman and Jordan, with encouraging waves of their guns, had made it clear that what you had better do if you were Toby Inman was take a deep breath, become a zombie professional, and read it.

So the eleven o'clock news went along as if nothing but another gonzo feature had happened for the three or four centuries it seemed to take to get to the 11:58 station-break extro.

The only way to get through those forty minutes was to stare straight into the camera eye through the transparent prompter, go into a trance state, and just *read the news* as if nothing existed but the camera lens, the words of the crawl, and his mouth.

Or anyway, that was how Toby got through it. When it was over, when Toby allowed himself to come out of his newsreader cafard, Jordan and Klingerman were gone, the woman called Helga and the man called Paulo were there, and they herded the four hostages up to the cafeteria.

Two tables in the center of the room had been shoved aside toward the toilet doors to make room for air mattresses that were already inflated and laid out beside each other on the grimy floor—

four of them, which, come to think of it, was a good sign that they hadn't dragged Franker off to be shot or something.

Helga and Paulo had thrown a stack of Styrofoam cups, a plastic jerry-can of water, and a big plastic bag of dried fruit and nuts unceremoniously down on one of the tables, then took up positions on chairs flanking the door, all with little more than grunts and gestures.

"You *really* think Eddie is okay?" Heather said. She seemed genuinely concerned about the old fart.

"As okay as we are anyway, Heather," Toby told her. "Look, see, there's a fourth mattress laid out for our little slumber party."

Heather's expression brightened somewhat. She reached into the plastic bag and scooped out a full handful of trail mix, which she had only picked at daintily before, picked up a big wad of it with her fingers, and began chewing heartily.

Toby went back to quietly eating the stuff himself, not so much because he was hungry but as an extro from the conversation.

For the truth of it was, that while he was indeed pretty sure that the terrorists hadn't done away with Franker, it was also true that if they had him on the phone trying to keep the FCC and the cops and whoever else was involved by now from yanking KLAX off the air, he certainly wouldn't want to change places with the station manager.

Mendoza was right, after all. "Pulling our plug" had indeed been an unfortunate turn of phrase.

For what it conjured up in Toby's head was the final scene of some old black-and-white movie he had seen once on late-night TV.

Warren Beatty, as a rundown comedian in deep shit with the mob, finds himself onstage in an empty nightclub, pinned in the spotlight. He can't see the audience, but he knows it's the mobster who's after his ass. As the movie ends, there he is, telling jokes for his life to dead silence, and more or less knowing it will end when he runs out of material or the invisible audience gets too bored, whichever comes first.

When they pull the plug on the limelight, they pull *his* plug too.

12:58 A.M.

IT FELT LIKE A weird sort of flashback to his good old middle-aged days to Eddie Franker as he sat there reclining in his swivel chair with his phone in his hand like a city-room potentate, giving what-for to a politician in no real position to give it back for the delectation of his reporters.

"One of these people just *killed himself on the air,* you stupid bastard!" he yelled into the handset. "Doesn't that maybe give you the vague idea that these people aren't bluffing?"

True, *this* little audience held him at gunpoint, and this was a lot more for real, but the pragmatic working situation had evolved into something strangely similar, captors and hostage or not.

"That's the whole point, Mr. Franker," the attorney general said. "We can't have . . . I mean . . . with children watching . . . the FCC . . . Surely you can appreciate our position. . . ."

"Appreciate *your* position, Kwan? What about *my* position, dickhead? I'm looking down the barrels of a couple of machine guns in the hands of people who *you* are pissing off!"

That was somewhat an exaggeration of the actual situation, since Horst and Kelly sat before his desk with their weapons in their laps, and, far from being pissed off, were watching him do his thing not without a certain grudging admiration for an old dog's news-hound tricks.

Eddie even mugged at Kelly. Why not? How he could not take a certain pleasure in a situation, life-or-death circumstances or not, that gave him license to call the attorney general of California a bastard and a dickhead?

Eddie had not been surprised when a politician rather than Calderon had finally called back, though he hadn't quite expected one this high up the statewide pecking order—though on second thought, why not?

He might have gone for George Kwan himself, for as politicians went, Kwan was at worst your average dickheaded bastard. The usual agro-industrial-real-estate money financed the usual sound-bite campaign, after which, except for executions, glamorous criminal cases, and what photo ops he could scrounge, Kwan, like your typical state attorney general with no ambition or credible case for higher office, stayed pretty much out of sight and probably even made a pass at doing his job.

And considering that Eddie had spent the last five minutes calling California's top legal official a schmuck and a bastard and a dickhead, Kwan's glacial calm had been impressive, an indication, maybe, that although he couldn't come out and say it, the policy he was enunciating was not one with which he agreed.

Eddie glanced at the air-feed monitor. Whichever terrorist was running things down there in the control room was filling the air-time with some moldy piece of crap out of the library called *Night of the Lepus*.

Which now gave Eddie an idea . . . things were falling into place. . . .

"Look, Kwan, if you turn on your TV, you'll see that all that KLAX is broadcasting now is a sci-fi stinker about giant killer rabbits," he said. "While it may not be doing much to elevate the cultural level of the masses, it's not exactly politically significant. . . ."

A long beat of silence.

"So?" said George Kwan carefully.

"Just a minute," Eddie said and put him on hold.

"Look," he told Klingerman, "I wanna buy us some time by telling this guy that if they don't cut our feed off the local transmitter, we . . . you . . . don't broadcast anything but old movies and sitcoms until . . . until. . . ." Eddie shrugged. "Until whenever. . . ."

"Until the six o'clock news tomorrow," Klingerman said.

Klingerman and Jordan exchanged glances. Then unsettling little Cheshire cat smiles. "We have nothing . . . *interesting* planned till then anyway," said Kelly Jordan.

"I think I've negotiated something we can all, uh, live with," Eddie told the attorney general, "something to buy us all some time to think. KLAX runs nothing but old shows and movies and you don't shut us off the transmitter as long as we do."

"Just a moment," the attorney general said, and then *he* put *Eddie* on hold.

"Now you will please explain what you are doing?" Horst Klingerman said with a certain threatening softness.

"Yeah, seeing as how *we're* the terrorists, and *you're* the hostage, we *would* appreciate being brought up to speed."

"Keeping KLAX on the air. Buying time."

"We haven't taken this station so we can broadcast wall-to-wall monster movies," Kelly said. "We go back on the air ourselves at six tomorrow, and that is nonnegotiable."

"Au contraire, kid," Eddie told her, "that's exactly what I'm in the process of negotiating."

George Kwan's just a moment stretched out into long tense minutes. "They . . . we . . . I . . . can agree to that," he said when he finally came back on the line. "But . . . ah . . . there's one other thing. We have . . . technical intelligence that KLAX has a live carrier-beam uplink still locked on to a StarNet satellite transponder. . . ."

"So?" said Eddie.

"We want it turned off," said the attorney general.

Eddie found himself shaking his head no at Horst Klingerman at the same time that Klingerman signed the same no at him.

"No way," he told the attorney general. "That's their insurance policy. You pull the plug on the local transmitter, they go right to live coverage, uplink it to StarNet, and—"

"We've already got an FCC order forbidding StarNet from downlinking anything from KLAX to its outlets."

"Then why make an issue out of the uplink?"

A long pause.

"Well, for some reason, we're having a problem getting anyone there with any authority on the phone. . . ."

"Really . . . ?" Eddie drawled. "Well, gee, it's about four A.M. on the East Coast, they've probably just all gone home to bed. . . . And I'm kind of running out of gas myself. So why don't we leave it where it is, try to get some sleep ourselves, and talk about it again in the morning?"

He held the handset out in front of his face for a beat, glanced at Horst and Kelly, grinned, and dropped it onto its cradle.

1:17 A.M.

HEATHER BLAKE WAS DRIFTING in a twilight state on the edge of sleep to the mantric drone of Toby Inman's and Carl Mendoza's snoring when a sudden sound jolted her into discombobulated wakefulness. For a moment, coming to consciousness in an unfamiliar darkness, she didn't know where she was or what was—

Then the fog cleared.

She was lying fully clothed on an air mattress on the floor of the KLAX cafeteria. The sound she had heard was the door opening, and in the light from the corridor, she could see three figures in silhouette, one of which she recognized.

"Eddie! Mr. Franker? You're all right?"

Eddie Franker stumbled uncertainly through the rearranged cafeteria furniture toward the air mattresses in the semidarkness as Toby and Carl rolled awake out of their sleep.

"Yeah, I'm okay, Heather," he whispered, but by that time, everyone was awake. Eddie plopped himself down on the vacant mattress beside Heather's. Carl and Toby groggily pried themselves up into squatting position, and the four of them hunkered in a circle on the floor, heads bent toward each other, like young girls at a living-room slumber party about to exchange juicy whispers in the dark.

"So?" said Carl.

Eddie looked back over his shoulder at the doorway, and following his gaze, Heather could see that the people who had brought him to the cafeteria were gone and the guards had resumed their seated positions flanking the closed door.

For a long moment the four of them stared silently and uncertainly across the room at the guards. Although she couldn't quite see their faces, Heather could sense them looking back.

"Do you mind if we talk?" she finally said in her best voice of bimboid innocence.

"Do vhat you like as long as you do not try to leave," said a woman's voice with a light German accent.

"Thank you," said Heather-the-airhead.

"Bitte sehr."

Eddie Franker gave her a strange look that she could not quite read in the semidarkness. "So we're still alive, and we're still on the air," he said. "Ferocious giant rabbits are rampaging on KLAX even as we speak."

"*What?*"

"I'm too exhausted to try and explain now, but I made a deal to keep us alive and on the air with old movies and reruns until. . . ."

"Until *what?*" said Toby. "Until *when?*"

Eddie Franker sighed. "Until the six o'clock news tomorrow," he said. "I think. I hope." He groaned, collapsed onto his mattress, rolled over on his side. "Anyway till morning," he muttered. "Long enough for a tired old man to get a little sleep."

"What happens at six?" Toby demanded.

"What really happened in—"

"Can't you see he's exhausted?" Heather hissed. "Let him sleep! We could all use some rest."

Eddie didn't answer, after a few unintelligible grumbles, Carl and Toby lay back down and drifted off, and soon enough Heather found herself serenaded by a curiously comforting trio of masculine snores. Carl Mendoza a deep bass rhythm, Toby Inman on intermittent tenor, and Eddie whistling counterpoints through his nose like a flute.

Nevertheless, Heather lay there in the darkness for quite a while, tired, but unable, or perhaps unwilling, to fall asleep, watching her own thoughts and reactions swimming across the screen of her mind like exotic tropical fish.

Am I frightened? Well sure, who wouldn't be? Am I excited? Yes, I guess I am. Am I somehow *getting off* on this?

That one was a weird creature, and that was the one Heather kept watching as she finally drifted off.

"See a movie, be a movie," some cinematic theorist had once said; it hadn't meant anything to Heather when she read it, and she suspected it hadn't meant very much to the person who said it, either.

Certainly not what it meant to her now.

For as she lay there in the darkness, there seemed to be at least four Heathers. There was the Heather whose life really was in danger in the real world. There was another Heather awake and aware in the darkness seeing it all as a movie. There was a third Heather,

Heather-the-actress, playing the airhead weathergirl hostage as a part.

And there was an elusive fourth Heather directing that actress, studying today's rushes even now on the edge of sleep; cool, detached, ambitious, calculating; somehow, in this moment, even a little frightening to herself.

"Be a movie, see a movie. . . ."

In some elusive way that Heather was far too grogged out to presently fathom, she sensed that there was some kind of survival wisdom in that.

2:35 P.M.

EDDIE FRANKER LEANED BACK in his swivel chair, sucking at his cigarette as he waited for the phone to ring. Horst paced the room nervously, peering out the windows from time to time at the cops in the parking lot and the barricades across Sunset. Kelly sat placidly on the couch with her feet up on the table, sipping coffee.

"What is delaying them?" Horst said irritably.

"Lots of bucks got to be passed, and that takes time," Eddie told him. "But don't worry, Horst, it's a lock, we've got 'em by the bottom line."

"We?" said Kelly dryly, vamping at Eddie over the lip of her Styrofoam coffee cup.

Eddie shrugged. "You, me, StarNet," he said, sipping at his own coffee. "As certain of my colleagues used to say back in the sixties, participatory journalism makes stranger bedfellows than politics."

What reporter *hadn't* fantasized himself kidnapped into the heart of a breaking story, visions of Pulitzers dancing in his head? But even in his days as a young would-be red-hot newshound, Eddie Franker had never imagined himself in circumstances quite as strange as this.

Anyone could probably imagine themselves in a hostage situation; who hadn't seen it on the tube? You got scared, you got brave, you got clever, you got killed, or you got rescued, run the credits, fade out on Warhol's famous fifteen minutes. . . .

But all those hostage stories on TV, news or fiction, had not prepared Eddie for what was happening here, for what he was *doing* here.

Less than twenty-four hours into this situation, he already thought of these two kids as "Kelly" and "Horst." They still had their guns, but they had long since stopped waving them around. He had taken over as their negotiator, and they had let him. He still didn't know what they were really after, but he was helping them get it, at least to the extent that it coincided with what *he* was after, namely to keep his station on the air and everyone concerned alive.

This wasn't the so-called Stockholm Syndrome either. He certainly hadn't started identifying with his captors or developed an emotional dependence!

How could he? He didn't really know much of anything about them at all.

They had seized the station. They were some kind of extremist ecological action group. They were clever enough and organized enough to run the station. They were lucky enough, or smart enough, or ruthless enough, or a combination of all three, to have found someone willing to blow himself up on live TV to make their point.

But that was just about all that Eddie knew about the Green Army Commandos. And about all that he knew about Kelly Jordan and Horst Klingerman was that she seemed to be an American and he seemed to be a European from some German- or Dutch- or Scandinavian-speaking country.

Nevertheless something *had* evolved between them that Eddie seriously doubted was in any of the textbooks—a pragmatic, professional, working relationship between captors and hostage, based, cynically or not, on shared self-interest. . . .

Eddie had slept like a brick till about ten, woken up stiff from sleeping on an air mattress on the floor like some goddamn Boy Scout, breakfasted on some dried New Age crap from a plastic bag and crummy cafeteria machine coffee, and taken his own sweet time gearing his old bones up for the day.

Horst and Kelly hadn't shown up to drag him to the office phone till nearly noon—three o'clock, and the end of even the longest wettest lunch hour in the East.

In California, however, the LAPD, and the attorney general,

and the governor, and whatever Federal authorities might be speaking through them by now had been up and awake forever, and were not amused.

Whoever was working his head by now, George Kwan was still doing the talking. "Where have you been?" he demanded. "We've been trying to get through to you for hours, and we've been unable to reach anyone in authority at StarNet either."

"I've been sleeping, what do you think I've been doing, hanging upside down from the ceiling like a bat or a politician?" Eddie grumbled at him to the visible amusement of Kelly.

There was a long pause on the other end of the line.

"You're not being quite frank with us, are you?" the attorney general said in a cooler voice. "You've told them not to talk to us, haven't you?"

Eddie let him eat a full ration of dead air.

"Mr. Franker . . . ?"

"It's a matter of self-interest, Kwan," he finally said. "StarNet has no self-interest in talking to you because they have no self-interest in hearing what you're going to say to them, and I have no self-interest in letting you cut the station off the air and get us killed."

"The decision is out of your hands, Franker," Kwan snapped.

"Is it? Tell you what, Kwan, you give me half an hour, and I guarantee Arlene Berkowski or someone even higher over there will be answering your calls, and then we will see what is in whose hands, okay?"

And he hung up without waiting for an answer, called StarNet, and of course got through to Berkowski immediately.

"We can't keep stonewalling them forever, Eddie," she said. "The phones are ringing off the hook."

"Who is *them*, Arlene?"

"FCC, FBI, Justice Department, people who say better-you-don't-know, and we've got writs and court orders pouring in through the faxes, our legal department is shitting pickles, I mean, once we do start talking to them, they're going to force us to cut your uplinks off the net."

"Are they?" Eddie said.

"Of course they are!"

"But they can't really do it, can they, Arlene?"

"Of course they can! The whole government—"

"I mean *physically,* not legally," Eddie told her. "KLAX has its own generator and a few days' worth of fuel, so short of storming the station, they can't cut our uplink to your satellite. And they can't stop you from downlinking our feed to the outlets short of zapping the satellite with a laser."

"Eddie! Be real! There are court orders, writs, injunctions—"

"And the First Amendment, Arlene. Ultimately, none of that stuff has a sustainable legal basis. I know that. You know that. They know that."

"But in the meantime—"

"In the meantime, you tell them to get stuffed. Because the bottom line is that they have no politically acceptable way of stopping you if you use their paper for ass wipes. What are they going to do, arrest you, lase your satellite, for exercising your First Amendment rights? They got writs and injunctions, you get writs and restraining orders, and the Supreme Court will eventually have to sort the whole mess out about five years from now."

"You have any idea of what the legal costs—"

"You have any idea of what keeping this story on the air can mean to StarNet?"

"The matter has been discussed," Arlene Berkowski said in quite another voice. "There are conditions under which even these legal costs might be absorbable. We would have to have an exclusive—"

"You already have—"

"I mean an *absolute* exclusive, Eddie," Arlene Berkowski said, and now Eddie could hear the enthusiasm stealing in, the hunger even, could almost see her slaver. "Worldwide. Total. CNN and the networks don't even get taped footage to replay. The BBC, the French, ZDF, whatever, all their stations buy our feed directly and credit StarNet, or they get no pictures at all."

"Jesus, Arlene, that's *really* hardball. . . ."

"Big stakes, big risk, big payoff, Eddie. This goes on long enough, it does for us in a small way what the Gulf War did for CNN. Not as big a story maybe, but the human-interest spin will mean even higher ratings if no one else can broadcast even delayed coverage of the inside action. And Hildebrandt doesn't intend to make the mistake Turner made. We do this, *we* control the coverage. The government tries to interfere, we smear them with shit."

"And our cut?"

"The usual airtime times audience formula on the world rights too, enough to make KLAX the richest independent TV station in the universe if this goes on for a week."

"Sounds like an offer we can't refuse."

"A deal then, Eddie?"

"Deal, Arlene."

"One other thing, Eddie," Arlene Berkowski had said. "Uh, look, could you, er, explain this to your . . . ah, captors? I mean, if they're going to do anything really spectacular, I mean, uh, like the . . . er, Ellingwood thing, I mean, ah, we *would* like it to happen about eight your time to cover the national prime-time spread. . . ."

Eddie's mouth fell open. There was nothing he could say to cap an extro line like that, so he hung up.

"She's *serious*?" Kelly said. "We throw a hostage off the roof or blow all of us to hell and gone, we're supposed to make sure we hit prime time?"

Eddie shrugged, leered at her sardonically. "At least we'll still be in show business," he said. Kelly groaned. Horst didn't get it.

"The cynicism of the West never ceases to exceed expectations," he had muttered instead as he stood there in front of Eddie's desk with an Uzi slung over his shoulder, and an explosive vest, and a look of perfect outraged innocence on his face.

"Don't knock the sacred bottom line," Eddie had told him. "It's what's going to keep us on the air."

Or so Eddie had hoped. But now it had been close to two hours since he had last talked to George Kwan, Kelly still sat there calmly drinking her coffee, but Horst's pacing was beginning to develop a certain—

The phone rang.

Eddie picked up the handset.

Horst froze in his tracks.

Kelly put down her cup and stood up.

Eddie hit the speaker button.

"Kwan?" he said.

"This is Elton Carswell, deputy director of the Federal Bureau of Investigation, speaking, Mr. Franker," said a flat, somewhat prim voice that Eddie had not heard before. "This matter has now been placed under our jurisdiction, since violations of federal law have become involved."

"You've spoken to StarNet? To Arlene Berkowski? Or Hildebrandt?"

"Not directly. But I've been briefed on various discussions which have taken place between their attorneys and the Justice Department."

"The outcome of which . . . ?"

"I'd like to speak with a representative of the Green Army Commandos."

"This is Horst Klingerman."

"And Kelly Jordan, Mr. G-man."

"I don't suppose you'd care to discuss a release of your hostages in return for a guarantee of safe surrender and a fair trial . . . ?" Carswell said.

"I don't suppose you'd care to withdraw your forces in return for a guarantee that we won't throw them off the roof?" Kelly Jordan shot back. "You wanna discuss something connected with the real world?"

"We are prepared to offer a temporary stabilization of the situation," Carswell said thickly. Eddie could well imagine the amount of bile-eating that took. The stomach-acid fumes were probably steaming out of this guy's ears.

"If you have a proposal to make on behalf of your government, we are prepared to consider it on behalf of the Green Army Commandos," Horst said with a slightly supercilious fake diplomatic pomposity that hardly seemed calculated to lower Carswell's blood pressure either.

But Elton Carswell was a pro. No unseemly display of ireful humanity from the blue-suited minions of the FBI! Just the lines, ma'am, delivered as written.

"No attempt will be made to take the station by force as long as no hostages are harmed. KLAX will be allowed to remain on the air as long as no further violations of FCC regulations are committed. The Justice Department will announce that this arrangement has been reached by direct negotiation, and no assertions to the contrary will be broadcast."

Horst looked at Eddie in befuddlement. "One moment please, while we consider your proposal," he said, and hit the hold button. "This means what?"

Eddie thought about it. He tried to imagine the conversations between Berkowski and Kwan, between StarNet's lawyers and the FCC, between the FCC and the Justice Department, between Washington and Sacramento and Parker Center. . . .

He grinned. " 'Tis a far, far better thing they do from their own PR point of view to get some small credit for successfully negotiating *something* than to admit StarNet told the Justice Department to get stuffed, and is getting away with it," he said.

"Vas?" said Horst.

Eddie laughed. "What it means," he told them, "is we got 'em! What it means, kids, is you can't go wrong by relying on the first law of bureaucracy to prevail."

"Which is?" said Kelly.

Eddie laughed again. "What else?" he said. "Cover thine own ass!"

6:00 P.M.

"THE KLAX SIX O'CLOCK News—with Toby Inman, Heather Blake, and Carl Mendoza!"

Well, not exactly. The terrorists in the control booth had keyed up the standard taped intro, and Toby was indeed in the central anchor slot, but that was about as far as this insane pass at normalcy went.

Carl and Heather had been relegated to folding chairs at the far ends of the crescent-shaped set to make room for Horst Klingerman and Kelly Jordan, who sat flanking Toby instead. The two punkers, Nigel and Malcolm, manned the cameras. Eddie Franker sat on a folding chair well out of camera range, guarded by the not-quite Japanese-looking terrorist they called Hiroshi. Helga stood in front of the studio door stroking her Uzi.

Scary enough to be sure, but from Toby Inman's perspective as he sat there staring at the red light on the number-one camera, not nearly as terrifying as what was running on the prompter.

Namely nothing.

"A script? You want a script?" the one they called Warren had said. "You mean you guys don't really make it all up as you go along?"

Toby had hardly been surprised when Helga and Paulo had herded the three of them from the cafeteria into the green room, nor when this character told them that they were going on the air at six. Why keep the air personalities as hostages when they let everyone else but the station manager go if they didn't plan to use them?

Nor had Toby been surprised when Warren told him that he was going to interview Jordan and Klingerman for the top-of-the-hour lead. But when Toby asked to review the script before he went on, this jerk had given him a blank stare Toby could not quite tell was assholery or deadpan put-on.

Warren was sallow-skinned and somewhat pimply, like a night person who slept away most of the sunlit hours indoors, thirtyish, with longish receding blond hair, wire-rim specs; no pocket protector, maybe, but otherwise apparently your typical computer nerd. Except, of course, for the machine-pistol slung over his shoulder.

"I'm your tech director for the duration, guys," he had said by way of introduction. "Fear not, I can multitask the board, and the uplink and the mix and whistle Dixie on a bunch of satellite transponders at the same time and still have ten megs left free."

And yesterday he had been able to do just that and key the commercials and station breaks besides, with only one assistant in the control room. So the guy was a hardware wizard. But unless this was an idiot put-on, he understood nothing about a news operation.

"We make it all up?" Toby said. "The ball scores and the stock-market prices? The Supreme Court decisions and the celebrity sex scandals?"

"Oh, you mean the *wire stuff*! Hey, guy, no sweat, we can hack any wire feed you want off the sats and pipe it to your prompter, AP, Reuters, Novosti if you can handle Russian, you name it. . . ."

"I mean I need a script crawl on the prompter if I'm supposed to do an interview."

"You really can't just, you know, just make it up?"

"Make *what* up? I don't even know what's going on!"

Warren had shrugged at him. "Hey, I guess we just forgot to bring a *scriptwriter,* guy," he had said with a certain bland sarcasm, "so you're just gonna have to get used to making up your own lines. Just introduce 'em, and let 'em talk, and you'll be okay. Just be natural. You can do that, can't you? Or at least emulate it?"

And the asshole had laughed at his own dim nerdish joke.

It hadn't been the least bit funny to Toby then, and he certainly couldn't find much humor in it now, as he sat there staring through the clear empty plastic of the teleprompter at the live camera waiting for the script crawl that he had to remind himself was not going to come.

"Uh, at the top of tonight's news, KLAX, I mean, us, the hostage situation here at the station, and with me to . . . ah background the, er, breaking story—"

6:01 P.M.

Onscreen:

"—IS KELLY JORDAN, UH, what . . . ?"

"Minister of Information of the Green Army Commandos."

Toby Inman's nervous face is replaced by that of a handsome and quite young black woman via a sudden jump cut as she prompts him in a firm clear voice, smiling with a rather devilish amusement.

Back to a close-up on Inman, looking to his left. "Minister of Information of the Green Army Commandos," he repeats, turning quickly to face the camera as he realizes he's back in the shot.

"And Horst, ah, Kingle—"

"Klingerman," says a male voice-over with a certain exasperation as the camera raggedly pans right to a medium close-up on a fortyish blond man with clear blue eyes and a high forehead. "Horst Klingerman, Chairperson of the Green Army Commandos."

Another angle, a rather unnatural long shot including Inman, Jordan, and Klingerman. Kelly Jordan looks straight at the camera.

Horst Klingerman's eyes dart around nervously. Toby Inman stares off into space for a beat, as if waiting for a missing cue.

"Uh, for those of you who weren't tuned in yesterday, KLAX has been seized by a terrorist . . . uh, ecological action group calling itself the Green Army Commandos," he finally manages to say. "The station has, ah, been mined with high explosives and one of the Commandos has blown himself up, and . . . and. . . ."

He shrugs. He glances at Klingerman, then at Jordan. "Uh, as Minister of . . . ah, Information of the Green Army Commandos, Ms. Jordan, maybe you could, maybe you'd like to . . . maybe you could tell us. . . ."

Kelly Jordan's voice-over: "What this is all about?"

A sudden jump cut to a well-framed medium close-up on Kelly Jordan, looking earnestly right at the camera, as if this shot had been set up well beforehand but was gone to raggedly on her response rather than Inman's intro line.

"I'd be glad to, Toby," Kelly Jordan says. "Otherwise we wouldn't all be here, right?" There's an Uzi slung over her shoulder, and she's wearing designer combat fatigues, but she smiles like an actress about to launch into a commercial for dish detergent.

"Who are we? The Green Army Commandos are a direct action group. What are we doing? We're taking direct action! What do we want? To save the Earth! From who?"

She pauses for a beat, cocking her head at the camera, grinning impishly as she delivers the entirely un-impish line: "From you, of course, assholes!"

She maintains the same winsomely girlish smile as she launches into a tirade in a genial TV commercial voice.

"Who else is killing the biosphere? Have the cows really created the greenhouse with their farts? Are the dolphins secretly stripping the ozone layer to wipe out the land monsters that use their seas for a toxic toilet bowl? Are the rain forests committing suicide to get even by depriving us of their oxygen? Or, fellow monkey-people, is there some small chance that the death of the Earth will be the result of our own monkey business?"

The effect is in-your-face to the max, but somehow sweetly disarming.

Toby Inman's voice-over: "The death of the Earth? Isn't that a . . . uh, gross exaggeration?"

Kelly Jordan flicks a glance in his direction, but the shot doesn't change, and neither does her expression.

"Why no, Toby," she says in that same bright earnest voice, "it isn't. Any scientist who isn't on the payroll of something paying him biggo buckso to say otherwise will tell you that the biosphere of this planet is dying. The food chain's dying off in the ocean from the bottom up, and the food chain on the land has been gobbled from the top down by the agro-industrial complex, and the atmosphere is becoming extraterrestrial, and the ice is melting, and the coasts are flooding, but hey, what, we worry?"

A confused beat of silence close up on her before there's a cutaway to a reaction shot of Toby Inman, and a little bit longer before he manages to say anything.

When he does, it seems pretty pallid after Kelly Jordan's controlled manic energy. "It's, uh, not as if people aren't, er, doing anything about it. I mean, progress has been made, ecological awareness has never been greater—"

"—and the check is in your mouth, and I won't come in the mail!"

A quick cut back to Kelly Jordan as she snaps off the line.

She doesn't just smile at the camera, she beams, she radiates, she pushes it over the top into vicious sarcasm.

"Let's not bore the folks out there with the gory details, they've heard and seen it all a million times already, and they're all tubed out," she says. "We know what we've done, and we know how, and we know that we're still doing more of it. And we know what we've gotta do if we want this planet to have any biosphere at all by the middle of the next century."

An awkward two-shot on Inman and Jordan; he's looking at her, she's still playing to the camera as if she's still in close-up.

"We know it so well that we're tubed out on it too," Kelly Jordan says, and now the sarcasm is gone, and she seems to be speaking plainly and sincerely. "Stop burning fossil fuels that pump carbon dioxide into the atmosphere. Stop cutting down forests that supply the oxygen we breathe. Close down nuclear power plants. Ban the production of all atmospheric pollutants. Abandon industrial monocultural farming based on massive use of toxic pesticides, eat granola instead of beef, save the whales and the baby seals, blah, blah, blah. . . ."

"But, ah, if we did all those things, people would starve, and suffer, and all, wouldn't they?" Inman says.

Kelly Jordan smiles sweetly at the camera, reverts to her TV-commercial delivery. "Sure they would, Toby. First World industrial civilization would grind down to a crawl, tens of millions of people would lose their jobs, cities based on the car like Los Angeles would probably have to be abandoned, millions of people would starve, and Americans would have to get used to living like Third World people."

"That's horrible!"

Kelly Jordan's smile doesn't waver, but her voice hardens. "For who?" she says. "For the four percent of the world's people who are now gobbling up twenty-five percent of the planet's resources, or for the other ninety-six percent? There are just too many humans on this planet, Toby. Far too many pigging out on energy and resources in the rich Northern Hemisphere. The Earth's biosphere may be able to support three or four billion people living at Third World levels, or a billion living the way Americans and Europeans and Japanese live today, but not both at the same time."

"You're . . . you're saying that you want to see the population of the planet cut in half? Americans living like . . . like . . . African . . . uh . . . natives . . . ?"

"You got it, Toby. Because if that doesn't happen, the whole planet dies within the next century or two. And you won't find a reputable scientist to tell you otherwise."

"But . . . but . . . but that's all decades in the future, none of us—"

"Will be alive? That's right, Toby. We've all got to make big sacrifices, and we're not gonna be around to even know whether we succeeded. But if we don't, we murder the planet. We don't take drastic action, it *is* going to happen. Not thinking about it *won't* make it go away."

"But . . . but . . . but . . ."

"*But . . . but . . . but . . . but if we don't,*" Kelly Jordan mimics in a fair imitation of Porky Pig, "*th-th-th-that's all, folks!*"

"But you're talking about . . . about . . ."

Cut to a medium close-up on Kelly Jordan as she stares, suddenly hard-eyed, into the camera. "*Revolution,* Toby," she says, "a

Green Revolution, the real thing, not the Hollywood version. Sacrifice. Direct action. Maybe people getting killed."

She smiles with her mouth only, and it becomes quite sinister when she unslings her Uzi, slams it butt down onto the desk top, and sits there holding it upright.

"Maybe you haven't noticed," she says, "but we've started it already."

A long, long beat of silence as the camera slowly moves in for a more extreme close-up on Kelly Jordan, just her eyes, and her mouth, and the region between, sleek brown skin glistening in the shooting lights.

"We're *revolutionaries,*" she says rather matter-of-factly. "We're convinced that a Green Revolution is the only hope this planet's got left, and I'm talking about *mass direct action,* not more empty talk and demonstrations. We're here to set you an example, to show you that direct action works, that you really *can* do something if you understand how desperate the situation really is and act accordingly. That's why we have seized this television station, why we're using it to defeat the Seawater Referendum, and to hell with the personal consequences to ourselves or our hostages. . . ."

6:13 P.M.

". . . WE BELIEVE THAT NOTHING else is as important as the life and death of the planet, so if that makes us fanatics, okay, we're fanatics. . . ."

As he sat there on the far end of the set's mock-up desk listening to the woman rave on, Carl Mendoza felt the sweat forming on his balls, and the hollowness in the pit of his stomach, and the flutter of his asshole, and realized that now he really *was* scared.

A peculiar revelation, maybe, to occur to a guy after a full day of being held hostage by armed terrorists.

That was admittedly a kind of scary situation, but it was a *situation,* like the bases loaded with nobody out and three, four, and five coming up, or a deep patrol into NVA-held territory when you've gotta freeze in the grass on an anthill for an hour while a full division of regulars passes by. You hitched up your jock, kept your cool, screwed up your concentration, and did your best to handle it. A pro with a good attitude could make that kind of *situational* scariness work for him, pump up the juices, sharpen the senses, be here now.

". . . gonna be voting on the Seawater Referendum, an outrageous birdbrained scheme by the agro-industrial complex to pick your pockets for billions to build a string of nuclear time bombs on a fault line. . . ."

Scary *people,* though, were something else.

". . . end water rationing for a few years, maybe, go back to watering your lawns and growing your pine trees and your rosebushes. . . ."

Scary people like Charlie or the NVA or some of the sleazebags in Guatemala who were forthrightly out to get you weren't so bad, no worse than a power hitter with a .350 average coming up with men on.

". . . knowing the next earthquake, or the one after that, after you're dead if you're lucky, next Tuesday if you're not. . . ."

Even obvious nutcases, guys with the thousand-yard stare and heads you knew were full of broken glass, weren't as scary as people like *this.*

". . . or you can vote against it like a fanatic and take a first revolutionary step toward saving the Earth. . . ."

People who didn't gibber and drool and bite the heads off live chickens. People who sounded calm and sure and logical. People who believed sincerely in the ultimate goodness and the ultimate necessity of what they were doing. People who sincerely believed that *their* particular mission justified *any* means, and if your ass got in the way, well those were the breaks.

Carl had met people like that in Nam. They were the grunts you avoided, you volunteered to walk point rather than stand next to them in the jungle. They were the kind of officers and noncoms who tended to lead patrols that never came back. Or who expired from friendly fire in hasty self-defense.

They came in all races, religions, creeds, and, apparently, sexes —these logical, reasonable, idealistic, dedicated maniacs, and as far as Carl Mendoza's stomach, and nuts, and asshole could tell him, they were the scariest thing in any jungle.

6:20 P.M.

Onscreen:

KELLY JORDAN, IN MEDIUM close-up, seems to be coming to some kind of climax. With her skin sheened with sweat from the shooting lights, the upraised Uzi, the smartly tailored fatigues, the flak vest stuffed with explosives, the fine young features, she looks somehow miscast—a teenage ingenue playing a latter-day, black female Che.

But she does come to her rhetorical climax with a certain power and conviction.

". . . so before you pull down that little ol' lever, do remember that Anthony Ellingwood *killed himself* to defeat this stupid evil con job! Anthony Ellingwood gave what was left of his *life* to save the Earth! Can you vote for Proposition Seventeen on Tuesday and look in the mirror on Wednesday and *really* tell yourselves that your swimming pool and your garden and maybe even a little bit of your fat-assed way of life were too much to sacrifice so your children don't end up living in Chernobyl West?"

The camera holds on her for a long beat of silence as she stares resolutely into it. Another beat of silence. She glances to the side.

A somewhat hasty cut to a close-up on Toby Inman. Pro that he is, the camera doesn't seem to have caught him unaware; he's looking right into it, if a bit glassy-eyed.

"Well, that's very interesting, very persuasive, ah, Kelly, and I'm sure everyone out there is—"

A male voice-over, loud, but not very well miked, interrupts.

"I want to say something, Malcolm, you put the camera on me, yes. . . ."

The camera pans jerkily to the right, into a medium close-up on Horst Klingerman. His expression seems wooden after Kelly Jordan's performance, his eyes simultaneously furtive and hypnotically transfixed by the camera eye. His voice is somewhat harsh and thin, a bit too loud as if to compensate, making the light Germanic cadences somewhat more noticeable.

"My English is perhaps not so good, you must pardon me

please, this is why Kelly speaks for the Green Army Commandos. But . . . but . . . I must say something now. As a German, yes, our countries are not so unalike, but they are different, that is. . . ."

He pauses, visibly struggling to find the words.

"The Nazis, yes, they were evil people, and there were many of them, but they could not have committed the terrible crimes that they did if good people had taken direct action. The Stasi too, the Party, they were a police state yes, but when we showed our courage in the Opera Platz, they began to melt swiftly away. Parlor debating societies must take to the streets. There are times when even pacifists must fight. You cannot simply sit there with your fingers up your behinds drinking beer while atrocities are being committed in your name . . . You . . . you . . ."

He seems to realize he's lost it. He looks this way and that mutely, impaled in close-up for endless beats like a bug on a pin.

6:24 P.M.

IN A PERVERSE SORT of way, Toby found himself empathizing with the poor fucker.

Held captive by armed terrorists, and working entirely without a script, or even much of a clue as to what these people were going to do or say next, had certainly made this the hardest airtime Toby had ever served.

And now, here the three of them were, trapped in this eternal moment of dead air without a scripted extro from it on the prompter for any of them. Jordan had delivered her set piece, and Klingerman had swallowed his tongue.

That leaves *you*, Inman. You're gonna have to make it up yourself. Do an interview. Just be natural. Or at least emulate it.

6:25 P.M.

Onscreen:

A LONG SHOT ON Inman, Jordan, and Klingerman, Toby Inman's hands clearly visible trying to pull the camera toward him. A sudden, very ragged cut to a close-up on Toby Inman.

"Let's see if we can make it a little simpler for the folks out there, Horst," he says in show-biz talk-show tones that seem a wee bit mismatched with the material. "Uh, what you're saying is that the American people should, uh, what, take action to save—"

"What the United States does to the planet is not so different from what the Nazis did to Europe—"

"Hey, now wait a minute—"

"Whole species marched off to extinction, the atmosphere of the planet destroyed, life on Earth itself perhaps goes into the ovens this time," Klingerman declares excitedly as another camera moves in for a close-up. "The death of the Earth may be measured in your freeways and fast-food chains. If America magically disappeared, the world would begin to heal tomorrow."

Toby Inman's voice-over: "Come on, get rid of McDonald's and the Hollywood Freeway, and you'll save the world?"

"In a manner of speaking," Klingerman says thoughtfully, "yes, that is good."

"I didn't really mean—"

For some reason the camera remains locked on Klingerman during the back-and-forth with Toby Inman's off-camera voice, as if the terrorist were a politician and Inman a heckler in the studio audience. But Horst Klingerman looks away from the camera at him owlishly like a college lecturer fielding a dumb question from a student.

"I am not saying that all Americans are Nazis—"

"—that's very big of you—"

"—all Germans were not Nazis either. But the Nazis *were* Germans. And the greatest despoilers of the planet *are* Americans. And if we do not assume responsibility for what the worst of us do and have the courage to act accordingly, then we collaborate with them."

Toby Inman's voice-over: "Act accordingly?"

"First you must vote against this Seawater Referendum for all the good reasons that Kelly has explained."

Finally, the long-delayed cutaway to a traditional two-shot of interviewer and interviewee making eye contact with each other.

"But to vote against the Seawater Referendum is not enough."

"It isn't?"

"No, it is not! More Germans voted against Hitler than not. More people hated the Party than supported it. But when evil of such enormous magnitude is being done, a vote for good does not absolve anyone from the moral responsibility to take direct action."

"Direct action? You talk a lot about this *direct action* stuff—"

With neither Klingerman nor Inman looking at the camera, this cutaway seems endless too.

"What does it mean?" Klingerman says. He pauses, then looks in the direction of the camera, which moves in with somewhat unseemly haste for a close-up.

"*Anthony Ellingwood* took direct action," he says. "We may not all be willing to die to provide such an inspiration. But from such examples we must take courage to direct action of our own! We must not just defeat the Seawater Referendum, we must begin the Green Revolution to save the planet!"

Kelly Jordan's voice-over: "Hey Horst—"

"—we must commit more than our votes to the struggle. We must do more than talk! We must take to the streets!"

"Hey, come on, Horst, this wasn't—"

Klingerman looks to the side, shakes his head.

"No, Kelly, I must finish! Malcolm, you will keep the camera on me!"

Horst Klingerman seems a long way from the lecture halls of academe now. He has his hand on the sling of his Uzi, and consciously or not, it slides down to the grip.

"You must take direct action. You must pour out into the streets and make them your own! Surround this station with your bodies! Blockade the Long Beach nuclear reactor that killed Anthony Ellingwood! Shut it down! Storm it if you have to! Show yourselves the power of direct action! Show them that you are unafraid and they will melt away!"

"Jesus—"

"I have seen this happen! The Stasi could not stop us! The government collapsed!"

"Horst—"

Klingerman unslings the machine-pistol, holds it in his hand, points it at the ceiling.

"This is the power of direct action. This is how a successful revolution starts! When people truly awake from the nightmare, nothing can stop them!"

"Get—"

"Stop—"

"Cut!"

"That is why the Green Army Commandos have taken this station—"

"Cut! Cut! CUT! Roll the goddamn station-break commercials, or they'll cut us off the air!"

A beat of dead black screen—

"KLAX-TV, Los Angeles!"

Station logo.

A medium shot on a large gray-haired fat woman in a gingham apron and white chef's toque humming happily to herself as she feeds a huge zucchini into the hopper of a red plastic rotary cutter she's cranking away at. Out the business end slides a cornucopial avalanche of perfect slices.

"Zucchini chips!" she cries out in joy as she beams up into the camera. "Carrot chips! Pumpkin chips! Artichoke chips! Even jalapeño chips if you want! Why settle for stale old potato chips when you can slice *anything* into something ready to fresh fry to a light crispy turn yourself with Grandma McChip's home hand vegetable chipper?"

6:31 P.M.

IT WAS LIKE A sinister David Lynch remake of a Marx Brothers movie, Heather Blake could not keep herself from thinking as she sat there extreme stage left, somehow terrifying and comical all at once.

Eddie Franker hadn't stopped pounding on the control booth

window. The terrorists inside were still trying to read his lips. Hiroshi stood over him uncertainly, looking for orders from somewhere. Helga, guarding the door, waved her gun around as if trying to take charge, but no one was watching.

Carl Mendoza, extreme stage right, had his hands balled up into fists, looking like he might try to get stupidly physical. Poor Toby sat there between Klingerman and Jordan like a pole-axed lox.

Kelly Jordan rolled her eyes toward the ceiling, shaking her head in dismay at what she was hearing as Horst Klingerman raved on.

"That is why we take this direct action! To start the Green Revolution!"

The joke of it being that someone in the control room had *already* keyed the commercial loop, and a Pizza Hut ad was running, not Klingerman's act at all, as all of them would know if they glanced at the air-feed monitor.

As a gag, this was strictly a one-liner, it had long since become ridiculous, and it was about to become dangerous.

"They're running the station break now, Mr. Franker!" Heather shouted loudly but nonthreateningly in her best bimboid voice.

It worked.

The volume automatically drew everyone's attention to her, freezing the action for a beat.

"See?" Heather said with ditzy good humor, pointing at the air-feed monitor. "I'm sorry I interrupted, but it doesn't really matter," she burbled on with a birdbrain smile. "They're running the commercial break, so we can all relax."

Toby Inman rolled his eyes skyward. Carl gave her a measuring stare. Eddie heaved a sigh of relief and lurched toward the set.

Klingerman and Jordan glared at each other.

"That was really smasheroo, Horst," Jordan said. "I'm sure they loved you in Peoria."

"The desired effect will be achieved."

"*The desired effect,* goddamn it! Is the effect you desire to have us yanked off the air?"

Eddie Franker had reached the set and stood nose-to-nose with a somewhat stunned Horst Klingerman, who stood there with his machine-pistol still in his hand while Eddie read him out like an irate boss.

"You came *that* close, you know that?" Eddie said, holding his thumb and forefinger about half an inch apart under Horst's nose. "Another ten seconds and they would've pulled our plug!"

"What . . . what are you talking about?" Klingerman stammered. "We made an agreement with the authorities!"

"Which you just violated! Or don't you think the FCC rules cover incitement to violent revolution?"

"That's what I was trying to tell you, Horst," Kelly Jordan said. "You can't wave the flag of ripe red anarchy in the land of the brave and the home of the free! Not on TV you can't!"

"I was not advocating lethal force," Klingerman said peevishly. "I was advocating direct action."

Eddie Franker sighed, set his hands down on the desk top for support. "A nit-picking Talmudic legalism which Robby Hildebrandt's legal eagles can probably use to keep them from pulling the plug on us till the Supreme Court sorts it out, maybe," he told Klingerman with sudden weariness. "But not the sort of fine-tuning likely to occur to the LAPD or the FBI when they hear some yahoo calling for riots in the streets on TV!"

"I think you should remember that you are no longer in charge here," Klingerman snapped, bringing his machine-pistol to bear on Eddie's slight paunch. "And perhaps it is time we apprised the authorities of the true nature of the situation—"

"I don't think we should discuss *that* in front of the children, dear," Kelly Jordan said quickly.

"Look, we've got about twenty seconds to decide what we air next," Eddie said in a much weaker and older voice. "The station-break loop's running out. . . ."

"We're open to suggestions," Kelly said sardonically, "aren't we, Horst?"

"I—"

That was enough for Heather. She stood up. She waved her arms frantically at the control room, pointed at herself, then her prompter.

"What the hell are you doing, Heather?" Eddie Franker demanded.

She smiled innocently, gave all and sundry a bimboid prima donna pout.

"Why the weather, of course, Mr. Franker," she said. "It's time for my slot."

8:16 P.M.

AFTER GOOD OLD HEATHER had warped the broadcast back into insane normalcy by standing up to do the weather like a trouper, the terrorists in the control room had managed to pump up wire-service babble on the prompters for Inman and Mendoza, under cover of which Kelly had dragged Horst out of the studio to parts unknown.

When the news hour from hell was over, Helga and Hiroshi had hustled Eddie Franker and the air personalities into the green room, and there they had sat for about an hour under the baleful glare of Helga, who silenced all conversation in such tight quarters with the weight of her armed presence.

Kelly and Horst had come for Eddie at 8:05, and now here he was behind his desk with three lines flashing on his phone console, Klingerman and Jordan pacing in small circles and looking rather worried, and a minimum two out of the three probable callers not likely to say much of anything that Eddie wanted to hear.

"Any preferences, kids?" he asked with his finger poised over the buttons. When there was no response, he hit one at random.

It was Yancy Foster, his contact man at Sierra Communications, Incorporated.

"We are not overjoyed at this situation, Franker," Foster said by way of greeting. "You know damn well that SCI has a serious financial interest in the passage of the Seawater Referendum, so you can imagine how pleased the boys are that their own TV station is being used against it by these raving green assholes!"

"Jeez, Foster, I'm a *hostage* of the people you've just called raving green assholes, and they're listening to every word you say," Eddie groaned. "You think you might try and remember that?"

A beat of silence. "Look, Franker, I'm just a messenger boy, you know that," Foster finally said. "And the instapoll I'm seeing on CNN right now shows Proposition Seventeen down by five point five one points since six-thirty, and the boys—"

"Instapolls! Stick your instapolls, Foster!"

Eddie Franker detested instapolls under the best of circumstances, which these certainly were not. Voodoo journalism! The idea of setting up two 800 numbers for an unscientific call-in of yeas and nays was at least a generation old, but no one had taken it seriously until the computers were able to get a fix on the phone number of each caller.

By interfacing this list of names and billing addresses with databases whose accessing Eddie had always found constitutionally dubious, the instapoll software supposedly was able to construct a real-time model of public opinion accurate to two decimal places.

If that wasn't voodoo, what was? Worse still, it seemed to work.

Too damn well for the health of the body politic, as far as Eddie was concerned. It did not seem conducive to political courage for so-called leaders to know within a tenth of a percentage point what the electorate thought of their potential decisions before they managed to figure it out themselves.

"When *the boys* start pissing and moaning again over their precious instapolls, Foster, you remind them of the money we're racking up selling all this to StarNet, that's *my* message," Eddie said and hung up.

The next line he picked up was Arlene Berkowski.

"Great stuff, Eddie, the national ratings for the first half hour were the single highest StarNet has ever had, though it dropped off hard after the station break," she said. "But no one east of Nevada's going to be tuned in at eleven West Coast time unless—"

"Look, Arlene, there's really nothing I—"

"The networks and CNN are starting to swarm all over this like flies on horseshit, Eddie, they're moving in mobile units and choppers, they've got crowd shots of something going on down at Parker Center, they've even got stuff outside the station—"

"What do you expect me—"

"Inside stuff, Eddie, pictures from inside the station, thirty-second spots on the half hour hyping the eleven o'clock coverage, and something to back it up, I mean you've gotta put those terrorists back on the air at eleven, that's the one thing the nets can't match, the one thing that'll keep people back east watching after midnight. . . ."

Elton Carswell was on the third line. The FBI was not amused.

"That display by Mr. Klingerman violated our understanding with the Green Army Commandos," he said. "Can they hear what I'm saying?"

Horst stood over the speakerphone pick-up. Kelly sat down in front of the desk. Horst nodded.

"Hanging on your every word," Eddie drawled.

"We cannot tolerate televised incitement to riot, Mr. Klingerman," Carswell said.

"Has American democracy sunk so low that peaceful demonstration against dangerous and stupid policy by its leaders on the part of its citizens is now considered an illegal riot against the status quo, Mr. Carswell?" Horst asked him sardonically.

"I am not interested in debating with you, Mr. Klingerman," Carswell said rather thickly, as if around a mouthful of bile, or so it seemed to Eddie. "I'm here to tell you that if you attempt another such provocation we will use surgical force against your microwave relay antenna and your satellite dish. Do I make myself clear?"

"Quite clear," Horst said. "Now I make myself clear, yes? If you do any such thing I will personally detonate charges sufficient to vaporize this building."

"There's a high probability that you're bluffing, Klingerman," Carswell snapped. "Are you really brave enough to do it? Under certain circumstances we might very well be willing to bet not."

"You are questioning our sincerity?"

"Call it what you like."

"I call it not being polite, Mr. Carswell," Horst said in a soft silky voice that sent a chill through Eddie's gut. "You really *should* be more polite to us, Mr. Carswell, or we might be forced to be not so polite ourselves. . . ."

"What?"

Horst Klingerman glanced at Kelly Jordan. "Any objections *now*, Kelly?" he asked enigmatically. Kelly shrugged. "You're the man, my man," she said. "And I guess now is the hour."

Eddie glanced uneasily at the two of them. It felt like the room thermostat had suddenly been turned down ten degrees. Something bad hung in the air waiting to happen.

"Don't force us to create a panic, Mr. Carswell," Horst said. "We do not feel it would be productive at this time to reveal to the public what you now force us to reveal to you."

"What are you talking about, Klingerman?"

"The nature of the explosive charges with which this building is mined, Mr. Carswell. About a metric ton of sophisticated plastic explosive evenly salted with a kilo of finely powdered plutonium."

"P-p-plutonium . . . ?" Carswell stammered. "You expect us to believe you've got an *atomic bomb*?"

Eddie's mouth went dry. Was it possible? The collapse of the Soviet Union had certainly dumped an unknown quantity of the stuff on the black market, smugglers had actually been caught trying to peddle small amounts of enriched uranium in Poland and Germany, thirty thousand or so warheads in the hot little hands of an impoverished army whose troops had been known to drink the transmission fluid out of their tanks in the middle of a war zone. . . .

"Oh, no, Mr. Carswell, we do not have a nuclear explosive device, I wouldn't insult your intelligence by claiming that," Horst said. "A critical mass was far beyond our resources. All we were able to obtain was a kilo. If you force us to detonate the plastique in which it is embedded, there will be no nuclear explosion, merely a large chemical one which will disperse a cloud of finely divided plutonium over the area. Those who inhale a fleck will not die immediately. Many might survive for years."

"Preposterous . . ." stammered Carswell. "You expect us to believe something like that?"

Eddie began to sweat. That an international terrorist group could score themselves a mere kilo of plutonium seemed to him all too credible, and Carswell's tone of voice did little to convince him that the FBI man believed otherwise despite his words to the contrary.

"That a kilo of vaporized plutonium would kill several hundred thousand people?" Horst said pedantically. "There is ample literature on its carcinogenic toxicity in the journals."

"Come off it, Klingerman, even if you *do* have the plutonium, you expect us to believe you'll kill yourself to commit mass murder with it?"

"The probability is not great, but it is not zero, is it, Mr. Carswell?" Horst said.

A long moment of silence on the other end of the line.

"What Horst is trying to tell you, Mr. G-man," Kelly Jordan said with an unnervingly impish grin, "is that while the odds may be in your favor, the shit that will fall from the sky if by some chance we're not bluffing and you provoke such a catastrophe makes the risk too big for you to take just to keep us from exercising our free speech, now doesn't it?"

More silence.

"Perhaps you do not have the authority to make such grave decisions, Mr. Carswell?" Horst suggested. "Perhaps you are going to have to speak to your superiors before you are authorized to do anything so stupid?"

Carswell still didn't speak.

Horst smiled. "I thought not," he said. "We could of course go back on the air right now with this information before you could obtain authorization from higher authorities to use force, yes . . . ?"

"Look, Klingerman—"

"Which would no doubt result in just the sort of mass panic you seek to avoid whether we are telling the truth or not—"

"For the love of—"

"But we really don't want to have to do that, Mr. G-man," Kelly Jordan said. "If you agree, it can be our little secret, at least for the moment. You agree not to mess with our transmissions, and we agree not to freak the natives out. Now isn't that an offer you can't refuse?"

"You . . . you won't make this threat public?" Elton Carswell said in a very tightly controlled voice. "And we're supposed to trust you?"

"Well now, Mr. G-man," Kelly said, "we have to trust *each other,* now don't we? Call it a mutual confidence-building gesture. Call it mutual self-interest. You don't want five million freaked-out Angelenos trying to leave the city all at once, and we don't want to look like the bad guys. Do we have a deal?"

"Until I receive orders to the contrary and so inform you, you have my word on that much," muttered Elton Carswell, and then the deputy director of the Federal Bureau of Investigation hung up.

"Is this true?" Eddie demanded. "You've really loaded your bombs with plutonium dust?"

Horst always seemed to look serious in some way no matter what he was saying, and Kelly never quite did. Together, they hardly gave him a clue. Easy enough to believe they had the stuff, but would they really poison a whole city to save the planet? That did not exactly compute.

And the Seawater Project did?

Kelly Jordan laughed, smiled brightly at Eddie. "What do you care, Mr. Franker?" she said, toying with the closure of her vest. "If anyone makes us hit the panic buttons, you're as dead as we are, plutonium or not."

"You'd really do it?" Eddie said softly.

"We are serious people," said Horst.

But Eddie's gaze had locked on Kelly Jordan. She looked back. She wasn't smiling now, and the superciliousness seemed to have evaporated for the moment. Her eyes seemed to be telling the truth.

"Do any of us know what we'll really do in a situation like that?" she said. "We say we do, we think we do, but who really knows until push comes to shove?"

"Scary," Eddie muttered, for that admission, in this moment, somehow gave the whole thing the ring of truth.

"Hey, Mr. Franker, we're terrorists, we're *supposed* to be scary," Kelly said with a feral grin. "Scary enough to keep KLAX on the air."

"Do you think we've succeeded?" Horst said. "Do you think the FBI will keep its word?"

Eddie sighed, leaned back, lit up a cigarette, grateful somehow to slip back into a more comfortable pragmatic mode.

"Depends on how far you push them, I suppose," he said.

"And what in your opinion would be pushing too far?"

Good question, Eddie thought, and better not to find out the hard way. He took a thoughtful drag, looked across the room over their heads at the air-feed monitor on the far wall, presently showing an old *Simpsons,* then checked his watch.

In the absence of any ability to read the minds, such as they were, of whoever was running the show out there, perhaps a little experiment might be in order.

"Look," he said, "we're coming up on the eight-thirty station break. So why don't we goose them a bit and see how hard they squeal? And maybe do ourselves some good in the process."

Maybe he was testing his captors too, seeing how far they would go in allowing him to run the news operation for them. Maybe in some weird way he was testing himself. How much would he risk to keep scooping the competition on the story of his own captivity? Where was the borderline between covering the news and *making* the news?

Especially when continuing to make it might be a matter of saving your own ass. . . .

8:30 P.M.

Onscreen:

A SOMEWHAT SHAKY LONG shot out a high window on the police line across Sunset Boulevard west of the station. Sawhorse barricades close the street, SWAT teams, squad cars, a robot minitank, three police buses, are deployed between the barricades and the station. A line of police stands on the other side of the barricades, facing east on Sunset, where the sidewalks stretching three blocks westward toward Vine have become crowded with people, spilling over into the gutter, blocking traffic. No signs or banners, apparently simply a more or less spontaneous agglutination of rubberneckers.

Toby Inman's voice-over: "Citizens begin vigil outside KLAX, instapoll finds Seawater Referendum too close to call, more at eleven!"

8:33 P.M.

KELLY AND HORST HADN'T objected to sending one of their cameramen up to the top floor with a hand-held to shoot live coverage of the barricades on Sunset as visuals for the 8:30 news promo spot, nor had the FBI thus far responded with so much as a peep.

"What say we crank it up a notch?" Eddie suggested.

"What did you have in mind?" said Kelly.

Eddie thought about it. What was it Berkowski had said about something going on at Parker Center?

"It occurs to me we've still got mobile units out there on the street," Eddie said. "Why don't you let me use one?"

Klingerman and Jordan exchanged glances.

"To do what?" said Horst.

"To rattle the bars of the cage just a little bit more and see what happens."

9:00 P.M.

Onscreen:

A LONG ZOOM SHOT from slightly above on a small crowd clumped behind police sawhorses on the street in front of Parker Center, four cops in black-visored helmets looking on, the narrow angle allowing a couple of dozen people to fill the frame. A few fists being waved, some incoherent shouting, otherwise not much action.

Toby Inman's voice-over: "Demonstrators gather at police headquarters to safeguard KLAX and protest Seawater Referendum, complete coverage at eleven!"

9:04 P.M.

So FAR, so GOOD, Eddie Franker thought. Sort of.

The Green Army Commandos might still control the physical station, but Horst and Kelly, perhaps without realizing it, had easily enough let him take stepwise control of the news operation.

They had let him lead them down to the control room so he could get on the radio to a mobile unit, and Vinh had managed to get the van down through the traffic to Parker Center in time to shoot live footage for the nine o'clock break.

Eddie had expected that getting live mobile-unit coverage out on the air with no technical expertise of his own and two terrorists in the control room would be the hard part, but that had turned out easy.

Warren's assistant, Jaro, hardly said a word, but he turned out to have magic fingers on the mixing board, and Warren himself seemed to know all about the broadcast and relay equipment. When Eddie told them what he wanted, they did it with relative ease. Indeed, it was soon apparent that they were more at home in KLAX's tech country than the station's own manager.

Eddie called shots for Vinh on the van via radio, Vinh bounced the feed back to the station via sat link, Warren caught the signal, Jaro mixed it with live narration from Inman, then Warren pumped it out simultaneously to the local transmitter via microwave relay and to StarNet via the uplink dish on the roof.

Eddie might not be particularly technologically knowledgeable, but it did seem to him that this was a lot of airwave traffic, and that the FBI could have broken the links, or jammed them, or easily isolated the station from the mobile unit.

But they hadn't. So far, they had kept their word. They let the remote feed from Parker Center reach the station and go out on the air without even a pro forma complaint from Carswell.

Arlene Berkowski, on the other hand, was on the line by 9:06, and bitching.

"El stinko, Eddie, really lame footage—"

"What the hell do you expect, Arlene—"

"—but it gives me an idea. You've still got control of that mobile unit at Parker Center?"

"So far," Eddie told her.

"Great, look, we got stuff coming in that something's starting to happen down in Long Beach, some kind of crowd forming near the shore-side seawater-pumping station."

"How do you—?"

"Let's just say we have . . . ah, internal intelligence on certain of the competition's com channels. . . . CNN has a mobile unit on the way down from Westwood, but they're stuck in traffic. The local ABC outfit wanted to send their chopper, but the airspace has been declared off limits. What our people who know L.A. tell me is that you can probably get your unit down there from downtown first. . . ."

Eddie took the phone handset from his ear and glanced around the control room, which was getting to be pretty close quarters with five people in it.

"StarNet wants us to move the mobile unit," he said.

"To where?" said Horst.

"Long Beach. Apparently the *direct action* you were trying to incite is beginning to happen."

Horst smiled just a bit, then turned pensive. "Do you think they will allow us to broadcast such material?"

Eddie shrugged. "Only one way to find out," he said. "Hit them with thirty-second spots for the eleven o'clock broadcast and see what they do."

"Do it," said Horst.

Eddie nodded, put on the radio headset, and told Warren to put him through to the mobile unit. Crazy though it is, he suddenly realized, somewhere along the line I've started to *enjoy* this. This is the most fun this stupid job has ever been!

9:30 P.M.

Onscreen:

A LONG SHOT ON the KLAX parking lot, apparently shot from a high window inside the station, as the camera pans slowly back and forth, up and down, across an impressive display of manpower, machinery, and ordnance.

The periphery of the parking lot is rimmed on the three street sides by parked police buses, and there are at least two hundred helmeted cops armed with shotguns and automatic weapons standing around in front of them waiting for something to happen. Closer to the building, SWAT teams in flak jackets have set up a ring of firing positions behind sandbags. Each firing position is centered around a man who seems to have some kind of hand-held missile.

Between the SWAT team positions and the conventional LAPD forces are two open-bed Hummers painted in ominously military khaki-and-green camouflage patterns. On the bed of the HMVs, weapons that look like multiple rocket launchers or outsized Gatling guns, presided over by National Guard or regular Army troops and pointed right up at the camera.

Toby Inman's voice-over: "Mayor, Governor, deny reported plan to rocket KLAX satellite dish, but warn Green Army Commandos against further provocations, bulletins on the half hour, full coverage at eleven!"

10:00 P.M.

Onscreen:

A SHIMMERY ZOOM-LENS shot at maximum magnification on the Long Beach nuclear desalination plant, sitting way out across the bay shining in its own floodlights: a big grayish-white dome set in a ring of girders above the large central cavity of something that otherwise looks much like an offshore oil-drilling platform.

The camera reverse-zooms, and then changes angle into a shot down a long metal pier. Two large-diameter pipes emerge from the sea at the far end of the pier and run along its sides like outsize rails toward the camera. The camera dollies backwards, revealing the land end of the pier, where the pipes enter a complex pumping station, and more piping looping away from it into the ground. There is a high chain-link fence separating the pier from a parking lot, razor-wire atop the fence that looks as if it may be electrified, and a gate in the fence in the center of the shot.

In front of the fence is a line of about twenty-five cops in mirror-visored riot helmets. About half of them carry clear plastic shields and batons. The others are armed with repeating shotguns.

The camera dollies back further to a shot over the heads of a crowd of about two hundred people gathered in a field across the road from the parking lot.

Some of them carry well-made if somewhat faded and clearly

recycled placards—NO MORE NUKES, CITIZENS AGAINST PROPOSITION 17, SIERRA CLUB AGAINST SEAWATER REFERENDUM, UNION OF CONCERNED SCIENTISTS—old ecowarriors who look as if they've been through this a thousand times before.

Others, some of them younger and scruffier, tending toward the black and Hispanic, carry painted bedsheets with mushroom clouds, exploding buildings, Los Angeles as desert wasteland, some of it quite nicely done in instant wall-graffiti style.

Still others, more prosperous looking, tending to be white, Asian, more yuppified, carry instant banners printed out on long strands of fanfold computer paper—SAVE KLAX, NO TO WATER VAMPIRES, ANTHONY ELLINGWOOD DIED FOR YOUR SINS, VOTE NO TO NUCLEAR NIGHTMARES.

Toby Inman's voice-over: "Ecological activists mass near Seawater Project pilot, threaten march on pumping station, pictures at eleven, here on KLAX!"

10:30 P.M.

Onscreen:

A LONG SHOT ON the bay, with the globe of the nuclear desalination plant in the background, the camera whipping back and forth confusedly as it tries to track the action.

Three, or possibly four, small boats with outboard motors—it's hard to tell in all the flying spray at this distance—are buzzing back and forth through the spotlight beams of two big police speedboats as the camera tries unsuccessfully to follow them, the police cruisers more or less herding them away from the reactor platform.

Toby Inman's voice-over: "Harbor patrol foils demonstrators' attempts to board Seawater reactor platform—"

The camera reverse-zooms back along the service pier, over the fence separating the pumping station from the parking lot. It's wall-to-wall cops along the fence now, two deep, a solid line with shields and batons backed up by a line of shotguns. The camera zooms back further to reveal a third line of riot police at the front of the parking lot, where it meets the roadway.

The crowd has grown rather larger, and it has spilled out into the roadway to confront the front-line cops almost nose-to-nose.

"—while demonstration outside pumping station grows, full live coverage in half an hour at eleven, with commentary by Green Army Commandos, only *here*, on KLAX-TV, Los Angeles!"

11:00 P.M.

Onscreen:

"**THE KLAX ELEVEN O'CLOCK** News—with Toby Inman, Heather Blake, and Carl Mendoza!"

Toby Inman, in close-up, looks pretty rank. His blond hair has been neatly brushed, but his face is stubbly, and his suit and shirt look as if they've been slept in for a couple of days.

"Good evening, Los Angeles. Well, we're at the top of the news again, that is the situation here at KLAX, where station manager Edward Franker, weatherwoman Heather Blake, sportscaster Carl Mendoza, and myself have been held hostage for two days by an ecological action group calling itself the Green Army Commandos. . . ."

Cut to taped footage from earlier in the day, a shaky long shot out a high window on the police line across Sunset Boulevard west of KLAX: barricades, SWAT teams, squad cars, a robot minitank, police buses, a small crowd spilling off the sidewalks and into the gutter.

Toby Inman's voice-over: "Meanwhile, spontaneous, ah, protesters have gathered outside the KLAX building to, er, protest the Seawater Project and to, uh, express their support for continued, ah, restraint, on the part of the authorities. . . ."

Cut to taped footage from earlier in the day of the demonstration, such as it was, outside the entrance to police headquarters, the narrow angle allowing a few dozen people to fill the frame and create the illusion of an off-camera multitude.

Toby Inman's voice-over: ". . . while a larger and more organized demonstration took place outside Parker Center."

Back to a close-up on Toby Inman.

"But the big demonstration of the day is the one currently, uh, going on down in Long Beach by the pumping station and service dock for the pilot Seawater Project reactor. KLAX's mobile unit is on the scene, and we'll have live on-the-spot coverage for you in a moment. But first, a few words with the people who'll be, uh, helping me, er, provide commentary on it, the, ah, very people who have, uh, provoked all this action themselves, uh, the Green Army Commando's own Minister of Information, and, uh, Chairperson—Kelly Jordan and Horst Klingerman!"

A long shot on Toby Inman flanked by Kelly Jordan and Horst Klingerman, an awkwardly wide angle that includes the edges of some lighting fixtures above the set.

"Well, uh, before we go to live coverage, uh, Kelly, let's, uh, update the situation. . . ."

11:04 P.M.

TOBY INMAN GLANCED AT the teleprompter out of sheer reflex, but of course there was no script crawl there. He was on his own.

". . . the, ah, latest instapoll that we've seen shows the Seawater Referendum likely to be defeated by a narrow margin, so. . . ."

Some awful impulse made Toby peek at the studio air-feed monitor, where what he saw was his own face in the process of delivering these pitiful ad-libbed lines.

One of the first rules of live TV was *don't* look at the monitor, a rule that Toby had always lived by, but whose wisdom he truly appreciated only now, in the breach, as a caricature of himself as a brainless talking head seemed to stare right into his eyes from the screen.

". . . you might say that your, uh, action, ah, appears to be heading for success. . . ."

Toby broke eye contact with his yahoo alter ego, but he couldn't escape the vapidity of his own yammering, the hesitations, the phumphering, the sheer *unprofessionalism* he could hear in his own unscripted voice.

". . . so maybe, your, ah, it might be time to talk about the, uh, consequences, for the, er, situation, right here at KLAX-TV . . . ?"

I sound like a brain-dead asshole, Toby thought helplessly as the words dribbled out of his mouth. *It isn't fair!*

"I'm not sure I'm exactly getting your drift, Toby."

"Well, I mean, what happens to us when the election is over?"

"You mean, are we gonna kill you, or let you go, or what?"

I haven't been trained for this!

Right! He almost broke himself up on the air with that one.

You haven't been trained for this, Inman. You haven't been trained to interview people holding you hostage without a script. Through some mysterious oversight, they failed to include such a course in the communications major curriculum at LSU!

"Well, I, uh, do have some personal interest in the, uh, question, and, ah, I'm sure—"

Come on, Inman, pull your socks up! If you're gonna die, at least make *them* do it, don't do it to yourself on the air!

"What happens to you, happens to us too, this I can promise you," Horst Klingerman said.

"What's that supposed to mean?" Toby demanded, surprising himself with the anger in his voice.

"We don't want to have to hurt anybody," said Kelly Jordan, no more than touching the top of her explosive vest, "but we want everyone to understand that we're sincere. So if you have to go to save this planet, Toby, we go with you."

"Who died and made you God?" Toby snapped. "Save the planet or we'll blow ourselves up! All right, crazy or not, that's moral dedication. But threatening to kill *us* to save the Earth, that's just blackmail, that'd be murder, wouldn't it? Who gave you the right?"

Wow, where did *that* come from? Toby wondered. The diction had been clear, the hesitations gone; it was as if he had been reading a script off a teleprompter in his head.

"That's a good question, Toby—"

"And it deserves a good answer, don't you think, *Kelly*?" Toby shot back. "I mean, speaking as one of the people you're holding here at ground zero—"

"Hey, there's nothing personal—"

"Well that's nice to hear."

"A cause that is absolute enough to die for is absolute enough to kill for," Horst Klingerman said.

That was kind of a conversation stopper.

"Wha-a-at?" Toby said with exaggerated slowness after letting the dead silence go on dramatically for a full beat.

"A cause that is absolute enough to die for is absolute enough to kill for," Klingerman repeated in bizarrely neutral terms. "I will explain."

"Oh, will you?" Toby shot back.

Klingerman nodded. "Markowitz claims that achieving good by a calculated tactical suicide is the ultimate revolutionary act," he said like some professor lecturing a class at LSU on his pet theory. "But it can be argued that *killing* in the same cause is an even more revolutionary act. By destroying ourselves in the act of blowing up this building, we sacrifice our lives, but not our honor. By killing you in the process, we willingly take it upon ourselves to commit an evil act in the service of a greater good."

"Uh, Horst—"

"The end justifies the means, does it?" Toby snarled, cutting Jordan off with volume. "You've got to destroy the village to save it? Kill for peace?"

"Horst, maybe you better let me—"

"Some ends justify some means. Sometimes it is necessary to amputate the rotting leg to save the whole body from gangrene. Any act is justified when it comes to saving the biosphere itself from otherwise certain destruction. Ultimate ends justify any means."

11:07 P.M.

"WHAT HORST IS TRYING to say—"

"To be willing to die that others may live, this is the Christian ethic, not true?"

"Right! And the Bible says it's okay to *kill* that others may live too? I guess I slept through that part in Sunday school."

Talking heads go apeshit, pictures at eleven! Eddie Franker felt like he was about to have an embolism.

Instead, he sprang to his feet, pressed his face to the control-booth window, waved his arms, then began slicing his finger repeatedly across his throat in a frantic "cut" signal.

"Go to the mobile unit, damn it!" Eddie shot back over his shoulder, as if the armed terrorists in the control room with him were dim-witted flunkies.

"Go to mobile unit . . . ?" Jaro said confusedly in his slow Slavic-tinged English.

"Cue it up on their air-feed monitor, fer chrissakes!"

"But they not narrating this camera feed. . . ."

"I know that, damn it, but I want them to—"

"But I cannot—"

"Gotcha, guy, you wanna go to the pictures to extro your dude from this scene, right?" Warren said.

"Right," Eddie said, and he turned to glance at the control room's air-feed monitor, slaved to the one inside the studio, upon which Warren had pumped up the camera feed from the mobile unit in Long Beach.

Eddie waved frantically at Toby Inman, finally seemed to have caught his eye, pointed forcefully again and again at the studio air-feed monitor—

11:09 P.M.

Onscreen:

A **LONG SHOT OVER** the heads of a tightly packed crowd on the triple police line between these demonstrators and the fence surrounding the entrance to the pumping-station pier.

A line of cops brandishing batons stands shoulder to shoulder behind clear plastic riot shields between the demonstrators and the parking lot fronting the roadway. Another similarly equipped police line has been deployed against the fence. More cops, these armed with repeating shotguns, are scattered about the parking lot itself in small tactical groups.

The globe of the Long Beach nuclear desalination plant and the searchlights of police cruisers chasing small boats are vaguely visible in the background. The crowd waves banners, placards, the occasional fists, bursts into random rounds of cheering that seem to have something to do with the small-boat action in the bay.

The camera pans back and forth slowly across this scene, speeding up jerkily to avoid holding on a CNN mobile unit that intrudes in the lower-left corner of the frame.

Just a lot of crowd noise, speedboat sounds, general aural bedlam for nearly thirty seconds, then—

Toby Inman's voice-over: "Well, uh, I see we've gone to live coverage from the scene of the Long Beach demonstration, so I, er, guess we'll have to continue this, ah, philosophical discussion later, but right now, maybe we could, uh, have your, ah, commentary on—"

Kelly Jordan's voice-over: "I'd be glad to, Toby. What we're seeing here proves that the Green Army Commandos have done the right thing. These good folks wouldn't be out there taking direct action if we hadn't liberated KLAX. Their hearts were maybe in the right place all along, but we had to take their precious tube hostage to get them to *act*."

Toby Inman's voice-over: "But what is a demonstration like this really going to accomplish?"

His face appears in the upper-left-hand corner of the screen, a somewhat shimmery inset square framed in blue fringes. Kelly Jordan's face appears in a similar inset in the upper right, while the rest of the screen is filled by the mobile unit's live coverage of the demonstration, the camera panning around randomly but trying to avoid more than a second or two's inclusion in the shot of other stations' mobile units, of which there seem to be plenty.

"Defeat the Seawater Referendum."

"Is it? Aren't these all people who planned to vote against it anyway?"

"Sure. But now they're showing their power in the streets."

"Seems to me everything you've done has been counter-productive."

"Hey, come on, Toby, you can look at this wonderful mass public response, and say we're screwing up?"

11:13 P.M.

"**WHAT ABOUT PEOPLE WHO** don't like the Seawater Project any more than you do, but think that terrorism and kidnapping is maybe a major no-no?" Toby Inman shot back without thinking. "And who think that people who think otherwise are gangsters and thugs?"

Courage, anger, inspiration, whatever, it all seemed to emerge from a place he had never been before, a place that existed only in some elusive virtual TV reality.

"*We're* gangsters and thugs? And the agro-industrial-real-estate mob that drained the state dry and sold us all that desert acreage isn't? It's worse to hold a TV station for a few days to get the word out to the people than to build a buncha time bombs on a fault line that's sooner or later gonna turn California into a radioactive no-man's-land? What kind of *people* you talking about, Toby?"

"People like me, Kelly. People who probably would've voted against Proposition Seventeen anyway, but who *you've* now given second thoughts."

It was wise to avoid looking at the monitor when you were doing a solo talking head, but when your talking head was interviewing another one, and the interview itself was inset over live-action coverage, then you *had* to check the mix out from time to time, no matter how weird it felt. . . .

"You were going to vote against the Seawater Project, and now maybe you wouldn't? Why?"

And it felt very weird indeed.

"Because it feels like being marched into that voting booth with a gun at my head."

"Really juvenile, Toby. You'd do what you know is wrong to spite Mommy and Daddy because they're telling you to do what you know is right!"

Here he was, on the set interviewing Kelly Jordan, and *there* his talking head was on the monitor screen, mouthing the lines he fed into it in real time. For an eerie instant of reversal, the words his lips were forming here on the set seemed to be under the control of the image on the screen.

It was disorienting, hypnotically fascinating, it was getting hard to look away, hard not to get sucked into it, hard not to let it take over. . . .

Toby blinked, forced himself to make eye contact with the woman seated next to him in the flesh, orienting himself via chemistry.

"That's the way people vote, Kelly. All the instapolls prove it, they've got to feel good about what they're doing. You make 'em mad enough, and they'd vote against a free lunch just to get even."

Kelly looked right back at him and laughed winningly. "I gotta admit that I don't think I look too fine wearing a black hat, Toby," she said.

Chemistry? Some kind of electronic circuitry?

The words had been pretty confrontational, much more confrontational than he had been with Klingerman, Toby suddenly realized, but somehow the music of this interview, the rhythm of the exchange, made it work smoothly.

"Believe me, I'd rather see you wearing a white one, Kelly," he said. "And *I* gotta admit, I'll say it on the air right now, I wouldn't want anyone to vote *for* Proposition Seventeen out of misguided sympathy for the hostages here, don't get me wrong about that, folks."

"Maybe we're saying the same thing, Toby?"

"How's that, Kelly?"

There wasn't anything sexual about it. They didn't really have to even like each other. They didn't even have to work well with each other. They worked well *off* each other.

The girl was a natural in a way that Toby knew damn well he wasn't, or at least had thought he couldn't be. The words flowed freely from her mouth without hesitation, maybe without even thinking. She didn't need a script. She could wing it. She just had to be cued and off she went. And she knew when to throw him a cue line too.

"Grow up, folks, wake up, and use your brains when you vote

for a change. Who knows, you might even like it, don't listen to us, don't listen to them, listen to yourselves, and do the right thing."

And when she did, Toby realized, he was able to wing it without a script too.

11:15 P.M.

EDDIE FRANKER HAD TO admit he was impressed.

Impressed by the way Warren and Jaro were able to mix this composite shot and keep it going, and even more impressed by the way Toby Inman was handling himself under fire now.

There was some kind of synergy between Inman and Jordan that let them play off each other, that brought out the potential talk-show host in Toby Inman, the mirror image, somehow, of the vibes between Inman and Klingerman that flared into poisonous lunacy every time—

"Call for you, guy."

"Not now!"

"I can transfer it to your headset."

"Who?"

"Some guy named Hildebrandt, says it's—"

"Robby Hildebrandt himself?"

"You wanna—"

"Yeah, yeah, pipe him through!"

"Franker?" said a kind of rolling good-ol'-boy voice in Eddie's ear.

"Yeah."

Eddie had never met StarNet's mastermind and creator, had never even talked to Hildebrandt on the phone before, knew him only by reputation. Which was as an old print rewrite man and editor who had eased into management of a feature syndicator, then created StarNet with a minimum of cash and a maximum of fast talking when the company he was working for folded under him.

"Look, Eddie . . . Eddie's okay, isn't it?"

"Sure, Robby . . ."

"Well, Eddie, we got a problem. The stuff you're giving us now ain't that bad, you understand, and it's doin' fine on the Coast where it's a hot local story and there's still some people awake, but nationally, nobody's watching, and our delayed tapes ain't gonna be worth jack shit tomorrow unless . . ."

"Unless what?"

"Unless you can this Frick and Frack show right now, and give us something exclusive all those other units out there can't match."

"Like—"

"—like maybe you could have the Green Army Commandos speak to the demonstrators."

"What! We can't possibly do that!"

"Why not? You got a mobile unit out there, don't you, Eddie? An' it's probably got a PA or a bullhorn, don't it?"

"Well, yeah, I think so, but—"

"Well shoot, Eddie, you got these people miked in the studio, an' you got a comlink to your unit right, so—"

"But—"

"So what's the problem, Eddie? You just split the signal, y'know, uplink the studio audio to us, an' downlink it to the mobile unit PA, an' all the competition will get in public domain is squawk-box sound while we've got air quality."

"You don't think this maybe carries managing the news just a wee bit over the top into creating the story you're supposed to be covering, Robby?"

"An' what's so all-fired wrong about that, Eddie?" Hildebrandt said with what seemed like total sincerity. "Aren't you the fella who sold us this as a big-budget story in the first place? What with fightin' all these restrainin' orders and all, we're barely out of the red on this thing. There's somethin' wrong about two ol' newshounds like you an' me gettin' together t'turn a little honest profit?"

"But what about the FBI and the FCC and—"

Hildebrandt's hearty laugh rang a bit hollow.

"Shoot, Eddie, that's really touching, there you are held hostage an' all, and you're worryin' about how I'm goin' t'handle *those* boys? Don't you worry, Eddie, you just get me that footage of your Commandos deliverin' a good ol' stump speech to them demonstrators, and never you mind, *I'll* take care of *those* sons o' bitches."

11:20 P.M.

"DO WHAT?" TOBY INMAN said.

"It's not my bright idea, believe me," said Eddie Franker, "it's Robby Hildebrandt's."

"Who is Robby Hildebrandt?" Horst Klingerman asked innocently.

"The head of StarNet," Toby told him, reeling with the sudden jump cut no less than Klingerman or Jordan.

First Franker flashes him cut signals, then someone pumps up a station break and commercial loop in the middle of a sentence, then Eddie's in here telling Heather to pick up on it with the weather, then he drags us off the set to tell us *this* piece of craziness.

"He *wants* us to speak to the demonstrators?" Horst said. "I do not understand. What does he expect us to say?"

Franker threw up his hands. "Don't you get it?" he said. "He doesn't care."

"He doesn't care?"

"This is your fifteen minutes of fame, kids," Franker drawled sardonically. "Say what you want."

"Anything we want?" Horst Klingerman repeated, almost visibly rolling the words around in his mouth to taste the notion.

"And he'll turn it into a major national story? And make the big bad G-men go away too?" Kelly grinned like a schoolgirl with a mouth full of steel teeth. "Well, hey, Mr. Franker, that's great! Why you looking so paranoid? What do you think we're gonna do?"

"What *are* you gonna do?" Franker said.

". . . and we'll be back with live coverage of the Long Beach demonstration right after this," said Heather.

Warren rolled a commercial.

"We gotta get back to the set now, don't we, Mr. Franker?" Kelly said. "So I guess we're just gonna have to make it up as we go along, now aren't we?"

Oh shit.

She gave Toby a wink that was somehow less than reassuring. "Sorta like what they used to call the golden age of live television, isn't that right, Mr. Franker? A high-wire act without a net."

11:25 P.M.

Onscreen:

A LONG SHOT ON the Long Beach demonstration from behind the demonstrators, the camera panning back and forth across the frame slowly, banners and placards more or less illegible from this angle, mobile units from other stations impossible to exclude entirely from the shot now, the faces of the police ominously unreadable behind their mirrored visors and riot shields, a police van mounting a water cannon now visible in the parking lot between the two lines of riot police.

Just a lot of wild sound, crowd noises, boat engines, general bedlam, for a few beats, then—

Toby Inman's voice-over: "Well, uh, we're back here live at the big demonstration against Proposition Seventeen down here in Long Beach, and, uh, we're gonna try something really different, folks. . . ."

An inset close-up on Toby Inman appears in the upper-left corner of the screen, looking very nervous. He moves his mouth to say something, but—

A horrible ear-splitting feedback screech!

Apparently it's not just on the air, because the people on the scene at the demonstration hear it too, heads turn en masse toward the camera with angry pained expressions, as—

The feedback dies away into a coherent but rather echoey version of Toby Inman's voice.

". . . hear me? Can you hear me out there?"

Boos, shouts, yells, waved fists, indicate that the crowd is now receiving the KLAX mobile unit's tinny output audio.

"This is Toby Inman of KLAX-TV speaking to you live from our studio in downtown Hollywood—"

The crowd reaction is less than enthusiastic. In the background, previously immobile and poker-faced riot police are turning their heads to regard each other in visible consternation.

"—where we've been held hostage for two days by the Green Army Commandos, whose, uh, action, ah, seems to have sparked, er, your very demonstration against the Seawater Referendum. . . ."

The booing and shouting begin to die down, the crowd becomes quieter, more expectant.

". . . and, so we have the opportunity to . . . I mean we are forced . . . well, anyway, here, uh, she is, speaking live to the anti–Seawater Project Referendum demonstration, *only* on KLAX-TV Los Angeles, the Green Army Commandos' own minister of information—Kelly Jordan!"

The inset of Toby Inman's face in the upper-left corner of the screen is replaced by a close-up of Kelly Jordan.

"Hi there, yes, this is Kelly Jordan, and I can't tell you how deeply moved I am to see this vast crowd of you good people turned out here tonight to stand up for the peoples of the Earth against the Seawater Referendum!"

Her audio is as hollow and thin as Toby Inman's has been, like someone speaking way down at the other end of a long tinny tunnel, but then, as the inset close-up of Kelly Jordan drifts toward the center of the upper third of the screen trailing blue fringes, some kind of technical adjustment is made to the broadcast audio so that what goes out on the air now is studio-quality sound rather than what the demonstrators are hearing.

"Now tomorrow the fate of Proposition Seventeen is gonna be decided in the voting booth like it's supposed to be, but lookin' at you brave people out there, I say we've won a great victory together already. We've proven that direct action begets direct action, we've helped you prove to yourselves that you're not the dumb herd of sheep the agro-industrial complex thinks you are! So let's have a great big cheer, not for me, not for the Green Army Commandos, but for *yourselves,* people! You folks have earned it!"

She pauses, smiles, as the crowd cheers.

11:31 P.M.

THIS WAS CERTAINLY THE weirdest moment of airtime Toby Inman had ever experienced.

". . . and win, lose, or draw on the Seawater Referendum, tonight the Green Revolution has started. . . ."

There he sat on the set watching it all on the studio monitor.

There Kelly Jordan sat, staring at the monitor herself against all the rules of TV professionalism, watching the words emerge from the mouth of her own image as she delivered them in the studio, while simultaneously clocking the live audience reaction in Long Beach.

". . . are you popping a six-pack and tubing out like a tribe of brain-dead couch potatoes like all the cynical packagers and media manipulators said you would? No! You're out here taking direct action!"

Toby watched the crowd reacting with cheers, and shouts, and the waving of banners and placards, watched the little face on the screen smile, and pause, and suck up the crowd reaction, turned and watched the flesh-and-blood Kelly beside him mirror that smile, nod in satisfaction, watch the image on the screen nod. . . .

". . . are you gonna let them turn California into Chernobyl West? Or take direct action? And let them pick your pockets to do it? Or take direct action? Turn this planet into their toilet bowl? Or take direct action? You wanna choke to death on carbon dioxide? Or take direct action?"

Kelly's voice fell into a hypnotic cadence, her body rocked back and forth in her chair to it, her eyes glowed with the charge, and her image on the screen seemed to pick it up and bounce it back at her off the crowd, a feedback loop of amplification that had them swaying to the rhythm too.

Toby wouldn't have been human if he hadn't been jealous, if he hadn't felt the allure of this heady power, if he had been immune to the desire to feel it himself.

But it was also quite terrifying.

What if StarNet had carried it one step further? What if they had set up a giant rock concert stadium monitor down there so the demonstrators could watch themselves making their own television reality too?

Fortunately, not even Robby Hildebrandt had thought of that one, nor, watching Kelly Jordan sucking it up or vice versa, would Toby care to mention the mass-market possibilities of such video cocaine to those who might choose to cash in on it.

Scary shit!

And when he stole a peek at Horst Klingerman, what he saw was scarier still.

Horst was staring hypnotically at the monitor too, his body

rocking to the rhythm of Kelly's rap and the crowd moving to it on the screen, and Toby certainly didn't have to be a crystal-channeling Topanga psychic to know that he lusted after his own nice big hit of that video stardust too.

11:36 P.M.

Onscreen:

"... **WATCH WHAT'S LEFT OF** the ocean die? Or take direct action? Fry to a cancerous turn in the greenhouse sun? Or take direct action?"

The crowd cheers, banners and placards wave, at the back of the screen the line of police shuffle their feet nervously, and in the inset close-up centered in the top third of the frame, Kelly Jordan grins triumphantly.

"... *you've* given your answer! You're taking direct action right now! You're gonna defeat the Seawater Referendum tomorrow! You got the power! You have started the *Green Revolution!*"

A big cheer rises, begins to fall away as she falls silent and continues to mug at the camera for several awkward beats. Half the crowd still looks uncertainly toward the camera and the KLAX mobile unit, as if waiting for a cue that doesn't come; others turn around to face the police again with a certain amplified belligerence.

Then Toby Inman's face replaces that of Kelly Jordan in the close-up inset box at the top of the screen. "Well, that was—"

Horst Klingerman's off-camera voice, distant and tiny, interrupts.

"I would like to add a few words to what Kelly has said now."

"Well, Horst, I don't know if we have time for—"

"I will now speak! Nigel, you keep the camera on me!"

A sudden jump cut to a close-up on Horst Klingerman, looking to the left. He squints at what he sees, looks into the camera, seems totally confused.

"This is not right, Warren," he says. "I must see them."

Back to the composite shot, but with Horst Klingerman replacing Toby Inman in the inset box at the top center of the screen.

It seems as if this back-and-forth has gone out over the mobile unit's PA system, for a lot of the crowd is goggling at the camera with rather bemused expressions.

"Can you hear me out there?"

A rumble of crowd noise tells Klingerman that they can, but there's a certain sarcastic edge to it, to which he reacts with visible annoyance.

"Yes, I know I am not such a good speaker in this language, and Kelly has a way with words," he says almost petulantly. "For a long time I was such a professional talker in my own language that some accused me of being afraid to take direct action. Then also, I can speak for the Green Army Commandos who come from many peoples not conversant with English. . . ."

This is not going over well at all, the crowd's attention is drifting rapidly back toward the police.

". . . peoples without countries, peoples whose lands have been raped and pillaged to create your trash piles, peoples who are not so different from you as you think. . . ."

Klingerman pauses, sees all too easily that he's bombing out, seems to grope for words that don't come, as the crowd, like an amoeba of human bodies, begins to flow away from the camera.

11:38 P.M.

HORST KLINGERMAN STOOD UP slowly, never taking his eyes off the air-feed monitor, as if drawn to it by some magnetic force, as, Toby realized, you could say he really was.

Nigel widened the camera angle to accommodate the action, and as he did, Toby watched the composite shot on the monitor change. And so did Horst.

Now he saw himself filling the entire left half of the screen, Uzi and explosive vest clearly visible in the medium shot, looming over the crowd like a giant poster of himself.

". . . capitalism, socialism, monetarism, fascism, monarchism, it is all the same, and we are all its victims, all of us, all the peoples of the Earth. The lands and lives of the planet are devoured with no thought for tomorrow for the benefit of a few fat predators at the top of the food chain."

A mighty legend on a stadium concert screen!

But only in his own mind, Toby reminded himself with some difficulty. This was what *Horst* was seeing.

As far as the mob scene in Long Beach was concerned, all he was was a bad-quality voice on a mobile-unit bullhorn.

". . . the baron, the king, the stockholders, the Party, it doesn't matter what they call themselves, they are what they have always been. . . ."

Toby knew for a certainty that something very bad was about to happen.

There Horst was, mesmerized by his own image on the monitor, himself as the movie-poster terrorist on ten million TV screens, the Mighty Electronic Quinn towering above the multitude, and what he was seeing on the other half of the screen was that this selfsame multitude was no longer paying attention to him at all.

He just didn't seem to get it.

The crowd was milling around rather listlessly now, but no one in it was looking in the direction of the camera. They were all naturally looking in the direction of the police lines, the Seawater platform lit up by floodlights, the speedboat action in the bay.

The mobile-unit camera zoomed out over the heads of the crowd to a shot on the desalination plant's nuclear containment globe glowing like a dull white jewel in the floodlights, panned down the girders, and pulled back through a plume of spray—

". . . the pirates who traded slaves for sugar and rum, the Party bureaucrats with their dachas and crumbling reactors, the factories turning the rain forests into chopsticks and hamburgers—"

—into a full shot on the ranks of the police, a fearsome fence of bodies, with their riot shields, and their billies, and the faces under the helmets unreadable behind their mirrored visors.

"And the thugs they hire with your money to protect themselves from you!" Horst cried out, pointing at the monitor screen.

Oh shit!

The crowd, of course, saw no giant figure pointing an accusative finger, but they could hear the mobile-unit bullhorn, and so could the police, whose faces might still be unreadable but whose displeasure could be read quite clearly in the curling tighter of their hair-trigger body language.

"Yes, I'm talking about *you*, whatever you call yourselves now!"

The forward line of police started fidgeting. A couple of them raised their batons. The crowd quieted as they saw the cops reacting to Horst's voice.

Oh . . . fuck.

They couldn't see him, but they could hear him. And now he had their attention. And now Toby saw that he seemed to finally understand the situation. And he smiled, and he nodded, and he seemed not so confused at all. As if he had planned all this. As if he knew just what he was doing.

11:39 P.M.

Onscreen:

ON THE LEFT HALF of the screen, Horst Klingerman, enormous, armed and dangerous, pointing contemptuously to the lower right like a prosecuting attorney pinning a dockful of perpetrators.

"The Cheka, the Gestapo, the Stasi, the flics, the *pigs*!"

On the right half of the screen, a long shot on the demonstrators, beginning to turn like a field of video sunflowers toward the camera, toward the disembodied voice on the mobile-unit PA.

"No, no, watch out, they're behind you!" Klingerman says, "there they are!"

Almost as one, reflexively, the crowd responds to the amplified shout of warning, heads whip around to confront the police, and bink, he's got them, they're listening to him almost as if he's really there, as if they're seeing what he sees, a giant Horst Klingerman menacing the lilliputian police line from the left half of the screen.

"There they stand where they always have, between the rulers and their victims, between the predators and their prey!"

He's also definitely caught the attention of the police, and they are definitely not amused.

"Without their vopos to hide behind, the people who are destroying your planet are helpless! When the police refuse to shoot unarmed citizens, direct action is irresistible! In my country, a brutal and efficient tyranny was swept away!"

The cops and the crowd are staring at each other now across a narrow divide of maybe three feet, an aisle between them created by the potential reach of baton and shield.

"If your police will stand aside, you can take direct action right now! You can march right down that pier and occupy it as we have occupied this television station! You can hold the pumping station and shut the whole thing down!"

The crowd begins to ooze tentatively closer to the police line, shields go up, batons rise threateningly. . . .

On the right half of the screen, the mobile-unit camera zooms in for a tighter shot on the line of riot police and the front of what has now become a surly mob beginning to press tentatively against their clear-plastic riot shields. Horst Klingerman's face in close-up fills the left half of the screen, seeming to directly address the police.

"Surely you will not shoot down your own unarmed citizens! Stand aside and let the people pass!"

Something happens somewhere that the camera doesn't catch.

One moment the mob is pressing tentatively against the riot shields of the police line, and the next moment, there's a general melee, batons thrashing, shields thrusting forward, people turning to escape but caught in the crush, other people surging forward waving their fists, trying to batter at the police with their placards, screams, shouts, the crack of wood smashing against plastic, the thunk of plastic against flesh.

11:45 P.M.

TOBY INMAN POINTED TO Horst, made frantic cutting motions across his throat, pointed forcefully to his own mouth.

Glancing at the monitor, he saw that someone had apparently gotten the point. Klingerman had been yanked off the air, and hopefully off the bullhorn, and now there was just a full-screen feed from the mobile-unit camera, panning back and forth, zooming in and out, trying not too successfully to capture poignant moments of coherence in the chaotic violence.

Horst was still staring at the monitor, but there was a measured appraisal to his scrutiny, a thin little smile on his lips, and he sank slowly back into his seat.

"Now look what you've done!" Toby snapped at him. "You've started a riot!"

"A riot," said Klingerman, "is when a mob runs amok without discipline or purpose. Not when the police savage nonviolent demonstrators."

"You incited this!"

"I suggested a disciplined direct action," Klingerman said in a maddeningly reasonable tone. "I believed that this was a democracy. I hardly expected your police to behave like the Stasi or the Gestapo! This is *America,* is it not, not the Third Reich?"

"You gotta forgive Horst his innocence, folks," Kelly Jordan said sarcastically. "He's never met the LAPD!"

11:47 P.M.

Onscreen:

A LOT OF BACK and forth and in and out by the mobile-unit camera as it tries to convey some overall impression of what has degenerated into a series of disconnected fistfights and beatings, people trying to flee, people trying to get their hands on the police—

Horst Klingerman's voice-over, ruefully: "Perhaps I *should* have known that the police would be ordered to create a provocation."

Toby Inman's voice-over: "Provocation?"

Kelly Jordan's voice-over: "What else do you call it? The police were ordered to start a riot to discredit the anti–Proposition Seventeen forces!"

The camera steadies. It fixes on something out of focus moving toward it in the background.

Horst Klingerman's voice-over: "A desperate measure they

would only have taken to try to save their Seawater Project from certain defeat."

The camera focuses on the water-cannon van moving forward across the parking lot toward it.

Toby Inman's voice-over: "The police started it? I didn't—"

Kelly Jordan's voice-over: "Just started whacking people over the head, Toby, you folks out there saw it, now didn't you, how could you forget it, it was awful!"

Toby Inman's voice-over: "They planned it beforehand? I find that pretty hard to believe."

The center of the police line parts to admit the water-cannon van. The turret swings around slowly, the nozzle comes around to bear, the cops fall back, and—

Kelly Jordan's voice-over: "I do believe that's a water cannon, Toby. Care to explain to the folks at home why they brought it if they didn't expect to be using it?"

—the water cannon blasts into the mob with a hard fire-hose stream, staggering people, knocking some of them right off their feet. Spray, and stumbling, and panicked confusion, as the water cannon hoses back and forth across the front ranks, herding them back with hydraulic force, police pressing forward beside it with their shields, swinging their batons, bottles, cans, assorted debris sailing toward them from the rear.

Horst Klingerman's voice-over, apologetic: "I'm truly sorry, I would seem to have entirely underestimated the ruthlessness of your political leadership and the brutality of your police."

A reverse zoom into a shaky long shot on the water-cannon van pressing very slowly forward into the crowd, the heavy stream of water waving back and forth, cops flanking it, anonymous behind their mirrored visors, shoving people with their shields, whacking at them with their batons, the camera dollying backward as the mobile unit retreats before what is now a fleeing mob.

The screen splits. On the right half, the riot, the water cannon advancing toward the retreating camera of the mobile unit, police clubbing demonstrators, general pandemonium; on the left, an insanely incongruous two-shot on Toby Inman and Kelly Jordan, talking heads doing commentary on the newsroom set.

"This is awful," Toby Inman moans.

"It certainly is, Toby! And it's all our fault!"

"You admit it?"

A full-screen close-up on Kelly Jordan, young, and bright, and somehow innocent despite the combat suit and the Uzi, cocking her head at the camera like a babe born yesterday.

"We thought *we* were terrorists," she says. "Our idea of getting physical was a peaceful takeover of a TV station where no one got hurt. We haven't hurt anyone, have we, Toby?"

A tight reaction shot on Toby Inman, looking a bit drained, a bit dazed, more than a little confused, and all the more sincere for it.

"No, Kelly," he says, "I gotta admit you haven't."

Back to a somewhat tighter close-up on Kelly Jordan, just her smooth shining face and youthful idealism, with no combat gear in the frame, as she delivers her perfect extro.

"Think about it," she says. "Think about it in the voting booth tomorrow, folks. The people who brought you Love Canal and Chernobyl and Three Mile Island and the Ozone No Zone have just reminded us all who the *real* terrorists are."

Cut to a close-up on Toby Inman, somewhere in outer space. He blinks, he smiles, he gets professional.

"Well, Kelly," he says in a flawlessly delivered anchorman extro of his own, "we'll find out what the folks out there think tomorrow, now won't we? And we'll have it all, election coverage with a difference, right here, on KLAX-TV, Los Angeles!"

DAY 3

11:10 A.M.

"JEEZ, I'M GETTING SICK of this stuff, I think it's making me constipated," Toby Inman bitched, picking listlessly at the little pile of trail mix in front of him on the table.

There was no more coffee left in the cafeteria machine, Franker was up in his office, Heather was in the can, and Inman's morning personality was about as charming as Carl's ex-wife's had been.

Carl reached into the trail mix bag, pulled out a big handful, chewed heartily, smacked his lips, pretended to enjoy it.

"How do you *do* it?" Inman moaned.

Carl needled him with a sour little laugh. "Hey, there were times in Nam when I lived for days on boiled grass tea and refried cockroaches," he said, "and some of the burgers in those California League towns were *worse.*"

"Spare me the war stories, will you, Carl!"

Carl grunted. Maybe I'm not exactly Little Mary Sunshine this morning myself, he thought. Pretty lame, Mendoza. You got nothing better to do than pull this poor bubba's chain?

Two days and more without a shave or a shower and two nights of sleeping in his clothes had rubbed the gloss off KLAX's anchorman's blond Anglo pretty-boy image, and he smelled like day six of a patrol in the jungle. Still, Carl had to admit he had never liked the guy more.

In fact, this was about the first time he had liked Inman at all.

Inman had never impressed Carl as anything but a lightweight.

But he had to admit that Toby had showed him something last night.

One of those moments, maybe, when someone grows himself cojones under fire. Carl had seen it often enough before. Some punk who spent every patrol you ever been on with him pissing and moaning is the one who takes out the machine gun's got you all pinned down. Some kid hanging on as a .230 utility infielder gets beaned, gets mad, goes three for four, goes on a tear, makes it to the majors.

"Seriously, Carl, how long you think we're gonna have to keep eating this shit?" Inman . . . *Toby* said in a rather serious tone.

Carl nodded at Paulo and Helga, sitting in front of the door with their Uzis across their laps. "Maybe we could ask them to send out for a pizza," he drawled.

"Very funny. But that's not what I—"

"I know what you mean," Carl said. "But today's Election Day. Proposition Seventeen passes or it goes down. The Green Army Commandos get what they came for and got no more reason not to let us go. Or they don't, and. . . ."

"And . . . ?"

Carl grimaced. He shrugged. "Either way, it don't look like we'll be eating this stuff for breakfast again."

"Terrific," Toby groaned.

"Hey, lighten up, Toby," Carl said. "The instapolls showed Proposition Seventeen fading fast even *before* last night's action, and the good old LAPD didn't exactly do it any good."

The ladies'-room door opened; Heather emerged and made her way back across the cafeteria to the table.

"What were you guys talking about?" she said as she sat down.

Toby picked up a few fingerfuls of dried fruit and nuts, let them dribble back into the pile. "This stuff," he lied truthfully. "And how much longer we can stand eating it."

Carl found himself beginning to grimace and had to stop himself from showing it. *He* was supposed to be the old Latino mucho machismo jock, right? So why was Inman's protectively patronizing attitude toward Miss Tits and Ass starting to piss him off?

Heather scooped a bit of it into her mouth. "Not exactly the best I've ever had," she said blithely. "Could do with some cashews, and Brazils, some dates and dried bananas. There's a place in the Farmer's Market where you can get it with macadamias, and hazelnuts, and dried *raspberries*."

Carl gave her a narrow look.

Right. Sure.

Heather smiled her blond bimbo smile back.

Bullshit, muchacha.

Carl gave her a phony smile back. Heather's expression didn't change at all, she didn't even blink, but in that moment something passed between them, some acknowledgment, something that had nothing to do with sexual attraction, something that wasn't even exactly personal, a message without a gender at all. Carl couldn't even say exactly what it was.

But he knew it was there.

1:13 P.M.

WARREN STOOD BY THE window looking out at the scene down on Sunset, his Uzi slung over his right shoulder. Jaro, his taciturn control-room collaborator, sat in front of Eddie Franker's desk cradling his Uzi in his lap and doing a less-than-convincing job of playing soldier.

Not that Eddie was really paying much attention at the moment as he sat there with the telephone receiver jammed between his right ear and his shoulder while he lit another cigarette and tried to get Yancy Foster to do his job.

"Come on, Foster, you're supposed to be the legal eagle, can't you—"

"I could be Clarence Darrow with dirty videos of the entire Supreme Court in action, and I couldn't do anything, Franker," Foster drawled. "Not after last night."

Eddie finished lighting his cigarette, picked up his remote, once more began flipping reflexively through the competition's coverage on the TV across the room that was jacked into the cable. It was pointless, of course. He knew the bad news already.

Every station in town with a chopper or a mobile unit had a camera on the building, on the demonstrators that surrounded it, on the police deployment.

Every station but KLAX itself.

The FBI, or the LAPD, or someone, had confiscated the station's own two mobile units for the duration, and neither Sierra Communications Incorporated, nor their mouthpiece Yancy Foster seemed to have the ability or inclination to get them back.

An off-year primary election like this would ordinarily have been a lead story only in California, maybe good enough for fourth or fifth story down on the national nets on a slow day. But the hostage situation, and KLAX's live coverage of the Seawater riot with color commentary by the terrorists the authorities were blaming for starting it, had made the story today's number one national news event.

The local stations were using shots of the demonstrators outside KLAX as lead-ins and extros to their hourly election bulletins, CNN was opening every half-hour cycle of Headline News with it, the national nets had featured it on their morning news shows.

Flipping through the channels, Eddie could see it all. The police had established barricades all around the station, so that none of the crowd could come within two blocks just in case the whole place went up. Most of the signs and banners seemed to be pretty standard anti–Proposition 17 or general ecofreak stuff, but there were also a few placards featuring an arm holding a machine gun aloft in green silhouette or otherwise openly supporting the Green Army Commandos. There were also banners saying things like HANDS OFF KLAX, FREE TOBY INMAN, NO USE OF FORCE.

Heartwarming, Eddie thought sourly, but also maddening.

Here he was, all too literally in the middle of the biggest story of his career, the *only* national story of his career, the chance of a lifetime in more ways than he cared to think about, and all he had to cover it with was a studio full of talking heads and two amateur British punks shooting hand-held long shots out the window.

"They're *killing us* on the coverage, Foster," Eddie moaned. "I mean without a mobile unit, we're gonna run close to dead last at six o'clock! Can't you get a restraining order or an injunction or something?"

"Jeez, man, the terrorists used your goddamn mobile unit to

start a *police riot,* thanks to which you now got instapolls showing Proposition Seventeen doesn't have a prayer, which is mucho dinero out of the pockets of the very boys who pay your salary and my retainer, and they are not exactly overjoyed with the situation—"

"You tell *the boys* that the only way they can come out ahead on this on their goddamn balance sheet is if our ratings—"

"—and on top of all that it's *Election Day,* Franker, remember, so how the fuck do you expect me to find a judge at all today, let alone one crazy enough to see it your way, even if I was paid to want to, which I'm not, so I don't."

"Screw you too, Foster," Eddie said, and he hung up.

"Bad news?" asked Warren. Unlike Horst and Kelly, he hadn't insisted that Eddie pump every phone conversation up on the speakerphone, so he hadn't bothered.

"That asshole is seldom anything else," Eddie grumped. "Calls himself a lawyer, but all he really is is a high-priced errand boy for the owners—"

"—Sierra Communications Incorporated."

"You know that?" Eddie blurted, caught by surprise.

"No, man, we just picked this station's name out of the phone book," Warren drawled sarcastically. "We don't know dick about the people who own it, or how much bread they've put behind Proposition Seventeen."

Eddie studied the man who seemed to be the chief of the only crew he now had.

With his long messy blond hair, granny specs, slouchy build, and pasty skin, Warren looked like a cross between your typical computer nerd and the anachronistic old hippie he was too young to be. Except, of course, for the explosive vest and the Uzi, which on him took on the unconvincing air of props.

The kind of techie who ordinarily did his job and faded into the background, at least from Eddie's usual perspective. What do I really know about this guy? Eddie thought for the first time. He can run a control room almost single-handed. He obviously knows from satellite links. Cool in a crisis. Takes direction well. Doesn't get excited. Doesn't waste words. What else?

He's a terrorist, that's what else!

Somehow, in what Eddie suspected would have been Warren's own terms, it did not compute.

5:30 P.M.

WEIRD, THOUGHT HEATHER BLAKE, weird because not weird.

Except for the absence of Melanie to do their makeup and the presence of Helga and Paulo to keep them armed company, it seemed bizarrely like just another evening in KLAX's dingy little green room waiting to go on at six.

Carl slumped in a chair in front of the air-feed monitor, with the sound turned off as usual, zoning out into the exciting denouement of a peculiar old movie that somehow managed to feature cowboys and dinosaurs in the same shot. Toby was scanning a printout of wire-service stories he had managed to wangle out of Warren in lieu of his accustomed script.

Heather herself was reading a printout of the six o'clock weather report and thinking how odd it was to be doing so under the circumstances without it really seeming strange at all, when the green room door opened, Helga stood aside, and Kelly Jordan entered.

"Hey guys," she said rather gaily, "you'll be glad to hear that the exit polls confirm that it's tube city for the Seawater Referendum!"

"Then you'll release us after it's official?" Toby asked hopefully.

Kelly sat down in front of the makeup table, peered into the mirror, fluffed at her Afro. "After a few odds and ends are tied up," she muttered.

Carl managed to tear himself away from the dumb movie, not exactly an arduous effort. "Odds and ends?" he said in a somewhat suspicious tone.

"Well, we *do* have to successfully terminate the action. . . ."

"Terminate the action?"

Helga, who had been slouching by the door like a prison guard bored by the doings of the denizens of the yard, seemed to come to sudden alertness. Paulo, seated in the back of the room, a stone-faced enigma as usual, didn't do much more than blink, but Heather's instincts told her that his attention level had just risen.

"Negotiate our way out of here," Kelly said.

"You really think you can cut a deal?" Carl said in a tone of voice that quite clearly told that he thought otherwise.

"Oh yeah, we're holding the high cards," Kelly said blithely.

"Meaning us . . . ?" said Toby.

"And the plutonium."

"Plutonium?"

"What plutonium?"

"The plutonium powder in our plastic explosives," Kelly said with insane matter-of-factness. "Didn't Mr. Franker tell . . ."

Turning away from the mirror to confront the three of them, she clearly saw that he hadn't.

"We've told the FBI that the charges are laced with plutonium dust, not enough for a nuclear explosion, but enough to poison a large part of the city—"

"It's true?" Heather blurted. "You'd really do such an awful thing?"

Kelly Jordan smiled at her with fatuous blankness. "Would I tell you it was false if it's true? Would I tell you it's true if it's false? Either way, would you believe me?"

"You think you can bullshit the FBI like that?" Carl blurted, and then obviously wished he hadn't.

"Did I say it was bullshit?"

"You didn't say it wasn't."

Hard looks began to build between them. Heather caught it, Helga seemed to catch it, tightening her grip on her weapon, and Kelly seemed to catch *that*.

"Hey, come on," she said, "What're they gonna do, get you killed for sure, and risk contaminating a whole city for no gain, or play it safe and let us go?"

"Just like that, let you go?" Carl said dubiously.

"Well . . . maybe, uh, we could arrange something where we all leave here together or something, and . . . they let it look like we escaped, or—"

The door opened and Horst Klingerman stood in the doorway for a moment like Karloff's original portrayal of the Frankenstein monster—hulking, menacing, maybe, but also somehow touching in his psychic fumble-footedness, a monster, if such he really was, for whom Heather could feel sorry.

He glanced at Helga for just half a beat, but Helga's eyes narrowed as if she was acknowledging something. He crossed the room, flopped down in an overstuffed chair, and only then did he seem to focus on Kelly.

What's really going on here? Heather wondered.

"You've told them, Kelly?" he said.

"About your so-called plutonium?" Carl snapped.

Horst smiled at him rather strangely. "You think it is so difficult to acquire a kilo or two? You think your authorities will find it totally without credibility?"

Carl glared at him.

"You had better hope they do not," Horst said.

"Better I?"

"Oh yes, you—"

"What Horst means is that—"

Kelly had started to interrupt, but Horst cut her off. "I can speak for myself in this matter, Kelly, even if I lack your television personality—"

"Hey, Horst, I'm sorry, I only meant—"

"I know what you meant, Kelly, now you will please let me finish," Horst said evenly, but it was enough to reduce her to what she was, a girl twenty years or so younger than the apparent leader of the Green Army Commandos being forced to bow to his masculine authority.

"All our lives depend to a large degree on the authorities' belief in that plutonium, Mr. Mendoza," Horst said. "Or at least in their shadow of a doubt—"

"—because you do not go free if we do not," said Helga. "And if they attempt to take this building, we all die together, that is right, yes, Horst?"

"That is right, Helga," Horst said. *Her,* Heather realized, he allows to interrupt; it's *not* a question of male piggery.

Kelly, on the other hand, now seemed to be eyeing Horst suspiciously. "Hey, wait a minute, Horst, that's not what—"

"*Please,* Kelly," he snapped, "we will discuss this privately, later, yes?" And shut her up again. "What I was *trying* to ask you before all these interruptions," he said in another and peevishly professorial tone, "is whether you have told these people that they are to do their normal news broadcast at six without us?"

"Our *normal* broadcast?" said Toby.

"Just so," said Horst. "The Seawater Referendum would seem to be in the process of being defeated, so any further action on our part at this time would only be counterproductive. Isn't that right, Kelly?"

"If you say so, Horst."

What does this scene really mean? Heather wondered. Are there *factions* inside the Green Army Commandos?

Heather realized what a stupid question that was the moment she thought it.

You couldn't have ten people engaged in a mutual enterprise *without* factions developing—in a film class, the cast of a production, or a movie crew.

Of course a terrorist group would be no different.

6:00 P.M.

Onscreen:

"THE KLAX SIX O'CLOCK News—with Toby Inman, Heather Blake, and Carl Mendoza!"

Toby Inman in the standard opening close-up, if framed somewhat crookedly and a tad too tight. His sleek blond hair is well combed, though his shirt and jacket look rumpled and three days of blond beard give him a rakish sexiness.

"Good evening, Los Angeles, good evening, California, and good evening to all of you out there tuning in to KLAX's exclusive coverage of, ah, this rather unusual, uh, situation, and at the top of the news is the projected defeat of Proposition Seventeen on the California primary ballot, the Seawater Referendum, the, er, cause of the hostage situation here at KLAX in the first place. . . ."

He seems to be losing the thread for a moment, pauses for half a beat, stares resolutely into the camera through the teleprompter, recovers.

"With about two hours to go before the polls close, both the instapolls and the more traditional exit polls all show fifty-seven percent of the statewide vote going against Proposition Seventeen, plus or minus two percent, and nearly sixty-two percent of South-land voters turning thumbs-down on the plan to relieve the drought conditions by building a string of offshore nuclear desalination plants. . . ."

Cut to a somewhat shaky hand-held long shot from on high out one of the station's windows on the crowd on Sunset behind the police barricades, faces turned slightly upward almost as if they know they're in the shot. The camera zooms in and out, moves around rather fitfully, trying to catch close-ups on the placards and banners, but from this high angle it's pretty much impossible, all that it gets is illegible bits and pieces.

Toby Inman's voice-over: "Meanwhile, a large crowd has gath-ered here at KLAX, where our hostage situation continues, though since Proposition Seventeen seems certain to be defeated, there is reason to hope that our, er, ordeal will soon be ended. . . ."

6:15 P.M.

IF I THOUGHT ABOUT it, this whole goddamn thing would be totally surreal, Eddie Franker thought paradoxically, realizing in that mo-ment that he had, and it sure as shit was.

On the air-feed monitor, Mendoza was not only running down the ball scores but narrating the freebie game highlights supplied by the Major League Baseball media office. In Eddie's ear, via the headset, Arlene Berkowski was whining about the crummy audience share. On the set, Ahmed and Helga were on the cameras, with Nigel and Malcolm still ready to shoot from the top floor just in case, and Kelly and Horst sat behind the cameras riding shotgun, or rather Uzi, with their backs to the control-room window.

In the control-room itself, in what the naive might conceivably refer to as the real world, Warren was trying to get his relief camera people to frame their shots more professionally, while Jaro mixed the baseball tapes with the studio audio and Ahmed's off-center close-up of Carl.

". . . left a little, Ahmed. . . ."

". . . look, Arlene, what do you expect me to do, put the Green Army Commandos up to goading L.A.'s Finest into attacking the building so we can boost our audience share another seven points in the process of getting ourselves blown to bits?"

". . . wouldn't do any good, Eddie, not without decent pics, and everyone out there's got coverage except you. . . ."

". . . with three runs without a hit in a wild ninth inning, on two walks, a dropped fly ball, a throwing error, a balk, a passed ball, and a wild pitch . . ."

". . . okay guy, now come in a little. . . ."

"Very funny, Arlene. Now maybe if Hildebrandt could get my mobile units—"

"There are limits even to Robby's clout. Besides, who cares? *Everybody's* got their mobile units out there, what we need is more exclusive stuff. . . ."

". . . in Detroit, the red-hot Kazu Tomashi extended his hitting streak to nineteen games with a double and two singles to raise his league-leading average to three sixty-eight. . . ."

". . . no, no, Ahmed, we don't want to see his *tonsils*. . . ."

"Like what?"

"Like the only exclusive you've got, Eddie."

All at once, Eddie's fractured and fragmented consciousness snapped into sharp focus. Warren's direction, Carl's patter, faded into the aural background, and all he really heard was the woman's voice on the phone.

"You mean you want me to put the terrorists themselves back on the air?"

"What *else* do you have that CNN and the nets, and for that matter every crappy little independent in your market area, doesn't have?" Arlene Berkowski said. "Have Inman do an interview. But don't do it until . . . lessee . . . six-forty, your time. That'll give us time to alert the affiliates, and them enough time to hype it during their half-past station breaks."

"But Arlene, Klingerman's liable to freak the cops again, and this time—"

"No problem, Eddie, we don't really need him, just go with Jordan; anyway our instapolls show that *she's* the one the audience—"

"Arlene! These people are *terrorists*! We're their *hostages*! Klingerman is their *honcho*! I'm supposed to tell him he can't go on the air because he's bad for the ratings?"

"You want *me* to talk to him, Eddie? I've got the figures right here, I could explain the instapoll differential between his image and—"

"Fer chrissakes!"

"Look, I think I could get *Hildebrandt himself* to lay it out for him, if that's what it takes."

"I'm sure Klingerman would be just overwhelmed," Eddie drawled.

"You think so?" Arlene Berkowski said earnestly.

That piece of innocent cynicism was enough to shatter Eddie's attention back into fragments, back into the surreality of the *real* world, where Mendoza was winding down his sports segment, where Uzi-packing terrorists in vests stuffed with high explosives were manning the cameras, and the mixing board, and the sat links, where Eddie Franker himself could be blown to pieces if Horst Klingerman did anything to light a match under the powder keg of paranoid cops, National Guard troops, FBI agents, and god-knew-what-else brandishing all that heavy ordnance outside.

". . . okay, Ahmed, just hold that, don't try for anything fancy, okay. . . ."

". . . five runs on ten hits and no errors for the Yankees, three runs, six hits, and one error for the Red Sox. . . ."

The real world, where, on the other hand, the sons of bitches who owned the station were royally and unjustly pissed off at him for allowing the Green Army Commandos to torpedo Proposition Seventeen, as if there was anything he could have done about it if he had wanted to, and would probably fire his ass when all this was over if he didn't recoup enough of their real-estate losses for them by keeping the ratings up.

The real world, where the last thing Eddie wanted was to broker a conversation between Robby Hildebrandt and Horst Klingerman, in which the StarNet honcho would attempt to convince the Green Army Commando honcho to stay off the air by telling him how shitty his image looked in the instapolls.

Eddie sighed. "No need to disturb the Great Man with petty stuff like this," he said. "Leave it to me, and I'll do what I can."

6:38 P.M.

IN THE IMMORTAL WORDS of Yogi Berra, Toby Inman thought nervously, it's déjà vu all over again.

There he was again, with Horst Klingerman and Kelly Jordan in Carl's and Heather's usual slots flanking him, waiting for the station-break commercial loop to end.

Eddie, or Warren, whoever, had dropped an extra commercial cycle in right behind Carl's segment without the usual anchorman extro, under airtime cover of which the station manager had charged into the studio in a breathless sweat.

"Heather! You go on directly after this break! Stretch your segment to three minutes, then intro another station break, we need time to talk, you got that, can you do that, sure you can, that's my girl."

"Right, Mr. Franker," Heather said gamely, scarcely batting a beautiful eyebrow.

Franker had then pulled Toby off the set, behind the cameras, to where Horst and Kelly were sitting on folding chairs with their Uzis across their knees, and laid it out.

The ratings were going down the tubes. StarNet wanted a twenty-minute personality profile interview with Kelly Jordan to go on at 6:40.

"Jeez, Eddie, I'm a newsreader, I've never hosted a talk show."

"Think of it as a major career move, Toby," Franker had drawled half sarcastically. "StarNet's hyping the hell out of this in advance, you'll be auditioning in front of a big national audience. Make good, and you could be the next, uh, Oprah Winfrey."

"I do not like this," Klingerman said. "Putting us on the television again before the pollsis likely to be more counterproductive than anything else."

"Not *you*, just her," Franker told him. "The instapolls show that you come across as Mr. Bad Cop, but she plays as Ms. Good."

"Vas?"

"You scare the audience, Horst. You piss them off. They don't like you. *Her*, they like."

The look on Horst Klingerman's face was so pathetic that the poor bastard actually had Toby feeling sorry for him. "I am not a cop of any kind," he almost whined. "I wish only to save the biosphere of this planet for future generations. How does this make me a bad person? Why should this make people not like me?"

"It's not that you're a bad guy, Horst," Franker said soothingly. "It's just that you don't play well on the tube."

Horst Klingerman's face hardened. His hands stroked the Uzi meaningfully. Franker froze. Slowly, he turned his gaze to Kelly Jordan, as if searching for support. But Kelly wouldn't look at him. Instead she shook her head, looked at Horst, then reached out and touched his hand.

"No go, Mr. Franker," she said. "If this is some cheap shot to divide us, forget it. If I go on, Horst goes on. We're a team."

Franker fidgeted unhappily. "Then maybe we'd *better* just forget it," he sighed.

"You *already* forget," Klingerman said. "You forget that decisions are not now being made by you. And there are things that must be said to the people soon, anyway. So why not make your friends at StarNet happy and do it now, yes?"

And with that, the decision, such as it was, had been made. Toby had gone back on after Heather's segment to fill StarNet's setup time reading bibble off the wires, and now here he was in the hot seat, counting down the seconds to—in Eddie Franker's words—his chance to make good and become the next Oprah Winfrey. Or Phil Donahue. Or Ted Koppel.

Of course, neither Oprah, Donahue, Koppel, nor any other star talk-show host he had ever heard of had ever interviewed their own armed kidnappers live and unrehearsed.

Maybe Eddie Franker was righter than he knew. Maybe this really *was* the opportunity to make a major career move.

After all, a huge national audience *would* be watching, would be finding out if Toby Inman really had what it took to be more than a newsreader, more than a major-market anchorman, more, even, in some sense, than a Rather, or a Brokaw, or even a legendary Cronkite, even as Toby himself found out whether he had the inner star-quality stuff.

If he succeeded, the sky might be the limit.

If he bombed out. . . .

Not exactly a fortunate choice of phrase.

6:40 P.M.

Onscreen:

A FULL SHOT ON the newsroom set, Toby Inman in the central anchor slot, Horst Klingerman to his right, Kelly Jordan to his left, their Uzis slung over their shoulders, their explosive vests hanging open over their chests. Toby Inman looks into the camera for a silent beat, seems to be calling up something from somewhere, takes a visible breath before he speaks.

"Well, folks, it seems pretty clear now that the Seawater Referendum is going to be defeated, and that the actions of the Green Army Commandos are in large part responsible, and so, uh, while we, er, still have them in the studio, uh, as it were, let's try and learn something more about the, ah, real people behind the . . . ah . . . the . . . er . . . the news. . . ."

He half turns to face Kelly Jordan, and there is a sudden awkward cut to a somewhat strange two-shot, Toby Inman in profile, Kelly Jordan in a full frontal angle behind him.

"So, ah, why don't we start with you, Kelly Jordan? Why don't you tell the people out there something about yourself?"

Kelly Jordan grins at the camera. "Shoot," she says. She almost winks, but not quite. "I mean, where do you want me to start?"

Cut to a more conventional two-shot, Toby Inman and Kelly Jordan framed more or less dead center, he looking at her, she playing directly to the camera.

"Like, oh, something about your childhood, your hometown, your parents, where you grew up. . . ."

Jordan looks into the camera for a silent beat, then it moves in for just a close-up on her as she starts to speak.

"Well, I guess you'd have to say my hometown was the Air Force, Toby. I was born right here in Los Angeles, but I don't remember much about that, or the next few places. My father was ground crew, we moved around from base to base, Alaska, California, Okinawa, the Midwest, all over, but it was all Air Forceville for a kid—the base, the noncom family housing, the PX, the other Air Force brats without any real long-term friends. . . ."

Cut to a two-shot, emphasizing Kelly Jordan.

"You didn't find all that travel exciting, seeing the country, seeing the world?"

The camera moves in for a close-up on just Kelly Jordan as she sighs, as a sad faraway look comes into her eyes.

"The world?" she says.

She shrugs. "When I was a little kid, I lived in *Americaland,* the Disney version. My parents wanted to keep the kid *American.* The more foreign it is *out there,* the more American *you've* got to be, the Girl Scouts and Sesame Street, Mickey and Roger, the same brands from home in the same aisles in the same PXs . . . *more* American than the real thing, as American as the Air Force and apple pie. . . ."

An awkward cut to a two-shot from another angle, half a beat after Toby Inman starts to speak.

"But for a black kid . . . I mean, wasn't there any, er, ah . . ."

Kelly Jordan's nostrils flare for a moment, her eyes narrow, but it's just a quick flash. "Hey, my grandfather had an appliance store, my father was a master sergeant, and the only ghettos I saw as a kid were on TV. The Air Force . . . the Air Force bent over backward to keep any racial stuff to a minimum, besides which having a topkick for a daddy kinda gave the other Air Force brats a reason to stay polite. I didn't even know what the real world *was* when I was a kid! Not until Germany."

"Germany?"

"My dad got transferred to Mannheim in Germany when I was about thirteen, and we were in Germany for the next five years . . . that's where I really started growing up, where I was finally old enough to get out on my own in the world off base, whether the Air Force liked it or not, whether my parents liked it or not. . . ."

"That's when you met Horst Klingerman?"

6:43 P.M.

"No, **NOT FOR ANOTHER** couple of incarnations," Kelly Jordan said.

Toby's initial plan had been to do a one-on-one with Kelly, then another with Horst, cheat it toward giving Klingerman as little airtime as he could get away with.

Maybe it was the way Horst was fidgeting. Maybe it was the way his interview with Kelly was turning into her monologue.

Whatever. Toby didn't quite know why, but some instinct he had just discovered he had, some feeling in his gut that went straight to his mouth, was telling him to throw that whole plan out, take her line for an extro, and make the whole thing much more interactive. Wasn't that what a talk-show host was supposed to do?

"Well, why don't we hold *that* story for a bit later, Kelly, while we bring our audience up to, uh, speed, with some, ah, back story on our other, uh, guest tonight, Horst Klingerman," Toby said, turning his profile to the hot camera and his eyes on Klingerman. "What about it, Horst, why don't *you* tell us something about yourself?"

"About myself?" Horst said uncertainly.

"Your childhood, where you grew up. . . ."

"I grew up in Leipzig. My childhood was school, and youth activities, long hours of hard work, but otherwise rather boring, this was generally what it was like as small boy in the DDR."

"The DDR . . . ?"

"Deutsche Demokratische Republik. German Democratic Republic."

"You mean, uh, the former East Germany? The, uh, old Communist police state, if you'll pardon my saying so?"

Horst peered at Toby like a teacher at a hapless student who had just said something particularly stupid. "Where else did you imagine Leipzig to be, in Bavaria?" he snapped. "And why do you apologize for calling a spade a spade? It was indeed a police state. The Stasi had infiltrated everything like a nest of maggots in a piece of rotten meat."

Toby began to sweat under the shooting lights. This was not going to be like interviewing Kelly. This was going to be a ballbuster.

"So, ah, what did your parents do?"

"My parents were politically correct proletarians," Horst said. "My mother worked in an industrial laundry and my father in a sausage factory."

"A sausage factory . . . ?" Toby blurted, biting his lip to keep from breaking up.

"This is funny in English?" Klingerman snapped. "Believe me, it was no laughing matter in the DDR in those days! It was a leg up the ladder for me into Karl Marx University!"

"Karl Marx University?" Now a brief giggle *did* emerge from Toby's mask of professionalism.

"You find that funny also?" Klingerman said angrily. "You are one of these ignorant people who think a degree in history from Karl Marx University is a worthless credential? You imagine your own Western equivalents are free from ideological bias in the opposite direction? Our intellectual standards were as high as anything in the Bundesrepublik and then some!"

Jeez, what the hell did I say? Toby wondered. Whatever it was, he had better cool things off, and fast!

"Uh, no offense to your alma mater, Horst," Toby said hastily. "I'm sure it was a terrific school—"

"We were in the forefront of the Revolution! We started it when we marched into the Opera Platz! *We* were the ones who put ourselves at risk to make the Reunification, not the Wessies!"

"Opera Platz? Reunification? Wessies? What are you talking about?"

Horst goggled at Toby in apparent amazement. "What am I talking about?" he said incredulously. "What do you *think* I'm talking about?"

Toby shrugged. What else could he say? What else could he do?

He smiled his best hunky smile and told the truth.

"Frankly, Horst," he said, "I haven't the faintest idea."

6:44 P.M.

Onscreen:

A CLOSE-UP ON Horst Klingerman as his anger visibly fades, though the afterglow of some sort of pain in his eyes is slower to gutter out.

"I forget myself," he says. "I forget that these things mean nothing here." He even manages a little smile. "I forget that I am not in an Oranienburger Strasse café or lecturing my old students in Leipzig."

An awkward late cutaway to a close-up on Toby Inman, a beat after he starts to speak, so that his first few words come as voice-over behind Horst Klingerman's face.

"You were a schoolteacher?" he says.

An awkwardly early cut back to a close-up on Horst Klingerman, cutting off Inman's image on the next-to-last syllable in overeager anticipation of the reaction line.

"I was a *professor of history* at Karl Marx University myself when the Reunification came!" Klingerman proclaims proudly. Then, much more quietly: "Well, an instructor at any rate, I hadn't completed my dissertation when the Wall came down, and after that the academic world in the former DDR pretty much fell apart, and like so many other of my former compatriots, I innocently assumed that life would be grander for me in the land of bananas and Mercedeses."

A two-shot on Toby Inman and Horst Klingerman.

"Bananas and Mercedeses?"

The two of them seem to be making eye contact, but not much more.

"Wessieland. Deutsche mark, deutsche mark, über alles . . ."

"Uh, in words of one syllable, for the folks at home . . ."

Klingerman half turns to squint uncertainly at the camera, as if to make eye contact with the viewing audience.

"The Bundesrepublik," he says. "The former West Germany. I left Leipzig for Berlin. Go West, young man, go West! This is an American idiom, is it not?"

"Well, here we both are in L.A.!" Toby Inman says brightly. "I'm a boy from the East myself, the *Southeast,* that is, Georgia, where we went through our own Reconstruction, where some folks ain't been reconstructed yet, so I guess I sort of know what it can be like to be a boy from the boonies in the Big Town."

Klingerman looks back at him with a sudden searching respect.

"They think anyone with an accent like ours must be a little dim, right?" Toby Inman says.

"They treat us like poor relations arriving on a late train from the country at their feast. . . ."

"They think the food we eat is funny. . . ."

"They make it impossible to get a position worthy of one's academic qualifications. . . ."

"They do?" Toby Inman says, and some subtle rapport that had been beginning to build between them evaporates.

"A degree in history from Karl Marx University is a joke to the Wessies!" Klingerman snaps. "They believe that a Marxist education in the social sciences causes permanent brain damage! They're all for materialism, all right, they worship it, but they wouldn't dream of allowing their students to be contaminated by anyone who might approach it from a dialectical perspective."

"You mean they treated you like you were a Communist?" Toby Inman says. "But . . . but you *were* a Communist, weren't you, I mean . . . *Karl Marx University.* . . ."

"*Here* I must hear this too?" Klingerman shouts. "I cannot believe it!"

"I only meant—"

A close-up on Horst Klingerman, his fair skin flushed with indignation.

"It was a university in a Marxist state so *of course* we had to teach history from a Marxist perspective! And what is so terrible about that anyway, what makes it worse than the breast-beating self-serving apologies for capitalist manifest destiny that pass for historical analysis in the West? Say what you like about Marx as a prophet or a utopian, at least dialectical materialism provides an objective analysis of political and economic reality!"

A hasty cut to a close-up on Toby Inman, looking quite befuddled. "Then you *were* a Communist?"

A two-shot on Inman and Horst Klingerman as Klingerman pounds the table with his fist. "I was a *Marxist,* perhaps, I was educated to approach the material from certain perspective," he insists, "but I was *never* a member of the Party! I *loathed* the Party! I was there in the Opera Platz with the people bringing it down!"

"So you were actually in the, uh, resistance?"

"Of course I was! By that time the whole country was! The Wessies did not march in and free us, after all! For nearly half a century they did nothing! The people of the DDR liberated themselves by direct action! It was something to be proud of!"

"Well, uh, that's all very—"

"Yet they treated us like a conquered people! Like the people of the *former Confederacy* were treated here, and worse!"

"Well, uh, I guess I can understand that, I suppose," Toby

Inman says as the camera moves in for a close-up on him with perhaps somewhat unseemly haste. "And I can understand how all of this must be, uh, painful for you to talk about, Horst—"

Horst Klingerman's voice-over: "—they paid Ossies two-thirds wages, did you know that, they made it impossible for me to—"

"—so why don't we get back to *you* for a few moments, Kelly. You say you spent most of your teenage years in Germany, but you and Horst never met then?"

A sudden cut to a close-up on Kelly Jordan, watching the back-and-forth between Inman and Klingerman with more than a little distress.

"Uh, yeah, that's right, uh, Toby," she mutters distractedly.

Then she seems to realize that the camera is on her, pulls herself together, looks right at it, speaks to it almost professionally.

"Not until years later after I returned from exile, you might say, back home in the United States . . ."

6:47 P.M.

"**. . . SO YOU SEE, TOBY,** I discovered the *real world* for the first time as a teenager in Germany, Europe, and, in a kind of way, the real America that I had never seen."

"Maybe you'd better explain *that* one a bit to the folks out there, Kelly," Toby Inman said smoothly, smiling silkily into the camera, partly because it was the thing to do to keep the mood lightening, and partly out of genuine relief.

"About all I knew about the United States before I was old enough to start running with the Eurotrash was MTV, CNN, the Hollywood version, and the military version. Now, at least, I had another cartoon version, America, as the *Germans,* as the *Europeans,* as the *world* saw it. . . ."

What a relief it was to cruise along like this with someone who had the instincts, who seemed to have the moves, after falling down that black hole with Horst!

". . . sex, drugs, rock and roll, Disneyland fascism, Elvis in a flying saucer, Hell's Angels on wheels. Jazz and McDonald's. Beggars in the streets and its troops all over the world. Race riots in its cities and massive relief missions in Africa. The impoverished military overlord of the planet."

"Musta been confusing," Toby said.

Kelly laughed a warm young-girl laugh.

"Half of my friends were afraid I'd whip out a razor every time some skinhead looked at me cross-eyed, and the other half were disappointed when I didn't," she said. "And as far as the skins were concerned, I might be a nigger, but I was an *American,* which at least made me better than a Gypsy or a Turk. Yeah, you could say being a black American in dear old Deutschland was a little confusing, all right, Toby!"

Smooth as a duckling's butt, Toby thought. Looking good. Her I could interview forever.

But he knew it couldn't last forever, or even till seven o'clock. Glancing quickly over at Klingerman, he saw that Horst was wriggling in his seat like a kid who had to pee, like the author grudgingly granted the last five minutes of a major-league late-night talk show to promote his book watching the celebrity astrologer ahead of him eating into *his* slot.

6:49 P.M.

Onscreen:

". . . ON YEAH, THE EUROTRASH greenie-weenies, as Daddy called most of my friends when he wasn't calling them something worse, *loved* black Americans; I was about as politically correct and culturally chic as you could get. I was the belle of the ball, my parents tried to keep tabs on me, but by the time I was seventeen, I had been all over on my own, boyfriends' cars, hitching, the old Trans-Europe Express. . . ."

A two-shot on Toby Inman and Kelly Jordan smiling for each other in the direction of the camera. Brush out the Uzi and recolorize the combat suit, and it could be your standard show-biz pitter-pat.

"And Daddy was not amused?"

"If Daddy was white, he woulda turned purple," Kelly Jordan says, softening it to a sitcom line with a twinkle. "As far as he was concerned, my crowd were all drug-crazed pacifist Bolshevik econut sex maniacs."

"What *my* daddy used to call the 'whole tie-died ball of candle wax.' "

Kelly Jordan laughs. "Yeah, and Daddy was convinced that my 'activities,' as he called them, were having a 'negative impact' on his Air Force career. So you can imagine how happy he was when he got transferred back to the States and dragged the family with him, to Vandenberg, not so sure he didn't wangle it, though he never admitted—"

"And you?"

"Vandenberg? For me that meant finishing high school in *Lompoc*."

"That's about sixty or seventy miles north of Los Angeles, right?"

"And about sixty or seventy thousand light-years from civilization after bopping around Europe, Toby. I mean, there I was, in a small-town high school full of redneck lager louts of both sexes with the political consciousness of grunions whose idea of trendy sophistication was to get blotted, go down to the beach, and screw while hoping their daddies at the base would oblige them with a missile launch."

"Pretty hard to take after Europe, huh?"

"*I* was pretty hard to take, Toby, I made sure of that. I mean, I was *pissed off*. I showed 'em! I went looking as far as L.A. for the most extreme action groups I could find, the loonier-toonier the better, no tune was too loony for me, not the Animal Liberation Front or speedfreak clones of Greenpeace, or the Militant Anti-Nuclear Coalition, anything that would drive my father crazy."

The camera moves in for a close-up on Kelly Jordan as she shakes her head, grinning.

"I was a monster. It was so easy. Compared to what I was used to, these people were so pure and simple and innocent. All I had to do was tell them war stories about my days in the European political underground, babble a little German, and I had even the so-called adult leadership of outfits like MANC convinced I was a napalm-breathing terrorist on the lam with heavy-duty Baader-Meinhof connections!"

A close-up on Toby Inman from another angle.

"All just to get even with your father?"

A close-up on Kelly Jordan as she shrugs, then shakes her head. "Oh, there was more to it than that. We all knew that things were getting terminal, the ozone hole, the greenhouse, the coral dying, the beginning of this drought here, but we had about as much of an analysis of what had happened or what to do about it as Las Vegas awaiting the Second Coming of Elvis."

She smiles rather wickedly, but it is the gleeful wickedness of a happily naughty child.

"Besides which, I had an agenda. When I graduated and turned eighteen, I wanted to be sure that Daddy would be only too glad to send me back to Europe!"

6:51 P.M.

KLINGERMAN WAS PRACTICALLY JUMPING out of his skin; there were about ten minutes left, Toby knew he couldn't keep Horst off the air much longer, Kelly had given him a perfect segue line, maybe he could use it to control the interview, keep it light and chatty.

"And that's when you two met, right?" he said, looking away from Kelly and at Horst. "When Kelly returned to Europe?"

"Yes, that is right, but—"

"And where did you meet—"

"In Berlin, in the *Weimar Republik*—"

"The Weimar Republic? Wasn't that the government that was overthrown by Hitler?"

Horst actually laughed. "In this case, it was a cellar café just off Oranienburger Strasse in the former East Berlin, the name itself being the proprietor's idea of Weimar-era humor."

Keep it short, Toby thought, keep it fast, now turn into a three-way conversation.

"So you met Horst in a bar in Berlin?" he said, quickly turning his attention to Kelly. "What were you doing there?"

"Looking for terrorists," Kelly said brightly. "The place had that kind of reputation—"

"Not entirely without justification," said Horst.

"—sort of a terrorist union hiring hall—"

"You were looking to join a terrorist group?"

"No, Toby, actually I was looking to hire one, or put one together."

The material was getting pretty weird, but the pacing seemed to be working so far. Keep it going like this, Inman, and we get through these next few minutes bright and clean. . . .

6:52 P.M.

Onscreen:

A LONG THREE-SHOT on Kelly Jordan, Toby Inman, and Horst Klingerman, a bit too long, with an overhead shooting light flaring into the lens of the camera for a beat until it comes in a bit closer. Inman and Jordan making easy eye contact, Klingerman looking not so happy, beginning to get ants in his pants.

"Hire a terrorist group?" says Toby Inman. "For what?"

Kelly Jordan mugs at the camera. "To do just what we're doing right now, Toby," she says.

"Kelly—"

"To seize KLAX-TV?"

"To get Anthony Ellingwood's story on the air—"

"Kelly, I do not think—"

"You knew Ellingwood from California?"

"No, Toby, but when Ellingwood went to the Militant Anti-Nuclear Coalition, MANC came looking for me, hey, I was the only real terrorist they knew, right, and when they told me their story and gave me a budget, well, hey, what was I gonna do, admit I had bullshitted them? Besides—"

"That is quite enough, Kelly!" Klingerman snaps.

"Hey, Horst, I only—"

"I said *enough,* Kelly! You are letting your mouth run away with you! You are not a disc jockey now!"

Toby Inman jumps on this, assumes a show-bizzy tone.

"You were a disc jockey, Kelly?"

"Uh, sort of, Toby, clubs, a little radio, some cable TV, I had to do something, and a black American girl who could motormouth in English and German had a kind of—"

"This interview has become entirely frivolous! We did not seize this station to fill the air with empty blathering!"

A quick cut to a close-up on Toby Inman, looking rather discombobulated.

"Huh?"

A close-up on Horst Klingerman, frowning in strangely prim-seeming disapproval. "The intellectual level of this discussion is embarrassing," he says. "Why don't you ask some meaningful questions?"

A two-shot on Toby Inman and Horst Klingerman, glaring at each other, Klingerman disapprovingly, Inman with indignation.

"I suppose you think you can do better!"

"If I were conducting this interview, I would at least try to understand why I was being held prisoner."

The camera moves in for a close-up on Klingerman as he looks toward it, makes a wooden attempt to play to it.

"Perhaps the people out there would be interested in learning *why* an international direct-action group has seized a California TV station?" he says sardonically.

A two-shot on Klingerman and Inman from a different angle.

"I thought the idea was to defeat the Seawater Referendum."

"Why would we risk everything over a local issue in Southern California?"

"Who's doing the interviewing here, anyway!" Toby Inman says angrily.

Horst Klingerman smiles. "I'm trying to get *you* to do it . . . *Toby,*" he says, with a sarcastic emphasis on the name.

It's obviously false, but Toby Inman manages to smile back at him.

"All right, Horst," he says, "what *is* a nice terrorist group like you doing in a local issue like this?"

Klingerman manages to laugh. "Defeating this referendum is a concrete achievement, but it has a much larger meaning," he says. "It is the beginning of the Green Revolution. A new kind of revolution based on a new kind of revolutionary tactic."

"What you keep calling 'direct action,' right?" Toby Inman says. "But what's so new about taking hostages and threatening to blow things up?"

"Now *that*, Toby," Klingerman says with genuine approval, "*is* an interesting question. You call me a terrorist, but I am not a terrorist."

"And I suppose I'm not your hostage, either?" Toby Inman says dryly.

Klingerman ignores him, looks directly into the camera. "Terrorism uses physical force to compel adversaries to act against their own class self-interest. Direct action uses physical confrontation to inspire the people to do what they know is right. To take direct action of their own. The Communists of Eastern Europe used *terrorism* to seize and hold power. But when the people began to take *direct action*, it spread like a firestorm, and blew them away."

"Terrorism is for bad guys, and direct action is for good guys?" Toby Inman says. "Then how come you're holding us prisoner and threatening to kill us?"

"Direct action is not pacifism, Toby. You must be willing to put your life at risk. And the lives of others."

"To kill for peace, huh?"

"If that is what it takes. The biosphere of this planet is dying. For decades, parlor radicals and well-meaning Greens have spoken, and marched, and demonstrated, and run for office, and they have failed to stop this planetary genocide. The Green Army Commandos are prepared to kill and to die if we must for something much more important than peace on Earth."

"More important than peace? What the hell's more important than peace?"

Kelly Jordan's voice-over: "Hey, Toby, wake up, will you? How about the survival of life itself? I mean if we—"

Klingerman turns to glare at her interruption, but as he does, there is a sudden late cut to a close-up on Kelly.

Horst Klingerman's voice-over: "—if you don't mind, Kelly!"

"—turn the Earth into a dead ball of rock like we're doing, war and peace becomes kind of an obsolete problem!"

Toby Inman's voice-over, loudly: "So saving life on Earth is one end that justifies any means, is what you're saying, Kelly."

"You got it."

The camera moves around disjointedly for a fraction of a beat.

Toby Inman's voice-over, loudly: "But you know, Horst, you never did answer the question you wanted me to ask! Why the Seawater Referendum, why California? Why do your direct action thing in the United States in the first place?"

The camera settles into a standard frontal full shot on the three of them, and by the time it does, Toby Inman seems to have restored a kind of order, flipped it into a Sunday-morning political panel-show format.

"Because the United States is both the problem and its solution," Klingerman says. "The greatest biospheric criminal—"

"Hey, wait a minute, Horst, that's not fair!" Toby Inman says.

"—and the military overlord of the planet."

"The military overlord of the planet . . . ?" Toby Inman says, rolling the words slowly out over his tongue as the camera uses this setup line to move in for a close-up on Klingerman, playing now directly to it.

"No combination of nations can stand against you. Destiny has placed the power of life or death over our planet in *your* hands. Only you have the power to save the Earth. And that gives you the responsibility to use it. The United States must act directly and unilaterally to save the planet."

Just the close-up on Klingerman, looking deadly earnest, for a beat, and then a cut back to the standard frontal three-shot as Kelly Jordan and Toby Inman react.

"Say *what*—?"

Jordan goggles at Klingerman, rather wide-eyed.

"You're suggesting that the United States use *military force* to—"

Inman seems to be groping for some concept. ". . . To . . . to do *what*?"

"To do what must be done, Toby," Horst Klingerman says quite calmly. "To save life on Earth."

Inman looks at Klingerman, then at Jordan, who has been eyeing Horst peculiarly. She shrugs. "Hey, don't look at me, Toby," she says, "I haven't heard *this* one yet, either!"

"The Green Army Commandos have demonstrated that we are willing to resort to unilateral direct action to do what we can to save the biosphere," Horst Klingerman says as the camera slowly moves in for a close-up. "At the risk of our own lives and those of our hostages, we have seized this television station and used it to persuade you to do what is right and defeat the Seawater Referendum. We are good people willing to do necessary evil to save the Earth. And so we are called terrorists."

He shrugs. "Now you must make your government do necessary evil to save life on Earth from certain extinction. You will be called imperialists, fascists, militarists, a terrorist *country*."

The camera begins to slowly pull back as Horst Klingerman comes to the conclusion of this little speech.

"You must do it anyway. You must take these insults as a badge of honor. If life on Earth is to survive, you must become Green Army Commandos too."

By the time he has finished, the camera has pulled all the way back into a three-shot. Klingerman sits there staring into it earnestly. Kelly Jordan eyes him with a kind of stunned hero worship.

"Wow, Horst," she says softly, "that's a long way from what we set out to do."

"And a longer road ahead still, Kelly," Klingerman says. "The Green Revolution has just begun."

Toby Inman, who has been sitting there just listening, reacts to something off camera, nods.

A close-up on Toby Inman, a strange half-smile on his face. "Well, that's all we have time for, folks," he says in anchorman extro cadences. "But we'll be back at eleven with final election results, right here, live, on KLAX-TV, Los Angeles!"

9:15 P.M.

No **CHAMPAGNE, NO LUMPFISH** caviar canapés, nothing to drink but water and what soft drinks were left in the machines and nothing to eat but the same old trail mix, but somehow the scene reminded

Heather Blake of nothing so much as a combination of a wrap party on a shoot and the postcurtain scene backstage on the opening night of a play.

Except for Jaro, still in the control room tending the sat link and the air feed, and Ahmed and Paulo apparently doing guard duty on the building entrances, the whole cast and crew were gathered in the cafeteria.

Eddie Franker had plugged a cable feed into the big monitor on the wall between the toilet doors, and there he sat in front of it flicking through the channels nervously for election coverage like a producer waiting for the first reviews. Carl Mendoza stood behind him, watching over his shoulder.

Warren and Hiroshi sat on folding chairs guarding the door, but they had their machine-pistols in their laps, their body language was relaxed, and they were jackpotting like tired stagehands.

Nigel and Malcolm, the two punker cameramen, were off at a corner table by the water cooler doing something to one of their cameras.

Toby and Kelly sat together talking themselves down from the performance high like a couple of actors waiting expectantly for their notices.

At the table nearest the door, Horst and Helga sat whispering in a bubble of isolation like the nervous writer and his Machiavellian agent, she popping a pill into her mouth that might be Maalox or aspirin, then offering one to her client.

Heather found herself viewing it all through her filmmaker's eye, something she often did at wrap parties for TV shows or B-movies in which she had been a mere bit player.

In a way, this wasn't so different. Toby had gotten to do his big star turn on the air with the terrorists, and she and Carl had served as little more than cutaways.

Heather hadn't seen it through such show-biz-colored glasses while her life had seemed to be on the line, but now that the whole hostage situation seemed about to come to a safe conclusion, she felt free to wish, not without a certain sense of irony, perhaps, that her part had been bigger.

Toby Inman had never impressed her as anything but a competent newsreader, a male equivalent of the bimboid weathergirl *she* played. But tonight, under pressure, working without a script, Toby had looked pretty damned good, considering the circumstances.

A piece of work like that with such national exposure was bound to draw the attention of major producers, news magazines, heavyweight agents. Job offers were going to come Toby's way off this, the grand tour of the talk-show circuit; the cover of *People* was not out of the question.

I wouldn't be human if I didn't envy him, Heather admitted to herself. I wouldn't be human if I didn't wonder if *I* couldn't have done just as well or better if I had had the chance.

But I wouldn't be human if I didn't admit that he deserves whatever he gets out of this. I'd be a low form of life for sure if I couldn't admit that the guy *did* come through in the pinch, that he's earned it—

"Hey people, the fat lady just sang!" Eddie Franker shouted.

Everyone froze.

"CBS, CNN, and ABC have just called it. The Seawater Referendum loses, and it loses big, sixty-three percent against according to CBS, sixty-two percent according to CNN, with ABC calling it at sixty-five percent! It's all over!"

It was certainly a strange moment. A spontaneous cheer went up from terrorists and hostages alike, followed by a spattering of applause. Warren got up, went over to Eddie, and actually gave him a high five!

Heather found herself in the grip of a most peculiar emotion. It was natural, of course, to feel a flush of relief now that the goal of the Green Army Commandos had been achieved and release seemed imminent.

But how natural was this other thing that she felt, this weird and nameless sense of loss, this sudden drain of energy, this bizarre and seemingly entirely inappropriate frisson of *sadness* at the thought that these three days of terror were now winding down to a happy ending?

The Method actress in Heather tried to seek out its roots. Was it just an irrational letdown having more to do with hormone surges and psychic energy levels than content? Something like the famous Freudian postcoital depression she had never personally experienced?

The wannabe director in Heather scanned faces, trying to read whether or not any of them shared this strange bittersweet letdown.

Eddie just looked tired and happy. Carl's eyes seemed strangely guarded. Toby and Kelly were grinning at each other like a mixed-doubles team who had just won their long hard tennis match. Warren and the cameramen were flashing their own victory smiles. Hiroshi sat by the door with his gun in his lap, stone-faced as usual.

Horst and Helga glanced up at him cryptically. Hiroshi nodded almost imperceptibly. Helga's eyes seemed to narrow. Horst took the pill she had given him, wolfed it down dry, bent over, said something in her ear.

Then, as if he had felt the pressure of her eyes upon him, he looked up, and his eyes locked on Heather's across the width of the room.

Just for a moment. Just for a beat or two.

But in that moment, something passed between them.

Heather couldn't quite say what it was, and she doubted whether he could either. A mutual acknowledgment of something, maybe.

He couldn't read her mind.

She couldn't read his.

But she somehow knew that he was feeling what she felt.

And she knew that he knew it too.

11:00 P.M.

Onscreen:

''THE **KLAX** ELEVEN O'CLOCK News—with Toby Inman, Heather Blake, and Carl Mendoza!''

The standard head-and-shoulders shot of Toby Inman. His suit and shirt are rumpled, he looks tired, disheveled, badly in need of a shave, but there's an energy in his smile, and his stubble, instead of being grubby, combines with the highlights in his blond hair, makes him look golden, triumphant—a star.

"Good evening, Los Angeles," he says in a round announcer's

voice that nevertheless lets a certain giddiness burble through, "and at the top of the news this Election Day in California, and certainly for all of us here at KLAX, is the stunning landslide defeat of Proposition Seventeen, the Seawater Referendum, the proposal to build a string of offshore nuclear desalination plants up and down the California coast. With ninety-one percent of the precincts reporting, the voters of California have turned it down by a margin of sixty-three percent to thirty-seven percent. . . ."

The camera moves in for a tighter shot, just Toby Inman's face, fatigue lines evident, beard emphasized, emotion nakedly showing, more a shot of an actor in some film than coverage of a TV anchorman.

"For those of you following the hostage situation here at KLAX, I don't have to tell you what this means to Heather Blake, Carl Mendoza, station manager Edward Franker, and myself, ladies and gentlemen. It means that the Green Army Commandos have achieved their goal, so we should be freed as soon as a peaceful surrender can be arranged between them and the authorities. . . ."

He pauses. Either his voice cracks with emotion or he puts on a very good act.

"I . . . we . . . I know with my head that the Seawater Referendum was no doubt defeated on the merits, but . . . but . . . but just the same, my heart tells me that in a very real way, my life, our lives, were in *your* hands out there, and . . . and you didn't let us down, folks, you didn't let us down. . . . So thanks to all of you out there, from all of us in here. . . ."

He blinks, the camera pulls back into a standard head-and-shoulders shot, his voice smooths out, becomes that of the professional newsreader again, the moment passes.

"And in other local primary elections here in Southern California, and throughout the Golden State. . . ."

11:29 P.M.

". . . AND THAT'S SPORTS FOR tonight, so over to you, Toby," Carl Mendoza said, and his red camera light went off.

"Thank you, Carl, and we'll be back right after the station

break with a final interview with the leaders of the Green Army Commandos—Horst Klingerman and Kelly Jordan!''

They ran the station-break loop, under cover of which Carl and Heather stood up to leave the set, vacating their positions to make room for Klingerman and Jordan.

Franker had gone on and on about how this was going to be their last chance at milking what they could out of the situation from StarNet, Toby Inman had been only too glad to go on with the two of them one last time in what figured to be a cakewalk now, Jordan and Klingerman seemed to have caught the show-business bug, and Carl, feeling himself a minority of one, though he wasn't so sure about Heather, had kept his misgivings to himself.

"The fat lady just sang," Franker had said when the networks called the election. Proposition 17 had been defeated, and all that remained was to negotiate a release and surrender with the authorities.

Only *those* fat ladies hadn't sung at all. They hadn't even whistled. No phone calls from the LAPD, the FBI, or anyone else out there. Nada.

Carl didn't like it. No news was not always good news. It seemed to him that there should have been someone on the horn with Franker or Klingerman or someone long ago, negotiating the details of the release and surrender.

If that was what they intended.

Whoever *they* were by now.

Carl did not exactly consider himself a political sophisticate, but you didn't have to be the kind of guy who read the rest of the *Los Angeles Times* through from cover to cover before you even looked at the box scores to know that there must be some pretty pissed-off people calling the shots out there now.

The Green Army Commandos had faced down the LAPD to the point where the FBI had taken over, meaning raw meat down there on the street and hot tempers in Parker Center. They'd stymied the FBI too, meaning angry chains of command stretching all the way back to Washington.

And the politicians who supposedly gave their signals—caramba! Proposition 17 had been their baby. The money boys who financed their campaigns for them had poured mucho dinero into getting it passed, and now all that was down the willy hole thanks to a bunch of Uzi-toting crazies and their captive TV station.

Despite all the backslapping and high fives going on inside the station now, the fact of the matter, at least as Carl saw it, was that the people managing the blue team outside were probably in no mood to be good sports about it.

Horst Klingerman eased himself into Carl's slot as Carl slid by him. Their gazes slid past each other too, without really meeting.

Carl sure hoped Franker knew what he was doing. He hoped that the six o'clock news hadn't been a fluke, that Toby really did know how to keep this character from doing something provocative again.

Certain power hitters with more muscles than brains thought it was cute to rub it in. Such assholes came up after a couple three homers, and they swung from the heels on the first pitch just to give the finger to a poor pitcher having a bad day.

Cabrones like that had a tendency to draw more than a brushback or a knockdown from a humiliated pitcher on his way to the showers. From a certain viewpoint, they were just *asking* for a high hard one *behind* their heads, where reflex was likely to back them into it.

Carl had the awful feeling that whoever was managing the blue team out there would just love a good excuse to order up a beanball.

The truth of it is, Mendoza, *you'd* do it in their game situation, now wouldn't you?

11:31 P.M.

Onscreen:

AN ESTABLISHING THREE-SHOT on Toby Inman flanked by Kelly Jordan and Horst Klingerman for just a beat before the camera moves in for a head-and-shoulders shot of the KLAX anchorman.

"Well, here we are back on the air one last time, or so we hope, with Horst Klingerman and Kelly Jordan of the Green Army Commandos. What about it, Kelly, you have some closing thoughts on the defeat of the Seawater Referendum for the folks out there?"

Cut to a close-up on Kelly Jordan, looking happy, yes, but somewhat deenergized, uncharacteristically uncertain.

"Uh . . . yes, Toby, I'd like to, uh, thank all the people out there who understood our message and voted against the Seawater Referendum. But, uh, I'd also like you all to remember that the defeat of Proposition Seventeen is only the beginning of the Green Revolution, the first victory in a long hard battle to save life on Earth. . . ."

She seems to run down verbally, and after a beat of awkward silence, there is a cut to a close-up on Toby Inman.

"But you *would* say that the Green Army Commandos have succeeded in accomplishing the goal of this, uh, mission?"

A two-shot on Toby Inman and Kelly Jordan, she looking somewhat perplexed.

"Well sure, we defeated Proposition Seventeen. . . ."

"So there's really no point in continuing to hold KLAX hostage."

"Well, no, I guess not, I mean. . . ."

"And you *did* give your word before a national television audience that you would release us if Proposition Seventeen was defeated."

"Did we . . . ? Well, yeah, I guess we did. . . ."

Suddenly, Toby Inman looks worried. "You *do* intend to keep it?" he says.

Kelly Jordan glances at something off camera, back at Inman.

"Well, sure, Toby, as soon as we can, uh . . . negotiate the arrangements with the authorities."

Cut to a close-up on Toby Inman as he looks straight into the camera, pouncing on the intro line with embarrassingly obvious overeagerness.

"Well, you heard that out there. And as one of the hostages, I'd like to assure the police and the authorities that none of us have been harmed, and we have all been well treated—"

Kelly Jordan's voice-over: "—thank you, Toby—"

"—and that no property damage has been done either. So there's no reason why these people should not be allowed to surrender peacefully after they've released us."

Horst Klingerman's voice-over, quite calmly: "May I say something now, yes, Toby?"

"Sure, Horst."

A close-up on Horst Klingerman, looking quite placid and reasonable.

"When the Green Army Commandos began this action, we knew we all might die if it failed, and we knew we would no doubt all go to prison if it succeeded. . . ."

Toby Inman's voice-over: "But there'll be a fair trial and—"

"Which can only result in our conviction for kidnapping and doubtless other serious legal offenses."

A two-shot on Horst Klingerman and Toby Inman, Inman not at all liking what he's hearing.

"What . . . what are you saying?"

Klingerman shrugs. "In for a dime, in for a dollar, that is the American proverb, yes?"

"I don't—"

"I have been thinking."

From the look on Toby Inman's face, he does not find this revelation particularly reassuring. The camera moves in for a close-up on Horst Klingerman rather than linger longer on Toby Inman's stricken expression.

"I think history has been made tonight," Klingerman says. "We have done much more than defeat this Seawater Referendum. I have hope that we have aroused the American people to take direct action, to do what must be done to save our planet and restore your country's lost honor."

His voice slowly gets louder, his cadence a bit more grandiose, he's looking forthrightly into the eye of the camera, addressing the television audience directly, seguing into more or less of a formal speech.

"It was the direct action of the people of East Germany themselves that tore down the Wall, not Helmut Kohl and the Bundestag! It was the direct action of the Russian people that prevented a military coup, not one man posturing atop a tank! Direct action works! People *can* enforce their will on even dictatorial governments, given total and sincere commitment!"

He smiles at the camera, but there is something sarcastic about it, something just this side of sinister.

"How much easier in a democracy like the United States, yes?" he says. "No Stasi, no tanks in the street, and where the agro-industrial complex that is eating the future of our species has just been roundly defeated by a popular vote. How much easier and safer for the American people to take direct action on a far wider scale to save life on Earth! How much greater your shame if you do not! Even as—"

"I don't see what all this has to do with negotiating a peaceful end to this hostage crisis," Toby Inman breaks in loudly.

There is a somewhat sudden and disjointed cut to a three-shot. Klingerman has half risen to his feet. Inman seems rather peeved at this grandstanding filibuster. Kelly Jordan gives Horst the fish-eyed stare.

"Hey, Horst," she says, "you know, neither do I."

"I will explain," Klingerman says, relaxing back into his chair and reverting to a more conversational talk-show mode.

"As we all know, Toby, the Amazon rain forest is the largest on Earth, and it is essential to maintaining a breathable atmosphere. It is being destroyed at an alarming rate by clear-cutting, and worse, by burning, and should the rest of it be lost, there is general agreement that the present greenhouse will go critical and the Earth will come to resemble Venus."

"I don't see—"

"Most of this vital rain forest is in Brazil. For decades, governments, international agencies, and well-meaning debating societies have tried without dramatic success to persuade the Brazilian regime of the moment to preserve it. I suggest the time for talk is over. I suggest that the United States tell the Brazilian government in no uncertain terms that it must act forcefully to end all logging, ranching, and farming in the Amazon entirely and begin a program of massive reforestation or face direct action."

"*Direct action?* Old-fashioned gunboat diplomacy? Military intervention?"

"With life on Earth at stake, the American people should not shrink from demanding that their government use its military power if necessary."

"Jesus Chris—" Toby Inman begins to mutter, realizes what he's doing, cuts himself short.

"But this should *not* be necessary," Klingerman says airily. "After all, one of Brazil's most important exports is coffee, and the United States is the largest single customer for it. So all that the American people must do to save the Amazon rain forest is to boycott all Brazilian coffee, all blends that contain Brazilian beans, all companies that continue to package such blends, all stores that continue to sell them, and so forth, until the Brazilian government capitulates."

Cut to a close-up on Toby Inman, looking mightily relieved.

"Well, yeah, Horst, I can certainly see how that makes a kind of sense. . . ." He frowns. "But I don't see how any of this relates to ending this hostage—"

Kelly Jordan's voice-over: "Neither do I, Horst, what are you—"

"—in for a dime—"

"—doing—"

"—situation peacefully—"

"—in for a dollar—"

A messy series of disjointed cuts, a close-up on Kelly Jordan, a close-up on Horst Klingerman, a two-shot on Toby Inman and Klingerman as the cameras try to keep up with the overlapping lines, finally settling on a long three-shot on the newsroom set including all three of them.

"It's the logic of the situation," Horst says. "When we surrender to the authorities, we will all be arrested—"

"But what about the plu—?" Kelly Jordan catches herself in midsentence, exchanges quick glances with Klingerman.

"Well, uh, yeah, I suppose so. . . ." she says.

"So what is the hurry?"

"Huh?"

Klingerman looks away from her, directly into the camera, apparently anticipating, or calling for, a solo close-up on him that is not forthcoming. He mugs into the camera silently for a beat. In the long shot, his right hand is clearly visible trying to draw the camera in on himself. The camera finally moves in for a close-up.

Horst Klingerman looks into the eye of the camera, into the eyes of the television audience.

"It is very simple," he says. "The Green Army Commandos call upon the American people to boycott Brazilian coffee until the Brazilian government meets our demands to preserve the Amazon rain forest. And we will demonstrate *our* commitment with direct action."

He smiles, the cat having eaten the perfect canary.

"We are only ten people and they are the government of a nation of a hundred million. But they must surrender before we will."

DAY 4

11:15 A.M.

HEATHER WAS DRINKING SOME crappy brand-X orange soda out of the machine, Toby was staring across the cafeteria at some ancient *Kojak* on the air-feed monitor, and Carl Mendoza was methodically chowing down on dried fruit and nuts without really tasting the stuff when Eddie Franker returned to the cafeteria from what had become his regular morning phone contact with the outside world.

The *only* contact any of us have had with the outside world for the last three days, Carl Mendoza suddenly realized.

Carl had turned into something of a loner these last years, not that close to his family, no wife, no kids, no real steady girlfriend, no really tight buddies, and he knew nothing at all about Heather Blake's life outside the station. But he did know that Franker had a wife, and Toby Inman had a wife and a couple of kids, he was the kind of guy who carried the pictures around in his wallet.

Yet the four of them had slept together on the floor in this fucking cafeteria for three nights and no one had mentioned family. Franker bitched and moaned about the lack of decent coffee and his creaky old bones sleeping on an air mattress, Toby complained about the trail mix and how it was making him constipated, but as far as Carl could remember, no one had yet complained about the total denial of access to their folks outside. No one had even mentioned the wife and kiddies.

Carl was no family man and never really had been, but now that he thought about it, it seemed kind of unnatural.

Of course, there was nothing natural about the situation. And nothing in Carl's experience, even in Nam, to compare it to.

Except maybe what it felt like on a deep penetration patrol that through some fuckup had been made for being in the area, turning the trip back into a sequence of short little firefights and long periods of tense lurking.

While you were hunkered in the bushes thinking invisible, you had plenty of time to think about the World. But you didn't. Even when nothing was happening, the reality was so intense, more intense in a way than when something was actually happening, that nothing existed outside the mission. . . .

Franker glanced over his shoulder at the guards, Ahmed and Hiroshi on this shift, as he walked across the room to the table in front of the vending machines that had somehow become *their* table.

"Well, there's good news and there's bad news," he said in a voice just up from a phony stage whisper as he sat down. "Which do you want first?"

"The good news," said Heather.

"The bad news," said Toby.

They both spoke in unnaturally low voices, and Toby Inman hunched forward, looking down at the tabletop with his head almost below his shoulders, as if he was trying to prevent the guards from reading his lips.

"You might as well save the spinach for last, Franker," Carl said, annoyed to find that he had automatically lowered his voice to a near whisper too.

"Well, the good news is that Robby Hildebrandt himself was on the horn to tell me how happy he was at the numbers we drew last night—"

"Terrific," Carl drawled sourly.

"—and Yancy Foster says if we can keep the numbers up, it may be good enough to keep the owners from firing me when this is over—"

"Heartwarming."

"—and according to Arlene Berkowski, three big-time agencies called StarNet to find out if you had representation, Toby."

"Really?" Toby Inman blurted in a sudden excited return to vocal normalcy that rang out like a shout after all the whispering, causing Ahmed and Hiroshi to half rise off their folding chairs in reflex reaction.

"And the bad news?" Carl demanded.

Franker shrugged. "Nothing unpredictable, really," he said. "Needless to say, a lot of politicians and the money behind them are chewing a lot of Persian tapestry out there."

"Dog bites man," said Toby Inman. "That's news?"

"Well it seems like . . . higher circles are taking over the show. . . ."

"Higher circles?"

"The highest," said Franker.

"En inglés, por favor," said Carl.

"The White House."

"The White House?"

"Seems like the Brazilians have already filed a formal protest. Apparently *their* president had *our* President on the phone for an hour saying unprintable things in Portuguese, the gist of which in English is that if their coffee sales start to go down significantly, clearing Brazilian customs could become an endless, tedious, and very expensive process for American products."

"How the hell did you find that out, Eddie?" Toby said. "Something like that didn't get on the wires."

"Elton Carswell told me on his way out the door. Seems like the White House has taken jurisdiction away from the FBI, he didn't say much about it, but you could tell he was as pissed off as those guys let themselves get."

"And given it to who?" Carl said.

"Themselves," said Franker. "Near as Carswell was willing to tell, some White House legal eagle pointed out to the President, or the attorney general, or the secretary of state, whoever, that this Brazilian coffee boycott was a violation of the Logan Act, private citizens meddling in foreign policy, especially after the Brazilian president put it in terms of interference in the internal affairs of a friendly nation. And then the State Department and Justice got into a jurisdictional pissing match, which got resolved by putting things directly under the executive office of the President."

"The Secret Service?" said Toby.

Carl found himself stealing glances over his shoulder nervously at Ahmed and Hiroshi. He didn't like the sound of this. He didn't like it at all.

Eddie Franker shook his head. "Some kind of political operative from the mid-levels of the White House staff, a professional negotiator. They're flying him out to take over, probably landing about now," he said. "Guy named Coleman."

"C-Coleman?" stammered Carl.

It was a common enough Anglo name; there had been a lot of ballplayers named Coleman, Jerry Coleman, Joe Coleman, he had been on the same team with a Bobby Coleman in the California League, just a coincidence. . . .

"Yeah, Alex Coleman."

Oh shit.

Just a coincidence, right.

They wouldn't run every name involved with this situation through every data bank in Washington. The CIA computers wouldn't flag Carl Mendoza as having had a cup of coffee with the Agency. They wouldn't be able to retrieve the name of somebody still in the Company whom Carl would recognize. The White House wouldn't put the Agency in charge of this operation just because the FBI had been stymied and the Justice and State Departments were fighting over turf and the president of Brazil was throwing a shit-fit and billions of dollars in foreign trade were affected.

After all, it was *against the law* for the CIA to operate inside the United States.

Right.

And everybody knew that babies were dropped down the chimney by the stork.

Carl realized that Franker was staring at him. He must have been doing some staring into space himself.

"Name ring a bell, Carl?" Eddie Franker said.

Do I tell them?

Tell them what? That the CIA brought in Alex Coleman just to send me a spirit message that they were taking over the show?

But why would they do that in the first place?

The only answer was very scary indeed.

They had brought in Alex Coleman to coach third base, to play

Mr. Outside, because they knew that they had a potential Mr. Inside who knew his signs, knew who he was, would get the message that they couldn't send in clear.

Namely that the Agency was in charge now, that they were probably willing to terminate the situation with extreme prejudice to everyone concerned if they had no better alternative, and that Carl had better understand that and be ready to act accordingly if and when.

Do I tell them? Can they keep it to themselves? What happens if Klingerman finds out what he's really dealing with now?

Stupid questions.

Carl shrugged. "Common gringo name," he said. "Couldn't be the same guy. I seem to remember playing on the same team with a shortstop name of Alex Coleman . . . in the Guatemala winter league . . ."

So he had. It had only been a cup of coffee. But Carl had played on that team long enough to remember a piece of Company policy that he hadn't thought of much down there then but that certainly seemed like wisdom up here now.

Never put dangerous information inside the heads of amateurs without a need to know.

12:15 P.M.

PAULO HAD KEPT HIS Uzi pointed at Eddie Franker's back when he marched him back to his office. When he ushered Eddie inside, he exchanged some kind of meaningful glance with Horst before he departed but seemed to avoid eye contact with Kelly.

Horst himself seemed more distant than he had been in what Eddie surprised himself as thinking of as the good old days of twenty-four hours ago, when the three of them had seemed to be acting in concert toward common pragmatic goals, and something seemed to have soured between him and Kelly too.

The atmosphere inside the station was definitely turning tenser, and not just between captives and captors. Eddie sensed that there were potential fault lines in the unity of the Green Army Commandos along which the group could fracture under pressure of an armed standoff that now, thanks to what Horst had done last night, had no foreseeable end in sight.

"This is the new negotiator from Washington," Horst said, punching the call through on the speakerphone. "He wants to speak to a representative of the hostages to verify the situation." He exchanged a cryptic glance with Kelly Jordan. "And we have . . . decided it would not be counterproductive to permit this." Kelly's lip curled upward in a tiny sneer.

"My name is Coleman, Alex Coleman," said a soft, mellifluous, vaguely Southern voice on the telephone. "Y'all can call me Alex if you like, 'cause I'd like to get us on a first-name basis toot sweet. You got this on a speakerphone? You want to confirm who all I'm talking to?"

"Yes, it's on the speakerphone, Mr. Coleman," Eddie Franker said carefully, not ready just yet to first-name this guy. "I'm Edward Franker, the station manager, and I'm here in my office with—"

"Horst Klingerman, Chairperson of the Green Army Commandos," Klingerman broke in sharply.

"Kelly Jordan, Minister of Information."

"And I'm a special assistant to the President for special public relations problems, of which this sure seems to be one, now don't it," Coleman said.

He issued—and that did seem to be the word—a hearty good-old-boy laugh that somehow managed to set Eddie's teeth on edge. "That's quite a mouthful, but what it comes down to is I'm one of the boys they send around to tricky situations like this to see if we can't resolve things without a lot of stuff in the papers might hurt the administration in the polls, a professional ameliorator, if you want the hundred-dollar handle. . . ."

In other words, thought Eddie, a staff bullshit artist.

"We are not particularly concerned with the public image of your administration," Horst said dryly.

" 'Course you're not, Horst, why should you be?" Coleman said amiably. "It's not in your self-interest, now is it? Your self-interest lies in gettin' your asses out of this in one piece."

"*All* our *true* self-interest lies in stopping the destruction of the Amazon rain forest!" Horst snapped.

"Well now, would it surprise you to learn that the President himself agrees with you?"

"He *does*?" said Kelly.

Coleman gave another of those rolling hearty laughs. " 'Course he does. You really think there's anyone in Washington goin' around sayin' what a terrific service to humanity the Brazilians are doin' by burnin' and cuttin' all those trees, pumpin' all that carbon dioxide into the air, raisin' the sea level, screwin' with the oxygen balance, so's the Potomac can flood the Lincoln Memorial and we all get to choke and fry? What we got here is not a policy dispute, Horst, just a disagreement over method."

"Then why does your President not order the Brazilian government to stop under threat of naval blockade?"

"Be real, man, he can't do that! For one thing, there are lots of American jobs involved with exports to a big country like Brazil, which the Brazilians are threatenin' to cut off at the knees already, and for another the whole Third World would commence to yowl about Yankee Imperialism and cut us out of *their* markets too, and the Europeans and the Japs an' all would just lick their chops and move right in. Situation like that, he couldn't get himself reelected dogcatcher at a cat-lovers' convention!"

"Then what are we talking about, Mr. Coleman?" Kelly said.

"Like I said, ma'am, I'm a professional ameliorator, and my job is to try and negotiate a peaceful way out of this situation in a politically acceptable time frame. And the way to do that is identify areas of mutual self-interest, or anyway self-interests that don't conflict, satisfy them, and see if we can't build a settlement out of that before my bosses get tired of my motormouthin' and put this situation back in the hands of the blue meanies."

"This means what?" said Horst.

"This means we begin by exchanging mutual unilateral confidence-building gestures," Coleman said. "We prove to each other that our hearts are in the right place. And I'm gonna go first. I'm gonna give you somethin'. I'm gonna ask somethin' in return, but if I don't get it, I tell you up front, you get what I'm givin' anyway. Can't ask for a better deal than that, now can you?"

If Eddie couldn't quite warm to Alex Coleman, if the guy still seemed far too slick to be trusted, he certainly had to at least admire

his technique. Eddie couldn't quite fathom what Coleman was doing, but whatever it was, this good old boy was good at it.

"Now I've been watchin' you people on television, and no
offense, but you're beginnin' to look kinda rank. I'll bet y'all could
use a supply of soap, an' shampoo, an' towels, an' shavin' stuff, an'
toothpaste and brushes, an' you'll pardon me for mentionin' it,
maybe some deodorant. So we gonna put together some CARE
packages of this stuff and unarmed cops are gonna leave 'em on
your front doorstep and retreat to the police lines. All you gotta do
is bring 'em inside."

"How do we know they do not contain explosive devices?"

This time Coleman's laugh almost seemed genuine. "Son, we
decide we want to play it that way, we don't need no Trojan dopp-
kits, we got enough heavy artillery around this building to turn your
parking lot into Vietnam."

Even Eddie had to laugh at that one.

"An' once you've convinced yourselves we haven't stuffed the
shaving cream cans with Semtex, we'd like y'all to have lunch on us.
We got arrangements with some local outfits to do the caterin'.
They wouldn't mind gettin' some promotional considerations,
y'know what I mean, but that's not my job. We got fried chicken,
we got cheeseburgers, we got pizzas, we got Coke and Pepsi, but we
don't have beer or wine, sorry about that."

Eddie was certainly far from being a junk-food junkie, but after
three days of nothing but dried fruit and nuts, even the thought of
sinking his teeth into napalmed chicken, greaseburgers, and refried
pizzas set him salivating, and from the look of them, Kelly and
Horst were not exactly immune to a Big Mac attack at this stage
either.

"I don't suppose you could come up with some decent coffee,
Alex," he blurted.

"I think that might be arranged," Coleman said. He laughed.
"Certified one hundred percent Colombian, of course."

"This is all very, uh, *white,* of you, uh, Alex," Kelly drawled
suspiciously. "But what's your quo pro?"

"Not a thing, darlin', this is my unilateral humanitarian gesture. 'Course a unilateral humanitarian gesture on your part might
keep the ball rollin' in a mutually advantageous direction. . . ."

"What did you have in mind?" Horst asked guardedly.

"Well now, as you can imagine, I've got certain pressures in this situation," Coleman said. "Just between us chickens, I never said this, you understand, but opinion back in Washington is not exactly undivided. I hope that don't shock y'all, the White House staff, it's got its factions like any other bureaucracy bigger'n a bread box, and it don't make my job any easier. I gotta tell you there are those who figure you've done so much damage already and you ain't fixin' to stop that if I don't get you to come peacefully in, say, twenty-four hours, the only thing to do is call your bluff and terminate the situation one way or the other."

"We are not bluffing. If we even *think* you are going to storm this building, we will vaporize it, and a kilo of plutonium with it."

"Maybe you will, and maybe you won't. . . ."

"What do you mean by that?" Horst snapped.

There was a short silence at the other end of the line.

"Now don't you go takin' this personal, son, but there is a certain lack of unanimity on that one. The ability of a group like yours t'score itself a little subcritical mass on the open market is unfortunately all too credible, but those what calculate such things, an' believe me we got more of 'em than we know what to do with, put the odds on you actually killin' yourselves to make your point at less than one in five. . . ."

"You doubt our sincerity?" Horst cried. It seemed to Eddie that he was genuinely insulted. Kelly, though, smiled thinly where Horst wasn't looking.

"Oh, no, that ain't *me* talkin', ol' buddy," Coleman said hastily. "I believe you're totally committed idealists, else why would you have placed your nuts in this vise in the first place? But on the other hand, well, I don't see how you can take *this* as an insult, I *do* have a certain problem with the idea that people so pure green as yourselves would be willing to pump plutonium into the atmosphere an' kill a whole buncha people just to maintain postmortem credibility. I mean, even if you do prove what bad-asses you were, a couple hundred thousand cancer cases ain't exactly gonna make your cause look good."

"We will announce our intention beforehand and give people a chance to flee the city," Horst said.

"Yeah," said Kelly. "How about we do it right now?"

"Now you don't want to go do anything confrontational,"

Coleman said nervously. "We don't want to panic eight million people onto their already gridlocked freeways all at once, now do we? 'Cause they got a contingency plan calls for a ballistic takeout you start to try, and if L.A. *does* get contaminated, well, you were the one that did it, ol' buddy, no one sees the incoming missile."

"You would chance all those deaths? You would chance turning this city into a radioactive ghost town?"

"Hey, now *you're* insultin' *me,* ol' buddy!" Coleman said. "*I'm* not one of those trigger-happy assholes! And like I say, those fellas ain't the only faction. But it would sure help me keep the coon dogs on their leashes if you was to give me a little somethin' I could point to as a sign of the progress of sweet reason."

"Such as what?"

"Well now, you got four hostages in there got wives and kids and friends and family out here chewin' their fingernails an' all, you can imagine, so wouldn't it be nice if you'd let 'em all talk to each other on the telephone? I mean, what harm could that do?"

"That seems reasona—"

"No!" said Horst.

"Why not, if I may ask, son?"

"Messages could be passed—"

"Oh, come on, Horst!" Kelly said.

They glared at each other.

"This was not in the plan!"

"*Right.* And this coffee boycott, I suppose, was?"

"Hey, whoa, you two!" Coleman's voice boomed out over the speakerphone. "The last thing in the world I wanna do is start an argument between you and destabilize the situation. . . . Tell you what, y'all get yourselves nice and clean and smelling pretty, and do some serious eatin' before you get down to decidin' anything. I tell you, an' I'm speakin' now in my professional capacity as an ameliorator an' all-purpose conflict-resolving factotum, half of all the world's woes would melt away like the mornin' dew if people would just stop tryin' to reason together on empty stomachs."

2:15 P.M.

THE YELLOW STUFF MELTED over the cheeseburger might be a slab of what was known as "American cheese," smooth as babyshit and twice as gluey, and the origin of the gristly meat might be better you don't ask, but Carl Mendoza had to admit that even a five-dollar special with wilted lettuce and too much Thousand Island dressing sure hit the spot after three days of trail mix.

Nigel and Malcolm, having apparently pulled door-guard duty, had taken out buckets of fried chicken and king-size cups of Coke, but everyone else in the building was here in the cafeteria greedily wolfing down burgers and pizza slices and chicken. Even Jaro had left *Tom and Jerry, the Movie* running on its own to fill the airtime and joined the picnic.

Which was more or less what it was. Right now, at least, the factions had nothing to do with captives versus hostages, and everything to do with pizza versus chicken versus burgers. People plunked themselves down at whatever table held what they wanted to eat most at the moment, and when they were through, they went elsewhere.

Currently, Kelly, Franker, Helga, and Warren were scarfing it up at the chicken table; Toby, Heather, Ahmed, and Jaro were eating pizza with everything but the anchovies; leaving Horst, Paulo, Hiroshi, and Carl himself to take care of the cheeseburgers. The factions kept shifting. Paulo had helped himself to pizza and chicken already, Warren had been here with the burgers before moving on to the chicken, Carl himself had had a slice before this burger, and just might be able to find some room for a wing or a breast after he finished it.

After sponge baths, shaves, and teeth cleaning in relays in the toilets, Horst had let Paulo and Hiroshi fetch the goodies that Coleman had left on the front doorstep. A whiff of the first real food they had smelled in over three days had almost been universally overpowering.

Almost.

The unappetizing thought had immediately occurred to Carl that all this food could be loaded with knockout drops or something. Horst, of course, had thought of it too, and his solution had not exactly been a hardship.

The hostages got to taste everything first. Only when nothing happened to them did the captors get to the goodies.

Carl took another bite of burger. He had to admit that at the moment, at least, he was feeling pretty mellow toward the Agency.

Poisoned pizzas and southern-fried diversions hadn't been the Agency's style since the legendary days when they had tried to terminate Fidel Castro with exploding cigars and toxic scuba gear. From what Eddie Franker had told him while they were shaving, Coleman had laid on some kind of charming old shit-kicker number with a trowel and was trying to get the terrorists to open the phone lines to the hostages for friends and families.

What for?

According to Franker, Horst and Kelly had argued about it. . . .

A real nasty thought occurred to Carl. He took a quick sip of Coke to wash the taste out of his mouth, but he couldn't wash it out of his mind.

Which was that by now Alex Coleman must know one hell of a lot more about Kelly Jordan and Horst Klingerman than anyone inside this building did.

They were identified. Jordan was an Air Force brat. Her school records, personality profiles, would all be easily retrievable. They would have interviewed her parents. Klingerman seemed to have been involved with terrorist circles. Interpol might have stuff. German intelligence would certainly have his passport records, his school records, whatever might be in old Stasi files.

Whatever line Coleman was handing them, there would be thick files on Jordan and Klingerman and whole platoons of shrinks and experts back in Langley to interpret them. If the game was to try to open a rift between them, Coleman came equipped with psychological owner's manuals.

And another one on Carl Mendoza.

4:14 P.M.

"... DON'T GET IT, HORST, what's the harm...."

"... they hope to get out of it...."

"... a few lousy phone calls..."

"... totally naive..."

Eddie Franker sipped at the dregs of his by now thoroughly tepid giant-sized cup of real brewed coffee, pretended to be studying its depths. Toby Inman pretended deep interest in the pizza slice before him, teasing individual pieces of pepperoni off it with his fingers and popping them into his mouth one by one. Heather Blake pretended to be dozing torpidly.

All of them, of course, were trying to catch the gist of the conversation going on at the table across the room.

"... perhaps they are sincere...."

"... no harm can be done...."

Only Carl Mendoza seemed to have no patience or insufficient fear to pretend indifference. He sat there squirming nervously in his chair, glancing overtly at the terrorists every thirty seconds or so as if daring them to notice, his face screwed up in open frustration as he fruitlessly attempted to eavesdrop on what they were saying.

"... Chairman..."

"... *person*..."

"... food, didn't they..."

After the gobbling had slowed down to slow finger-licking and bone-nibbling, Horst Klingerman had ordered the hostages over to their usual table in front of the soda and candy machines and gathered the Green Army Commandos at another half out of earshot across the cafeteria by the toilets.

They had been at it for maybe half an hour now. Helga and Paulo had their chairs turned to keep an eye on the hostages, but the rest of them, all the terrorists in the building except Nigel and Malcolm, still apparently guarding the entrances, sat facing each other across the table.

"... nowhere!"

"... *their* timetable, not ours!"

Not surprisingly, Horst and Kelly seemed to be doing most of the talking. Some kind of agitated discussion, maybe even an argument, was obviously going on.

Or so at least it seemed to Eddie—from the body language, the rising and falling of the vocal tones, the snatches of audible phrases cresting randomly out of the sea of angry muttering.

". . . must reply . . ."

". . . bluff . . ."

". . . *what* reason . . ."

"This is making me real nervous," Carl Mendoza muttered sotto voce.

"So I noticed," said Eddie.

"You were on the phone to . . . to this guy Coleman with them, Franker. Just what did he say?"

Eddie shrugged. "I *told* you, he's trying to get them to let us take personal phone calls—"

"What's the matter with you, Carl?" Toby said.

Mendoza completely ignored him, stared intently at Eddie. "Come on, Franker, what *else* did the guy say?"

"A great ream of charming bullshit, how the President really supports saving the rain forest in his heart, factions on the White House staff—"

"What?"

"Usual good-cop, bad-cop stuff, kind of begging them to open the phones to, how did he put it, 'help him keep the coon dogs on their leashes' . . ."

"Think, Franker, think, try to remember specifics. What are these . . . these *coon dogs* gonna do if they *don't* give Coleman this Milkbone to toss to them?"

"You mind telling me what this is all about?" Eddie said.

"Yeah, I do."

"Hey, Carl, what the—"

"Shut up, Toby!"

There was more intensity in Carl Mendoza's eyes than Eddie had ever seen there before. Carl had always showed up, read the sports, never gave trouble, went home, never really called attention to himself. Now he had suddenly become a . . . a *presence,* capable of silencing the anchorman with a single leaden glance.

"Humor me, Franker," he said.

All of a sudden there was something frightening about Mendoza, something that told Eddie that humoring him right now might not be such a bad idea.

"I think what he said was the coon dogs, or the blue meanies, whatever, were talking about calling the Commandos' bluff."

"Fuck," said Carl Mendoza, quite softly.

His whole demeanor changed. The take-charge presence was gone. Eddie had the feeling that were he an Anglo, his face would have suddenly gone pasty pale. Mendoza, far from being frightening now, seemed frightened himself.

Somehow Eddie found that a good deal less than reassuring.

4:17 P.M.

"**. . . TALK ABOUT *UNILATERALISM*, HORST. . . .**"

". . . golden target of opportunity . . ."

". . . no thought at all!"

Carl sat there for a long silent moment trying to figure out what the hell to do. Toby glared at him angrily. Franker looked at him as if convinced he was nuts. Who could blame them? Only Heather's face was expectantly neutral, waiting for some other shoe she somehow knew he was holding to drop.

Can I tell them? Can I trust them to sit on it?

A crusty old fart of a newsman like Franker could probably keep his mouth shut. Heather he had the feeling contained all kinds of secrets already. Three days ago, he wouldn't have trusted Toby Inman with the key to the men's room, let alone his life, but the guy had showed some stuff under fire, and now. . . .

Now, Carl finally forced himself to admit, there really wasn't any other choice.

"We are in very serious trouble, people," he said in a voice just above a whisper.

"Tell us something we don't know," Toby drawled sarcastically.

Carl stared hard into his eyes. "I'm going to do just that," he said. "But you better be prepared not to show any reaction they can read from over there. Not a word. Not a peep. Be cool."

Toby Inman stared back hostilely.

Carl hesitated, took a deep breath.

"I know this guy Coleman," he said. "He's Company. They've put the CIA in charge."

Toby's eyes widened; he flinched but to his credit made not a sound.

"But they're not allowed to operate inside the country!" Franker said. "It's illegal—"

"Well, then I guess Coleman will just have to stick to his little cover story, now won't he?"

"How do you know this, Carl?" Heather said.

"I was with the Agency for a little while after I was convinced I was finished as a pitcher and before I got into sportscasting. Alex Coleman was the guy who recruited me."

"And they just *happened* to pick him to . . ." Franker began. Then the light bulb went on behind his eyes.

"Oh," he said.

"Oh," said Carl.

"I don't get it," said Toby.

"I'm not sure I get all of it either," Carl told him. "For sure they chose Coleman to send me the message that the Company has taken charge of the operation. Maybe part of this open phone stuff is just so they can talk to me."

"Why?" said Heather.

"To flash me the bunt sign before they start the runners."

"Huh?"

Carl sighed. "Look, why would they turn this into a covert CIA operation unless they were getting ready to use force? The Agency's probably got long files on Kelly and Horst. My guess is they figure it's a reasonable bet Kelly won't use her remote detonator. So if I can take Horst as they move in—"

"But there are *eight other terrorists* with guns and explosive vests!" Toby said. "How can they expect. . . ." He stopped. He was silent for a moment.

"Shit," he said.

"For sure. The deep dark stuff. And we're in it. From their point of view, the four of us have become acceptable casualties. That's another reason to put the Company in charge. They give the orders, the LAPD takes the PR fall for anything that happens to us, and the White House has its deniability. That's what the Agency is *for.*"

"Isn't there anything we can do?" said Franker.

Carl glanced over at the chicken table, where it was beginning to get a bit hot and heavy by the look of it.

"About all we can do is pray that they *do* decide to open the phones the way Coleman wants," he said. "Coleman wasn't *that* bad a guy, the Agency doesn't go in for *unnecessary* lies. So maybe he was kind of telling the truth. Maybe there really *are* factions out there, maybe only one of them is ready for some rock and roll, maybe Coleman *can* hold them off if he gets his little gesture. . . . If not . . ."

"If not?"

Carl sighed. He shrugged. "If not, I think Coleman gets ordered to storm the building anyway, without even signaling me when."

"And if that happens, we've got no chance at all, do we?" Heather said. "We're expendable. We're dead meat."

She said it so coolly, so matter-of-factly . . . so . . . so professionally, that Carl had a flash that he was back in Nam, discussing the unfortunate probabilities with a patrol commander in the deep boonies. Not, in a certain sense, that he wasn't.

Still, this was a beautiful blond lady trying to be brave, and Carl still had enough machismo to acknowledge it with a little of the Brit stiff upper, though he couldn't quite meet her eyes in the process of slinging such manteca.

"Well, if there's enough confusion, if Horst hesitates long enough before he sets off the main charges . . . maybe I can get to him anyway, worth a try, and if Kelly chickens out, if the rest of you are lucky enough to be in the right place at the wrong time, if . . ."

"You don't really believe a word of that, do you, Carl?" Heather said very coldly.

Now Carl did look into her eyes, and what he saw there was not so much bravery as a calculating steel-hard realism he had not seen since Nam, and certainly never thought to see in the eyes of any blond Anglo princess. In other circumstances, it might almost have been enough to make him fall in love with her. In these, it seemed to require the courtesy of replying to her as an equal.

"No," he said. "Action starts, and we can all probably kiss our asses good-bye." He shrugged. He smiled. He cocked his head at her. "On the other hand," he said, "you got a better idea?"

"Yes," said Heather Blake, "I do believe I do."

4:21 P.M.

"**LET'S DO A TEARJERKER,**" Heather said. She glanced over at the terrorists, still chewing things over endlessly and getting nowhere by the look of them. "I'll bet I can sell it to *them,* and I'll bet your friend Coleman will go along with it, because he'll sort of be getting what he's asking for, if he *really* doesn't want to be ordered to shoot his way in."

"What the hell are you talking about, Heather?" Toby said dismissively.

"A tearjerker. Our family and friends get to talk to us just the way the CIA wants, but—"

"Christ, Heather, what do you think they've been arguing about over there for—?"

"—on the air!"

Toby Inman shut up.

Eddie Franker leaned closer, almost smiled. "On the air?" he said slowly.

"Sure. Maybe we can even get Coleman to give us back our mobile units, Eddie, so we can have pictures. After the news, in prime time. An hour or two of the hostages talking with their loved ones while the whole country watches."

Eddie's eyes just about lit up in dollar signs. "Robby Hildebrandt would cream in his jeans. . . ."

"That would be nice, I suppose, but the point is, it would make it awful hard for the people outside to go ahead and do anything that's going to get poor little us killed, I mean, after we trot out the wives, and kiddies, and parents, and all to tug at the national heart-strings. Hey, I have a friend out there who could *coach* them, and just to be sure, we could have them rub *onion juice* under their eyes. . . ."

"Diabolical," Eddie whispered in admiration.

"Well, what do *you* think, Carl? Would that put a muzzle on the pit bulls?"

Carl managed a laugh. *"Coon dogs,"* he said.

"Whatever. Wouldn't it be just *terrible* public relations if they were to get trigger-happy and get us killed after the Green Army Commandos were so *sweet and reasonable* letting us talk to our grief-stricken teary-eyed loved ones?"

"You are something else, Heather." Carl sighed. He frowned. He nodded across the cafeteria in the direction of the Green Army Commandos. "Only thing is, how do we get *them* to go along with it?"

"Well, it's in their interest too, isn't it? I mean, if they don't, according to you, the CIA will probably—"

"Jeez, Heather, we can't tell them it's *the Company* out there!" Carl hissed.

"We can't? Why not?"

"Tell them it's the CIA out there? Tell we know this because *I* used to work with Coleman in the Agency?"

"I guess not," Heather said. "But . . . but I've got an idea, let me handle it," she said, bolting to her feet.

"Heather—"

"Hey," she called out loudly at the terrorists across the room, "I want talk to you!"

Actually, she didn't have an idea in the world of how she was going to do this. But having gone this far, there was no turning back, and that in itself was an idea, or at least a piece of direction she had just given herself.

The argument at the terrorist table had stopped for a beat. Helga and Paulo were out of their chairs with their machine-pistols half raised.

"Sit down!" Horst shouted.

Reduce your IQ thirty points, Heather-the-director told Heather-the-actress. Lick your lips and make them glossy. Arch your back and stick out your tits. Roll your hips and take silly little mincing steps from the ankles. Look like a frightened little bird trying to be brave against her nature.

"If I don't sit down and be quiet like a good little girl," Heather said in a kind of ditzy Marilyn Monroe voice, "what are you going to do, show what a big tough man you are by telling your friends here to shoot me?"

Slowly, keeping her eyes locked on Horst Klingerman, she began walking across the cafeteria, one little mincing step after another.

"Stop!"

Heather spread her arms wide in a Christlike gesture, seemed to close her eyes as if against oncoming bullets, though actually lidding them open far enough to avoid stumbling as she continued to walk forward.

"Well, go ahead and do it then, and see if I care, I . . . I . . . I'm not afraid of you."

Through her lidded eyes, Heather could see Helga and Paulo glancing at each other uncertainly, then back at Horst. None of the other Commandos had gotten up or touched their weapons. Horst himself shot confused glances at Kelly, who gave him nothing much back.

Heather breathed a little easier. Who, after all, was going to machine-gun a brave terrified sexy little dumb blonde who obviously couldn't hurt a fly just for walking across a room to have a little chitchat?

"What . . . what do you want?" Horst Klingerman stammered, and in that moment, though she had no idea of quite what she was going to say or do next, Heather knew that she had him.

"All I want is to have a little talk," she cooed, all the while closing the space between them. "I mean, we've been sitting there *forever* listening to you *arguing* with each other, and you know, it's very *frightening*. . . ."

"It has nothing to do with you," Horst said harshly.

Heather-the-actress was almost to their table now, about on her mark, and that was a good intro line. Time for a nervous breakdown, hon, Heather-the-director told her.

"Nothing to do with us!" she shrieked in a blubbery howl, shaking her head wildly, bugging her eyes, waving her arms like an impotent wild woman as she delivered the lines.

"You hold us prisoner for four days in a building surrounded by a million crazy cops with machine guns and you keep threatening to blow us to pieces and now you're fighting with each other and maybe you're gonna get us all killed and you say *it's got nothing to do with us*!"

"Control yourself!"

"*Control myself*! I'm cooped up in this building for four days with a bunch of homicidal maniacs and you're telling me to *control myself*! I'm scared shitless, aren't you human enough to understand that? I can't take it anymore! I don't want to die! I don't want to die!"

She had reached the table now, blubbering and screaming; she pushed past Helga and Paulo, put her palms on the table, leaned forward into Horst Klingerman's body space, and howled in his face, deliberately spraying spittle. "I don't want to die! Please don't kill me!"

An Academy Award performance, it certainly wasn't, and she probably *would* have died if anyone from the Actors Studio Workshop had been around to witness such kitschy histrionics, but it was good enough for the audience under the circumstances.

Horst leaned backward, aghast and appalled. Jaro sat there more or less stone-faced, but Warren was half out of his seat with a look of nerdish horror at such an unseemly expression of naked emotion.

Kelly Jordan, with an expression of sisterly concern, or maybe distaste for Horst's display of masculine piggishness, reached out a tender hand and laid it on Heather's shoulder. Nobody went for their guns.

"It's all right, it's all right, no one's going to hurt you. . . ." Kelly soothed.

Heather froze under her touch for a beat, then allowed herself to slowly be gentled like a skittish horse, catching her breath, rubbing at her eyes, sinking down into the nearest available chair as if in sudden emotional exhaustion.

Glancing behind her, she saw that Eddie, Toby, and Carl had crossed the room, blocked a few feet behind her by Helga and Paulo, who stood in front of them with their machine-pistols held across their chests.

"I'm sorry," Heather said in a wee little frightened voice, "but the strain, it's been so terrible, and now . . . and now . . ." She let her voice break up toward the edge of hysteria.

"Please," said Horst in a most uncomfortable tone, wiping at his face with the back of his hand. "No more hysterics, yes. . . ."

"I'll try." Heather sniffed. "But . . . we couldn't help hear you arguing, and we're afraid that you're deciding to . . . to . . . to . . ."

"We are discussing tactical matters that are none of your concern."

"Oh come on, guy, can't you see she's freaking?" said Warren.

"You're deciding whether or not to kill us!" Heather whined.

"No, we're not," Kelly insisted, "we're just trying to decide whether or not to let you have a few phone calls from people outside."

Bingo!

"That's what Eddie *told* us," Heather said in a somewhat calmer tone, "but I just didn't believe him."

"You gonna let us talk to our folks or not?" Eddie called out past Helga and Paulo.

All the Green Army Commandos within Heather's eyesight flicked silent glances at each other in a webwork of complex reaction shots with no speaking lines.

"That is the subject of this discussion," Horst finally said rather lamely.

"Well look . . ." Heather began. She caught herself short, glanced over her shoulder. "Could you let them through so we can talk together for a minute?"

Horst frowned silently.

"Oh for chrissakes, Horst!" Kelly Jordan snapped.

Horst shrugged, sighed. "Very well," he said. "If you have something to say, I suppose it will do no harm to listen."

"Well look," said Heather, "you're the terrorists, and we're your hostages, but maybe we do have one interest in common, like none of us really wants to get killed?"

"For sure," said Warren. Jaro nodded. No one else reacted.

"Well, there are cops and soldiers and whatever surrounding this building and they've got *machine guns* and *cannons* and all, and if somebody *sneezes* at the wrong time, they're liable to start shooting, and then you start blowing things up, and . . . and . . ."

Heather made like she was fighting for composure for a beat or two, then let herself win. "I'm sorry," she said in a controlled voice, "but all this is so upsetting. And Eddie . . . Mr. Franker . . . seems to think that the authorities don't *care* whether we get killed anymore, that . . . that it's more important to them to just *end* the takeover, that StarNet won't . . . that . . . I don't really understand all this stuff, maybe you could explain it, Mr. Franker?"

Eddie Franker had been allowed to approach the table close enough for Heather to cue him with a swift kick to the ankle, though she found herself wishing she had thought to rehearse this scene beforehand.

But Eddie, bless him, picked up his cue and ad-libbed like a trouper.

"The thing of it is, our fifteen minutes of Andy Warhol time are up, the big story is over as far as StarNet is concerned, the national coverage is worth maybe a three-minute cameo on the 'ongoing hostage crisis in Los Angeles' after the second commercial break, and the nets maybe even less. . . ."

"I fail to see how this is our concern," said Horst.

"What if there really *are* people in Washington who want to destroy the station in order to liberate it? We've got no mobile unit. And in a few hours, the majors will pull theirs, no one leaves them in place very long unless they're feeding fresh photo ops. So they wait until the cameras leave, and then they go in, and as far as national TV coverage is concerned, it never happens. They can claim you started shooting out the windows. They can claim they didn't do anything till you started setting off explosions and then made a desperate unsuccessful attempt to save the hostages."

"We are not stupid," said Horst. "We have thought of that. But I don't see how allowing you phone calls would do anything to stop them."

"What if we turn it into a soap opera?" Heather said.

"Soap opera?" said Kelly.

"We take the phone calls from our friends and family on *television,* in *prime time,* maybe we have pictures too, we make it a big TV show, we play it with gypsy violins and lots of handkerchiefs . . ."

"I do not understand," said Horst.

But Kelly Jordan smiled knowingly. "But I do!" she said. "It'd be a big media event, it'd keep the national attention—"

"All our friends and family will tell the whole country how *wonderful* we all are, cry and blubber, and tear their hair, and all, and . . ."

"And plead with the television audience to call their congress-creatures and whatever to demand that the authorities negotiate a peaceful solution at all costs!" exclaimed Kelly Jordan.

"Brilliant," Heather murmured. She hadn't thought of that one.

"Don't you get it, Horst?" Kelly burbled excitedly. "Audience participation! Save the whales! Save the cute little baby seals! Save the KLAX hostages! It'd be a public relations *disaster* if they storm the station after that, it'd be like Bambi getting machine-gunned in a police shootout with drug dealers on national TV! They wouldn't dare! We could hold this station, stay on the air for weeks and weeks, we really *could* keep it going till the Brazilians capitulate."

"True . . ." Horst said thoughtfully.

Uh-oh, Heather thought. She hadn't thought of that one either.

"Cool," said Warren.

"Yah," said Jaro.

"Smart," said Ahmed.

"And it settles our internal dispute, Horst," said Kelly. "We give Coleman his phone calls, but we use them to tie him up in knots, PR-wise."

Horst shrugged. "Yes, I must admit that this is clever," he admitted.

Slowly, he turned toward Heather, fixed her with those icy-blue eyes. "*Very* clever," he said. He continued to stare at Heather, his expression hard and unreadable.

"This . . . this hysterical performance . . . these tears . . . this was all so you could get to propose this stratagem?"

Heather stared back just as blankly and said nothing.

"You could have been killed . . . or at least you must have feared so, yes?"

"I could get killed no matter what I do, now couldn't I?" Heather said coldly.

Horst's eyes narrowed.

"You were just . . . playacting. . . ."

"I really *was* scared."

"But you did it anyway," Horst muttered. He frowned. "You played me like a fish on a line!" he said much more sharply.

Heather smiled her warmest, sexiest bimboid smile at him, turned it into a cartoon version by batting her eyebrows in languid slow motion, did a thick world-weary Dietrich.

"Don't feel so bad, darlink, you vere had by a professional."

Horst Klingerman's eyebrows rose, held there for a beat as he scowled menacingly at her.

Then broke up into gales of laughter.

7:05 P.M.

Onscreen:

A SPLIT-SCREEN SHOT:

On the right half of the screen, Toby Inman sits on a green couch before a maple coffee table speaking into a telephone receiver. Behind the couch, Ahmed and Hiroshi stand at ease, legs spread, Uzis held across their chests barrel up, staring into space, perfect movie-poster terrorists in khakis, webbing, and explosive vests.

On the left half of the screen, a dark-haired woman sits on a black leather couch in a suburban living room, a sun-seared rear garden dimly visible through the window behind her. Fine-featured, but a shade blowsy, wearing a blue sleeveless summer shift and apparently no makeup, she is just this side of striking, an American beauty rose just beginning to lose her bloom.

"Toby?" she says in a wavering lilt. "Toby, can you hear me?"

"I can hear you, Claire. And I can see you on the monitor. Are you all right? Are . . . are you and the boys taking good care of each other?"

"We're . . . doing all right as we can without you, honey, are you okay?"

"As good as can be expected. . . ."

7:08 P.M.

THE TWISTED INVERSIONS OF television and domestic realities were maddening, and the distance between Claire and himself seemed enormous. There Toby sat in studio B, the all-purpose talk-show set, talking to his wife on the phone, watching *her* on television, on the monitor, trying to find out what was going on at home after four days' absence while every word they said went out to a national audience.

Are the boys giving you shit? Did you pay the Visa bill? Are you keeping it under control, or are you getting blotto?

He could hardly ask questions like that on national television. Nor could he reach out and touch her. And while this conversation hadn't exactly been scripted, Heather *had* prepped Claire on the phone beforehand.

"I miss you very much, Toby, I'm so lonely at night. . . ."

"I miss you too, Claire," Toby replied dutifully. In one sense it was true, but in another sense, he realized, it wasn't, not exactly. She somehow didn't seem quite real. He somehow didn't feel emotionally connected.

It was not that he thought any less of his wife, not even that he didn't sincerely long to be sitting right there beside her in their own living room, and certainly not that he wasn't worried about how she was handling the boys and the bottle in his absence.

"You tell those terrorists to treat my man all right, you hear," Claire said in a quavery gentry accent, sniffing a little, daubing at her cheek with an actual hankie. It was Claire's words, there was sincerity in the way she said it, she might even have cried anyway, especially if she had had a couple beforehand, but she had been coached into delivering this cue line, and Heather had told her to rub onion juice into the handkerchief.

"They're not gonna hurt me, honey, they haven't hurt anybody, they don't want anyone to get hurt, and nobody's gonna get hurt unless someone does something stupid," Toby said, as he was more or less supposed to.

But it was as if he had been dipped in some kind of video novocaine. For four days, he had been cut off from the world outside the cafeteria and the studio.

And now he was watching it on television. On the monitor's

split screen, he was watching *himself* watch it on television, while twenty or thirty million people watched him do it.

Who was he? The image of himself on the monitor? The husband and father? Someone playing himself?

Or somehow someone else?

A creature of the only world he had known for four days—the hostage of a building full of armed terrorists, KLAX anchorman Toby Inman, speaking to you live from his own captivity.

Sitting there in the studio with two machine-gun-toting terrorists dressing the set and two more on the cameras, Uzis and explosives and all, only that reality was immediate and vivid.

After four days, *that* was what seemed normal.

7:13 P.M.

Onscreen:

A SPLIT-SCREEN SHOT with Toby Inman on the right, Claire Inman on the left. She's crying now, wiping at her eyes with a handkerchief, but she gamely faces right into the camera, the brave wife and mother fighting back her tears.

"It's going to be all right, Toby, we're all with you. . . ."

"I know you are, honey . . . try to be brave. . . ."

A long beat of mutual silence.

Claire Inman squints at something off camera to the right, nods almost imperceptibly, looks back at the camera.

"Uh . . . Ellis and Billy would . . . like to say hello."

Two young boys sort of stagger into the frame from the right.

The elder, about ten, wears a dirty white T-shirt and tan hiking shorts. He's got blond hair like his father, worn ear-length like a surfer, a slightly sullen expression and a tendency to chub. He sprawls down on the couch to the left of his mother, flinches, and screws up his nose as she conspicuously lays a protective arm around his shoulders.

The younger boy, maybe eight, dark-haired like his mother, wears a cute little blue Dodger jacket and cutoff blue jeans, is thinner, more kinetic looking. He squirms himself down on the edge of the couch and sits there vibrating.

"Say hello to your father."

The two boys look around in confusion.

Claire Inman points toward the camera. "Just look over there and talk," she hisses.

"Hi, Daddy!" pipes the younger one. "Am I on television now?"

"Bil-*lee*," groans his older brother, rolling his eyes.

"Yes, Billy, you're on television," Toby Inman says, a small smile crinkling his lips.

"Hello, Dad," the older boy says, pitching his voice deliberately and artificially low to emphasize *his* maturity. "Are you okay? Is everything coo-el? They're not torturing you, are they?"

"No, Ellis, they're not torturing me, they're—"

"But if they *were* torturing you, they could be making you say that. So how do we know—?"

"Ellis!"

"They're not torturing me, Ellis, they're not even such bad people—"

Billy makes a gun with his hand, pokes it at the camera. "Machine guns, *brrrrrrr!*" he rasps.

"Billy!"

On the left side of the screen the camera moves in rather quickly for a tighter angle on Claire Inman, cutting the kids out of the shot. Something going on outside the frame seems to anger her, but her eyes are still red and teary as she manages to focus on the camera.

"They're too young to really understand, Toby," she says. "But they've been . . . brave."

"And I know you've been brave too, honey," Toby Inman says tenderly. "Try and keep it up. I'll be okay, this'll all be over soon."

Claire Inman's lips tremble; she wipes at her teary eyes with her handkerchief, but it only seems to make things worse. "Will it, Toby? Will it really?"

"Sure it will. . . ."

"I've seen all the police around the station, all those guns, and people saying . . . people saying . . ."

"They're *not* going to attack the station, Claire, they've been *talking* to the Green Army Commandos. As long as everybody stays patient, nobody will get hurt."

"*You* stay patient, y'hear, Toby?"

"You too, babe . . . I've gotta go now, the rest of the hostages are waiting to talk to their folks too."

"I love you, Toby!" Claire Inman shouts, and then starts really bawling.

"I love you too!" Toby Inman says, not nearly as loudly, looking a bit taken aback. He hesitates, blows her a kiss across the split-screen dividing line.

She looks straight into the camera, eyes streaming tears, nostrils reddened, mucus glistening above her upper lip, a horrid, pathetic, heartrending sight, as she puckers her lips and blows her man a good-bye kiss too.

7:17 P.M.

IF EDDIE FRANKER HADN'T known Ellie for thirty-one years, he might very well have believed that she had a foot and a half in the grave. There she sat with a shawl over her knees in a rocking chair, her gray hair teased up into a fright-wig, her eyes and nose red and rheumy, every wrinkle on her unmade-up face emphasized and deepened into a grand canyon by the cruel, harsh, frontal lighting. Her hands trembled as she kneaded her handkerchief. Her lips wavered like a senile old biddy's when she spoke.

"Edward Franker, how many of those dreadful cigarettes have you used this awful situation as an excuse to smoke today?"

But of course, Eddie *had* known Ellie for thirty-one years. She might have her problems with the asthma and a touch of varicose veins, but she was hardly this doddery old grandma. She wouldn't be caught dead wearing her hair like that, if anything, she had become addicted to an excess of makeup the last few years, they didn't even *own* a rocking chair, and though she did give him grief about his smoking often enough, she *never* called him "Edward."

Eddie smiled at the apparition on the left half of the air-feed monitor and did his best to keep his own image on the right half from breaking up and giving it all away. Oh yes, he had known Ellie for thirty-one years, well enough to know that despite the situation, or maybe in some perverse way because of it, she was enjoying this hugely.

"You'll be happy to hear that I've cut down to three packs a day," he said.

"That's not funny, Edward Franker. You're just ragging me to keep my spirits up."

Despite the armed terrorists on the cameras, the terrorists behind him, the phoniness of the whole situation, Eddie Franker felt a surge of genuine warmth and didn't give a damn if his television image showed it.

That line, though delivered in the same silly foxy grandma voice, was definitely out of character for the ancient invalid she had decided to play, and very much the real Ellie, an acknowledgment of the truth slipped in there just for him.

They had known each other so long that they could communicate like this, via TV hookup, with the whole world watching, putting on phony voices, playing silly parts, crocheting grumpily at each other like the crabby old farts they certainly had not yet quite become, and all the while just telling each other to keep on truckin', saying I love you in secret alphabets.

7:21 P.M.

Onscreen:

A SPLIT-SCREEN SHOT: on the right half of the screen, Edward Franker, balding, slightly wizened, wide ears, big nose, cynical mouth that seems like it should have a cigarette stuck in one corner, looks like a tough old businessman, the kind who has spent his life dealing with real products like clothes, or meat, or electrical supplies, not the pushing of corporate paper.

On the left half of the screen, Ellie Franker, a gray-haired little old lady rocking fitfully on a sun-drenched porch framed by parched brown chaparral, the wooden railing lined with pots of dying flowers. She seems about ten years older than her husband, frail and aged.

"How's the asthma?" he says.

"Had two attacks yesterday," she says in a weak whiny voice. "You know what the doctor says about stress setting it off."

A look of deep concern appears on Edward Franker's face.

"And the arthritis is acting up too, they say it's the pollution, not to mention the heart palpitations I get every time I turn on the TV to see if you're still alive, and of course, I just can't stay regular eatin' frozen TV dinners all the time without you here to help me make a real dinner. . . . Sciatica comin' back too. . . ."

For some strange reason, this litany of medical woe seems to relieve Edward Franker's concern, or at least he looks strangely relieved as he inquires after further symptoms.

"That trick knee giving you any problems lately, Ellie?"

"I haven't been up and around that much to notice."

"That ulcer acting up?"

"Good as can be expected."

A flash of devilment in his eyes for a beat.

"You still got that awful boil on your butt?"

"Eddie Franker!" she snaps in quite another voice.

His face softens.

"Just making a little joke, Ellie."

Ellie Franker sits up in her rocker hesitantly, shakily, like a frail creature trying to put on a show of youthful vanity.

"In front of all these people?" she says, mopping her wet lips with her handkerchief, dabbing at the tip of her rheumy nose. "I may not be feeling too well, I may not be up and about much these days, but I will not have all those people thinking I've really got a big ugly boil on my . . . on my . . . on my you-know-what! You tell them I don't, Edward Franker, or I swear, when you come home . . . when you come home . . ."

She bursts into tears, rubs at her eyes with her handkerchief, stares sobbing into the camera.

"I'm sorry," she whines piteously, "I know I should be braver, but I'm coming to my wits' end, Edward, I'm just not a well woman, you know that, and without you to take care of me, well, the neighbors they come by and help sometimes, but . . . but . . ."

Edward Franker looks into the camera tenderly. "I'm sorry too, Ellie," he says softly. "And I want everybody watching out there to know that my wife does not now nor has she ever had a big red boil on her sweet little old butt. Okay, Ellie, is that what you want?"

"Oh, Eddie, Eddie, all I want is for you to come home in one piece! I don't care about the ozone or the Brazilians or whatever all these people say this awful business is all about! Why can't they just let these people go if they let you go first? Who cares? They haven't hurt anyone, have they? Not yet."

For a moment, the emotional intensity of the moment seems to have fanned her fading fires, caused the remembered persona of a younger, stronger self to flare up out of the dying embers.

"Not yet . . ." she says much more softly, and the moment passes, her strength fades, she daubs at her streaming eyes, shrivels back under her shawl, coughs fitfully.

"Oh, Edward, Edward," she wails. "I'm so afraid. If . . . if something should happen to you, I wouldn't last six weeks, and you know it. . . ."

"Don't talk like that, Ellie, asthma, and ulcer, and heart murmurs, and all, you'll end up outliving me by twenty years."

Ellie Franker's eyes are still teary, she's sunk back in her rocker in near exhaustion, but something of the woman she once must have been flares up once more.

"Bite your tongue, Eddie Franker, how can you talk like that under *these* circumstances?" she says with surprising strength. "That's not what I want, and you know it!"

"Take it easy, Ellie, you know it's not good for your blood pressure."

They look at each other silently for a beat across the divide of the split screen.

"You come home to me, Edward, you hear," she says in an older, frailer voice.

She forces a brave lorn little smile. "It just wouldn't be right if anything happened to you now. What a waste it would be, you stinking up the house with those disgusting cigarettes all these years, and not getting to die about twenty-five years from now of lung cancer."

7:31 P.M.

A TELEVISED CONVERSATION WITH Carl Mendoza's ex-wife Maria figured, like their marriage, to be nasty, brutal, and short. He didn't really have a current girlfriend. No really close buddies. His brothers were not much to write home about.

It was kind of depressing to admit it to himself, let alone to Heather, but his best bet as a heartstring-tugger, after forty years and more on the planet, was still Mama Mendoza.

He might not be an MVP-class son exactly, or even Mamacita's sole means of support after Papa died, but he *had* kept the bank from foreclosing on the old house in Silverlake, and he *did* see to it that she didn't want for anything serious, and he *would* come over for a home-cooked dinner three or four times a month, and they *did* get along okay, and, hey, she was his *mother*, wasn't she? And knowing Mamacita, she'd get a charge out of being on TV.

And so there he was in the hotseat after Franker's truly strange conversation with his truly strange wife, and there Mama was on the left half of the studio-monitor screen, sitting at the big oiled redwood table in the kitchen, the eternal mug of coffee in her hand, her dyed-black hair all brushed and shiny, wearing the fancy embroidered white campesino blouse Carl himself had bought her a few Christmases back.

"Hey, Carl, you don't look so bad for terrorista tuna salad, hijito. . . ."

Carl had to laugh. Mamacita always had a mouth on her, not nasty, not exactly sarcastic, really, but reliably weird.

"You're lookin' good too, Mamacita."

And for a woman her age, she was. The skin might be wrinkled, the cheeks might be chubby, and the tight blouses she wore when he was a kid were definitely not in order, but the old lady still had her teeth, and her smile, and those tough brown eyes.

"They feeding you okay, Carl? You look a little thin, like one of those macrobiotic Catholics give up meat for Lent and then forget when it's over."

"I always look a little thin to you, Mamacita. But actually, they've been feeding me a lot of crap." He grinned at her. "I could go for a nice big bowl of your menudo right now." Actually, he hated the stuff.

Mamacita scowled back. She knew it.

"You listen to me, hijito, you're your poor old Mamacita's major meal ticket, so you better take care of yourself."

Carl, somewhat to his own surprise, actually felt himself *enjoying* this. Heather had tried to brief Mamacita on how to play this, but the old lady wasn't having any and had her own suggestions as to what Heather could do with her onion-juice-soaked hankie.

"When I need advice on how to talk to my own son with his butt in a bear trap, I'll look it up in my horoscope, muchacha, and don't you know onion juice makes your mascara run?" Mamacita had told her. "Once in my life, I get to go on television, and you want me to look like a bruja with a nose cold?"

That was Mamacita, big as life and mucho más picante. Better the real thing than some sob-sister Disney version.

7:36 P.M.

Onscreen:

A SPLIT-SCREEN SHOT:

Carl Mendoza on the right, a somewhat gaunt, dark-skinned, hard-eyed old jock, his eyes twinkling a tiny bit, the corners of his very serious mouth crinkling upward as he shoots the shit with rather affecting little-boy amusement with his mother.

On the left, Mama Mendoza, her thin slightly arched nose, large full-lipped mouth, deep-set dark eyes, a softer, older, feminine version of her son's features, sips from the coffee cup in her left hand, waves the forefinger of her right hand at the camera as she declaims into it.

"Those cops out there, those puberdas in soldier suits, I drove down Sunset and had a look myself—"

"You drove down to the station yourself?"

"You think I'm too old to handle a five-speed gearbox? You think the groceries walk themselves up the hill? For sure I had to go there myself, hijito, you *know* you can't trust what you see on television—"

"*I'm* on television, Mama—"

"—'cause you can't *smell* it. And I don't like the smell of 'em, smell like hair grease and cheap drugstore after-shave, like too much gun oil, like firecrackers waiting to go off, like. . . . Caramba, you know the smell of the LAPD, Carl, a lot of overweight macho squeezed into pants too tight for their cojones frying like frijoles in their own juices watchin' the clock for some action to happen or time to go have a beer. . . ."

Carl Mendoza breaks up.

"Hey, that's L.A.'s Finest you're talking about, Mamacita!"

"Hey, hijito, if that's their finest, remind me to be halfway to Taxco when they send in the B-team!"

As they both break up together, Mama Mendoza looks off camera to the left, scowls, nods, mutters something, then looks back at the camera.

"Got a surprise for you, Carl. Your old amigo from Vietnam Charley Bird is here, wants to say hello, just showed up here after the TV people."

On the left half of the screen, the camera pans across the kitchen table to the right as a black man wearing a nattily tailored blue-and-white seersucker suit walks into the frame, smiles at the camera, sits down. His hair is cut somewhere between military crew and Afro. He's got a big friendly smile, but there's something strangely neutral about his rather predatory eyes. He's got a red handkerchief tucked into his breast pocket. No tie. No jewelry. He could be anywhere from thirty-eight to fifty years old.

"Hey, Fireball, I tried to call you at work, but all I got was a bad connection to the Hanoi Hilton," he says in a warm, hearty voice, "so I thought I'd better try sending in clear. I just had to tell you I was here for you, buddy. Parker doesn't forget who his boonie buddies were."

On the right half of the screen, Carl Mendoza looks a bit embarrassed, as if he can't place this guy but can't really admit it.

"Good to see you, Charley," he says. "But how did you get my mother's address?"

"Don't you remember, Fireball? You gave it to me the last time we got together, at that barbecue party in Manhattan Beach, you drank a lot of beer, man, but you *do* remember, don't you? Louie was there, and Angel, and the Hulk. All the old team except Murph, remember, he had to go to his grandmother's funeral . . . ?"

Carl Mendoza seems to be searching his memory, finally connects with something, a smile paints itself across his face.

"Oh yeah, *now* I remember, Charley . . . *Parker,* guess I did have a few too many. . . ."

Charley Bird laughs. "A few too many? Hey, we were all tighter than fourth and goal from midfield with twenty-four on the clock and no time-outs left!"

"To what do I owe the honor, Parker?"

Charley Bird shakes his head, looks at someone off camera, probably Mama Mendoza. "Will you listen to this guy?" he says with a grin. "He saves my life, and he's surprised when I show up to let him know the guys from the old company are *stand up*! That's the kind of son you've got, ma'am!"

On the left side of the screen, the camera pulls back to a wider angle that includes Charley Bird and Mama Mendoza as she reacts in surprise.

"Carl saved your life?"

Charley Bird shakes his head again, ruefully. "He never told you about it?" He looks at the camera as it moves in for a closer shot, just on him. "You never told her about it, did you, Fireball?" he says. "What a guy! A Hall-of-Fame performance, and you don't even tell your own mom!"

On the right half of the screen, Carl Mendoza shrugs. "You know how it is, Parker . . . maybe better than I do. . . ."

Charley Bird nods, smiles, but his eyes have a certain cool hard stare, as if he's out there in memory, as if he's seeing it all again from the analytical distance of survival. Who he's really speaking to seems elusive: Carl, Mama Mendoza, the TV audience, the memory of his younger self . . . ?

"It was a deep penetration patrol, real deep, remember, end

run through Cambodia north of the DMZ. We get all the way back into country before we run out of luck, and then we don't even get made by NVA, it's a bunch of semipros in black pajamas, and there can't be more than a dozen of 'em, embarrassing, ain't it, Carl? There's a running firefight, and Carl and me get captured. They drag us to a hooch in some boonieville, and they're probably sending out for an NVA interrogator, 'cause they know they've bagged themselves a brace of LURP."

He looks into the camera with that thousand-yard stare. "Remember, Carl? Remember that little bastard with the grenades all up and down his chest? Remember the chick with the M-sixteen? Remember the pig turds in that crappy little hooch?"

Carl Mendoza goes a bit dreamy-eyed, as if he's been drawn back there too, back to Vietnam, back to another captivity, back there into memory's jungle.

"Like it was yesterday . . . Parker, or tomorrow, right. . . ."

"Five by five, my man, five by five," says Charley Bird with a strangely humorless little grin, and pauses for half a beat of silence before plunging back into his war story.

"Well, the rest of the team, they're out there, aren't they, Carl? They're out there in the jungle with the sun going down, and when it gets dark, you can hear bird songs never heard in the Nam, the screeches of scrub jays and the cooing of street-trash pigeons, and Louie goin' *schmuck! schmuck! schmuck!*"

"That Louie always was a smartass," Carl Mendoza says.

"Ain't it the truth? He almost gives it all away. Maybe he *does* give it away, 'cause our guards are getting real restless, they've lived in this jungle all their lives, and those birds out there sure don't sound right. . . . And then . . . and then . . . and then long about ten P.M. on that dark moonless night, ten P.M. exactly, as a matter of fact, 'cause the Words from the Birds ain't just to keep the natives nervous, they're the home team's signals. . . ."

Charley Bird pauses. "Why don't you tell the rest, Carl? You're the hero of the tale. . . ."

"Wouldn't think of it, old buddy, you're doing a better job than I ever could. Why don't you tell the people out there how it goes down?"

"Well, there's who knows how many of 'em outside, but one way and another, our boys are lowering the odds silently. And the two guards inside the hooch, the dude with all the grenades, and the chick with the M-sixteen. . . ."

Charley Bird pauses, smiles. "Come on, man, why don't you tell it yourself?"

"I guess . . . I guess I'm just too shy, know what I mean?"

Charley Bird shakes his head in wonder. "Will you listen to that? You sure aren't shy when push comes to shove, my man! Well, what happens is that someone screws up, no one will cop to it later, and there's this gurgling scream from out there in the jungle, gets cut off quick, but it's too late. . . . Firefight breaks out, our guys rush the hooch, Mr. Black Pajamas whips out one of his grenades, pulls the pin, lays the sucker right upside my head, shoves me out the doorway into the night yelling something in dink, the gist of which, no doubt, is come any closer, and your buddy and me get blown to dogmeat. . . ."

On the right half of the screen, Carl Mendoza has broken into a sweat, his eyes hooded, his jaw set tensely, as if he's living through it all over again, as if Charley Bird's story is calling up a kind of combat flashback.

"Well, I don't see it happen, and when you tell me later, Carl, you remember, I can't hardly believe it, but I'm still there, so it must be true. Carl, he runs toward the doorway, backkicking the chick in the crotch, and before the dude with the grenade can react, Carl coldcocks him on top of his head with his fist, catches the grenade as it's dropping, pivots like a second baseman, pegs the sucker into the jungle, comes around, lands a haymaker on the girl's jaw just as she's about to bring the M-sixteen up. The grenade goes off, the guys reach the hooch, and it's all over."

On the left half of the screen, the camera pulls back to include Mama Mendoza in the shot, her eyes wide in wonder.

"You did all that, Carl? You played hot potato with a hand grenade? You kicked a girl inna pants and socked her inna teeth? That why you never told me?"

On the right half of the screen, Carl Mendoza still seems a little shaky, not yet free of the memory. "It was Nam, Mamacita, lots of crazy things happened no one back in the World would ever believe 'em. . . ."

"Ain't it the truth?" Charley Bird says as the camera moves back in for a close-up on him.

"Ain't it. . . ." Carl Mendoza repeats in a rather strange tone of voice.

" 'Course that was a long time ago, wasn't it, Fireball? Now you're a sportscaster pushing forty from the wrong side, and old Charley Bird, he's got a steady company job. But you know what, old buddy?"

"What, Parker?"

Charley Bird smiles at Carl Mendoza, at the camera, but something in his eyes seems cold as oiled steel in January. "I do believe that if the old home team was fourth and goal with twenty-four on the clock all over again, when the ball was snapped, old Fireball would still have what it takes to make that pivot."

"You really think so, Parker?"

"I'd bet my life on it all over again, Fireball, wouldn't you? That's what I came here to tell you, my man! Hang tough, Carl. The old team's still in there rooting for you!"

"That's . . . that's really heartwarming, Parker," Carl Mendoza mutters. "I . . . really don't know what to say."

"Hey, my man, you don't have to say anything! Times like these, you find out just what old friends are for!"

7:51 P.M.

"So long, Mom . . . so long, Dad. . . ."

"You take care of yourself . . . *Heather.* . . ."

"We're praying for you, dear. . . ."

So far, so good, better than she had expected in some ways, but Heather Blake was still worrying how her sketch with Nancy Clarke was going to play as she said good-bye to Mom and Dad.

The problems she *had* anticipated hadn't materialized. Alex Coleman *had* bought the idea of the show, he *had* released the KLAX mobile units, and StarNet *had* been able to rent a third one on short notice, and with a lot of frantic driving, three units *had* been enough to cover four locations in an hour. Horst *had* let her use the phone to coach these performances.

Even her parents hadn't screwed things up.

StarNet had set up a remote feed from the Gluck living room

via a local station in Cedar Rapids, and after not too much argument considering, Heather *had* been able to use the undeniable fact that their little girl's life was in dire danger to persuade them to please, please, let themselves be the "Blakes" for the duration.

They had been pretty wooden, which Heather had expected, but at least they *had* gotten through the whole thing without slipping once and calling her "Hester."

But . . .

Heather had set the whole thing up so that the big payoff would be the end of her concluding segment, a set piece played by two professional actresses capping the whole hour with a direct appeal to the national television audience to flood Washington with calls and faxes demanding that the hostage crisis be ended without violence.

After talking to Claire Inman, Ellie Franker, and Mama Mendoza, Heather had set up the order of phone conversations, figuring that Carl's segment with his slightly wacky mother would be the best relatively light lead-in to her tear-jerking capper with Nancy.

But then this Charley Bird had showed up unannounced, and the segment had unexpectedly stolen the show. What terrific television! Who could top it?

Well, she and Nancy were just going to have to try.

And to make the situation worse, much worse, the sketch they had worked out was *another* this-poor-hostage-saved-my-life schtick! And one that was going to seem pretty damn hokey after the real thing.

Get ahold of yourself, Heather, get professional! she told herself as Nancy Clarke's heavily made-up face appeared on the monitor.

When you come right down to it, you and Nancy are probably the only ones who are really going to care that this schmaltzy little scene has already had the show stolen out from under it.

7:55 P.M.

Onscreen:

A **SPLIT-SCREEN SHOT:** on the right half of the screen, Heather Blake; blond, beautiful, a bit haggard, a brave little false smile determinedly plastered on her face, looking therefore touchingly vulnerable as she speaks into her hand-held telephone receiver.

On the left half of the screen, an artificially well-preserved woman in her sixties; heavy powder over leathery wrinkled skin, lots of eye makeup, pinkish white lip gloss, beehive-coiffed thinning hair a somewhat garish tone of auburn. She's wearing a lime-green jumpsuit with puffed sleeves that hide her upper arms. She's sitting on a tan Naugahyde couch in a vaguely institutional-looking parlor, pale yellow walls, a floral lithograph visible on the wall behind her.

"Hello, Heather," she says in a raspy, whispery voice, a lot weaker than she looks. "Remember me?"

Heather Blake squints at the camera, searching her memory, looks embarrassed. "Mrs. Simpson?" she finally says uncertainly, looking rather nervous for some reason.

Mrs. Simpson smiles. "Yes, it's Arlene Simpson. When the TV said they were going to let you take calls, I just *had* to try, and that nice Miss Jordan said it would be all right. For a . . . a terrorist, she doesn't seem such a bad sort. . . ."

Heather Blake seems more and more embarrassed, squirming in her seat. "She isn't . . ." she stammers distractedly. "But . . . but . . ." Almost blushing now.

Mrs. Simpson's lips quiver. Her eyes are moist. She dabs at the corner of the left one with a lace handkerchief. She looks like she's fighting back tears.

"I never *could* understand you, Heather, you . . . you gave me these last five years of life—"

"—*please,* Mrs. Simpson!"

"—and I've had enough operations to know how painful that marrow extraction was, you should be proud. Why have you always been so *secretive* about it, child?"

Heather Blake's eyes seem to have lost their professional ability to meet the eye of the camera; she looks down, up, sideways, everywhere but into the lens. "I really wish you *wouldn't* . . ." she moans.

Tears well up in Mrs. Simpson's eyes. "Ordinarily, I wouldn't, you know that, Heather, never said a word to the press, not even when you became the regular KLAX weathergirl, now did I?"

"No you didn't," Heather Blake admits in a tiny voice.

"But this is different!" Mrs. Simpson says, a slight edge of hysteria leaking into her voice. "Now it's *your* life that's in danger, and I just can't sit here in this hospital and say nothing just because you're such a modest creature, Heather Blake!"

"Hospital?" Heather Blake says sharply, a sudden shock of concern.

They look at each other across the split-screen line for a silent beat.

"It's come back," Mrs. Simpson says softly.

"Oh no! Look, when I get out of here, they can—"

"I couldn't ask you to go through that again."

"You wouldn't have to!"

"I wouldn't *let* you, not this time. The doctors don't think it would work again, not even with a tissue type as closely matched as yours, I couldn't let you go through all that pain again for nothing."

"They could try!"

Mrs. Simpson's lips quaver. "I didn't call to talk about *my* leukemia," she says with audible bravery, "I called to tell all those people out there about *you*."

"Mrs. Simpson, *please,* this is so *embarrassing*!" Heather Blake moans, and she really seems to mean it. "It was no big deal."

"No big deal! Without your bone marrow, I'd have died five years ago!"

"I mean *anyone* would have done it. I was the only close match they could find."

Big tears roll down Mrs. Simpson's cheeks. "You really sincerely believe that, don't you?"

"Well, sure, I mean what kind of person . . ."

Mrs. Simpson looks directly into the camera, which moves in for a tight close-up on her as the split-screen line wipes right, erasing Heather Blake's image.

"I'll tell you what kind of person *this* is," she says directly to the viewing audience. "I needed a bone-marrow transplant for my leukemia. The UCLA Medical Center went through all their student records and came up with only three close enough tissue matches—"

Heather Blake's voice-over: "I thought I was the only—"

"No you weren't, child, there were two others. They asked them both first, and when they learned what was involved, they both refused to go through it to save the life of a total stranger."

Heather Blake's voice-over: "That's awful!"

"Just a college girl, with her whole life ahead of her. She understood the risks. She knew how painful it was going to be. She . . . she . . ."

Mrs. Simpson breaks up into tears for a beat, wipes at her streaming eyes. The screen splits again, showing Heather Blake on the right half, looking almost ready to cry herself. Mrs. Simpson recovers enough of her composure to go on, but she can't quite stop weeping, and as she speaks, the split-screen line slowly wipes left into a full-screen close-up on Heather Blake, her lips trembling, her eyes unable to look into the camera.

"Wouldn't take a dime. Didn't tell anyone. And now that she's a big-time celebrity, she won't even use it to get her name in the *People* magazine. . . ."

"I *did* let you pay the hospital bill, Mrs. Simpson," Heather Blake says in a tiny voice. "And you *do* send me those wonderful homemade fruitcakes every Christmas."

The screen splits again, Heather Blake in the right half, Mrs. Simpson in the left.

"Ever since then, I've followed this girl's career, I think I've seen every little part she's ever had in a TV show or a commercial," Mrs. Simpson says, blinking back tears. "After all, she really *is* a part of me. And I tell you, this girl is going to be a real star, unless . . . unless . . ."

She breaks up into sobs again, fights for control, looks right into the camera with the tears pouring down her cheeks. "But we're not going to let that happen, are we?" she says in a quavery but somehow still powerful voice.

"I'm talking to *you* out there looking at your TV sets, that's why I really called, to talk to you. This girl just wouldn't let me die. She wouldn't take a word of public credit for saving my life, and I'm afraid I've made her cross with me right now for coming on the TV and telling her secret story. Well, I'm truly sorry about that. But it's *her* life in danger now, and I just *couldn't* sit here in this hospital waiting to die and doing nothing, now could I? You wouldn't, now would you?"

The split screen wipes right into a full-screen close-up on Mrs. Simpson. "Of course you won't! I just *know* there are thousands and thousands of good people out there just like Heather listening to me right now. I'm not asking any of you to go through the terrible pain of a bone-marrow extraction to save a life. All *you* have to do is use your telephone or your fax machine or send a telegram if the Western Union is still in business and you let the people in charge know that it's more important to save *one good girl's life* than to kill or punish a thousand really bad people let alone a few misguided fools who just want to do good as *they* see it and really haven't hurt anyone."

A split-screen shot, Heather Blake on the right half of the screen, Mrs. Simpson on the left. Tears are streaming down both their cheeks.

"And I'll tell you what, Heather, maybe it's wicked to do this, but I'm going to make a deal with the Good Lord Himself if He'll let me. . . . You listening, Lord? Because I'm praying, and here's my prayer. You let this girl walk out of that building safe and sound, and I promise, no matter what it takes, I'll keep those Christmas fruitcakes coming to her for *another* five years! Just let her live, Lord, You hear—"

"Oh, Mrs. Simpson!"

The two of them break up sobbing, reaching futilely for each other as if to hug across the barrier of the split-screen line.

Fade out.

"KLAX-TV, Los Angeles!"

8:45 P.M.

"WELL, HERE'S TO TONIGHT'S better two-thirds of the KLAX-TV news team," Toby Inman said, holding his paper cup of Pepsi aloft over the remains of the pizza. "Here's to the two heroes who have

probably saved our asses. You guys deserve champagne, but this'll
have to do!"

Coleman had let the same fast-food benefactors supply the
same pizza, chicken, and burgers, and while it sure beat trail mix,
Toby had a feeling that a few more days of this stuff could also get
pretty tedious.

The previous picnic atmosphere had not materialized tonight.
Nigel and Malcolm sat guarding the door with most of the chicken
on the floor between them, the rest having disappeared along with
all of the burgers and the rest of the Green Army Commandos,
leaving Toby, Heather, Carl, and Eddie Franker to eat pizza and like
it. Or not, as the case might be.

"Come on, Toby," Heather said with a little grin, "you know
as well as I do that that whole scene was a phony, onion-juice tears
and all."

"Well, sure," Toby said, "but from where I'm sitting, it deserves an Emmy."

Heather groaned. "Soap-opera schlock!"

"High art maybe it wasn't, Heather," Eddie Franker said, "but
I'll bet there weren't too many dry eyes out there in the audience.
Or dry jeans over at StarNet, let me tell you!"

"No way in the world they'll dare try to storm the station after
tonight," Toby burbled. "I can just see those faxes and phone calls
pouring into Washington. . . ."

"Save the whales, save the planet, save the KLAX-TV hostages,
keep those cards and letters coming in, folks," Carl Mendoza muttered sarcastically.

It was about the first thing Mendoza had said since the broadcast. He had sat there staring silently and morosely at his pizza for
the last half hour, not managing to get down more than a slice.

At first, Carl's depression had seemed pretty strange, but
though Toby had never known combat, he had seen plenty of TV
shows and movies about people who had. This was probably what
they called a flashback. Talking to Charley Bird after all these years
had flashed poor Carl back to those awful moments in the jungle,
and while it had ended happily, with Carl a hero, the experience
itself had no doubt felt pretty terrifying at the time.

"Hey, come on, Carl, lighten up," Toby said soothingly.

"Lighten up. . . ." Mendoza repeated in funereal tones.

"Yeah, Carl," said Heather, "*I* was the one playing the phony modest hero, but you're the real thing."

"The real thing," Carl practically snarled.

"What's the matter with you, Carl?" Toby said. "You back there in that jungle with your buddy Charley Bird or something?"

"My *buddy* Charley Bird . . ."

"What the fuck's the matter with you?" Toby snapped irritably. "It all went great! Your segment was terrific! Why are you so depressed?"

"Because of the Word from the Bird."

"The Word from the Bird?" said Heather. "You mean your friend Charley? But all he did was thank you for saving his life."

"Like *your friend* Mrs. Simpson, Heather?"

Carl Mendoza's words hung there in the silence for a long moment as Heather's expression changed, as Eddie Franker's mouth opened vacantly, as dread slowly blossomed in Toby's gut.

Carl glanced over at Nigel and Malcolm occupied with their fried-chicken parts, leaned closer, lowered his voice.

"Give the Emmy to Parker, or whatever his name is," he said. "I never knew any Angel, Hulk, Murph, or Louie in Nam. I was never captured. And I never saw that cock-sucking Agency son of a bitch before in my life."

DAY 5

10:38 A.M.

FRANKER HAD BEEN DRAGGED to his office to field incoming phone calls, and Heather was in the toilet, so for the moment Carl Mendoza sat across the cafeteria table from Toby Inman with no one else in the room but Hiroshi and Ahmed, well out of earshot, guarding the door.

As he chewed slowly on his breakfast of trail mix, he chewed over the spirit message from the Company yet one more time.

. . . fourth and goal from midfield with twenty-four on the clock and no time-outs left. . . .

That was clear, all "Parker" had been sending there was the number itself and the game situation, a day before the ball would be snapped.

He had asked for a confirm anyway. "Like it was yesterday . . . *or tomorrow, right . . . ?*"

And had gotten it.

Five by five, my man, five by five.

And the time: *. . . long about ten P.M. on that dark moonless night,* ten P.M. *exactly . . .*

And a confirm on that in the same sentence: *'Cause the Words from the Birds . . . they're the home team's signals. . . .*

And the general scenario . . . the man with the grenade, the hostage, the girl with the gun, the storming of the hut, the move they expected him to make . . .

Ten P.M. tonight, they were going to storm the building, and

that's when they expected him to try to take Horst. And if he didn't
. . . well, Charley Bird hadn't asked for a confirmation. They were
just going to make their move to end the situation, and end it
would, one way or another, whether old "Fireball" tried to play
Lone Ranger or not.

He sure could use a Tonto to improve the odds.

Franker was a tough old bird, but his age made it out of the
question. Heather was young, looked to be in good shape, and
there was little doubt about her courage, but Carl had enough machismo left not to trust an unblooded woman in a combat situation
unless he knew she had at least middle-level martial arts training.

That left Toby Inman.

Carl studied the anchorman as he picked pieces of dried apricot
and raisins out of his trail mix. Medium-sized. No more than ten
pounds over his ideal weight. Probably a little soft. But it would
improve the odds greatly if Toby had the balls for it.

"You ever been in a fight, Toby?" Carl said cautiously. "I mean
a real one?"

"Huh?"

"One where there was a risk of serious bodily harm?"

"Nothing worse than some schoolyard stuff when I was a
kid . . ." Inman said, eyeing him peculiarly. "What's this all about,
Carl?"

"Can I trust you to keep your mouth shut if I tell you something dangerous? Can you sit on it and not tell Heather or
Franker?"

Toby Inman's eyes hardened. "This is about that CIA phone
call last night, isn't it?" he said. "You didn't tell us everything, did
you? All that sportspeak and Namvet chitchat was some kind of
code."

"Sort of. . . ."

"Well, you've made me paranoid already, Carl, so if you want
this kept between you and me, you better spit it out before Heather
comes back from the can."

Toby had a point. He had really made his decision when he
opened his mouth. Carl had to keep reminding himself that this
good old boy was sharper than he looked.

"They're going to rush the station at ten o'clock tonight. They figure Kelly doesn't have what it takes to detonate the main charges. They want me to take out Horst."

"She-yit," Toby said rather levelly. "But . . . but what if you don't? What if you're not even in the same room with him when it starts? What if . . . what if . . . ?"

Toby Inman's mouth ran down as Carl opened his to expose a toothy smile of exaggerated falseness, pursed his lips, and made a silent *poof.* "Oh," he said.

Carl nodded. "Looks like the powers that be have told them that ending the situation by the deadline one way or the other is priority uno. Saving the four of us too would be nice, so, since we're all dead if Horst gets to his detonators anyway, from a Company viewpoint, we might as well give it the old college try."

"We?"

"Maybe I won't be anywhere near Klingerman at ten, maybe you will. . . . If both of us are, it would improve the odds if we made our move together, I mean, I hate to remind you, but the guy *is* packing an Uzi."

"And if neither of us is anywhere near him?"

Carl shrugged.

"Fuck," Toby Inman observed. A certain somewhat frantic look came into his eyes. "Look, Carl, this all happened before Heather's segment after all, and by now there must be trillions of calls and faxes dumped on Washington," he babbled. "I mean, maybe they'll be forced to call it off, that's a possibility, isn't it?"

"Maybe," Carl said. "Maybe Horst will trip over his shoelaces, fall down a flight of stairs, and kill himself. Maybe a lightning bolt will strike him dead."

Heather emerged from the toilet, walked across the room toward them.

"But if none of that shit happens by ten o'clock tonight, Inman," he hissed, "you willing to go out trying if that's how it comes down, or just sit on your ass and go out for sure with a nice big bang?"

Toby Inman met Carl's gaze. His expression seemed to firm up. He cocked his head to the left, shrugged almost imperceptibly.

"Well, when you put it that way. . . ."

Heather reached the table, sat down.

Carl continued to stare at Toby.

Toby made a fist with his right hand, raised it about three inches above the table, then let it relax.

11:02 A.M.

No sooner had Eddie gotten off the phone with Arlene Berkowski than he was on it again with Alex Coleman.

Berkowski had been the good news. Relatively speaking.

The ratings for last night's hostage friends-and-family feature had been very nice, considering that it had been up against big-budget prime-time programming everywhere east of Las Vegas. They wanted more.

"More what?" Eddie had asked.

"More of the same, Eddie. More human-interest features on the KLAX hostage crisis that can pull the same numbers."

"Like *what*?"

A long silence on the other end of the phone.

"That's up to you, I guess, I'm not a programmer," Berkowski finally said. "The point is, as a straight ongoing news story, this thing isn't worth the hassle anymore—"

"Hassle?"

"Washington is leaning on us. They want us to discontinue downlinking your feeds to the affiliates. Our position is that we'll sell whatever coverage the affiliates will buy as news, freedom of the press and all that stuff, but that's only three minutes a night now on average. Accounting tells us that the only way we don't show red ink fighting all these injunctions is with hourlong features that capture a significant national market share."

Horst and Kelly, as usual, had been listening in on the squawk box, she sitting down in front of Eddie's desk, he pacing nervously.

But as was certainly *not* usual, Horst stopped, sat down, stared at the speakerphone as if it were the person in question, and spoke directly to the StarNet executive.

"I have the solution. We will speak directly with the people."

"*We*? Who is this?"

"Horst Klingerman. We will answer telephone calls from around the country. We will let the American people speak directly with the Green Army Commandos."

His voice was animated, excited, in love with his own idea, or so it seemed to Eddie.

A pause on the other end before Arlene Berkowski spoke. "I dunno . . . what you're talking about sounds like talk *radio* to me."

Horst frowned, pursed his lips, glanced at Kelly, looking pathetically disappointed and pissed off at the same time.

Kelly herself seemed obviously taken with his idea, or perhaps, what with all the airtime she had had in the past four days, had just been bitten by the show-biz bug.

"Hey, come on, it's the same format that made Larry King a mover and shaper!" she said.

"You're not exactly him," Berkowski pointed out. "Besides which, you don't have any celebrities to interview on camera."

"Hey, *we're* the celebrities! You *really* don't think there are people out there *dying* to talk with us personally on national TV?"

"Well . . . seems kind of thin for prime time to me. . . ."

If these kids hadn't been wrapped in explosive vests and been wearing machine-pistols slung over their shoulders, Eddie would have burst out laughing at the way they were unconsciously mimicking schlockmeister producers pitching a format.

As it was, he almost did anyway. From a certain perverted perspective, the guns, and the bombs, and the fatigue suits were the whole point of the joke. Entertainment, news, politics, planetary survival; these days even armed terrorists found themselves forced to pitch themselves to the masters of the tube.

These days, there's no business *but* show business, and we are all in it!

Horst, however, apparently thought otherwise.

"You forget that *we* are in control of this television station," he pointed out. "We do not answer to you. We can broadcast anything we please."

"In *Los Angeles*," said Arlene Berkowski. "*We* control the satellite downlink to the rest of the country, remember? Without StarNet, your national market share is zilch."

"We are not interested in market share or profitability, we are interested in saving life on Earth!"

"Commendable," drawled Arlene Berkowski. "But if a tree is saved in the forest, and there's only a market share of two percent to see it, does it really happen?"

"Vas?"

"On the other hand, I gotta admit no one's come up with anything better," Berkowski said thoughtfully. "Look, tell you what, I'll run it past the affiliate buyers, project a potential market share, and get back to you later."

And she had hung up.

At which point, the phone immediately rang again, and the bad news, in the person of Alex Coleman, came pouring through the squawk box.

"I may be a professional ameliorator, folks, but I got to tell you, I'm not feelin' all that ameliorative right now, not with all the grief I'm catchin' over that little ol' scam you foxed me into lettin' you pull off!"

"Scam—?"

"The resident spin doctors do not appreciate being buried under a heap of calls and faxes paintin' their bosses' images brown, and the shit has been flowin' downhill in the general direction of yours truly."

"I have no idea what you're talking about . . . Alex," Eddie said disingenuously.

"Don't try to goosegrease this old gander," Coleman said. "It really *is* counterproductive to bullshit me, Eddie."

"And of course, you've been playing straight with us all along!" Eddie snapped back peevishly at the damned CIA bullshit artist, and then almost bit his tongue.

Eddie knew that Coleman was CIA, he was dying to let old Alex know that he was no longer putting one over on him, but it definitely *would* be counterproductive and possibly fatal to Carl Mendoza for Kelly and Horst to find out.

Coleman's voice slowed down, dropped half an octave, became plaintive, positively wounded. "You sayin' I haven't? Didn't I send in the soap and shampoo and shaving gear and all? Didn't I get you pizza and fried chicken and cheeseburgers?"

"And you received your quid pro quo," Horst pointed out to

Eddie's perverse satisfaction. "We permitted our hostages to speak to their friends and family on the phone as you requested."

"I wasn't exactly askin' for a three handkerchief hearts-and-flowers circus to dump all those 'let Tinkerbell live or lose twenty points in the polls' calls and faxes in the mailbox at sixteen hundred Pennsylvania Avenue."

"Jesus Christ, Coleman, what did you expect?" Eddie snapped. "Our friends and relatives to go on and demand a bloodbath? Didn't you get what you said you wanted, something to prevent—what did you call 'em, the *pit bulls?*—from breaking their leashes?"

"*Coon dogs,*" said Coleman, "and the idea was certainly not to have them droolin' and gnashin' this close to my ass! Lettin' you pull off that phony interview's got 'em bayin' at *my* moon!"

"Phony interview—"

"So the home folks get prepped, so there's onion juice in the hankies, well, okay, I've been on the other end of the transaction too often to get a constricted sphincter over a little creative management in *your* end of the news business, Eddie, but I gotta agree with the blue meanies that puttin' out an interview with someone that flat out don't exist to ram it up their backsides, *that's* a tad over the top."

Oh shit, Eddie thought. "I don't understand what you're talking about . . ." he stammered stupidly.

"I'm talking about poor old Mrs. Simpson!" Coleman snapped with an uncharacteristic lack of country-boy charm. "Who don't exist. Who is an actress name of Nancy Clarke worked out the whole scene beforehand with your weathergirl."

"To know all that you'd have to be tapping our phones!"

"Oh, dearie me, perish the very thought," Coleman drawled. "After all, all we got here is terrorists taking over a TV station, usin' it to foment a riot that kills a major construction project worth billions of dollars and a whole buncha jobs, and tryin' to blackmail the United States government into startin' a fuckin' war with Brazil over their own goddamn jungle! Of course none of these high-spirited boyish pranks is any excuse for the government of the United States to do anything so sleazy as listen in on your phone conversations! You believe that, Eddie, I'll bet you bought yourself an Edsel once from Richard Milhous Nixon."

"But then why—"

This time, Eddie's teeth *did* actually come down on his tongue, though he managed not to bite it.

Why did you let us do it if you knew what was going to happen all along, Alex?

Not a question for Alex Coleman to answer in front of Kelly and Horst. Because the answer was obvious. Coleman hadn't interfered because he too had used the format to put on a ringer, Mendoza's nonexistent buddy from Nam. All this wounded outrage was a cover, about as real as Charley Bird.

But *why* Charley Bird in the first place?

That was another question Eddie knew he didn't want Coleman to answer in front of the terrorists. The suspicious look on Horst's face was scary enough as it was.

"So you are displeased with us and you are listening to our phone conversations," Horst said. "Neither comes as a great revelation. So what is the point of this conversation?"

"The point is that my shit-kicker accent notwithstanding, there are necks a whole lot redder than mine frying under the toxic sun back there in Washington."

"Vas? I do not grasp the idiom."

"What I'm trying to tell you in my downhome colorful manner is that I am what stands between you and all that heavy ordnance outside you may notice if you stick your head out the window—"

"At the first sign of—"

"Yeah, yeah, I know, you'll blow the whole shitpile and turn Los Angeles into Chernobyl West."

"You doubt—"

"Look, Horst, what I'm tryin' to get through your thick head is that there are a lotta Potomac life-forms who don't want to believe you've got any plutonium, or if you do that you'll use it, because—how can I put this?—they *don't really give a shit*. Whose reptilian calculation is that gettin' you people off the air one way or another is preferable to letting this situation fester like a pustule and waiting to see what other mischief you manage to dream up next. Whose standing has not exactly been diminished in council by the Mrs. Simpson caper. Who are whispering in sympathetic ears and screamin' in mine to release the phone tapes to the press and expose the whole thing."

"You will not do that, Mr. Coleman," Horst said with a weird toneless certainty.

"Oh, I won't, huh? What makes you so all-fired sure, if I may ask?"

"Because if you do, *we* will tell the press that the explosives with which this building is mined contain plutonium, and that your government has known it all along."

"How many people you think are gonna believe *that*?"

Horst Klingerman smiled. "Enough to generate quite a local panic, wouldn't you think?" he said. "The truth of it is, Mr. Coleman, that we have both been less than fully frank with the public, have we not?"

"Now you really *do* wanna take that move back, Klingerman."

"Do I? May I ask why?"

"Because was I to relay such a birdbrained threat to those stink-tank lizards, they would order me to blow you to hell and gone about ninety seconds later to preclude your implementation," Coleman shot back.

Then, much more softly: "Fortunately for you and all concerned, I am of the fuzzy pink liberal opinion that at the moment the coon-dog pack does not have a need to know. I mean, maybe you have, and maybe you haven't, maybe you would, and maybe you wouldn't, but, unlike certain others I could mention, I am not a scientific enough poker player to ante a hundred thousand lives to call even with the odds in my favor, if I can avoid it."

"A conspiracy of silence, yes, Mr. Coleman . . . ?"

Eddie's head began to ache. His ass began to sweat. Something here just did not compute. He fished out one of his few remaining cigarettes, lit it, dragged deep.

Alex Coleman was surely the most accomplished liar he had ever encountered, yet the genius of his talent for falsehood was the extent to which it was buttressed by his employment of truth.

He had admitted to the phone taps up front. His picture of the factional situation back in Washington had the ring of truth. Maybe he really *was* trying to keep the coon dogs at bay.

"Up to the point where I become the voice of reason cryin' out in the wilderness, ol' buddy," Coleman said. "There's a point beyond which even ol' Alex must bow down to the sacred first law of bureaucracy, which is graven in stone upon the Gates of the Beltway and which reads 'Cover thine own ass.' Do I make myself clear? Do you read me?"

And even *knowing* the extent of the guy's duplicity, Eddie simply couldn't help himself from *liking* Alex Coleman on some gut level.

Or was that the slickest con of all?

Horst was silent. But the words came unbidden to Eddie's lips, the Words from Alex Coleman's very own Bird.

"Five by five, my man," he said, "five by five."

12:41 P.M.

CONSIDERING THAT IN THE interim she and her assistants would have had to have been on the horn to maybe forty or fifty affiliate buyers, it did not take Arlene Berkowski long to call back.

"Well, I'm afraid that the consensus among those we'd have to be selling it to is that a prime-time televised radio talk show would bite the big one," she said without preliminaries.

Kelly pouted. Horst was not about to take no for an answer.

"Then we will just have to do it locally here in—"

"—*However,* for a two-hour *afternoon* slot, say two P.M. to four P.M. your time, five P.M. to seven P.M. in the east, when all it's going to be up against is other talk shows, soaps, reruns, crummy old movies, and kiddie programming, we've got something viable. We're even willing to let it use one of our eight hundred numbers to let it be nationally interactive, and boost the time rate to the affiliates to cover it."

Horst regarded Eddie with some perplexity. "This is a good arrangement?" he asked.

Eddie shrugged. "Smaller audience in Los Angeles, but bigger one nationwide," he said. "The eight hundred number is a big plus. Without it, people from outside the local area code just aren't going to sit on hold on their own nickel."

"Just one thing," Berkowski said. "We can live without a time delay, but we have to have a neutral MC and button man."

"Button man?" said Horst.

"They want a third person on the air to moderate and control the incoming phone calls," Eddie told him. "Keep the flow going and cut calls off if they start getting dirty, libelous, or boring."

"Who?" said Kelly.

An experienced radio talk-show host was what was called for, but no such talent was in the building. Carl had no proven ability to do anything but read the sports. Heather might be able to handle it but wouldn't have the weight. Eddie himself was hardly an air personality. . . .

"It's got to be Toby Inman," he said.

"That's just who we had in mind," Berkowski said. "I mean, who *else* is there? And besides, the guy's scored well on the instapoll profiles, and we got agents calling here all day trying to sign him. He pulls this one off, you won't be able to afford to keep him, Eddie."

"I can live with it," Eddie said.

An unfortunate choice of words, he realized immediately.

For Eddie had the uncanny feeling that somehow more than market share was going to be riding on Toby Inman's performance.

Competent newsreaders were a dime a dozen, and he could certainly live with a stellar performance from Toby that would move his anchorman's career on to greater and more lucrative glory.

He was sure he could live with it.

But the corollary was less than reassuring.

Things being what they were, Eddie Franker was a good deal less sure that he could live *without* it.

1:59 P.M.

TOBY INMAN HAD NEVER had stage fright before, and he doubted that this was really it either, but for the first time in his life, he felt, well, *fear* as he sat there looking into the camera with his intro smile already plastered across his puss, waiting for the red light to come on.

On the other hand, he thought, who wouldn't?

After all, there he was on the couch of the studio-B talk-show set, cozily flanked by two armed terrorists, and it was going to be his job to *moderate* (what a word!) between them and whatever came in over the telephones.

Worse still, he had a five-button phone console in front of him, and all five lights were already blinking with calls. True, this was not exactly an advanced piece of technology, but true too that he had never done a phone show before, let alone been in charge of controlling the calls on the air in real time.

And that was only the physical format. Behind it was the question of what kind of calls were going to be coming in.

Eddie had managed to tell him that the CIA was tapping the station's phone lines, not exactly an awesome revelation if you thought about it for ten seconds. Toby had considered for a good deal longer than ten seconds whether to tell Franker what Carl had told him—namely that the CIA intended to replace words with action if the situation was not resolved in its favor before 10:00 P.M. tonight—before deciding against it.

No need to know, as Mendoza no doubt would have put it.

Toby found himself comprehending the concept all too well. For when he added one and one together, he came up with knowledge he could well do without.

He might be a technological naif, and the incoming calls were supposed to stack up on his console in order of connect time, but he wasn't so technologically naive as to be able to believe that the Agency had no way of manipulating the holding pattern to their own ends, whatever those might be, if they wanted to.

How fearless would the legendary talk-show hosts of yore be under *these* circumstances? Wouldn't Edward R. Murrow have gone through a pack of cigarettes in the last half hour? Wouldn't Oprah have sweated off ten pounds of water weight? Would Larry King's suspenders snap with the tension? Could even *Carson* have kept his cool any better?

Worse still, or in some perverse way better, there was a *positive* hit of adrenaline redoubling his tension, for terrifying as these circumstances might be, they amounted to his Big Break, his shot at a major career move into their exalted company if he could show the world and himself that he had what it took to make it.

And of course, live to cash in on it afterward.

The red light winked on.

Toby stared manfully into the camera.

"Good afternoon, America, this is Toby Inman, coming to you live from KLAX-TV in Los Angeles, where the Green Army Commandos have been holding us hostage and calling the shots for five days now. But for the next two hours, it's going to be *your* show, folks, *your* chance to speak directly with . . . uh, America's best-known, ah . . . terrorists, Kelly Jordan and Horst Klingerman. Call eight hundred, nine oh one, eighty-nine eighty-nine. The phones are ringing off the hook already, so we'll take the first call right . . ."

Toby paused, for dramatic effect, to take a deep breath and pray to the gods of chance, poised his finger above button number three at random—

"*. . . now!*"

—and hit it.

2:08 P.M.

Onscreen:

A **FULL SHOT, TOBY** Inman sitting on a green couch, Horst Klingerman on his right, Kelly Jordan on his left. Nothing behind them but a neutral cream background. There's a maple coffee table in front of them, and on it, in front of Inman, a dark brown multiline phone console—a receiver and a set of five buttons. The receiver is in its cradle. Four of the buttons are flashing. The fifth glows a steady yellow-white.

Female caller's voice-over, with a slight loss of sound quality:

". . . don't know what business some damn kraut has telling us what to do inside our own country!"

A hasty cut to a close-up on Horst Klingerman as Toby Inman punches her out. Considering the provocation, his expression is impressively neutral.

Back to the full shot on the three of them as Toby Inman hits the next button. "Hello, you're on the air!"

Male caller's voice-over, a tad ethereal, possibly stoned:

"Hey, I know what's *really* taking out the ozone layer. . . ."

"Yeah," says Kelly Jordan, "it's—"

Caller's voice-over: "The Vegans!"

"The *what*?"

"The Vegans! They're doing it with the exhaust fumes from all those flying saucers! It's deliberate, see, they're immune to ultraviolet radiation, they *get off on it*, they're Vegaforming our planet, and when they're finished—"

Inman, Klingerman, and Jordan goggle at each other.

"Next!" says Toby Inman.

Female voice-over: "Hi there, Horst, hi there, Kelly, I just wanted you guys to know that there *are* people out here who *do* appreciate what you're doing, a lot of us *have* stopped buying Brazilian coffee!"

Kelly Jordan: "Well, uh, thank you!"

"But you know, it doesn't seem fair, I mean, sure the Brazilians got to be stopped from destroying their rain forests, and yeah, we the ones got the power to make them do it, but, like, *we Americans* are the biggest ecopigs of all, so what right do we have to tell other people what to do until we clean up our own environmental act?"

"A good—"

"The point is—"

"—question—"

"—we can't—"

Horst Klingerman and Kelly Jordan talk over each other for a couple of beats, stare at each other in confusion. Toby Inman holds up his right hand, smiles. "Kelly?" he says, and the camera moves in for a close-up on Kelly Jordan.

"Maybe we don't have the right, but the Earth will die unless *someone* kicks ass," she says. "And only America has the power to do it. What do you want, moral purity, or planetary survival?"

She shrugs, smiles rather engagingly. "Me, I'll take planetary survival. By whatever means necessary." She laughs. "So call me a terrorist," she says. "It really *is* a dirty job, but someone really *does* have to do it—"

She glances to the right in some consternation as Horst Klingerman's voice-over interrupts: "—and it is the job that you Americans must make your government do—"

A quick cut to a three-shot on Toby Inman, Kelly Jordan, and Horst Klingerman. Jordan has recovered from her annoyance and is listening to Horst with a thin smile plastered across her face and her eyes looking sincerely into the camera.

"—neither because you are purer than anyone else, nor because you are the worst sinners, but because no one else can do it!"

Female caller's voice-over: "But . . . but the world would *hate us* for it, they'd call us international outlaws, racists, imperialists, warmongers. . . ."

"That is right," says Horst Klingerman. "You would not be about to win any planetary popularity contest."

"But, like, you're saying we *should be* a terrorist nation!"

"Quite correct."

"But . . . but . . ."

Horst Klingerman reaches back over his shoulder, brings his Uzi forward for a moment without unslinging it.

"You must remember, madam," he says in a somewhat sinister voice, "we are not television talk-show personalities, after all. We ourselves are terrorists."

An unsettling moment that hangs there for a long beat, leaving Toby Inman looking somewhat pallid.

"Uh . . . but on the other hand, this *is* a TV talk show after all," he finally says, "so we, ah, really *should* go on to our next caller."

And hits a button at random.

"Hello, this is KLAX-TV, and you're on the air live, with Kelly Jordan and Horst Klingerman!"

Male caller's voice-over: "I am . . . ? Well, uh, hi there, my name is Ron and I'm calling from Austin, and, uh, well, I don't know much about this ecology stuff, but I work on a *cattle ranch,* and, well, it sounds kinda gross, but I saw on the television, this fella said that these, uh, greenhouse gases, they didn't come so much from cars and all, but, well, ah, from, well shoot, *cows fartin'.* . . ."

2:43 P.M.

HEATHER BLAKE YAWNED. BESIDE her, Carl Mendoza's eyes had a glazed look as he stared in the general direction of the cafeteria air-feed monitor. Ahmed and Hiroshi also looked less than focused on the proceedings as they sat at the table to their right, machine-pistols in their laps, bleering at the tube, and whispering to each other occasionally.

What a bomb!

Earnest ecological activists, a flying saucer nut, a right-wing loony who thought the whole greenhouse crisis was a Communist plot to bankrupt America, a left-wing loony who thought the Green Army Commandos were CIA agents trying to give the Pentagon an excuse to start a war in Brazil to preserve the defense budget from the next round of cuts, a vegetarian who insisted that the planet could be saved if only everyone would give up meat-eating, some woman blathering on about the skin cancer plague being the wrath of God upon sinners displaying their nakedness. . . .

And Horst and Kelly Jordan used each caller as an intro to the same limited repertoire of recycled minispeeches. Boycott Brazilian coffee. Commit yourselves to direct action. Make the American government throw its weight around to save the planet. It's necessary to do some evil to serve the greater good. The planet is dying. The ice caps are melting. Direct action. Save the oceanic plankton. Boycott Brazilian coffee. . . .

Toby Inman was probably doing as well as anyone could under the circumstances, keeping the flow moving and cutting off the most boring callers smoothly and quickly; certainly Heather did not delude herself that she could do any better, given the material and the format.

". . . come on, Klingerman, admit it, you enjoy it, you're just in it for kicks, aren't you?"

"I don't see—"

"You gotta be pushing thirty-five, maybe forty, Klingerman? Where you *been* all those years?"

"In Germany."

"I mean where you *been*, what've you *done* with your life? Got a wife? Got a family? Got a career? Got a job? Got a life at all?"

Heather's attention was suddenly sucked into what was happening on the monitor. A nasty, insinuating male voice was needling Horst Klingerman and doing a pretty good job of it by the look on Klingerman's reddening face, by the way his features seemed to squirm under the assault.

"I . . . I do not see what this—"

"You're no idealist, Klingerman, you're a phony. What do you do when you're not kidnapping people, hang around bars cadging drinks from other losers and trying to pick up teenaged groupies like Miss Kelly? Admit it, Klingerman, it's all just a scam to get your feeble rocks—"

"You should talk, fella," Toby said and punched the caller off the air. "Next!"

Male caller's voice-over, in a dumb stage-German accent: "Jawohl, Herr Klingerman, I vood like to know vezzer your fatter vas in der Resistance or vedder he vas—"

"Next!" Toby Inman shouted as he cut the call off. Horst Klingerman's flush deepened.

Heather glanced at Hiroshi and Ahmed. Now they were sitting bolt upright, jaws clenched with tension, Ahmed unconsciously stroking the barrel of his machine-pistol.

"Yes, I'd like to know why it's always some blond white guy on top, and the black girl is the, uh, *spear carrier*. . . ."

Jesus!

Carl Mendoza's eyes narrowed for a beat when he caught her looking in his direction. He grimaced, shook his head almost imperceptibly.

Heather's attention was drawn back to the monitor now with a sudden keenness of interest. This was no longer dull talk-show chit-chat. Something had certainly changed, and not for the better.

3:01 P.M.

Onscreen:

A **FULL SHOT ON** Toby Inman, Horst Klingerman, and Kelly Jordan as Inman punches in a caller. "Hello, you're on the air!"

Female caller's voice-over: "Yes, I'd like to know whether you two are lovers."

"What?" shouts Inman.

Klingerman and Jordan look at each other in embarrassment.

"None of your business!" Kelly Jordan snaps.

Female caller's voice-over, insinuating: "Oh, come on, I'm sure we'd all like to—"

"We're supposed to be discussing serious issues here," Toby Inman snaps, "not indulging your prurient interest!"

"This *is* serious, it's mythic, the big blond Aryan hunk and the black—"

"You're twisted, sister!" Toby Inman says as he punches the caller out with something of a flourish. "Next! And could we keep our hands out of our pants and our attention on the subject please!"

3:02 P.M.

"**THIS IS KLAX-TV, TALK** with the Green Army Commandos," Eddie Franker said as he plugged the next caller in the stack into his headset.

"Hello, is this Toby?" a male voice said. "Hey, I don't hear myself on the TV—"

"No, this isn't Toby Inman, and you're not on the air yet," Eddie said. "This is the, ah, producer, and my job is to get an idea of what you're planning to talk about, I mean, we can't have pervos on the air, or people who are gonna try to sell something. . . ."

"Oh," said the caller, sounding somewhat disappointed and slightly dim, "I guess I can understand that . . . all I want to ask is how you can tell Brazilian coffee, you know, I mean, they mark 'Colombian Coffee' on the package, but. . . . Look, I've never been on TV, and I'd really like—"

"Okay, okay, you'll do," Eddie said, "stay on the line and I'll put you on Toby's stack."

Another con job? Eddie wondered. All too probable. But what the hell am I supposed to do about it?

Eddie had never screened calls for a phone show before, and he certainly hadn't planned to do it for *this* one. For the first forty minutes or so, he had been content (if that was the word) to sit on a stool in the control room and watch the proceedings.

But then the calls had started turning nasty. Not just nasty, but pointedly so—anti-German, racist, full of sniggering sexual innuendo, sneeringly anti-Horst, as if the collective TV audience zeitgeist was trying to provoke Klingerman, the way similar crowds of yahoos delighted in rattling the bars of the monkey cage.

Eddie had decided that someone had better screen this stuff, and since Jaro was not exactly the verbal type and Warren had his hands full, that had to be him.

Eddie was no pro at this, and he certainly wished he had someone on these phones who *was*. Was this shit normal? Did callers to phone shows *usually* sound reasonable to the screener and then turn into vicious monsters once they got on the air? How were you supposed to deal with it?

Eddie could believe that people would do just about anything to hear their own voices on television; he could *almost* believe that a majority of the people out there really did want to push Horst Klingerman's buttons for the sick pleasure of freaking him out.

But that so many of them were *able* to bullshit their way past him by playing dumb Dr. Jekyll in order to turn into Hyde on the air defied the laws of mathematical probability.

And some of them, anyway, seemed to have a little too good a fix on the *location* of Horst's buttons.

Maybe a couple three of them were legitimate loonies, but the rest of them had to be *acting*. There *was* a pattern to this shit. And once you accepted that, it wasn't hard to see the general purpose, namely to provoke Klingerman into demonizing himself. And there was only one . . . Agency out there with the resources and any conceivable reason to be doing this.

But why would Coleman want to provoke Klingerman on the air?

Unless . . . unless it's those coon dogs of his trying to corner their quarry. . . .

And what the fuck can I do about it?

Eddie sighed, plugged in the next caller. Not a damn thing but what I'm doing already. "This is KLAX-TV, talk with the Green Army Commandos. . . ."

3:05 P.M.

Onscreen:

A FULL SHOT ON Toby Inman, Kelly Jordan, and Horst Klingerman. All three of them are sweating. Jordan has a bit of a glazed look. Klingerman, grim, frazzled around the edges, eyes narrowed, jaw tight, with the look of a man whose digestion has been soured by swallowing far too much of his own bile, wipes his hand across his mouth nervously.

Toby Inman has a jumpy no-more-Mr.-Nice-Guy look as he punches in the next call.

"KLAX-TV, you're on the air with Kelly Jordan and Horst Klingerman, and I *do* hope you've got something more important on your mind than hearing the sound of your own voice on TV."

Male caller's voice-over: "I sure do, Toby. I'd like Horst and Kelly to look *you* in the eye, and then look *us* in the eye, and tell us whether they could really kill you."

Toby Inman pales for a beat. Kelly Jordan freezes. Horst Klingerman's face is unreadable. A long beat of deadly silence.

"What kind of question is that?" Kelly Jordan finally says. "I don't see—"

"The *real* question, now ain't it?" the caller's voice says silkily. "You talk a lot about blowing things up and killing people and you look real cute with your exploding vests and machine guns. But could you really *do it?*"

A close-up on Toby Inman, sweating harder now, looking not into the camera but to the right, apparently at Horst Klingerman.

Caller's voice-over: "You got what it takes, or you just a couple of bigmouth pussies? One picture's worth a thousand words. So look Toby in the eye, look us out here in the eye, look yourselves in the eye—know what I mean?—and say whether you could really kill—"

"Why don't you go back to rubbernecking freeway pile-ups, ghoul-boy?" Toby Inman snaps rather shrilly as his hand starts to move toward the button console—

A hard jerky cut to a shot on Inman and Klingerman as Horst Klingerman grabs it.

"No!" Klingerman says. "I am not afraid to answer!"

Another awkward cut, this one into a full shot on the three of them as Kelly Jordan tries to reach across Toby Inman to touch Horst Klingerman, fails.

"Hey, cool it, Horst, this creep—"

"No, Kelly, our credibility has been questioned, and so we must answer!"

"It's some kind of trap, Horst, it's a trick, we don't—"

Male caller's voice-over: "Are you killers, or are you liars?"

3:07 P.M.

TOBY INMAN'S AWARENESS OF the camera faded. He no longer saw the control-room window, the set, the monitor. He had totally lost that old familiar feeling of *being on television.*

He was sitting on a couch next to a man with a machine-pistol. Who had just palmed some kind of pill into his mouth. He could smell Horst's sweat, all but feel his body heat. Horst's eyes looked straight into his, the pupils dilated, the irises pale blue. But they didn't seem icy, they didn't seem hostile, indeed there seemed to be something like pain behind them.

And that was what made them so terrifying. That was what gave them a dreadful sincerity.

Horst Klingerman looked into Toby's eyes for what a part of him knew was just a beat or two but what another part experienced as an eternity. Klingerman's nervous fingers moved to the closure of his explosive vest, slipped inside.

"Could I shoot you in cold blood?" he said. "In all honesty, I am not sure. But I am sure that if necessary to save life on Earth, I could certainly blow up this building and kill everyone in it."

And Toby believed him.

3:08 P.M.

Onscreen:

A QUICK CUT FROM a close-up on Toby Inman to a close-up on Horst Klingerman in the act of turning away from Inman to look directly into the camera with a dreadful calm and clarity.

"It would be an evil act," he says. "It would be murder. But I could do it because I would be punished for such murders in the very act of committing them. Sometimes one must do necessary evil in the service of greater good. But one must acknowledge that evil and be prepared to accept the justice of punishment. And if you inflict it upon yourself at the moment of the evil's commission . . ."

He pauses for a beat. His eyes become almost dreamy. Rather than looking *at* the camera, he seems to be looking through it, to a vision beyond. His lips tremble. They almost seem to smile.

"Then one's conscience is clean," he says, "and the act becomes pure."

He almost sounds happy.

3:09 P.M.

"AND YOU, KELLY?" PURRED the voice of the caller. "*You* got what it takes?"

"Up yours, creep!" said Kelly Jordan. "You don't get to play your sicko game with me!"

Toby Inman blinked, shuddered, realized he had been staring into space for long beats of dead air.

The caller laughed, a horrid, somehow mechanical sound. "Well, I guess that tells us what we want to know, doesn't it?" he said. "You don't even have the guts to look him in the eye and answer the question!"

"Back to the rock you crawled out from under, scuzzball!" Toby snarled as he punched the bastard out.

But how could he help looking at Kelly Jordan with the very

same question in his eyes? How could she not meet them? How could she possibly face him in this moment without revealing the answer?

3:10 P.M.

Onscreen:

A TIGHT TWO-SHOT on Toby Inman and Kelly Jordan as their eyes meet. A long beat of motionless silence.

Kelly Jordan blinks, once, twice, thrice, looks down into her lap as Toby Inman exhales visibly.

The camera moves in for a close-up on Kelly Jordan. With her shoulders hunched, and her eyes downcast, and her lower lip trembling, the Uzi and the explosive vest seem entirely unconvincing.

She looks up into the camera. Her face is bathed in sweat. Her eyes seem furtive. She looks in this moment like nothing more than a young girl caught playing terrorist games on television.

A hard cut to a full shot on Kelly Jordan, Toby Inman, and Horst Klingerman.

Inman, seated between Jordan and Klingerman, seems to recede backward against the cushions, as if trying to disappear from the shot. Kelly Jordan looks at Horst Klingerman across his body.

Klingerman stares back at her with the mixture of genuine anger and genuine regret of a schoolteacher forced in all honor to fail his prize student.

She cocks her head to one side, shrugs, looks away, an entirely girlish gesture.

An eternity of dead air.

3:11 P.M.

TOBY INMAN STARED AT the air-feed monitor, at a full shot on three silent zombies. Kelly seemed almost on the edge of tears. Horst seemed to have withdrawn into some private somewhere, staring expressionless into the camera. Without any attempt at stealth this time, he reached into a shirt pocket, pulled out another white pill, popped it into his mouth. Toby himself gaped stupidly at Toby gaping at Toby gaping at—

Jesus Christ!

The camera . . . the audience . . .

How long had this been going on?

He didn't know. He couldn't remember.

What was he supposed to do *now*?

He looked down at his phone console, where all five button lights were blinking insistently.

What else *could* he do?

He smiled stupidly into the camera, deliberately exaggerating his expression into a goofy cartoon of itself.

"And now for something totally different," he said in a voice as supercilious as he could manage as he hit a random phone button. "We hope."

"Oh wow, like that was, you know, *gross*!" said a ditzy Valley-girl voice, "I mean, don't evil dorks like that just make you want to *puke*?"

Toby laughed at the accent in sheer relief, because what the hell else was there to do? "Oh yeah, it's people like that who make this job disgusting!" he said.

3:30 P.M.

". . . WOULDN'T YOU SAY, KELLY, I mean, the caller *does* have a point; as far as I know our northwestern rain forest *is* in worse shape than the Amazon. . . ."

Carl Mendoza found himself tuning the show out mentally, and he had a feeling he wasn't the only one. The confrontations between Klingerman and Inman, Inman and Jordan, that had been the real thing, that had been like watching the ninth inning of a no-hitter, or the heavyweight championship of the world changing hands by a knockout in the last round.

What could you really follow that with?

Not much more than what Inman and Jordan had been doing for the last twenty minutes or so—volleying ecobabble back and forth across the net of innocuous phone calls like a team of sportscasters filling the dead airtime after the fourth-round knockout of the heavyweight champ.

Hiroshi and Ahmed were paying no more attention to this stuff than he was, whispering to each other in words he couldn't make out, but whose unhappy music was all too plain.

And *they* didn't even know what had really happened.

But Carl was pretty sure he did.

Coleman's ringers had done their jobs: they had goaded Klingerman into playing Mr. Monster on TV, confirmed that Jordan didn't have what it took to use her remote detonator, and maybe opened up a split between the two of them too.

And as if Coleman was sending him a confirm, as if to say, *scenario proceeding nominally, Mendoza,* the Agency must have let go of whatever it had been doing to the incoming lines, for now Inman and Jordan were fielding nothing worse than the usual random radio phone-show audience while Klingerman sulked and glowered silently in the background, like a starter knocked out of the game in the sixth with a nice lead watching from the bench as a succession of ineffective relievers who had already blown it for him continued to get their brains beat out.

And all the while the clock was ticking toward ten o'clock with, so it seemed, no time-outs left. . . .

3:47 P.M.

Onscreen:

". . . AND YOU'RE ON THE air!"

A two-shot on Toby Inman and Kelly Jordan as he punches up the next caller.

Male voice-over, reedy, vaguely asthmatic, like someone sucking on a joint: "Yeah, I'd like to have a word with my bro there Horst."

Inman and Jordan look at each other nervously for a beat. Cut to a medium close-up on Horst Klingerman, sullen, spaced, out of it.

Caller's voice-over: "Yo, Horst, can you hear me?"

A beat of dead air.

Toby Inman's voice-over: "Horst . . . ?"

Horst Klingerman's expression seems to slowly begin to swim back into focus. "Yes," he says in a flat de-energized voice, "I am here."

"You and me got a lot in common, Horst, you're sorta like a spiritual son, carrying the torch, know what I mean, you don't need a Weatherman to know which way the wind blows. . . ."

No response.

"Famous long ago . . . ?"

"Look, caller, would you mind getting to the point?" Toby Inman says, and as he does, there is a cut to a two-shot on him and Klingerman.

"Yeah, well, direct action *is* the point, always has been, ain't that right, Horst? Way back in the sixties, there was a lot of mass action in the streets, against the war, against the Establishment, against the pigs, people were a lot more ready to act directly, I mean, people *then* knew for sure that the ecopigs were killing the planet, there'da been marches on Washington and riots in the streets. . . ."

A spark seems to ignite beneath the surface of Horst Klingerman's eyes.

"The Prague Spring . . . the antiwar movement . . . civil rights marches in the American South . . . May in Paris . . ." he says somewhat dreamily. "Even in the DDR we knew of these things."

He frowns. "But the tanks rolled into Prague, and Kennedy and King were assassinated, and direct action died, and—"

"Because it was all a damn Children's Crusade, Horst, a lot of spoiled bourgeois brats getting loaded and playing revolutionary! Only a few of us had the courage to be the real thing like you, to kill if we had to and accept the consequences!"

Now Horst comes fully alert. "The Weathermen, yes," he says sharply. "The Weather Underground! I have heard—"

"Yeah, I was Weather. We were *real* revolutionaries! We were the cutting edge!"

"The Weathermen . . . ?" says Toby Inman. "Weren't they some kind of bomb-throwing anarchists?"

The caller laughs. "Anarchists? *Those* pussies? Hey, we were *Marxists,* boy, and proud of it! We were the Children of Che! We didn't *throw* half-assed bombs like a bunch of amateur jerks, we constructed well-designed explosive devices and planted them where they'd do the most good!"

He laughs again, a wild, gurgling, demented sound.

A full shot on Toby Inman, Kelly Jordan, and Horst Klingerman. Klingerman seems to have somehow loomed forward without moving. Inman appears quite grossed out. Kelly Jordan exchanges uncertain glances with him.

"People got killed, didn't they . . . ?" she says. "Innocent people . . . and there were explosions in bomb factories killed some of your people too. . . ."

"Yeah, we took some casualties, but like Lenin said, and I don't mean wimpy old John, you can't make a revolution without cracking heads."

"But your revolution failed," Toby Inman says. "You were defeated, wiped out, arrested. . . ."

"Oh, there are still a few old farts like me hiding out in the woodwork. But you're right, peace got drafted, love caught the clap, Tricky Dick became fuehrer and then Ronald Raygun, the pigs and spooks and fascists won, and now here we are, gorked in front of the tube with our thumbs up our butts like a good little nation of sheep, while the capitalist imperialist exploiters gobble up the planet and crap out death."

Toby Inman's jaw hangs open.

"Uh . . . that's a pretty extreme statement," he manages to say.

"Extremism in the pursuit of liberty is no vice, you know who said that, Toby?"

"Uh . . . Karl Marx?"

"*Barry Goldwater,* haw! haw! haw! I remember when he was a

fascist. Way things are today they'd be calling him a Communist like you just did, and he'd probably be enlisting in the Green Army Commandos himself!"

"Well, that's very interesting, I suppose," Toby Inman says as his hand moves toward the phone console, "but we *do* only have a few minutes left, and there *are* a lot of other—"

"Wait!" shouts Horst Klingerman as he reaches out and grabs Inman's wrist with his right hand. They glare at each other for a beat. Then Klingerman reaches across his chest with his left hand, brings down the Uzi slung across his shoulder rather awkwardly, aims it shakily at Toby Inman's face.

"I would like to continue this conversation if you don't mind, Toby," he says much more softly, letting go of Inman's wrist.

"Way to go, Horst!" the caller cackles. "Ah, I tell you, I had given up hope till you guys took over this TV station! Don't give up, man! You got an army of supporters out here waitin' for the word!"

Cut to a close-up on Horst Klingerman, just a head-and-shoulders shot, the Uzi and whatever he may be doing with it discreetly off camera now. "The word?"

"Well, sure this Brazilian coffee boycott is all fine and dandy, but we both know that the *real* enemy of planetary survival is the U.S. of A, the imperialist overlord of the planet, the big green free-enterprise death machine that does more damage in a year than the Third World could in a century, ain't that right, Horst?"

"Yes, that is certainly so!" Klingerman says.

"So what we gotta do is bring the Amerikan ecodeath machine to an ass-grinding halt, wouldn't you say?"

"Yes, you are right, but—"

"And only Americans can do it, *we* gotta smash the monster we've made 'cause no one else got the power!" the caller says, his voice segueing into a chanting cadence like a tent-revival preacher as the camera holds close-up on Horst Klingerman, as the words and the beat pass through him.

"So you tell us, Horst, you tell us, man, gotta be twenty million people listening to you right now, oh yeah, most of them the fat-assed middle-American couch potatoes and moral morons who let their slavemasters make this mess in the first place, for sure, but there's thousands of us still left out here ready to take *direct action*! Do it, man! Be our Fidel! Be our Mao! Be our Che! Point us in the right direction! Give us a mission! We're out here and we're ready to move when the word is given!"

Klingerman nods almost imperceptibly during all this, up and down, up and down, hypnotically, rhythmically, and when it climaxes into a long heat of silence, he seems hypnotized for a moment himself, blinking rapidly into the camera as if emerging from a trance, searching for words to say.

"If . . . if . . . if Americans were to give up their automobiles . . ."

He stammers uncertainly at first, but his voice becomes firmer, more resolute. "Yes, yes, that is the single most effective direct action Americans can take to save life on Earth! American automobiles pump more carbon dioxide into the atmosphere than any other source on the planet!"

"Right on, Horst, right on! But Americans *love* their cars, they'd *ball* them if they could, and some of them probably do! Just as well ask them to give up their *guns*! We're gonna have to *make* 'em do it, right, take *direct* action, yeah!"

"Yes!" Horst exclaims. "There was once a truck driver's protest that paralyzed France, a few thousand people was all it took, they parked their trucks on the highways and refused to move them. The government finally had to use force to drive them away!"

"And they couldn't have done that if the truckers had set their rigs on fire, could they? If ten or twenty thousand Americans used their landwhales to block the freeways and then dropped matches in the gas tanks!"

"True. And petrol stations are also highly flammable!"

"Right on!"

"Horst—"

"Oil refineries!"

"Horst, please—"

The camera has been holding a tight close-up on Horst Klingerman as his voice rises; now it pulls back jerkily into a wider shot, still just on Klingerman. He is on his feet shouting now, the Uzi's sling still around his right shoulder, the gun clenched by its grip in his right hand, the caller's voice-over egging him on.

"Molotov cocktails to the people!"

"We must paralyze the automotive infrastructure to *force* Americans out of their cars!"

"Do it! Direct action!"

3:53 P.M.

EINSTEIN WAS RIGHT, TIME *is* relative, Toby found himself realizing inanely as he ran his finger across his throat again and again frantically, calling for Franker, or whoever was in charge in the control room, to cut Klingerman off the air.

Everything was happening all at once, yet from the fragmented perspective of his speeded-up perceptions, it all seemed to be happening in slo-mo.

Through the control-room window, he could see Eddie Franker arguing with Warren. On the set, Nigel's camera was live, holding the shot on Horst. Malcolm had set his for a long shot. The monitor still showed Horst, on his feet, raving, with his gun in his hand.

The same Horst Klingerman who stood about a foot away in the flesh.

While Kelly Jordan stared at Toby in horror, her eyes imploring him to *do something*!

"We must show the American people their own power to resist!"

"Bite out the guts of the belly of the beast!"

If Toby had had any doubt left that the CIA was feeding these phone calls into his holding stack, this phony lunatic had certainly wiped it away.

Children of Che! Capitalist imperialist exploiters! The big green free-enterprise death machine!

Fat-assed middle-American couch potatoes and moral morons . . .

Toby could just see the support for sweet reason melting away, instapoll point by instapoll point, could just see those selfsame tens of millions of fat-assed middle-American couch potatoes, with their collective feet up on the collective national coffee table as they stared grinning into their TVs, swilling from their collective national six-pack, and cheering as they watched the troops move in and the station blow sky-high at ten o'clock.

And Horst had even gone Coleman one better all by himself.

Just in case being called morons and fat-assed couch potatoes wasn't enough to set their All-American blood boiling, he had to threaten to destroy their *cars!*

Do something?

Do what?

"Bring the planetary death machine to an ass-grinding—"

Fuck it! Toby thought, and punched out the Agency son of a bitch in midsentence.

Horst Klingerman whirled, his eyes wild, his face reddening, pointing his Uzi straight at Toby's head.

3:55 P.M.

Onscreen:

"Go AHEAD, DO IT, asshole, pull the trigger!"

"Horst, for chrissakes, chill out, man, look at the monitor!"

A full shot on Toby Inman, Horst Klingerman, and Kelly Jordan. Klingerman grips his Uzi at nipple level, pointing it at Inman's face no more than two feet away. Toby Inman seems about to bolt off the couch as he screams at Klingerman. Kelly Jordan has stood up, moves toward Klingerman, touches him gingerly on the shoulder.

The three of them freeze like that for a beat.

Horst Klingerman slowly looks away from Toby Inman off camera to the right.

His expression slowly changes. The rage leaks out of it, replaced by embarrassment, then a flush of shame. His posture softens, he slowly lowers the Uzi, holds it slackly; it seems to sit there in his hands like a detumescing penis, and Horst stands there looking not unlike a naughty boy caught by the camera with his dick in his hand.

Kelly Jordan takes his free hand, gently pulls him back down onto the couch beside her as Toby Inman sits down to the left, about as far away from the two of them as he can get.

A close-up on Toby Inman, the flush fading from his face, panting lightly and blinking for a couple of beats as his eyes come to focus on the camera.

"Well . . . uh . . ."

A long moment of dead air.

"Ah . . . I . . . uh, guess we have time to . . . er . . . take one more call . . ." he finally says, shrugging, rolling his eyes upward as if in prayer, and punching a button on the phone console.

3:56 P.M.

"GOODNESS, TOBY, THAT WAS just *awful*. Are you all right?"

The caller's voice was female, wispy, grandmotherly, soothing to Toby's ears, calming to his racing heartbeat. Thank God!

"Yes, ma'am, I'm okay," he said, feeling his pulse rate dropping back toward at least a semblance of normal. "This is, uh . . . kind of a tense situation for everyone, and—"

"Would it be all right if I spoke with Kelly Jordan for a moment now?"

Sweet, concerned, almost dripping with good old downhome feminine courtesy.

"Sure," Toby said.

He could have hugged her. About four minutes of this nightmare left, and there he sat, soaked in sour sweat, feeling suddenly lightheaded from the adrenal backwash. Horst Klingerman sat there sullenly like a bad little boy caught doing something nasty to a cat in the corner of the schoolyard. Kelly, at least, seemed calm and relatively on top of things, and as far as Toby was concerned, she could extro this mess without him saying another word.

"Hello there, Kelly, can you hear me?" the grandmotherly voice said.

"Yes, ma'am."

"Well now, dear, I'll be seventy-eight next October, so I don't suppose I'm going to live long enough to see all the coastlines flooded and the atmosphere become unbreathable, but I *do* have five grandchildren, so I try to do my little part to save the planet for their sake. I don't use my air conditioner any more than I really have to, I'm too creaky these days to drive at all, I try not to waste water, I recycle glass and papers, I compost the kitchen scraps for my garden, I do my best to be what you young folks call *green*. . . ."

Toby watched Kelly's face relaxing stepwise as she listened to this, and at the end of the caller's little monologue, she was actually smiling into the camera.

"Hey, that's terrific, if everybody would do the same, we'd be more than halfway there. . . ."

"And I think what *you're* doing is commendable too, Kelly . . . up to a point," the caller's voice said.

Uh-oh. Something in the timing of that pregnant pause was a little too professional, a tad too slick.

"Up to a point?" Kelly said, walking right into it.

"Well, as a Christian, I can't condone violence, or holding people prisoner, and as an American I'm deeply offended by all the terrible things that Mr. Klingerman and that last caller said, couch potatoes and moral morons indeed!"

That definitely *did* sound like something read off a script. Foxy Grandma was almost certainly another of Coleman's ringers. But what—

"I'm sure Horst didn't mean people like *you*, ma'am," Kelly said soothingly. Was she onto it, or—

"I am capable of speaking for myself, Kelly!" Horst snapped, suddenly and unfortunately roused from his funk.

"Goodness knows you've certainly proven *that*, young man!" the caller chided primly. "But are you capable of showing some common courtesy? It doesn't do your cause much good to be rude and insulting to the very people you're trying to convince."

Horst's anger transformed into a kind of quizzical bemusement. "Rude and insulting!" he muttered.

Toby couldn't help it. "Emily Post *does* say it's crude to stick a machine gun in your host's face," he pointed out. "You could look it up."

Kelly actually managed a laugh.

"Uh, you were saying, ma'am?" she said.

"I was trying to say that I *do* believe you have a good heart, my dear, and I *do* believe that what you want us to do is the right thing. Why, I've even stopped buying Brazilian coffee myself! But don't you see that what you're doing is *wrong?* The ends can *never* justify the means."

"We defeated the Seawater Referendum, didn't we? And we convinced *you* to boycott Brazilian coffee."

"But not by shooting people or blowing things up!"

"We haven't hurt anybody, not really."

"Not yet, Kelly. So don't you think it's time to be reasonable now, before you really *do?*"

"Reasonable . . . ?" Kelly said, and Toby could all but see the Agency actress playing the Nice Old Lady pounce on the cue line.

"Yes, child, you've done everything you really can. You've defeated the Seawater Referendum and you've started the Brazilian coffee boycott and you've managed to do it without hurting anyone. But this thing about people's cars—"

Horst tried to get a word in edgewise, but the professional grandma swatted him down like an annoying insect.

"The American auto—"

"Hush up, and stop interrupting your elders, young man, don't you have any manners at all?"

Kelly grinned at the camera, maybe a bit too winningly.

"People aren't going to give up their cars overnight," the caller said, "and they certainly aren't going to have any sympathy for people who want to burn them, and block the freeways, and set gas stations on fire. You can see that, Kelly, now can't you?"

Kelly hesitated, maybe finally beginning to realize that this sweet little old lady was dribbling her like a basketball.

"Well . . . I suppose so . . ." she finally said in a small voice.

"So there's really nothing to be gained by continuing this foolishness any further and endangering innocent lives, now is there?"

"What are you trying to say, ma'am?"

"That it's not too late."

"Not too late for what?"

"I'm just an ordinary old woman, a good American, a good Christian, a parent and a grandparent, who *does* want to do her part to save this planet for future generations, who *does* appreciate what you've been trying to do, and I'm sure there are millions and millions of people just like me who would be more than willing to be merciful. . . ."

The setup, the dribble down the lane . . .

"We're about out of time," Toby said, glancing at the studio clock.

"Merciful . . . ?" Kelly Jordan muttered almost hopefully.

"If you did the right thing. . . ."

"The right thing?"

But just enough time left for a slam dunk at the buzzer!

"Release your hostages, take your medicine, and give your-selves up."

"Well thank you for calling, ma'am, but that's all we have time for," Toby said, punching out the caller. "I don't know about you out there, folks, but as far as I'm concerned, it's been quite enough."

The red light on Malcolm's camera winked out, and the station-break loop replaced his video image on the monitor.

For a beat, Toby just sat there, not quite connecting up with the reality that the phone show from hell was actually over. Then he blinked and mopped the sweat from his forehead with the back of his hand.

Malcolm and Nigel shut their cameras down, unplugged their headsets, hung them on the camera handles, then directed fish-eyed stares at Kelly and Horst.

Kelly, her eyes focused on some inner landscape, didn't even seem to notice. Horst seemed zombified too, but there was a sullen edge to it that made Toby feel, well, somehow sad.

"What are you two staring at?" he finally said.

Malcolm glanced down at his feet, then up again at nothing in particular. *"Arrr . . ."* he growled softly.

Nigel shrugged, shuffled his feet, but didn't look away. "Bloody fookin' hell, Horst," he said, "I mean the dingo act *was* a bit thick, dinnya think?"

"Vas?"

"All that ravin' on about burning cars an' all," Malcolm said. "When all's said an', the old Granny was right, wasn't she, these fookin' Yanks'd as soon cuttit off as give 'em up. Like callin' their mums fookin' hoors."

"Not quite the way to make us their fave raves, mate!"

"We did not begin this action with the idea of winning a popularity contest—"

"Didn't we?" Kelly said.

"What?" Horst snapped, glaring at her.

"The whole idea was to defeat the Seawater Referendum, to win an election. That's not a popularity contest?"

"That was only stage one," Horst said.

"So what the fook is stage two?"

"The Brazilian coffee boycott."

"Which you just sort of made up as we went along, right?" Kelly said.

"This was a bad idea?"

"No . . . but—"

"But if stage three is ta convince the fookin' Yanks ta climb out of their bloody cars an' piss off down the road on bikes like fookin' Dutchmen," said Nigel, "we'll be here till our bungholes learn ta fart the Jimi Hendrix version of 'The Star-Spangled Banner'!"

"Wasn't even *your* dumb idea, now was it, mate?" Malcolm said. "Was that droolin' maniac on the phone, now wasn't it?"

"This may be so," Horst admitted sullenly, "but what is done cannot be undone. We are committed."

"Ta bloody *what*?"

"Unless . . ." Kelly muttered slowly.

"Unless *what*?" said Malcolm.

"Well . . . why *don't* we just declare victory and negotiate our asses out of here. I mean that was the original plan, wasn't it?"

"Fookin' A!"

"This is nonsense, Kelly, totally wishful thinking," Klingerman said.

"But you said—"

"The ol' plutonium—"

"Enough!" Horst shouted. He stood up, glanced meaningfully at Toby. "If we must continue this discussion," he said, "let us keep it to ourselves!"

Nigel nodded, unslung his Uzi, waved it perfunctorily at Toby, pointed it toward the studio exit. "After you, mate," he said.

Toby knew that by any sane adult logic he should not be taking Horst Klingerman's side in any of this. Kelly and the punkers wanted to surrender, Horst didn't, and if Klingerman had his way, *he* was the guy Toby and Mendoza would have to fight in a few hours with everyone's lives on the line.

Yet as Nigel marched him off the set, Toby found himself reacting with the prepubescent emotional logic of the schoolyard, found himself *feeling sorry* for Horst Klingerman.

The poor bastard had been thoroughly jobbed, turned into the Bad Little Boy to foil for the Good Little Girl, and he *still* had no idea what had really been done to him, let alone by whom and why.

4:10 P.M.

IF CARL MENDOZA HAD allowed himself any lingering doubts that the Agency was going to storm the building there was no doubt at all now that this stupid phone show was over. When they went in tonight, he and Inman either succeeded in stopping Horst from blowing the place to pieces or they didn't.

If they did, there would be a couple of live heroes, and probably a movie that would do for the Agency what the Entebbe action did for the Israelis.

And if they didn't, well, Horst Klingerman had been a maniac, now hadn't he? Blow up gas stations, burn cars, fuck up the freeway rush hour even worse than usual—what more could you ask to prove that you had been dealing with an Abu Nidal, a Carlos, a crazy motherfucker . . . ?

Carl knew how *he'd* do it.

Blow the sat dish off the roof from a distance, a rocket from a gunship orbiting a few miles away or fired from a position in the Hollywood Hills; claim it was in answer to fire from inside the building. Who could say otherwise with KLAX off the air except the surviving terrorists afterward, if there were any, which, one way or the other, would not be likely?

Then about ten seconds later, a frontal assault on the building by SWAT teams, commandos dropped on the roof by choppers, tear gas and concussion grenades through every window, hope for the best. . . .

What were the odds?

Face it, cholo, slim and none.

If he and Inman happened to be close enough to Klingerman at ten, *if* they could disarm him before he blew them away, *if* he didn't simply stick his hand inside his vest at the first sign of anything, *if* they could do it all in a shitstorm of tear gas and shock waves—

Sure.

Hiroshi and Ahmed were having what might have been an argument or just a heated discussion at the next table, it was hard to tell with two guys hissing and whispering to each other in two differently accented versions of English. Heather was staring at some terrible old Mexican vampire movie on the monitor for want of anything better to do.

And all at once, Carl realized that as far as his old nonbuddy Alex Coleman was concerned, everyone in the building was dead meat already.

Charley Bird, all the elaborate signals flashed to him from the third-base coach, were just the kind of shot you might as well take across the whole court from under your own basket down two points with nothing left on the clock. If by some million-to-one chance it went in, hey, pop the champagne, boys, and when it didn't, well, what the fuck, it was a lost game anyway.

"A peso for your thoughts," Heather said.

"A politically incorrect remark."

"Seriously."

"Seriously?"

And all at once, Carl felt his prick stiffen. How weird. There she was where she had always been, the blond Anglo princess with the big tits, the supposed wet dream of Chicano manhood, but only now, with the clock on their lives maybe running out, with the fantasy completely impossible to accomplish under the present circumstances, did it occur to him that it might be rather nice to fuck her.

I must be getting old, he thought.

Or at the very least, approaching some sort of half-assed maturity.

"I'm thinking we're in deep shit," he told her. *Deeper and darker than I've got the balls to tell you.*

Heather leaned closer to him, cocked her head. "There's something you're not telling me, isn't there, Carl?" she said in a half whisper.

Caramba! Is she a mind reader, or is it just so damn obvious?

Carl studied Heather Blake for a long moment, not as a potential sex object, or even something soft needing masculine protection, but as he might size up a batter he had watched hit a few times but had never himself faced before.

Heather Blake, on the record, was a tougher customer than Inman. Physical strength aside, of the three potential allies he had in here, *Heather* was the one Carl would have trusted furthest in the clutch.

"What are you looking at so hard?" she said.

"A very pretty lady . . ." Carl muttered inanely.

Heather's only reply was a slight wrinkling of her nose, a curling of her upper lip.

Carl sighed. This must be what those feminists mean by dumb well-meaning piggery, he thought. I told Inman, I'd tell Franker if I had any reason to, but *her* I gotta protect from the truth like a real macho, as if it's going to do any good when it all hits the fan.

He glanced over his shoulder at Hiroshi and Ahmed, who were still deep in whatever and not paying them much attention. On the other hand, better safe than sorry . . .

"Lean closer," he whispered. "Smile, and nod, and bat your eyelids like a good little bimbo while we talk, like I'm coming on to you and you're thinking about it."

"What?" she hissed.

"Just do it, Heather, you'll understand later."

Heather shrugged, leaned forward, eased into Carl's body space, smiled vapidly. Carl plastered a dumb hard-on smile across his face, laid a conspicuous hand on her arm as he whispered to her.

"They're gonna move in in force on the station tonight at ten."

Heather's eyes widened, but she showed no other reaction. Tough lady. "How do you know that?" she hissed around her painted smile.

"All that gabble from old Charley Bird was code in clear. You had to be me and Coleman to get it. They go in at ten, they want me to take Horst when they do."

"How do they know you can? How do they know you'll even be around—"

Heather caught herself short. She frowned. "Oh," she said.

"Right," Carl whispered around a sappy grin. "Win or lose, as far as we're concerned, from where *they're* sitting, it's all over when the fat lady sings."

"You're going to try it anyway?"

"If I get the chance."

"You think you can do it?"

"No."

"Then why . . . ?"

"You got a better idea?"

Heather stared deeply into Carl's eyes for a long moment, smiling foolishly, even batting her eyelids as she had been instructed, but all the while he could hear the machinery whirring beneath those baby blues.

"Maybe," she finally said without moving or changing expression.

"Well?"

Heather blinked, once, twice, licked her lower lip thoughtfully. "Well," she said, "you *could* take a chance and tell them. . . ."

"Tell who what?"

"Tell Horst and Kelly, or maybe all of them, what's going to happen."

"What the hell for?" Carl hissed.

"So maybe they'll surrender first. Or do something else before the CIA makes their move. *Anything* would be better than just sitting here waiting for it to happen."

"Why would they even believe me?"

Heather's eyes narrowed. She was silent for a moment. "You'd have to tell them everything."

"Everything?"

Heather widened her stupid grin even further, nodded. "That you were once with the CIA. That Coleman sent you a message to try to overpower Horst at ten o'clock."

It took a mighty effort for Carl to keep playing the game, to grin like a horny ape as he hissed: "That's a crazy chance to take! Horst'd be liable to waste me!"

Heather pouted prettily. "Right," she said. "It's a stupid, crazy, dangerous thing for you to admit to. Therefore a lie you'd have no reason to tell. That's why they'll believe you."

"Fuck," Carl grunted in amazement, in a kind of admiration.

Heather smiled at him with a perfect expression of fatuous innocence.

"You really think they'd surrender if they believed me?"

"Probably not."

"So . . . ?"

"So consider the alternative."

Carl thought about it for about twenty seconds. If the Agency *did* storm the building, their chances, *his* chances, of living through it were maybe a hundred to one. Looked at that way, Heather's plan, ten-to-one shot though it probably was, looked relatively attractive.

"You *really* this stony cold, lady?" he whispered.

Heather Blake let something slip behind her eyes, and there was a quaver in her voice and maybe a little tremor in her lower lip, but otherwise her face could have been a magazine ad for toothpaste or sugar-free chewing gum.

"No, actually I'm really terrified, Carl," she whispered sincerely without a change of expression. "But I also *am* a pretty damn good actress."

5:05 P.M.

"**WHY THE HELL DIDN'T** you tell me, Mendoza?" Eddie Franker hissed angrily. "I *am* the goddamn station manager, remember!"

"Keep it down, Eddie!" Inman whispered nervously, glancing across the cafeteria at Hiroshi, Ahmed, Nigel, and Warren, who were absorbed in their own hushed and hunkered conclave.

"What difference would it have made?"

"Shit," Eddie moaned. "And now you want to tell Kelly . . . and *Horst*?"

Carl Mendoza grimaced. "Unless, of course, *you* can think of something better, Franker," he said.

Eddie tried. And came up dry. The revelation that Coleman was preparing to use force explained an awful lot in retrospect.

Arlene Berkowski had waxed enthusiastic about the nightmarish phone show, worse, had even wanted a national prime-time en-core.

"Forget everything I said about the format being too thin for prime time, Eddie, we're ready to go with it for ninety minutes starting at eight your time, we're gonna download the best footage to the affiliates as early news coverage, and by the time you go on, the demographics will be fantastic. . . ."

Eddie would have sooner been dragged through a mile of sour owlshit than screen the calls for another such nightmare, but how could he have tried to talk Horst and Kelly out of it without re-vealing Alex Coleman's true identity and the nature of the Machia-vellian game he was playing?

He just might have tried anyway if he hadn't assumed that Coleman, tapping the phones, would call and ax Berkowski's idea.

But there had been nothing from that quarter but a puzzling silence. A silence that Mendoza's revelation explained all too omi-nously.

Coleman hadn't called to protest the results of the phone show because they were exactly what he had wanted. And he wouldn't protest a repeat in prime time because he would have no need to.

Eddie sighed. "Your call, Carl," he said. "Either way, you're the one who's gonna be putting his life at immediate risk, whether you play it Coleman's way or Heather's."

5:09 P.M.

"WELL, THEN THERE'S NO point in putting it off any longer, is there?" Carl said. He slid his chair heavily across the floor with a loud screech that caused the terrorists at the side of the room to turn their heads reflexively in his direction, and as they did, he slowly stood up.

"I want to talk to you," he said.

"Sit down," said Ahmed.

"I *have* to talk to you."

Slowly, Ahmed stood up, unslung his Uzi, and pointed it at Carl. "Sit down and be silent," he said.

Carl didn't move. "You gonna kill me for telling you something that maybe saves your own life?" he said.

"What the fook is this?" Nigel said.

Carl took a deep breath. "It's about the CIA," he said, "that's the Central—"

"We know what the bloody initials stand for, arsehole."

"That's who's out there. That's who's in command of all that ordnance."

"So fookin' what?"

"So they intend to use it real soon."

"They told you this themselves, I suppose?" Warren said.

"As a matter of fact they did."

"What did they fookin' do, send you fookin' messages onna TV like this bloke I knew convinced he was getting marchin' orders from fookin' old Guns N' Roses videos?"

"Look, the bottom line is that the so-called hostage negotiator running things out there is a CIA agent name of Alex Coleman. I know this because he recruited me."

Hiroshi, who had sat there stone-faced as usual through all this, got slowly to his feet, brought his Uzi to bear on Carl's midsection. Ahmed's eyes narrowed and his fingers danced speculatively around the grip of his own weapon in an unsettling manner.

Well, Carl thought sardonically, at least I've gotten their attention.

"You out of your bloody mind, mate?"

"You are *admitting to us* that you are a CIA agent?"

"*Was* a CIA agent," Carl said, "for a few months, long ago, in a country far, far away. Enough to make me like the Agency about as much as you guys do. And believe me, what's going to happen tonight isn't going to make any of us like the sons of bitches any better."

"I don't get it, guy, why are you *telling* us this?"

Carl looked Warren directly in the eyes. "To save my own ass," he said with utter truthful sincerity. "And all of yours too in the bargain."

5:21 P.M.

PROFESSIONALLY SPEAKING, HEATHER BLAKE thought, Carl had given an excellent performance. Gaining initial attention safely by dragging his chair loudly across the floor before standing up had been a nice piece of business, the calm tough-guy tone that stopped short of smartass had been just right, and the punch line had been perfect.

Of course a movie would have jump cut from there to the arrival of Horst and Kelly instead of including these dead minutes while Hiroshi went to fetch them, but—

—the cafeteria door slammed open.

In stomped Horst Klingerman, machine-pistol unslung and scowling like a proper terrorist, the shot that *should* have followed Carl's last line. Behind him came Hiroshi, then Helga and Jaro, she looking like something out of *Ilsa, She Wolf of the SS,* he looking rather uncinematically tentative.

Behind *them,* not at all how Heather would have shot it, was Kelly Jordan, moving slowly, looking distracted, and even politely closing the door behind her.

"What is all this about the Central Intelligence Agency?" Horst demanded as he strode across the room toward the hostages' table with the others trailing behind him.

Carl stood up before Horst had a chance to loom over him, met his gaze levelly. "Coleman is CIA," he said, "and they chose him to run this operation because I knew him in Nam, because he recruited me later. My buddy, Charley Bird? Never knew any such person. The whole bullshit combat story he told? Never happened. The whole thing was Coleman's way of sending me a message—they're coming in tonight at ten, and I'm supposed to jump you when they do."

"Vas?" exclaimed Horst Klingerman, gaping at Carl for a long frozen moment. "If this is true . . . or . . . or even if it is not," he stammered, "why . . . why are you *telling me* this?"

Carl Mendoza stood there nose-to-nose with Horst Klingerman like Clint Eastwood and Lee Van Cleef sizing each other up in some spaghetti western.

"Maybe I could take you, maybe not, you've got the weapon, I've got the combat training and I'd have surprise, might be interesting," Carl said. "But me take you out before you get your hand inside your vest and blow the whole shitpile?"

He shrugged. He smiled thinly. "No way, José," he said. "I know it, and so does that cocksucker Coleman."

"I do not understand. . . ."

Carl Mendoza took a subtle half-step backwards, or maybe just arched his back in a way that created the illusion. His body language changed subtly, became laconic, languid, the old gunfighter ending the confrontation by slowly holstering his pistol.

He broke eye contact with Horst Klingerman, looked slowly around the room before him, calming the saloon.

"Why don't we all sit down and I'll try and explain it," he said, and he pulled up a chair from behind him, flipped it out in front of him backrest forward, and sat down.

Heather doubted whether Eastwood, or Kirk Douglas, or for that matter even Paul Newman or Spencer Tracy could have done it better.

5:31 P.M.

CARL MENDOZA WAS *NOT* one of those sportscasters who picked up extra income as an after-dinner speaker or awards-show MC. He hated the very thought of speaking to a roomful of people.

But he was doing it now.

Franker, Inman, and Heather sat flanking him. Nigel, Warren, Jaro, and Ahmed sat at the other side of the next cafeteria table. Klingerman had pulled a chair up close and sat on it in reversed position, mimicking Carl, maintaining an intense eye contact. Jordan sat beside Klingerman, leaning against her backrest in a normal manner. Only Helga and Hiroshi remained standing, bracketing Horst and Kelly, with their feet spread and their unslung weapons pointed down but in his general direction.

"The timing, what I'm supposed to do, it was all there," Carl continued.

"In extremely cryptic form," said Klingerman. "You *could* be reading meaning where none exists."

"And why did you wait till now to say anything?" Kelly Jordan said. Carl checked her with a glance but went right back to eye contact with Klingerman.

"Yes, why?" Klingerman said.

"*Why*? What was I supposed to do, hold up my hand like a kid has to take a piss, and say, pardon me, that's the CIA out there, and the reason I know is 'cause I used to be with 'em and they just sent me a message they're comin' in and the only chance I have of living through it is by jumping you, my man?"

"But you were going to try it, weren't you?" Klingerman said shrewdly. "From your point of view, it *was* the only chance you had. *That* is why you held your silence, yes."

"You got me, muchacho."

"So what changed your mind?"

"The fuckin' phone show. The way they set you up. It kind of clarified my thinking."

"Set me up?" Horst said slowly.

"Get it through your head who and what you're dealing with out there," Carl told him. "These people are sharp, they're ruthless, they got resources you can't imagine. You think they don't have the tech to control what comes in over an eight hundred number? You think they don't have platoons of shrinks and media experts to figure out just what kind of raving on your part is gonna turn the maximum number of people against you? You think they can't come up with a script to push your buttons to make you do it? You really think that old hippie Weatherman got you screaming to burn cars and block freeways, for instance, was the real thing?"

"What . . . what are you saying?"

"You've been *had*!" Carl said, snapping it off. "And *I* was gonna be had too! We're all *already* dead meat to Coleman and his bosses in Washington! Why the fuck would I take the chance of telling you all this if I wasn't totally convinced that this is the *only* chance I or any of us have of living through the night?"

"Even if all this is true, it does not change anything."

Kelly was looking green around the gills, Hiroshi and Helga gritted their teeth and clutched their weapons over at the other table, Nigel and Warren looking like maybe they were getting it, old Jaro poker-faced as usual, Ahmed's eyes narrowing. . . .

"Goddamn it, this is *real*!" Carl shouted, bolting suddenly to his feet. "You surrender, or *we all die*!"

Horst was standing before Carl knew it, his Uzi pointed straight at Carl's navel.

"Go ahead, do it, if you want to," Carl said icily. "Now, later, what's the difference?"

He raked his gaze around the room. "None of my business, maybe," he said, "but are you guys gonna let der Fuehrer here decide whether you all live or die all by his own perfect self, or do you think it might at least be a good idea to talk about it?"

"Fookin' right!"

"Never bargained—"

"Got a point!"

"Yeah, Horst—"

"—trick to divide us—"

All of them were suddenly yammering at each other at once. But while the Green Army Commandos broke up into squalling little groups, Horst maintained eye contact with Carl, even smiled a little like a hitter acknowledging a killer pitch with a move of his hand in the direction of the bill of his cap.

Kind of a show of class, Carl had to admit. But also a reminder that the ball game was far from over.

6:02 P.M.

". . . THE ISRAELIS MIGHT BE capable of acting on such cold calculations, but it is hard to credit the Americans. . . ."

"My arse!"

". . . done all we can anyway . . ."

". . . didn't sign on for this shit . . ."

". . . bourgeois adventurers!"

This was not going as Heather had planned, to the extent that she had planned anything. What she had hoped, she supposed, was that Carl's revelation would convince all the Green Army Commandos, Horst included, that their only real choices were timely surrender or certain death.

"How did you *expect* this action to end anyway?"

"Question of will . . ."

". . . knew that going in . . ."

But instead, they had ordered the hostages to the table in front of the soda machine, sequestered themselves at the table under the air-feed monitor across the length of the cafeteria, and there they had sat arguing among themselves ever since.

While Heather could only catch bits and pieces of dialogue, from their body language and who seemed to be talking to whom when, she could read, or anyway thought she could read, the drift of the group dynamics.

Kelly was apparently arguing for surrender, and Warren and Nigel, seated on her side of the table, seemed to be with her, forming the soft core. Helga and Hiroshi flanked Horst on the other side of the table, apparently the hard core. Ahmed, seated on Horst's side, but whose attention seemed to swivel back and forth like a man watching a tennis match, and Jaro, who sat there quietly beside Warren taking it all in, appeared to be the swing group. Of the two missing Commandos no doubt guarding the station entrances, Malcolm would probably side with his friend Nigel, and Paulo was a total unknown.

". . . could start negotiations ourselves . . ."

". . . sign of weakness!"

". . . fookin' ego trip . . ."

Carl leaned across their own table, closer to Heather. "This doesn't seem to be working too well, does it?" he said.

"Given time, I think a majority of them will surrender, only Horst, Helga, Hiroshi, maybe—"

"Time we don't have much of, Heather!" Toby hissed. "And Horst is the one that counts! This was really a dumb—"

"Lay off her, Toby!" Eddie Franker snapped. "I didn't hear you come up with anything better."

"Yeah," growled Carl, "*I'm* the one that risked getting my ass blown away, not you, so shut the fuck up!"

". . . really killed anyone . . . ?"

". . . counterproductive anyway . . ."

". . . co-opted by the media . . ."

"Listen to us," Heather said, "we're starting to sound like *them*! And we can't afford it."

Toby looked chastened. Carl nodded. Eddie Franker patted her arm paternally. "Not your fault, Heather," he said, "but maybe we *have* miscalculated . . . not that there was really any better chance, I suppose . . ."

". . . never really thought this out to the end, Horst!"

". . . pleased with yourself on television!"

". . . yeah, well *your* performance . . ."

"This is not *playacting,* Kelly!"

"What do you call *this* bullshit, Horst?"

The sound level across the cafeteria had suddenly risen. Horst and Kelly were shouting at each other across the table, and the rest of the Green Army Commandos had been converted into an unwilling and seemingly appalled audience.

"You want us all to spend the rest of our lives in prison?"

"You want us all to die?"

"This is a bluff!"

"And the plutonium isn't?"

And so were Heather and the other three hostages witnesses to the rather terrifying spectacle of the two terrorist leaders working themselves up into a state approaching pop-eyed and spittle-spraying ire.

"Listen to you! This result is just what the Americans intended!"

"*I'm* an American, remember!"

"And you are proving it with your naivete!"

"Shit," Toby moaned, "this is all we need now."

"It *is* starting to get dicey," Carl said as Horst Klingerman stood up suddenly, pounded his fist on the table.

"Some of us are *sincere* about direct action! To some of us it's more than an excuse to preen on television!"

"Jesus Christ," Eddie groaned.

Kelly Jordan got up too, stood there trembling. "Low, Horst, really low!" she shouted.

"But the truth, Kelly, you have become enamored of your own image!"

"Hey, guy, come on—"

Warren was on his feet trying to calm Horst Klingerman. Nigel had Kelly Jordan by the elbow.

"Fookin' bloody hell, not in front of the children!"

"You're just jealous!"

"Of *what*?"

Helga stood up, Hiroshi, Ahmed. Only the opaque Jaro just sat there.

"You hate playing the villain!"

"Do you suppose all this is some stupid cowboys and Indians movie? Have you been *that* corrupted?"

Heather found herself on her feet, not quite sure when she had stood up, why she was doing this, what it was she was doing, or what she was about to do next.

But a strange fearlessness seemed to possess her, as if this were only a film she was directing, and the actors had somehow drifted far from the script and the scene had gotten totally out of control.

A part of her knew that this was quite insane, but another part of her knew that this was the role she was being called upon to play now, the role, paradoxically enough, of the director of this real life-and-death movie.

Heather Blake threaded her way through the chairs and tables about halfway across the cafeteria. She stopped, put her hands on her hips, took a deep breath, and shouted with as much strength and authority as her well-trained voice could muster:

"CUT! STOP! SHUT UP! CUT! CUT! THIS IS AWFUL!"

The scene froze for a long silent beat.

Kelly, Warren, Nigel, and Jaro, who had been facing her, gaped.

Horst, whose back had been to her, whirled around, fury on his face, followed a half-beat later by Helga, Hiroshi, and Ahmed.

"Listen to yourselves!" Heather shouted before any of them could get in a reaction line. "You're gibbering like idiots!"

Eight astonished and outraged terrorists faced her. They had machine-pistols, but they had no script and no direction to prepare them for a move like this, and Heather knew that as long as she could talk faster than they could think and play the role of the director with convincing authority, she would control the action.

Such was the Method in this madness.

"You're doing just what the CIA has programmed you to do like a stupid bunch of audio-animatronic terrorists in Disneyland!" she said in the same authoritative voice, walking forward toward them slowly.

"You're breaking up into factions! You're playing right into their hands! We're all gonna die and everything you think you've accomplished is going to be blown away with you because as far as public opinion is concerned you'll all have been a gang of murderous anti-American blood-crazed monsters!"

Heather delivered these lines in a rapid mesmeric cadence that left no room for reaction dialogue or action, and by the time she had finished she was standing maybe a yard away from Horst Klingerman.

She took two firm deliberate steps forward, reached out slowly, and poked him in the chest with a forefinger.

"Stop this stupid childish behavior!" she said in the same director's voice, glowering at Horst like an exasperated producer. "You better listen to a professional who knows what she's talking about."

Nobody moved. Horst's face was a mask of anger, but only a mask now. He might have the gun, but she was in control, and she had been from the opening line of this scene.

The anger faded from Horst's face, and something almost approaching mirth began to steal into his blue eyes.

Now he knew it.

"This . . . this has been another of your acting tricks, yes . . . ?" he stammered.

Heather smiled at him, winked broadly. "No," she said, "*this* is called directing."

Horst shook his head ruefully, almost smiled. "I suppose if you wish to say something to us *that* badly," he said, "we might as well listen."

The moment broke, and with it Heather's sense of directorial mastery of the situation. She had gained the center of attention, all right, any decent actress could have done it, but now what was she supposed to do with it?

The truth of it was that she had acted entirely off her gut instinct, without any idea of what she would do next.

Playing for time, Heather walked over to the terrorists' table, pulled out a chair, dragged it to one narrow end and sat down—another little directorial trick, creating a head of the table and putting herself at it.

Slowly, everyone took seats, hostages and terrorists alike, all of them looking to her, united for the moment at least on a human level, eleven people hoping they were about to be told a way out of what seemed to be an impossible and deadly situation.

And that was when it came to her.

"Look," Heather said, "I don't have a hot new idea. But I do have an old one that worked before, so I don't see why it shouldn't work again. Let's do another tearjerker. Let's make it impossible for the government to get away with using violence."

"Jesus Christ, Heather," Toby moaned rather sneeringly. "We're about out of friends and relatives, and they'd never let us do it again anyway."

"That's *not* what I mean," Heather said. "Look, right now, as far as the American public is concerned, the Green Army Commandos are really Kelly Jordan and Horst Klingerman, right, with Horst cast as the heavy. So if the CIA attacks the station, the explosives go off, and everybody dies, it all gets blamed on this awful guy last seen foaming at the mouth and telling hoodlums to burn cars and gas stations."

"So?" Horst muttered sourly.

"So let's differentiate the spear carriers, let's give them lines, let's let them all have their time in center stage."

"*Spear carriers?* I do not understand the idiom."

Slowly, one by one, Heather made eye contact with each of them, not with an anonymous bunch of terrorists, but with Warren, Helga, Jaro, Hiroshi, Nigel, and Ahmed, with six individuals, however presently opaque and mysterious, six *real people* who were not spear carriers in *their own* movies, six human beings whose lives people could be made to care for if their stories were well told.

"We could call it something like, oh, *Meet the Green Army Commandos*," Heather said. "An interview of about ten minutes each with the eight anonymous terrorists the public hasn't gotten to meet."

She looked at Eddie. "What do you say, Mr. Franker? Is that something you could sell to StarNet?"

Eddie just grinned.

"I think I could handle it," Toby said.

"Fuck you, Toby Inman!" Heather snarled, taking a certain pleasure in showing herself plain. "This one's *mine!*"

"This is very interesting, yes," Horst said, "but I do not understand how this will prevent the CIA from doing what they have planned."

"Yeah," said Kelly, "I don't get it."

Heather grinned. "Picture it . . . about eighty minutes of sympathetic interviews with these idealistic people from all over the world risking their lives to save the planet. . . . And at the end, and as the capper . . ."

She paused for a beat, a second beat, a third, waiting for a cue line, a rather cheap trick, but always an effective one.

"And as the capper?" Warren finally said.

"And as the capper, as the grand finale, after Mrs. and Mr. America have met all you wonderful people and seen what is in your hearts . . ."

Another dramatic pause, Heather could hardly resist it, less still could she resist grinning like a triumphant ape.

Beat.

"And as the capper," she said, *the hostages come on camera and plead for their captors' lives!*"

"Far fookin' out!"

8:00 P.M.

Onscreen:

A CLOSE-UP ON HEATHER Blake, KLAX's prototypical blond good-looking Southern Californian weathergirl . . . but there's an unfamiliar intensity in her eyes, a more mature quality to her voice, that makes her seem about ten years older than her video image.

"Good evening. As most of you know, I'm Heather Blake, KLAX-TV's regular meteorologist, and currently a hostage of the Green Army Commandos. You've been hearing a lot about the Green Army Commandos these last five days, and you probably think you know more than you want to know. But actually, even those of us being held hostage know very little. We know Horst Klingerman and Kelly Jordan, but what do we really know about the *other* eight members of the terrorist group that has seized this televi-

sion station? Well tonight, we're going to find out, you and I. . . .
Tonight we're going to *meet the Green Army Commandos!*"

As she pauses, a cut to a head-and-shoulders shot of a man in
his thirties; pale, rather bad complexion, near-shoulder-length
scraggly blond hair balding at the crown, wire-rimmed granny
glasses, a nerd with an Uzi slung over his shoulder.

Heather Blake's voice-over: "And we'll begin with Warren Davies. . . ."

A two-shot on Heather Blake and Warren Davies, sitting side
by side on a green couch in front of a maple coffee table against a
neutral cream background.

"Tell us something about yourself, Warren."

"Uh . . . like what?"

"Where you grew up, where you came from, your parents, you
know. . . ."

Warren Davies squints uncertainly at the camera as it moves in
for a close-up. "Grew up in Mendocino, California, around there
anyway, my parents, I guess you'd say they were hippies, communes,
dope farms, natural granola, you know, moved to San Rafael finally,
where I went to high school, couple years at UC Berkeley, dropped
out. . . ."

A two-shot on Heather Blake and Warren Davies from a different angle as he pauses, shrugs. "That what you want to know?"

"And after you dropped out of college, what did you do, I
mean to make a living and all?"

"Electronics . . . computers . . . that sorta stuff."

"*What* with computers?"

"You know. . . ."

"No I don't."

"This and that. . . ."

"This and *what*?"

Warren Davies squirms nervously in his chair. "Stuff . . ." he
mutters. "Hacks . . . this and that with, uh, credit cards . . . setting up, ah, systems, consulting, software, hardware. . . ."

"You mean you made your living as an underground computer
hacker?"

Warren Davies becomes much more animated.

"Hey, a lot more than *that*!" he says almost indignantly.
"Those guys are like so *narrow*. You wanna call me an *electronic*

hacker, I can cop to it. Always had an electric thumb, you know, chips, circuits, software, juice goes through it, Warren can do it! Sure, I did my share of system hacking but I teched for electronic groups, video processing, troubleshooting two-byte FM stations, little programs for this and that, uh, satellite stuff, gray cable hookups. . . ."

Cut to a close-up on Warren Davies as he breaks into a little grin. His voice firmer and clearer. "My hippie-dip folks called me a cybernerd or worse, I mean, they thought a baby harp seal died every time you booted up! But if I was a cyberpunk, I was a cyberpunk Bay Area style."

Heather Blake's voice-over: *"Bay Area style?"*

"Hey, like the Sixties never ended up there inside the fog bank . . . maybe twenty years of all that dope smoke did something permanent to the atmosphere, I mean like everything there has to be *underground* to be *overground* . . . like the Grateful Dead outlasted two generations up there, I mean, *geriatric rock stars* and tie-dyed neon, and. . . ."

Cut to a two-shot on Heather Blake and Warren Davies.

"For Mr. and Mrs. Middle America . . . ?" Heather says gently.

Warren Davies shrugs. "Like Bob Dylan was my parents' *Lawrence Welk*. . . . Kids like me, we grew up thinking like all that stuff was *normal*, I mean, we wanted to rebel, we could become *Republican stockbrokers*."

A close-up on Warren Davies as he smiles rather affectingly into the camera. "Not *really*," he says, "I mean what we *really* hated was all that Sixties *technophobia*, not sex, drugs, rock and roll, or radical politics, so when *we* did our countertake on the Bay Area counter-culture thing, we went *electronic*."

He laughs. "Or you could say when we did our trendy cyberpunk trip, we did it to the usual funky old Bay Area beat."

Cut to a close-up on Heather Blake, looking a bit bemused by all this. "So how did a nice technohippie like you end up in a terror-ist group like the Green Army Commandos?" she says.

A close-up on Warren Davies, his eyes narrowing behind his glasses, his face becoming rather guarded.

"On the net . . ."

Heather Blake's voice-over: "The net?"

"One of the trendy words for it, you know, the net, the matrix, cyberspace, virtual reality," Davies says. He shrugs. " 'Course all it *really* is is terminals, com lines, data banks, and what goes on between 'em. Phones, computers, modems, TV sets. Phone lines and sat links. The net's all of this stuff and none of it. It's everywhere and nowhere. It's the interface, and the dudes surfing it."

Heather Blake's voice-over: "Marshall McLuhan's electronic global village, right?"

"Sorta," says Warren Davies. "More like the global electronic Sierra Maestra, you might say, or anyway my folks would if they understood it."

He looks down away from the camera, his eyes becoming evasive.

"I mean, you gotta be pretty dumb to *pay* for all that connect time, so many ways to hack yourself as much as you can eat, an hour on an underground board in Tokyo or Moscow's just as free as an hour on the same down in San José, boards inside of boards inside of boards, people using handles, half the time you don't really know who you're interfacing with or even where they really are. . . ."

Heather Blake's voice-over: "You linked up with the Green Army Commandos electronically before you even *met* any of the others?"

Warren Davies nods.

"I was heavy into the international boards, maybe just 'cause I knew what I was getting free was like so *expensive,* just because I *could,* I mean because I was using . . ."

Davies pauses suddenly. "Well, never mind. Anyway, I got on this underground board, worldwide, and, uh, *transparent* to the ·billing software of all the carriers. Known as 'Fruits and Nuts,' 'cause that's like what it was, all sorts of *really* weird forums and areas, I mean, transsexual soccer freaks, Ninja Nazis, Chinese Imperial Restorationists, Zen Communists, leather lesbian transcendental masturbators, Militant Carnivores, you name it, what a zoo!"

He laughs. "Better than two hundred channels of pirated pornsat! And a lot more interactive. I spent a couple weeks playing around on it, and then I logged onto an area called Anarchy."

"*Anarchy*? You mean as in guys with long mustaches in black raincoats throwing bombs shaped like bowling balls?"

A two-shot on Warren Davies and Heather Blake, a certain chemistry in evidence as he laughs at her line.

"Seemed like that to me at first too," he says. "A whole load of forums and sub-boards leading who knew where, Bakuninists, Left Trots, Right Trots, Fox Trots, plans for bombs, atomic ones even, booby-traps, how to drop an airliner, where to score Semtex, Stingers, plutonium. . . ."

Heather Blake looks rather appalled. "You were seriously interested in . . . in *killing people?*"

"Hey, who could take stuff like that *seriously?*" he says. "I mean, far as I was concerned, it was just a blood-sausage custard pie . . . and then . . ."

A close-up on Warren Davies, his expression gone all serious. "And then I logged onto a subarea called Earthdeath, and inside it was a forum called Bad Boys, and inside *that* . . ."

8:13 P.M.

"YEAH, LOOV, THAT WAS us," Malcolm Macklin said. "Fookin' bloody bad, bad boys we wuz!"

"Please!" Heather said. "Remember, we're on the air, and the—"

"Ah yes," said Nigel Edwards, "the bloody fookin' Carlin rule! The seven bloody fookin' words yer not supposed to utter on the air in bloody fookin' Yankland! Shall we dispose of this bloody fookin' matter so we can converse freely inna bloody fookin' civilized manner, Malcolm?"

"Bloody fookin' capital idea, Nigel. Shall I?"

"Afta you, mate!"

"Fuck, shit, cock, cunt, prick, bastard, motherfucker. Have I forgotten something?"

"Please . . ." Heather moaned.

"Ah, that's right, innit, a cock-sucking Yank TV station could lose its bloody fookin' license for lettin' a couple of shitty pricks like us use such foul language on television."

"Too true, mate! Their bloody fookin' FCC is a buncha motherfookin' old lady fascists!"

"Cunts, that is."

They both broke up into raucous laughter.

It was not so easy for Heather not to break up with them. After all, the CIA *was* going to storm the station in less than two hours if this didn't work, and everyone inside it *would* probably die, so it *was* bloody fookin' ridiculous to worry about the Carlin rule under such circumstances, which, from a certain viewpoint, were an invitation to flout it flagrantly.

"You were saying, before we got sidetracked onto the bloody fookin' Carlin rule . . . ?" she said rather gaily in a fair imitation of their accent.

Nigel laughed. "*We* was the Bad Boys, I was saying, hidin' down there under all that parlor anarchist crap, like one of those trapdoor spiders waitin' for a nice fat fly, or whatever it is them boogers eat. . . ."

Heather had already thrown her mental script away. . . .

"Warren was yer electronic whiz, but wiff the political consciousness of an earthworm. . . ."

Her original notion had been to simply do a series of disconnected personality profiles, and she had decided to start with Warren only because she thought leading off with an American would be the best intro for the audience, and she had planned to go to Helga next. . . .

"Yer typical Yank hacker, wiff his bits and bytes inna right place, but his vision of the planetary future up his own arsehole."

"So fookin' disconnected from the real world it was just another video game—"

"Like wassit, Peter Sellers innat movie, this guy knows nothing but the tube, goes out onna street with his remote, mugger accosts him seriously, he don't get why the booger don't disappear when he presses the button ta change channels."

But when Warren's segment led so naturally in this direction, she had Eddie put Jaro and Ahmed on the cameras and segued straight from Warren to the British cameramen themselves, letting the thread unwind backwards, let the story tell itself. . . .

8:16 P.M.

Onscreen:

A TWO-SHOT ON Malcolm Macklin and Nigel Edwards, two ominous-looking young punks in a stereotypical way—Macklin pale and pasty-faced with a rather unkempt mousy Mohawk running down the center of his shaved head and half a dozen metal rings through each ear, Edwards with a chubby and beefy-complexioned John Bull face and rotten teeth set off by a much more impressive crest of bright red spikes, both of them wearing the inevitable black leather jackets encrusted with chrome fetishwork, and both with Uzis slung over their shoulders to complete the Bad Boys kit.

And yet . . .

"Matter of leading a bloke like that along by 'is joystick, so to speak. . . ."

"Gettin' him to download educational material by convincing him it's *secret knowledge,* them types rather get inta that than a hot pair a tightpants. . . ."

And yet there is something charming about them, something affecting about the way they so manifestly enjoy doing their grossout routine on television.

A three-shot, Malcolm and Nigel on the left, Heather Blake on the right, beauty and the beasts, as it were, except she doesn't seem to feel threatened, and they don't seem to be trying.

"What sort of . . . educational material?" she asks.

"Ecological stuff at first, carbon dioxide count, ozone depletion, death o' th' oceans an' all, only kind of buried inna form of suppressed government reports, pirated landsat footage, an' whatever, even though anyone who gave a shit could find it all out by watchin' the telly, but with blokes like that—"

"You gotta turn it into a tease, like a nice paira tits is somehow more, ah, *titillating* peekin' out some black lace than out there in clear, at least for certain sortsa blokes."

"An' then, after he gets it that the technology which created the problem had fookin' bloody well better be part of the solution, we get down to the old gritty titty—the Big A."

"The Big A? Anarchism?"

"Right! Startin' with practical stuff, an' progressing to theory."

"Bomb plans, how ta penetrate secure satellite transponders, wipin' corporate data banks . . ." Nigel winks. "You know, the kind boys like!"

Heather Blake laughs, then regards them more seriously. "You're *really* anarchists?"

A two-shot on Malcolm and Nigel as they exchange somewhat supercilious glances.

"Loov, we grew up workin' poor in Maggie Thatcher's and John Major's bloody fookin' England—"

"*Workin'* poor my arse!"

"I had a job once."

"When?"

"Uh . . . I fookin' forget."

Nigel laughs. "What my colleague here is tryin' ta say is we grew up working *class* inna Midlands, only by that time there wasn't much fookin' *work* ta be had—"

"An' no fookin' *class* inna country either, what Major called th' classless society, an' he should know, seein' as how the booger had absolutely none himself—"

"Point is, the bloody fookin' government was run by no-neck clots an' upper-class twits wiff broomsticks up their arses without a break since before we were born—"

"Leadin' anyone who could listen ta the radio and smoke dope at the same time to the logical conclusion that just maybe *government* itself was a bloody fookin' con game by means of which this gang of vampire toadies continued to suck the blood of the working class—"

"Namely us."

"And when you wake up that far, which, you gotta admit ain't much," Malcolm said, "you are already an anarchist even if you don't know it."

"At which point all you gotta do is watcha BBC, what with the Kurds stompina Wheys, anna Jugs goin' bugs, anna Sunny ragheads givin' it ta the Shits and visa versa, ta get the bigger picture, namely that all these fookin' national states an' half-arsed tribes a suckers is just the same government con game writ global, by means of which the bastards what gobbles caviar an' swills champagne in Number

Ten Kremlin White House Palace gets to keep their fookin' corner on alla goodies."

"Anarchism in one easy lesson, Heather, from those what learned the hard way!"

A close-up on Heather Blake, the blond surfer-girl ingenue confronted by a deeper and harsher reality on the one hand and a cool hard intellect learning fast on the other.

"Leading to the conclusion that violence is justified to smash the system?" she says.

A three-shot on Malcolm Macklin, Nigel Edwards, and Heather Blake as Edwards shrugs, smiles with a mouthful of rotten teeth.

"In theory," he says. "After all, loov, the fookin' state is armed ta the teeth, now innit, an' it ain't at all reluctant ta use what it's got on other fookin' nation-states, or the likes a us. . . ."

"But in practice, loov, it's not too bright ta walk up ta a twelve-foot gorilla an' whack it inna nuts with your purse, now is it?"

"So it's more like an *attitude,* a target of opportunity presents itself, you take it, you steal it, you hack it, you trash it, whatever—"

"You can't smash the state, at least you don't let the state smash *you.*"

"No more than it fookin' has already!"

"And *this* is the stuff you recruited Warren Davies with?" Heather Blake says dubiously.

Malcolm laughs. "Shit no, that's primitive, loov, just the old outlaw attitude wiff a bit of rationale for gravy!"

"By the time we went fishin' inna electronic frog pond fer a Yankland cyberwhiz, we had already evolved ta a higher level."

"I mean that up-against-the-wall shit is pretty far fer a couple of uneducated yobs boosted themselves computers and vidcams an' all and learned ta play with 'em, but when all's said an' done, it's all pretty fookin' negative, now innit?"

"Smash the state, fook the pigs, rip off the goodies, it's all well an' good, seein' as how the state needs smashing, the pigs need fookin', an' we all need our goodies, but wiffout a vision of how it can be made to serve some kind of positive evolution, it's just a fookin' good excuse for a criminal attitude, now ain't it?"

"And that's what we more or less were, a couple criminal-minded little boogers wiff a cellar fulla stolen gear, makin' dumb videos for stupid groups went nowhere, hacking into systems, deludin' ourselves that we were hot revolutionary shit."

"Struttin' our stuff an' beatin' our electronic chests like a coupla anarchist gorillas onna Fruit and Nuts board."

"Finally settin' up our own Bad Boys forum fer transnational pig-fookers, system-smashers, an' general underground riffraff such as ourselves."

"An' then we start gettin' uploads from somewhere from this bloke goes by the handle of Green Army Commando. . . ."

"Which turns out to be old Jaro out there in Czechland. . . ."

8:23 P.M.

JARO OLGAR SAT THERE stock-still, smiling a false wooden smile at Heather, at the camera, only his right leg, well out of the frame, twitching nervously to reveal his stage fright.

He had always seemed taciturn and unreadable, but not until she started interviewing him on the air had it occurred to Heather that it might be because he lacked a confident command of English.

"First Slovak, then Czech, same language, but Slovaks don't admit, Russian in school, everyone hates, but what can do, then German, English only in Prague after Velvet Revolution, so is fourth or fifth for me, not so good maybe yet. . . ."

"You're doing fine, Jaro," Heather lied encouragingly. "And you were able to communicate easily enough with Malcolm and Nigel now, weren't you . . . ?"

"Is easy on board . . . write . . . save . . . edit . . . up-load . . . download answer . . . *this* I could do in Serbo-Croatian or Danish if had to."

"You were trying to recruit people for the Green Army Commandos?"

"Jah. We need for mission how is the English words, technical know-what. . . ."

"Know-how."

"Know-*how*. I have. Need more. Find Fruits and Nuts board.

Bad Boys area. Nigel and Malcolm. They have. Politically naive, ecologically ignorant, but right spirit. Not hard convincing."

"And how did *you* hook up with the Green Army Commandos?"

"Hook up?"

"Join, get recruited."

Jaro squirmed, fidgeted, frowned. "Long story, complicated," he said. "Maybe not . . . *adequate* English . . . ?"

"Don't worry, Jaro, you're doing fine, and I'm here to help you tell your story to the folks out there," Heather said soothingly, flashing him a warm, friendly smile.

Nor, she realized, was it entirely feigned.

This was a bitch, tougher than most pro talk-show interviewers would dare try, but Heather sensed that Jaro *was* getting through, did come across as sympathetic, if only because *she* found herself warming to the guy herself.

Heather might not be the naive middle-American ingenue she spent so much time playing, but when it came to all this cyberpunk stuff, all this European politics, all this multilingual personal reality, her ignorance was really not *that* far behind that of the mass American audience this show was supposed to be reaching.

And by not getting too far out in front of the identification figure she was playing, she hoped she could take them along with her. . . .

8:29 P.M.

Onscreen:

". . . SLOVAK, YES, BORN IN Bratislava . . . but this nationalism to me is so stupid. . . . Not Czech, not Slovak, *Czechoslovak*, this I think myself under Communists. . . ."

A close-up on Jaro Olgar, in his thirties perhaps, neatly combed medium-length straight black hair, wide forehead, thick lips, high cheekbones, gray eyes, closely shaven—only the Uzi slung over his shoulder marks him as anything less than respectable.

He speaks haltingly, in a thick accent, and he looks almost petrified by the eye of the camera, but conviction, emotion, seems to come through by act of will.

". . . I go to university in Prague, Czech Republic, best film school—"

Cut to a tight two-shot on Jaro Olgar and Heather Blake. She's leaning deeper into his body space than the normal one-on-one interview, as if trying to support him with her body language.

"You went to film school! So did I! UCLA!"

"UCLA!" Jaro Olgar exclaims. He positively beams at her. "We hear of this place even under Communists! Spielberg! Lucas!"

Heather laughs. "A bit before my time," she says. "But I would have thought that a film school under the Communists—"

"Is strange, Czechoslovak film, video, theater, all advanced, all very . . . avant-garde, even under Communists, even before *Dubček,* is said . . . of course . . . political content must hide or be punished . . . Havel himself goes often to prison."

A close-up on Jaro Olgar, his face stays animated, his eyes remain brightly alive, but something about his expression becomes faraway and dreamy.

"I graduate into time of perestroika . . . join underground . . . make videos . . . time of Velvet Revolution . . . everyone not dead in spirit does this. . . . Wonderful time! Is wonderful time to be . . . not Czech, not Slovak, *Czechoslovak!* Communists fall! Revolution wins! Havel President! Old Dubček himself back from exile! He is Slovak too, you know, Communist, yes, but *Czechoslovak* patriot!"

A tight two-shot on Heather Blake and Jaro Olgar as he frowns heavily, shrugs, squirms, seems to be struggling with something other than the language. Heather Blake leans even further forward, actually pats his knee.

"What's wrong? What's the matter?"

"What wrong? What *right*? Is . . . how you say . . . hang-dog, morning after . . . Revolution finished. Meciar and his stupid Slovak nationalists! Is shown in . . . you say, polls of opinion? Majority of Czechs not want. Majority of *Slovaks* not want either! But happens! Dream finished! Czechoslovakia finished! All we work and fight for finished!"

A close-up on Jaro Olgar, angry now, bitter. "I am *Czechoslovak*! Care nothing for this chauvinist . . . bullshit! And film, TV industry, is all in Prague, in Czech Republic, where I cannot be Czechoslovak, where I am stupid *Slovak*!"

A tight two-shot on Jaro Olgar and Heather Blake. "There wasn't much of an industry back in, uh, Slovakia?" she says.

"In *Slovakia*? Slovakia is . . . weapons factory for Russians! Military industrial . . . water closet! Coal mines! Chemical plants! Nuclear reactors! Dead rivers color of piss! And nationalists like Communists! Censor boards! Control all budgets! No money anyway! Slovakian cinema is like . . . like . . . like North Korean rock and roll!"

Heather Blake breaks up.

But Jaro Olgar, his tirade over, becomes quite wistful. "*Prague* . . . this is my city . . . my home . . . heart of my soul . . . center of my spirit . . . and now . . . in my Prague, I become *foreigner*. . . ."

"So, uh, how did you become a Green Army Commando?"

"Is no money for Slovak to make films in Prague. . . . But I speak good German. Get small job to . . . make footage in Berlin for independent television . . . give me camcorder, second-class train ticket, room in not-so-good hotel . . . story is about Oranienburger district . . . you have heard?"

"I'm afraid not, and I'm sure the folks out there haven't either."

The camera moves in slowly for a close-up on Jaro Olgar.

"Is very interesting. Is district around Oranienburger Strasse, this is in the old East Berlin, old prostitution place like Reeperbahn, but very . . . slum . . . dirty old buildings which crumble . . . after Reunification, taken over by artists, anarchists, cafés, cellars, you say . . . you say . . . ?"

He seems stuck for a word. Cut to a two-shot on Jaro Olgar and Heather Blake as she tries to help him.

"Bohemian?"

He looks puzzled.

"Bohemian? Bohemia is part of Czech Republic, not in Germany. . . ."

"Uh, well, *underground*? A kind of . . . tough scene? Artists and writers and actors without much money? Little theaters and galleries? Drug traffic? Political radicals? People hiding out from the police?"

"Yes! Yes! Underground! Is good word! I am to shoot footage about Oranienburger *underground*!"

Back to a close-up on Jaro Olgar, nodding enthusiastically.

"I shoot street scenes, cafés, galleries, restored synagogue . . . talk to people . . . hear about *Weimar Republik*. . . ."

Heather Blake's voice-over: "The *Weimar Republik*? Isn't that the bar where Horst met Kelly?"

"Yes. Yes. Is cellar bar. Has reputation as . . . you say hangout? . . . for radical political people, old Baader-Meinhoffers, Black Septembrists, terrorists from groups no longer exist . . . some say is, what you would call it, terrorist union hiring hall."

A two-shot on Heather Blake and Jaro Olgar.

"Sounds like a pretty ominous scene," Heather says.

Jaro nods, grins happily.

"Is great footage!" he says. "Dirty bar in basement! Smoke. Hashish. Like black-and-white movie from Thirties with Marlene Dietrich. All kinds people! Germans. Arabs. Turks. Bosnians. People who will not say. Strange dress. Many boasts. People say were members of Red Army Faction, Japanese Red Army, Fatah, Sendero Luminoso, groups no one ever hears about. Many liars, I think. Many, how you say, philosophers of the saloon, who tell stories for to have people buy them drinks. But some, these I think are real, like Helga Mueller. . . ."

"And the Green Army Commandos? They hung out there?"

"Horst, Ahmed, Paulo, Hiroshi, these I meet there later, and then Kelly, first is Helga, is very . . . cautioned . . . tell me of mission . . . is some money for budget . . . from MANC, American ecology group . . . could be . . . much important footage for . . . for right person with courage. . . ."

8:38 P.M.

IF JARO OLGAR HAD seemed the most opaque of the Green Army Commandos, Helga Mueller had seemed like the most unsympathetic as far as Heather was concerned, nor was this interview doing much to change her opinion.

"So you recruited Jaro . . . ?"

"We needed technical expertise in certain matters."

"Such as?"

"Such as what we are doing now."

"Which is?"

"Running a television station."

There was something about the woman that set Heather's teeth on edge. Worse, she could hear herself being turned into some kind of interrogator, for Helga seemed to react to every lead line as if she was indeed being interrogated by some police agency, and extracting information, let alone human interest, was like pulling teeth.

"Why Jaro?"

"He had what we needed. He was willing. For him, the opportunity to perhaps secure videotape of the proceedings was sufficient motive."

Helga shrugged. She grinned entirely mirthlessly.

"Like you people. A show-business person. A mercenary."

"And you're not?"

"Yes and no."

"Yes *and* no? How is that possible?"

Helga regarded Heather with a look of such lofty contempt that Heather found herself actually wanting to *slug* the fookin' cunt.

"You are American," she said, in that sharp, precise, vaguely nasal voice, in English enunciated so perfectly it somehow seemed intended as an insult. "You cannot possibly understand."

"Try me," Heather said, trying to stay professional. "This *is* American television, and you *are* on it."

8:39 P.M.

Onscreen:

A **CLOSE-UP ON** Helga Mueller, straight mousy-brown hair streaked with gray, cold-eyed, clean-featured, full lips that seem to be sucked deliberately inward in an attempt to negate any hint of sensuality. To a man, she might seem to be a lesbian. To a woman, she would not.

"It was Hiroshi who said it correctly," she says. "Ronin, he called us. Masterless samurai. Looking for—"

"A leader?"

"Horst Klingerman?" Helga Mueller snapped, scowling. "Full of ideas, full of passion too perhaps, but not the sort of person experienced operatives would choose to follow into an armed confrontation, if he had not latched onto Jordan and her American funding—"

Helga Mueller stops in midsentence. Her eyes narrow.

"I say too much."

A two-shot on Helga Mueller and Heather Blake, eyeing each other warily.

"Horst didn't start the Green Army Commandos? You did?"

Helga shrugs. "Horst was certainly an interesting theoretician, and a great talker, no doubt about that. I am neither. He could go on and on about direct action. I had spent my life living it. Without him, no Green Army Commandos. Without me, no Green Army Commandos. Without innocent little Kelly shopping for terrorists like an American heiress out to spend Pappa's money on furs and jewels, no Green Army Commandos either. It . . . came together."

Helga pauses, and now she smiles a smile that seems almost wistful. "Ronin, Hiroshi called us," she said. "Warriors whose reasons for being had died. Looking for . . . looking for . . ."

"A new cause?"

"Perhaps. Or a way to serve the old one in this changed world."

"Which was . . . ?"

"The best question you have asked so far. I used to think I

knew the answer clearly. International working-class solidarity. The revolution of the oppressed against the oppressors. Socialist idealism against capitalist exploitation."

"You're talking like . . . like some kind of *Communist*. . . ."

Helga Mueller laughs, a not particularly mirthful sound. "Perhaps because I was, and would like to think I still *am*. Not a Leninist, not a Stalinist, a bit of a Maoist perhaps, with a certain sympathy for the doctrines of Sendero Luminoso and Trotsky, but basically a rather old-fashioned straightforward Marxist transnationalist revolutionary with little interest in such dialectical hairsplitting. An old Marxist samurai, as Hiroshi would say."

A quick cut to a close-up on Heather Blake, reacting to this with her mouth hanging open, then a close-up on Helga Mueller, laughing again, but this time somehow more sympathetically.

"You Americans! You believe that Communists must have horns and tails! You cannot imagine someone admitting to being one on television! And being proud of it!"

A two-shot on Helga Mueller and Heather Blake, Heather leaning toward her a bit, studying her with a somewhat softer attitude.

"But . . . Communism failed . . . it's dead. The West won the Cold War, didn't it . . . ?"

"Has it? Is it? Did it? Over a billion people still live under Communism in Asia. As for European Communism . . ."

A close-up on Helga Mueller as she sighs, as her face softens. "It was never truly tried, never more than a cruel Stalinist farce, a series of unloved puppet regimes imposed on conquered peoples by the Red Army. If Dubček had succeeded, if Yeltsin had not overthrown Gorbachev . . ." She shrugs. "Perhaps it does not really matter."

A two-shot on Heather Blake and Helga Mueller, emphasizing Helga Mueller, something changing in the chemistry between them.

"Doesn't matter?"

"When you believe something is right, when you *know* something is right, when you commit your life totally to an ideal, do you abandon that cause just because it has been defeated?"

"I don't think I understand. . . ."

"How could you? Your country has never been defeated on its own territory, never committed crimes so monstrous that justice demanded it be crushed utterly. Perhaps that is why we Germans are the strongest transnational idealists, such fervent Greens, why we make the most dedicated international revolutionaries. Where else on this planet has tribal chauvinism and predatory capitalism revealed its true face so nakedly, discredited itself so completely?"

"You mean you became a Communist revolutionary out of some kind of . . . ancestral guilt over the Nazis and the Holocaust?"

"Freudian rubbish!" Helga Mueller snaps rather shrilly. "Bourgeois sentimentalism! Spoken like a Social Democrat!"

"Then why?"

"Why not? It was an entirely rational decision based on the objective conditions. I grew up in the Federal Republic, a rich, fat, self-satisfied land which had successfully expunged its past to become the least nationalistic of states, a people owing their highest allegiance to the luxurious Mercedes and the powerful Porsche and the almighty deutsche mark."

"Is that so bad?"

"It was and is poisonous to the spirit!"

A close-up on Helga Mueller as she fairly grins. "Ah yes, it surprises you to hear a Marxist speak of the spirit! Dialectical materialism is supposed to deny all that! But it doesn't. I'm not talking about God, and the soul, and the rest of that mystical claptrap, but simply the *human* spirit, what people feel right here right now on this planet."

Her voice grows harder, more angrily passionate, the grin is replaced by a contemptuous sneer. "And when all that people care about is food, sex, drink, riches, they feel *nothing,* they have no spirit. They are perfectly content to cram beer and wurst down their throats till they are about to burst and poison the land with the excreted residue while billions starve elsewhere and their supposed fellow Germans in the DDR suffer!"

A two-shot on Heather Blake and Helga Mueller, Heather taken somewhat aback by this outburst, Helga rather abruptly calming herself.

"And of course I was a fat little child of this culture before my university days," she admits in quite another tone. "Only then did I meet young people who were committed to something beyond their own self-gratification."

"Communists? Marxists?"

Helga shrugs. "Communists, Marxists, Trotskyites, Anarchists, Greens, all kinds . . . all arguing so passionately over tactics and theory and doctrine . . . but what they all shared . . . what they all shared . . ."

A close-up on Helga Mueller as she pauses, seems to survey some inner landscape.

"What they all shared was a vision, though among the factions, they would never admit it . . . what I now know was the *planetary* vision, a solidarity not with nation or culture, but with the exploited Earth and its suffering peoples, divided into tribes and factions and classes by a small egoistic elite, who themselves follow no higher purpose than their own blind tropism to gobble, to gobble, and gobble, until they swallow the whole world and shit it all out as one final monstrous poisonous turd."

A two-shot on Helga Mueller and Heather Blake.

"*That's* in *The Communist Manifesto?*" Heather says.

Helga laughs wholeheartedly. "That's the Green Army Commando speaking, that's Horst Klingerman, not Karl Marx!" she says.

"You met Horst at the university?"

"Oh no, not until well after the Reunification, when he was the reigning barroom theoretician in the *Weimar Republik* and I had little to do but drink beer with the rest of them and listen! In those days, I wouldn't have given the time of day to such a feckless intellectual. In those days, I was a *real* terrorist!"

Heather nods toward the Uzi slung over Helga's shoulder.

"And now you're not?" she says dryly.

The camera slowly moves in for a close-up on Helga Mueller as her face hardens, and her eyes grow cold, and something frightening paints itself across her lips as the hideous semblance of a smile.

"This is nothing," she says. "I drifted in and out of many action groups before I found myself in the Red Army Faction. Sometimes known in the popular press as the Baader-Meinhof Gang. Baader-Meinhof you have perhaps heard of . . . ?"

A two-shot on Heather Blake and Helga Mueller. Heather looking quite ill at ease.

"They . . . you . . . kidnapped people, robbed banks, blew things up, deliberately *murdered* people, didn't you . . . ?"

"Yes we did." Cold as ice.

"How could you—?"

"Because we were idealists."

"How could—"

"How could idealists kidnap and murder and rob and blow up precious private property? Because it was *necessary*. It was necessary to awaken people from their stupor. It was therefore necessary to force the capitalist fascist statist elite to show its true colors, to resort to open oppression. Only then would people be sufficiently provoked to rise against their masters. And only a reign of terror would force the ruling classes into such a fatal error."

"That's not only immoral, it's insane."

"Is it? Would Kenya have gained its independence without the Mau-Mau? Did not your own American counterculture provoke Richard Nixon into the Watergate plot which destroyed him? As a tactic, it is not without its successes."

"But it didn't work for *you*, now did it?" Heather says. "There was never any Communist revolution in West Germany. Instead, the Communists in East Germany were kicked out, the Wall came down, the country was reunified, and everyone more or less lived happily ever after."

"Happily ever after! Yes, the Stalinist regime in the DDR was a historical monstrosity, yes it betrayed Marxist idealism, but still a whole world died with it, a world of secret solidarity against the Stasi, a world of art and literature nourished by state subsidies yet made strong and subtle by the dialectic of disguised opposition, a world of socialist idealism despite it all, a world, at least, which valued a sense of solidarity with one's fellow humans over a kilo of wurst and a liter of beer!"

"Aren't you romanticizing this stuff, the way some people here romanticize, oh . . . the Old South, with Rhett and Scarlett, and stately old paddle wheelers, and minstrel shows, and happy darkies strumming banjos? But it was really a lot of white guys with whips treating black people like *farm animals*, now wasn't it?"

The camera moves in very slowly for a close-up on Helga Mueller as she regards Heather Blake silently for a long beat, her eyes narrowing, her expression transforming into one that clearly says *you are a lot more sophisticated than you look*.

"Point taken," she says. She grimaces. "Indeed, even worse

than you know. When the Wall came down, and journalists began nosing through the old files, it turned out that the Red Army Faction itself had had secret Stasi controllers! Perhaps we *were* all naive romantics in the old international revolutionary underground, those of us who were idealistically committed to violent means, to risking our own lives . . . Red Army Faction . . . Black September . . . Japanese Red Army . . . IRA . . . Abu Nidal . . . still . . ."

She smiles almost dreamily, like some suburban hausfrau remembering golden girlhood summers of wine and roses.

"Many causes, many groups, much doctrinal dispute, but solidarity too, a sense of common spirit, we were all comrades together. . . ."

She shrugs. "You cannot possibly understand," she says wistfully.

Cut away to a close-up on Heather Blake, studying Helga Mueller intently, rather sympathetically. "Try me," she says softly.

Back to the close-up on Helga Mueller, not exactly looking at the camera, viewing some inner landscape with that same sweet nostalgic smile.

"We were all part of one great revolutionary cause, the downtrodden of the Earth against their oppressors, we were like a large extended family, the sons and daughters of Che. . . ."

Her mouth hardens, her eyes snap back into present focus. "And then the Wall came down, the Soviet Union disintegrated, European Marxism collapsed, the Israelis began negotiating seriously with the Palestinians, Germany was reunited on Western terms. . . ."

A two-shot on Helga Mueller and Heather Blake.

"And there you all were, all dressed up on Saturday night with no place left to go," Heather says.

"How American!" Helga Mueller says dryly. She shrugs. "But apt."

"And while the rest of the world was celebrating, you and your terrorist friends were crying in your beer. You had lost and freedom had won."

Helga Mueller sneers, makes a wordless snorting sound.

"Yes, we lost," she says with naked bitterness. "But *what* won? Now the nationalists and chauvinists were free to slaughter each other's peoples to their hearts' content. And the capitalists and monetarists and free-market buccaneers were free to pauperize the masses of the world. And the developed countries were free to suck the Third World dry. And all of them were free to murder life on Earth itself!"

"So you became . . . an ecologist . . . ?"

"*Ecologist!* What a stupid word! I'm a *revolutionary!* A doer, not a talker! Still a Marxist samurai at heart!"

"Still crazy after all these years," Heather Blake says warmly.

"You Americans *do* have a way with words!" Helga Mueller says. But for the first time there is real eye contact between her and Heather Blake, a flash of human connection.

"We do not call ourselves Green *Party,* or Green *Peace,* but *Green Army Commandos,*" she says. "The concept may have been Horst's, but the name was mine."

A close-up on Helga Mueller as she shrugs. "And not many of us were ready to listen to a character like Horst Klingerman. . . . Most of my comrades in the struggle went down fighting for their old lost causes, or, like bitter old soldiers, just faded away. . . ."

A two-shot on Heather Blake and Helga Mueller, a rather strange look on Heather's face as she looks straight into the camera.

"I don't know about you folks out there," she says, "and I'm not sure why, but it sort of makes me sad."

"Ich hatte Kameraden," says Helga Mueller. "They took one path and I took another. Nevertheless, I salute them."

The camera moves in for a close-up on Helga Mueller as she moves her right hand toward her forehead in a phantom salute.

"Someone once said that the real moral struggles are never between good and evil, but between different concepts of good," she says.

She stares directly into the eye of the camera. "Think about it, sister. Think about it, Mr. and Mrs. America. Perhaps some day you will come to understand."

9:02 P.M.

"YES," SAID AHMED JIHAD, "those of us who fought hardest for Palestine, the children of the camps who had grown up with a Kalashnikov in the cradle, who had known nothing but the struggle, who had lived their whole lives for the cause, were precisely those who were denied the sweet fruit of their own victory."

After Heather's emotional roller-coaster ride through her interview with Helga Mueller, she found this one with the Palestinian who called himself "Ahmed Jihad" rather de-energized despite all the tales of bloodshed and violence, perhaps because it was so emotionally monotonous, so depressing, so unrelievedly sad.

What an awful life! An endless string of atrocities, as victim and perpetrator, one horrible war story after another. Hardly a real life at all. Even the name was a nom de guerre.

Born in a refugee camp in Lebanon, father a guerrilla killed by the Israelis trying to cross the border when Ahmed was eight, mother killed in an air raid five years later, given a machine gun as soon as he was old enough to carry one, trained as a guerrilla fighter at an age when American kids were going to junior high, killed his first Israeli before his sixteenth birthday, infiltrations, escapes, bombs, firefights, massacres, atrocities, wounds, plots. . . .

By his own admission, he had lost count of how many people he had killed, or rather had never really kept a tally of his victims in the first place. They were just Jews. Israelis. An enemy as faceless to him as he was to them.

And yet . . .

And yet Heather found it somehow impossible to hate Ahmed Jihad, or even to avoid understanding him. Maybe it was the Method training. Maybe it was this whole process of interviewing her captors and trying to humanize them for all those ordinary Americans out there in order to save her own ass. . . .

Maybe it was just the title of an ancient Rolling Stones song.

"Like Moses standing on the mountain and looking down on the Promised Land from afar after all those years in the desert and knowing he will never get there himself. . . ."

Sympathy for the Devil.

"Funny, I do not look Jewish," Ahmed Jihad said. "Or do I?"

He couldn't bring himself to laugh at his own lame joke any

more than Heather could. The best he could manage was a grimace and a nod at the bitter irony of it.

"The British say that dogs come to resemble their masters. It is also said that no fight is as savage as that between brothers."

"We Americans say, we have met the enemy, and he is us."

Now Ahmed Jihad did venture a thin little smile.

"A turtle and a scorpion meet on the bank of the Jordan River," he said, "and both wish to cross to the other side. 'Take me across on your back,' says the scorpion. 'Surely not,' says the turtle, 'it is your nature to sting me to death.' 'Have no fear,' says the scorpion. 'After all, if I sting you in the middle of the river, we will both die.' The turtle is won over by this logic, allows the scorpion to climb upon his back, and swims out into the river. In the middle of the river, the scorpion stings the turtle, and as they both sink beneath the waters to their death, the turtle looks up at the scorpion and utters the single word—*why?*'"

Ahmed paused, shrugged.

"'What did you expect?' says the scorpion. 'This is the Middle East.'"

9:34 P.M.

Onscreen:

A **CLOSE-UP ON** Ahmed Jihad, an olive-skinned young man in his late twenties with oily black hair and intense dark eyes, explosive vest, battle fatigues, machine-pistol slung over his shoulder, the prototypical Arab terrorist. But there is something else in his voice besides the standard bitterness, a certain realism, a wise irony beyond his chronological years.

"We were that scorpion, Black September, the PLF, Al Fatah, the PLO itself. Terrorists. Warriors. We had known no other life. Could the scorpion be trusted to beat its stinger into a plowshare?"

A two-shot on Ahmed Jihad and Heather Blake, her expression not unsympathetic.

"If you can ask that question . . ."

Ahmed Jihad shrugs. "We were fedayin, the Holy Warriors of the Palestinian Revolution, we and the children of the Intifada were the necessary monsters that our politicians used to bring the Israelis to the peace table. It was perhaps necessary for them to betray us."

"The Israelis?"

Ahmed Jihad laughs bitterly. "The Palestinians. Our own people who we had brought to the border of the Promised Land. But we could not be allowed to cross the Jordan with them. No return of terrorists from the Diaspora. That was the price the Israelis demanded. We had given our lives, and now we had to make the final sacrifice so that Palestine might be reborn. . . ."

A close-up on Ahmed Jihad as he sighs. "Who can say it was just? But in the end, who can say it was not right? What could I have done in a land of uneasy peace? How could I have earned my bread? What did I know? What skills did I have? Weapons. Explosives. Small-unit tactics. It would have been like Afghanistan after the fall of Najibullah."

A two-shot on Ahmed Jihad and Heather Blake.

"And afterward?" she says.

Ahmed Jihad smiles, a thin smile, but seemingly genuine. "Happily, and surprisingly, there *was* no afterward. What I learned was that Palestine had never been my true country. I had not been born there, I had never lived there, I had only set foot on its soil in secret, to fight and to kill. . . . When I faced the fact that I could never go home, I realized that I was home already, that I had always been there. . . ."

"Been *where*?"

"Where indeed? I had spent my life on the move, training camps in the Bekaa, in Libya, Syria, missions inside Israel, around the Mediterranean, Europe, everyone I knew and cared the slightest for was an international terrorist like myself . . . Palestinians . . . IRA . . . Baader-Meinhof . . . Japanese Red Army . . . *these* were truly my people, all of them, *this* was my country, my world . . . the Revolution itself."

"The Revolution? *Which* revolution?"

A close-up on Ahmed Jihad as his smile widens, as a certain fire steals into his previously hooded eyes.

"*The* Revolution!" he declares quite passionately. "Mao was right, but in a way he had not imagined. Permanent revolution *was* possible, but only for those who had nothing else. And for us, no *other* life was possible. One struggle was over, and it was time to seek out the next. . . ."

A two-shot on Ahmed Jihad and Heather Blake.

"And that was when you joined the Green Army Commandos?"

"That was when I drifted toward Berlin, became one of the denizens of places like the *Weimar Republik,* so many of us there at loose ends. . . ."

Ahmed Jihad laughs. "No, we *were* the loose ends, the human war-surplus sale of all the old struggles, lost and won, fedayin, mujadin, Communists, revolutionaries dispossessed by victory or defeat or the disappearance of our enemies. And there were those who still had employment for our skills . . . Sendero Luminoso . . . the cartels of Medellin and Cali . . . Muslim Slavs . . . Kurds . . . Kashmiris . . . obscure national liberation movements in places which even *we* had never heard of. . . ."

"But you chose the Green Army Commandos. Why?"

Ahmed Jihad shrugs. "I wanted more than . . . employment. . . . I wanted . . . I wanted . . ."

"To fight for something you could really believe in?" Heather Blake says knowingly. "The way you had believed in Palestine? Something that could make a life without personal ambition seem worthwhile?"

Ahmed Jihad glances at her suddenly, sharply. Heather Blake smiles at him.

"We all seek that feeling, or something like it, I think," she says. "Not all of us find it. Most of us don't even know we're looking for it. And you found it in the Green Army Commandos?"

A close-up on Ahmed Jihad, as he nods, shrugs.

"*It* found *me,*" he says. "On an aimless night in the *Weimar Republik* that promised to be no different than all the others. . . ."

9:10 P.M.

Onscreen:

"NOT JAPANESE!" HIROSHI IGARAMU insists belligerently. "I am *Ainu!*"

He certainly looks Japanese in close-up, the straight black hair, the East Asian eyes, the flattened cheekbones, and his English has the sharp and distinct cadences of the native Japanese speaker.

But perhaps there *is* something not quite Japanese if you look for it—that too-prominent nose, that Caucasoid skin tone, that heavy five-o'clock shadow grubby with shooting light sweat.

A two-shot on Hiroshi Igaramu—cold, hard, and angry—and Heather Blake—frowning, hesitant—as if she *knows* he can only take what she must say badly.

"Ainu? What's that?"

Hiroshi Igaramu's eyes do not react, but his voice becomes scornful and distant, hurt hiding behind contempt.

"Ainu? What is that?" he mimics. "Everywhere but Japan, I hear this question. In Japan, they have answer. Ainu is *nigger*. Hairy monkey-man."

"This isn't Japan, Hiroshi," Heather Blake says softly. She nods toward the camera eye. "And all those people out there will never know what it means to be Ainu unless you explain it to them."

"So," Hiroshi Igaramu hisses. "So . . ." he mutters more thoughtfully, as the camera moves in for a close-up.

"So . . . I explain. Ainu are original people of Japanese islands. Like your red Indians. Japanese do to us what you do to them. Take our land, land where we followed the way of the hunter and the gatherer. Fill it with themselves. Millions of them. Chop down forests. Build big cities. Industry. Poison. Destruction. Filth."

He pauses, grunts. "Old story, ne? Same all over world. Push us up to Hokkaido to die away. But Japanese come there too. *Develop* the island, as is their way. Some want Ainu to survive like your Indians on reservation. Wear traditional clothing for expensive cameras of tourists. Like monkeys in zoo. Ainu Disneyland exhibit . . ."

Cut to a two-shot on Hiroshi Igaramu and Heather Blake. She seems sincerely outraged.

"That sounds really awful!" she says. "But you weren't having any? You, uh, didn't accept this for yourself?"

Hiroshi nods. "Hai. We have television. We have schools. I know outside world. I am told I can be modern Japanese. I believe this. Go to Tokyo. Where I learn I am *Ainu,* nigger, lower than Korean. Can never be good salaryman. Never become Japanese. Low jobs. No job. I learn what is to be Ainu in Japan. . . ."

The camera moves in for a close-up as he just about snarls.

"And learn what is to be *Japanese*! Pretty flower arrangements. Shinto. Buddhism. Shrines to nature. Japanese *pretend* to seek harmony with spirit of the Earth. But they lie! Destroy the land and cover it with concrete. Poison the air to build Sonys and Toyotas. Victims of Hiroshima and Nagasaki bring to the land *plutonium* to make power to run their televisions and video games. Breed and shit like rats in warehouse full of grain. And we, Ainu, seek only to survive as children of the land, *we* are barbarians!"

A close-up on Heather Blake, reacting to this outburst with a certain politically correct horror. "Uh . . . we certainly hear a lot of Japanese bashing over here, but I never thought I'd hear a Japa—"

"I am *not Japanese*!" Hiroshi Igaramu shouts as there is a hard jerky cut to a close-up on his angry face.

Heather Blake's voice-over: "I only meant—"

"I tell you story. True story. Changes my life. I read in Tokyo newspapers, see on television. Scientist publishes study shows original samurais, brave Japanese knights, shining heroes of movies, image of honorable Japanese spirit, ideal of Japanese manhood, were . . . *Ainu*!"

A two-shot on Hiroshi Igaramu and Heather Blake, a rather vicious satisfaction in his eyes as he delivers his next line. "And what happens?"

"They denied it all, didn't they?" Heather says. "They pretended it wasn't true and went on making samurai movies."

Hiroshi's eyes widen in amazement. "How did you know?" he hisses.

Heather shrugs. "That's show business," she says. She laughs. He doesn't.

Instead, he seems to reel the scene back, ignore the joke he doesn't understand.

"For Japanese, nothing changes," he says. "For me, everything changes. Is satori. I am Ainu. Samurai are Ainu, not Japanese. I must become *Ainu samurai*. Follow way of Bushido, but serve cause of *my* people. I swear samurai oath in my heart to destroy evil civilization of these false samurai, these salarymen, these thieves of our land and rapists of its spirit, these Japanese!"

"You . . . uh . . . declared war on Japan?"

"Hai! In my soul."

"You, uh, thought you could defeat the Japanese all by yourself?"

"I am Ainu samurai. I dedicate my spirit to this struggle. Not important to win. Important to fight."

"And what did you do next, look for a master to serve?"

Hiroshi's face lights up with unabashed astonishment. "How did you know?"

"I was a film major," Heather says dryly. "I'm sure I've seen more samurai movies than you have. *Magnificent Seven*. Toshiro Mifune. *Throne of Blood* and all that."

She laughs. "Besides which, this is *Southern California*."

Hiroshi squints at her, not getting it at all.

"I look for . . . others like me. Way to serve cause I am sworn to serve." He frowns. "Do not find. Other Ainu do not understand, think is bad joke. Japanese are . . . Japanese . . . then . . . "

"And then . . . ?"

"Then *I* am . . . sought. I drink too much, maybe, speak too freely in Ginza bars, in Rappongi . . . they have ears . . . they have eyes . . . they find me. . . ."

"They?"

"Japanese Red Army. You have heard?"

"Uh . . . people have been mentioning them all night, but—"

"They are samurai!" Hiroshi exclaims as the camera moves in

for a close-up. "Not Ainu samurai, not Japanese samurai . . . Marxist samurai!"

Heather Blake's voice-over: "*Marxist* samurai!"

"Hai! Not Japanese! Not Ainu! Loyal only to cause of oppressed people of Earth. Have doctrine. Have discipline. They are Marxist knights of Bushido."

A two-shot on Hiroshi Igaramu and Heather Blake. "Uh . . . but they were also . . . ah . . . extreme violent terrorists, weren't they?" she asks carefully. "They . . . uh . . . killed a lot of innocent people, didn't they?"

Hiroshi Igaramu smiles a most unpleasant smile. "Hai! Most extreme! Left of Communists! Left of Maoists! Left of everyone!"

"And you *believed* in this extreme Communist philosophy?"

He shrugs. "Philosophy not important. Destroy system. Destroy oppressors. Destroy status quo. Destroy capitalist exploiters. Destroy America . . ." He pauses for a beat. "Destroy . . . *Japan*."

"But that's so totally negative!"

"Makes us strong. Ruthless. Dedicated to the warrior's way. Japanese Red Army were true samurai! Ready to serve all who fought same enemy . . . PLO, Baader-Meinhof, Black September. . . . We were strongest of the strong, hardest of the hard, bravest of the brave, missions no one else takes were our treasures of the spirit. . . ."

A close-up on Heather Blake, clearly shaken by all this, but visibly making an effort to try to understand.

"You went out on these missions? You killed people yourself?"

A close-up on Hiroshi Igaramu, his face devoid of all expression, made so, perhaps, by deliberate act of will.

"I was samurai."

The camera holds this close-up for a long silent beat.

Cut to a two-shot on Hiroshi Igaramu and Heather Blake, emphasizing Heather Blake, her eyes searching for some kind of extro.

"So . . . uh, how did you end up leaving the Japanese Red Army and joining the Green Army Commandos, then?" she says. "I mean, the Green Army Commandos don't seem quite like . . . uh . . . the same sort of . . . er, murderous group. . . ."

A close-up on Hiroshi Igaramu, something guarded in his expression.

"Cold War ends. All international police agencies after us. No regime gives sanctuary. We must all scatter and run."

It sounds like the truth, but there is a tentativeness, an undertone of dissembling.

"Cyprus. Athens. Paris. Amsterdam. Berlin. Better there. Police busy chasing Stasis, neo-Nazis, easier to disappear. . . ."

He shrugs, his eyes become even more evasive. "Bad time . . . drink too much, maybe. . . ." He pauses, his expression brightens, perhaps by act of will.

"Meet Paulo Pereido. Drink in *Weimar Republik*. Talk. Meet Horst. Helga. Talk. Find . . . find . . ."

Cut to a two-shot on Hiroshi Igaramu and Heather Blake as he struggles for words.

"A new master to serve? A new cause?"

Back to the close-up on Hiroshi Igaramu, reacting; an enthusiastic nod, a hesitation, words that seem . . . crafted.

"Green Army Commandos not samurai, not like Japanese Red Army. But cause . . . hai! This I learn from Paulo. This I learn from Horst. Survival of whole planet . . . this is eternal battle. Never final victory."

His smile, though, seems genuine.

"I am Green Army Commando. I fight to save life on Earth. Is *perfect* cause for Ainu Marxist samurai, ne?"

9:17 P.M.

"HIROSHI IS NOT A bad man," Paulo Pereido said in that soft mellifluous voice. "He is a spirit in pain. He was much worse when I met him. Then he had nothing but the fury of a man betrayed."

"Betrayed?" said Heather. "He didn't say anything about being betrayed. By who?"

Paulo shrugged gently.

"An Ainu and a Yanomami, meeting in a café in Berlin, becoming drunk together just as the white people imagine we would. . . . To *me* he could admit what he could never say to a pretty white lady like you."

"Which was?"

"His comrades in the Japanese Red Army were false. In their minds, with their mouths, they believed that all oppressed people were brothers, but they abandoned him when their group began to come apart, for in their hearts, they were still Japanese, and he was still Ainu."

Paulo smiled that shy engaging little smile of his. "That is why he is so still so angry. He has found a cause to serve, but he has no true home in this world. Like me."

"But *you* don't seem like an angry person, Paulo," Heather said.

"I am a very angry person," he replied in the same calm voice. "That is why I found him so simple to understand. We are so much alike."

What a relief!

Warren, the underground hacker next door, could even have been your kid, Mom and Dad. Nigel and Malcolm had been outrageous but engaging. Jaro had been just a language problem. Helga had been a challenge, but Heather was proud of how she had handled that one. Even Ahmed was at least someone Mr. and Mrs. Middle America could feel sorry for. . . .

But there was no way to make Hiroshi Igaramu, unrepentant Japanese Red Army terrorist killer, come across as sympathetic to an American mass audience. And for this whole thing to work, the interviews had to end on a warm empathetic note, or at least something a lot better than the chill Hiroshi had left in the media air.

Fortunately, she had left Paulo Pereido for last, and so far, the Brazilian Indian was proving to be the ideal capper. Not only did he seem oddly calm and gentle for a terrorist with a machine-pistol slung over his shoulder, not only did he exude the sort of Noble Savage Buddhism that the American audience expected from The-Indian-as-Good-Guy, he even seemed to be able to make *Hiroshi* look a little better after the fact. . . .

"You certainly don't *seem* much alike. . . ."

"But we are. He is Ainu. I am Yanomami. We are both . . . both . . . what is the word . . . native people . . . arbor . . . abor . . . ?"

"Aboriginals?"

Paulo nodded. "*Ab-originals* . . . it is a good word. Original peoples. People of the forests and plain and rivers. The original children of the planet who remain close to its spirit."

For the first time in the interview, Paulo frowned. "Better than *Third World* people," he said. "*We* are the First World. After all, *we* were here first."

"I never thought of it that way," Heather said.

"We fished, we hunted, we gathered fruits and roots, we grew some things. We remained few not because we were so wise, but because we could not feed more. We knew no better. We knew no worse. We were in harmony with nature because we were *part* of nature. We and the Earth could have gone on like this forever."

9:19 P.M.

Onscreen:

A TWO-SHOT ON Heather Blake and Paulo Pereido, a wide, squat mesomorph of a man with straight black hair falling down past his earlobes, blunt Indian features, sharp black eyes.

"For the first thirteen years of my life, I lived with my family in a small village in the forest, where we fished, and hunted, and grew simple crops, and walked around in our innocence wearing almost nothing at all," he says. "We Yanomami were noble savages."

Heather eyes him suspiciously.

"Isn't this what your audience wants to hear?"

A half-beat of silence, then Pereido laughs.

"Yes, that is the image you prefer," he says. "The Catholic mission school is not shown in the picture. The children wearing T-shirts with the emblems of First World sodas and rock groups and rubber sandals from Japan. The Walkmen and the portable radios. The tin roofs on the traditional huts. The Marlboro butts on the jungle trails."

"I think everyone agrees that what's happened to the Amazon Indians is awful, the burning, and the clear-cutting, hillsides sluiced away by miners, the killings, and stolen lands and disease—"

"Your concern is very touching," Paulo interrupts, firmly but evenly.

"I didn't mean—"

"Yes you did."

A close-up on Paulo Pereido, his eyes sparkling with intensity, the rest of his face eerily, glacially, preternaturally calm.

"You meant well. The missionaries meant well. The rubber tappers who believed they were supporting our cause meant well. But we would have been better off with enemies who admitted they wanted to destroy us. Maybe we could not defeat them, but they could at least be fought."

Cut to a close-up on Heather Blake's earnest, confused, sincere face. "I don't understand. . . ."

Back to the close-up on Paulo Pereido.

"To be a Yanomami of my generation is *not* to be a noble savage. That world was gone before I was born. Perhaps it never was. How should I know? I had the words of my father's generation, blurred with drink, confused with idleness, and the books and television and radio of your world."

A two-shot on Paulo Pereido and Heather Blake, slightly emphasizing Heather, who leans toward him slightly trying to establish empathy for the camera's eye.

"So you were caught between two worlds?" she says.

"Caught in *no* world. The forests being torn down around me, the villages of the Yanomami disappearing, the old people wasting away with disease, the men seeking to become cheap labor for the Brazilians, the women becoming whores or the victims of rape, the fires, the gold prospectors, the rubber tappers . . ."

He shrugs. "*This* was my world, a disappearing forest, a disintegrating tribe, mud, and ash, and disease, a world whose soul had been slain before I was born and whose carcass was being devoured by the beetles and the flies. . . ."

"And the missionary school and the media showed you that other world, *our* world . . . ?"

Paulo Pereido nods. "The dreamworld . . . the dreamworld of airplanes and Hollywood and rockets to the moon . . . Coca-Cola and Carnival and Ipanema . . ."

The camera moves in slowly for a close-up as he sighs. "My

father was killed by a truck, my mother died of influenza, I became an orphan, a child of the Church. Be good, the priests told me, study, work hard, and you will become a citizen of the rising giant, not a Yanomami of the forest, but a *Brazilian* of the world. . . ."

He pauses, he shrugs, for the first time a thin trace of irony creases his lips. "So I did. I become the mission school's prize student, proof that they could turn an Indian of the forest into a modern Brazilian. They sent me to a boarding school in Manaus like one of your American high schools. . . ."

9:22 P.M.

HEATHER FOUND HERSELF DRIFTING a bit from her role of interviewer, becoming part of the audience as Paulo Pereido spun out his tale.

The school that graduated him with a liberal education in nothing in particular into an inflation-ridden economy where he could find only the most occasional and menial of low-paying jobs, the wanderings to Brasilia, to São Paulo, finally to Rio and a foul hillside favela where the Third World looked down in hopeless longing on the glittering riches of the First. . . .

"So I became a thief . . . a very well educated thief, but not such a good one, and soon enough I was running from the police, back into the Amazon, back to the land of the Yanomami. . . ."

Paulo shrugged. His eyes narrowed. For the first time, Heather could sense a hardness and even a bitterness behind all that eerie calm.

"Your world in its guilt had decided to be good to the Yanomami. An area of ruined forest was set aside as a reservation, where we could follow the forgotten ways of our ancestors and slowly starve to death in peace."

He sighed. "There was no place for me there," he said. "There was no place for *anyone* there, really, but I had lived in the dreamworld, I had been blessed or cursed with the education to know it."

Heather glanced at the studio clock. Time was running out. In more ways than one.

"But how on earth did you get from the Amazon forest to Berlin?" she asked, trying to force the jump cut. "That *is* where you joined the Green Army Commandos, isn't it?"

"Yes . . . it is a long story if a stupid one. . . . I robbed a gold miner of his nuggets, he fought, there was a killing . . . I had to flee across the border into Surinam, buy an airline ticket to Holland and a false passport . . . most of the money was gone after a few months in Amsterdam . . . I tried burglary, drug dealing . . . *other things* . . . more trouble with the police. . . ."

A bit of that strange calm sweetness seemed to return. "One more dark-skinned little Third World street criminal lost in the white man's world. . . ."

"So why Berlin?" Heather said, growing desperate to hurry things along.

9:24 P.M.

Onscreen:

A CLOSE-UP ON Paulo Pereido.

"What with the confusion of the Reunification, the rioting skinheads, the neo-Nazis, the anarchists, the squatters, Berlin seemed like a forest where the police would have much more important things to do than pay attention to a small predator like me."

A two-shot on Paulo Pereido and Heather Blake, Heather glancing at something off camera, looking rather agitated.

"Look, Paulo, I'm afraid we're running out of time—"

"Yes, yes, you are the masters of the world, and the slaves of the clock!"

"—so how did you end up in the Green Army Commandos?"

Paulo Pereido laughs. "By being very stupid," he says.

"Stupid?"

"I tried to rob Helga Mueller. It was dark. Maybe I was drunk. How was I to know that this white German lady was carrying a gun?"

A close-up on Paulo Pereido, a certain wistfulness, a nostalgic memory of wonder steals upon his characteristically impassive face.

"I understood later why she could not turn me over to the police," he says. "But she could have killed me, and I learned later that she had killed people before."

He shrugs, he smiles, he almost laughs. "Instead, she offers to buy me a drink! Well, not *offers*. She still has the gun. I flatter myself that perhaps she wants sex. She is older. She is not so attractive. But instead of taking me to her room, we go to the *Weimar Republik* and she talks. Of putting my anger to use. Of things that an educated Yanomami street criminal adrift in the cities of Europe could understand . . . and begin to believe in. . . ."

Heather Blake's hurried voice-over: "Which *were*? I'm afraid we really *are* about out of time!"

Paulo Pereido laughs.

"Yes, just that," he says, "we are *all* really out of time."

And then his expression hardens, and his voice develops a cadence building to a certain oratorical crescendo as he realizes that his time before the camera is indeed coming to an end.

"The Yanomami wasting away in their reservation. The Brazilians in their shining cities and the favelados looking down on them in envy. The Third World street people of Europe. The people who call us niggers and wogs. The starving Africans. The Ainu who hate the Japanese. The Japanese who despise the Ainu. You Americans, poisoning the planet in your innocent greed. We are all out of time. We do not have the time to learn to love each other. We must first save life on Earth from ourselves if we want to live even long enough to continue to hate each other. We must be Green Army Commandos together. First World or Third World, the only alternative is No World."

Cut to a close-up on Heather Blake, clearly in a rush.

"Well, that's as good a last word from the Green Army Commandos as any," she babbles too rapidly.

Then, she takes a long deep breath, slows down, looks right into the camera, smiles a bit—vulnerable, brave, tender, innocent, Mr. and Mrs. America's darling threatened cheerleader daughter.

"Okay, folks, so now you've met all the Green Army Commandos," she says in a slightly tremulous voice. "Americans and Englishmen and Germans and Arabs and Slovaks and Yanomami and Jap—*Ainu*. Communists and terrorists and criminals."

She shrugs affectingly.

"Not the kind of people you *really* want your kids to bring home to dinner, I guess," she says. "Not the kind of people *we* like being locked up with for this five-day slumber party either, I suppose. . . ."

The camera creeps in a bit closer for an extreme close-up on this plucky American beauty rose.

"But I *have* brought them home for dinner, now haven't I?" she says. "Or at least into your living room for some non-Brazilian coffee and apple pie. You've gotten to listen to them and look into their eyes as they've told their stories, and, I hope, seen what's in their hearts. And so have I."

She pauses, her lower lip trembles. She nibbles at it, a gallant gesture, somehow. Are those tears that come to her eyes?

"I don't know about you folks out there, but me, after getting to know them as *real people* instead of just heavies from central casting with a bad attitude and guns. . . ."

She pauses again, and a single fat wet tear glides down her right cheek.

"Maybe I'm going to die with them," she says bravely. "There are people out there with guns who think it's somehow more important to kill us all than let this situation go on. . . ."

The camera begins to slowly creep backward, widening the angle of the close-up on Heather Blake.

"Well, I'll tell you something, folks, if I've gotta die, and I guess we all do, now don't we, I could think of a lot worse company to do it in, couldn't you?"

The camera pulls back jerkily into a long shot, revealing Edward Franker, Toby Inman, and Carl Mendoza standing well behind Heather Blake against the cream-colored backdrop curtain . . .

. . . which is revealed as such as the camera pulls back even further into an unnaturally long shot, including the overhead lights, the scrims, the technological bric-a-brac of a working set.

Heather motions with her hand, and, one by one, looking rather ill at ease, the foot soldiers of the Green Army Commandos— Malcolm Macklin, Warren Davies, Jaro Olgar, Helga Mueller, Ahmed Jihad, Hiroshi Igaramu, Paulo Pereido—troop dutifully onto the set and pose, Uzis slung over their shoulders, in front of their hostages, looking for all the world like a bunch of football players posing for a team photo, or a small-town graduating class mugging glumly out of a high-school yearbook.

Heather gestures again, more insistently, and a figure steps in front of the camera, blocking the shot for a couple of beats. Then Nigel Edwards, black leather jacket, red spike hairdo, chrome fetish items and all, kneels down in front of Heather with a foolish grin full of rotten teeth, for all the world like a team mascot, to complete the tableau.

"Now the Bible tells us to love our enemies, and forgive those who trespass against us," Heather says. "Well, I don't know if I'm a good enough Christian to do *that,* but I don't really believe that I have to be. Because these people are not our enemies. They're just like you and me. They're good people trying to do what they think is the right thing in a bad world."

Heather turns to face her three fellow hostages. "What do you say, guys?" she says. "Tell the folks out there. Tell all those millions of people out their in front of their television sets. Tell the men with the guns. Tell the politicians back in Washington. You're their hostages. If it was up to you, if it was up to us, would you forgive these people and let them go? Or do you want to see them die for going too far to try and save us all from what we all know we're doing to our planet and ourselves?"

No cameraman, no close-ups, no proper miking.

Edward Franker places a hand on the shoulder of Jaro Olgar. Toby Inman does the same for Warren Davies. Carl Mendoza seems about to let his hand come down on the shoulder of Paulo Pereido, hesitates, and, to her obvious surprise, touches Helga Mueller instead.

"Well, there you have it folks, that's how *we* feel," Heather Blake says. "What about *you?*"

She gets up, steps around the coffee table, around the kneeling Nigel Edwards, walks toward the camera and right into a self-directed extreme close-up, beautiful even from this revealing angle, moisture visible on her soft vulnerable lips, eyes all but making love to the lens.

"We hear that there are people out there who feel different. People who are about to do something cynical and stupid. People who would rather see us all die tonight than let these rabble-rousers continue to speak to the American people," she says. "People who don't believe it's safe for you to hear what they have to say. Well, maybe it isn't. But speaking with a lot more at stake than they have, I say I'd rather leave it up to you. This is a democracy, isn't it?"

Heather Blake backs slowly out of the extreme close-up, pauses, hesitates.

"We don't want the Green Army Commandos killed in *our* names, in a misguided attempt to rescue us!" she says. "Do you want us all killed in *yours*? Pick up your telephone! Get on your fax! Tell them how you *really* feel! Do it *right now*! Before it's too late!"

Then she turns and walks rapidly away from the camera, back into the static long shot on the terrorists and their hostages, takes her place as one of them.

"From all of us here at KLAX-TV Los Angeles, to all of you out there, thank you, and good night."

DAY 6

10:19 A.M.

TOBY INMAN SAT THERE by himself glumly picking at the goddamn trail mix while Heather Blake danced around the cafeteria doing her star turn with her supporting cast of terrorists.

The Green Army Commandos hadn't put away their guns, but it no longer seemed like a game of prisoners and jailers. The ass-saving success of last night's show had changed everything.

Although the instapolls had delivered the verdict by 9:45—65.05 percent against *any* use of force to take the station, a whopping 72.11 percent should anyone get killed—nobody had dared say a word as everyone counted down the final fifteen minutes in the cafeteria.

9:59 . . . 10:00 . . . 10:01 . . . 10:02 . . .

"Hey, folks, I do believe it's over," Franker finally said at 10:06. "The will of the people as expressed by the self-fulfilling infallibility of the instapolls has prevailed. The Fat Lady ain't gonna sing!"

"It's all over but the shouting," Heather said, "so we might as well!"

And they all did.

All that had been missing was champagne to turn the scene into some kind of weird cast party. Nigel and Malcolm had turned into comedians. Warren had gone around babbling about media power. Jaro and Paulo hadn't exactly become loquacious, but did reveal an unexpected ability to smile. Helga, Hiroshi, and Ahmed might not have exactly turned into party animals, but at least they had stopped seeming so ominous. Kelly bubbled. Even Horst had turned into something resembling a human being.

Nothing like a reprieve from the governor's office to lighten up the atmosphere on Death Row.

All thanks to Heather.

Heather Blake was the heroine of this movie. The star of the show. The belle of the media ball.

You're jealous as all hell, aren't you, Inman? You're green with envy, old son!

Well maybe I am.

Don't I have a right to be?

Toby had little doubt that he could have handled those eight terrorist interviews as well as Heather had. When you came right down to it, all she had really done was wind them up and let them talk. And he *was* the anchorman; by rights those golden ninety minutes of national prime-time exposure should have been his, not some *weathergirl's.* What did Heather have that he didn't except tits, ass, and those midwestern cheerleader good looks?

Toby sighed. Low, Inman, really low.

Heather Blake was obviously not the airheaded little popsicle her looks had always led him to believe. *She* had come up with the format, as she had with the previous tearjerker, now hadn't she?

Besides, Inman, he reminded himself, you've already had plenty of major prime-time exposure to sweet ratings yourself. There'll be plenty of fat offers to go around when this mess is finally over.

And now, for the first time, it seemed clearly a matter of *when,* not *if.* Over 70 percent of the people out there would be pissed off at any politician held responsible for getting any of them killed. No one was going to stick their political neck out *that* far. Even these terrorists could read numbers like that. Saved by the ratings, no question about it.

Toby frowned. Only thing was, they still wouldn't let the hostages use the phone. And according to Arlene Berkowski, there were major agents out there lining up to talk to him. And once they were released, the offers were going to be thick as flies on horseshit.

And when it comes to *those* kinds of numbers, salary, signing bonus, points, structuring a contract to maximum tax advantage,

I'm still a country boy from Georgia. I'm going to have to be strong. Promise yourself this right now, Inman. You gonna hold them all off until you get yourself an agent. You gonna smile, and mutter, and kick that ol' shit around, and sign nothing by yourself no matter how sweet it looks.

Old Jefferson, or Paine, or whichever of those Tom guys it was, had the right idea.

No legal obligation without major agency representation!

10:25 A.M.

HORST KLINGERMAN STEPPED ASIDE to let Franker open the door to his own office, gestured for Carl to precede him, then entered after him, with Kelly Jordan bringing up the rear.

Franker crossed the room and sat down behind his desk while Horst and Kelly took seats in front of it with the familiarity of a shortstop and a second baseman moving into double-play position after five seasons together, while Carl stood there like a rookie centerfielder considering where to position his ass.

Funny, he thought, *they* walk in here like they own the place, but all this time working here, and this is the first time *I've* seen the inside of the station manager's office.

Not that he had exactly missed a treat for the eyes, and certainly not for the nose. A desk cluttered with phone console, computer, papers, old Styrofoam coffee cups filled with soggy cigarette butts. An air-feed monitor, a TV plugged into the cable system, a VCR, assorted institutional chairs, tables, bookcases, dusty brown industrial carpeting, lime-green walls stuck with corkboards dripping outdated old notes and photos, and after five days without cleaning or the disposal of Franker's cigarette remains, the air-conditioned sealed atmosphere stank like a minor-league locker room after a twinight doubleheader.

But the windows . . .

Light poured into the room from two directions through the two big windows, almost literally poured, for the dust motes swirling in the conditioned air rendered it visible, gave it a syrupy moving substance. Vision told Carl that it should have been blazing hot but the air-conditioning kept his skin at a cool seventy. After five days of nothing but the windowless studio and cafeteria, the sight of so much sunlight, of sunlight that seemed to have *volume,* was quite overwhelming.

And it reminded Carl with sudden impact that he *had* spent the last five days sealed up in here like a submarine sailor, without any contact at all with the natural world. Even now, all he could feel on his skin was the air-conditioning, all he could smell was the crappy recycled air.

He almost laughed aloud. Here I am, he thought, after five days in here with these armed terrorists, and now I *really* feel like a prisoner!

"Now remember, Mendoza," Franker said. "We don't even want him to know you're *listening* until the time is right, *we* want to control this one, that's why *we're* calling *him*."

"That is right," Horst said, "you are our . . . ace card down—"

"Ace in the hole," said Kelly.

"—and it would be poor strategy to reveal too much too soon, you agree with this, yes, do you not, Carl?"

"Five by five, my man, five by five," Carl said dryly, as he pulled up a chair between Kelly and Horst well in range of the speakerphone pickup.

That, of course, had been a bit of mumbo jumbo between himself and the nonexistent Charley Bird, and here he was flipping it to Horst Klingerman like a phantom high five!

Carl doubted that any of the rest of them appreciated the humor of it. His experience in the minors had taught him that team spirit could suddenly arise out of the most unlikely chemistry. Pitcher gets traded to a club whose hitters have generally been beating his brains out and ducking hard ones under the chin in return, you figure on bad blood, but it doesn't take long for all concerned to realize that now that they've been thrown together, they better start concentrating on winning the game.

"You know this guy, Carl," Kelly said. "Why hasn't *he* called *us* after what happened last night? What do they do next?"

"I don't really know Coleman all that well," Carl said, "but since he doesn't know that *you* know that anything was *supposed* to go down, however pissed off he might be at the way we stopped it, I don't see how he can admit that anything really happened for him to react *to*. Which is maybe why he hasn't. What do they do next . . . ?"

He shrugged. "Quién sabe? Best not to give anything away, and let old Alex do the talking, which he tends to do anyway. . . ."

"Seems to me, talking is *all* he can do now," Franker said. "It's a standoff. You saw the instapolls. No politician in America is going to buck numbers like that."

Horst shook his head like a man who had fallen into the wrong cartoon. "Instapolls . . . rating numbers . . . You really believe this is how the *Central Intelligence Agency* makes decisions?"

"It's sure how *elected officials* in this country, up to and certainly including the President, have been making decisions at least since George Bush," Franker said. "And I don't really believe they've lost control of the CIA on this one."

"It has been known to happen," Horst said dubiously.

"Not on something like this. This is *all* about polls and numbers, and spin control. If it wasn't, the Feds wouldn't have risked putting the CIA in charge, they would have just let the LAPD do what comes naturally and take the blame for the bloodbath."

"It is hard to believe that the leadership of the military overlord of the planet makes such decisions like . . . like . . . like this Arlene Berkowski, like . . . like . . . television executives."

"Think of it as electronic democracy in action," Franker said cynically.

"It is entirely *appalling*!" Klingerman said primly.

Franker laughed. Kelly laughed. Looking at this terrorist sitting there with his explosive vest and Uzi, and such a look of righteous indignation, Carl could only laugh too.

But still, Carl knew what he meant.

There was indeed something disgusting about those spineless fuckers in Washington making decisions about whether people lived or died, about whether *Carl Mendoza* lived or died, solely on the basis of how the instapolls showed the results were going to look in their own personal popularity box scores.

In some crazy way, Alex Coleman and the Agency were *better* than their bosses, better than the ball-less bastards whose hot-dog concern for looking good in the polls was what would have seemed to have saved his own ass.

For a moment, his eyes met Horst Klingerman's, and something passed between them in body language, in Carl's almost imperceptible shrug and nod. Not only was Klingerman right, terrorist or not, *he* was better than those cabrones sin cojones too.

10:31 A.M.

"WELL NOW, FOLKS, I gotta admit that last night's show was about as cute as a baby panda's asshole," was Alex Coleman's opening line when Eddie Franker finally got him on the phone. " 'Course, you *did* miss one bet. . . ."

"What was that . . . Alex?"

"How come y'all didn't sing 'We Shall Overcome' at the fade-out?"

Eddie had to laugh, Carl grinned thinly, Kelly broke up, only Horst didn't seem to get it.

"Glad to see you haven't lost your sense of humor," Eddie said dryly.

"Oh, I'm just slappin' my thighs and gigglin' like a stoned schoolgirl! We got yahoos torchin' gas stations and parkin' instant car bodies on freeway ramps, we got the Brazilians threatenin' to recall their ambassador unless their coffee sales stabilize by next week, and now we got Latin American generalissimos proclaimin' that the Green Army Commandos are a sinister CIA plot to use this First World ecology bullshit as an excuse to justify American intervention in their squalid little bailiwicks."

Even Horst laughed at that one. Coleman, ignorant of their knowledge of his true identity, the knowledge that so enriched the irony, raved on.

"And now we got polls that indicate that there'd be a hot market for lovable Green Army Commando Kewpie dolls, be the first on your block to collect the whole set! And who do you think is catchin' the crap for this friggin' fiasco? Do you imagine that our Peerless Leader is hoggin' the blame for himself? Do you picture the White House staff stuffin' themselves into hair shirts and wailin' mea culpa? You think the fire-eaters who wanted to end all this with Donner an' Blitzen are too timid to bellow 'We told you so' at the top of their leatherneck lungs? Do you believe anyone but yours truly, the voice of amelioration and sweet reason, has been nominated as the wimp responsible?"

"The point of which is?" Eddie said.

"The point of which is? The point of which is, *how could you guys do such a thing*? Hell's bells, we all heard of the Stockholm Syndrome, but don't you think you've carried identification with your captors a tad over the top? Is there not even a rudimentary remnant of patriotism left with you people? Which side are you on?"

"The side of saving our own asses," Eddie snapped. "The side of . . . living through the night."

There was a long beat of silence on the other end of the phone. Carl Mendoza walked his chair closer to the speakerphone pickup, cocked an inquisitive eyebrow. Eddie raised his right palm in a "hold" signal.

"Living through the night?" Coleman said in a voice upon whose tongue butter would not melt. Almost. "Aren't we gettin' a wee bit melodramatic here?"

"Are we, Alex?"

A beat of silence.

Eddie nodded at Carl Mendoza, brought down his hand.

10:34 A.M.

"HELLO, COLEMAN," CARL SAID. "You know who this is?"

A slight pause, during which Carl could visualize Coleman's dark green eyes narrowing above that big loose mouth probably still frozen in the shit-kicker grin that had made the guy look like some dim slow plowboy, that hid a mind as sharp and swift as a Nolan Ryan fastball.

Carl knew damn well that Alex Coleman recognized his voice; it might have been twenty years since they'd talked, but not since Coleman had heard him on the tube. This hesitation was no riffle down the Rolodex of memory lane. Coleman was pondering just what Carl's advent on the phone meant, and what should be his spontaneous good-old-boy response.

"That's Carl . . . *Mendoza,* ain't it? The sports guy?"

"Charley Bird's old buddy himself. How's old Parker doing, Coleman? You got any more of my old friends from the phantom platoon out there with you? Or they all gone back to the Company town?"

Carl didn't quite know why he was playing this little game with Coleman, or what he expected the comeback would be, but when Coleman fired an unexpected fastball right down the middle, it froze him with his bat on his shoulder.

"All right, Carl, let's can the cutesy-poo, shall we?" Alex Coleman said in a harder voice. "You've been somewhat less brilliant than you think, Mendoza. You've made a seriously counterproductive move. For all of us."

"Have I?" Carl said. He tried to put some bravado into it, but he sounded lame even to himself. Something in Alex Coleman's voice told him that he had already lost control of this situation. He couldn't imagine how, but he had a sinking feeling in his gut that he was about to find out.

"You have told these people about our brief previous relationship, haven't you, Mendoza?" Coleman said without any vehemence. "They now all know the dreadful truth that yours truly, far from being a pantywaist flak from the White House staff, is a big ol' bear in the employ of the Gnomes of Langley, an' all that ordnance pointed out there is therefore under the command of the wicked ol' CIA."

Carl stared at the speakerphone with his mouth hanging open and not a thought in his head of what to say.

Alex Coleman laughed. "An' you probably told them that Charley Bird was just a message from me to you lettin' you know we were gonna exercise our ultimate option at ten last night. Thus the tug at the heartstrings of Mr. an' Mrs. Instapoll, so said terminal option would be foreclosed by the prospect of a mass public-opinion shit-fit in the event of casualties attributable to friendly fire. This, in your chickenshit unpatriotic manner, you preferred to the admitted long shot of attempting to whack ol' Horst upside the head like a good little expendable hero before he could pull a trigger or flip a switch. How'm I doin', Mendoza? You care to critique my analysis for the record?"

Carl just sat there feeling more stupid than he ever had in his life. "You . . . you . . ."

"Stop flappin' your lip with your finger and feelin' like such a macaroon, Mendoza," Coleman told him with a shit-eating grin in his voice. "You won. Congratulations. Unfortunately, we all now gotta deal with the consequences."

"The consequences . . . ?" Carl stammered.

Coleman laughed sourly. "Oh yes, *that* is where you have been a prime dickhead," he said. "You never considered the other side's next move in the unlikely event of what you in your childlike innocence imagined to be victory, now did you? You never considered the endgame at all."

"The endgame . . . ?"

"It never dawned on you that one way or another this situation *had* to end, and soon, now did it? It never dawned on you that all those spin doctors up there in the bowels of sixteen hundred Pennsylvania Avenue are paid to *doctor spin*. It never dawned on you that these people were not merely reptiles, but *professional* reptiles with their jobs on the line. That when you foreclosed a nice clean military solution, they would be ordered to present the powers that be with a menu of options severely limited by the unfortunate circumstances and ruthlessly calculated as to political impact to two decimal points. That the President himself, instead of consulting his Ouija board or the entrails of the last fried-chicken dinner to be placed before him, might indeed hold his nose, grit his teeth, and be forced to pick the least objectionable scenario, such as it is."

Carl had had just about enough. "What the fuck are you talking about, Coleman?" he demanded. "Will you just cut the bullshit and get down to the bottom line?"

"I thought you'd never ask," Coleman said with sweet sarcasm. "Welcome to the wonderful world of realpolitik, folks. The Word has come down from On High, and thanks to you, thanks to my inability to produce anything better, I have been removed from the policy loop and reduced to its humble instrument."

"En inglés, por favor."

"En inglés, muchacho mio, the point of terminal official exasperation has been reached. Within forty-eight hours, one of two things is going to happen, as surely as the inexorable law of political gravity causes shit to flow downhill. The Green Army Commandos are going to release their hostages unharmed and surrender themselves to the tender mercy of the duly constituted authorities, or an unfortunate accident due to an interaction between the amateurish nature of the remote radio-controlled detonators of the explosive charges in the KLAX building and some sort of chance electronic artifact yet to be determined is going to blow the whole shitpile to hell and gone."

"You're bluffing, Coleman!" Franker cut in. "No one will believe obvious ass-covering crap like that! It'd be a political disaster!"

"And what do you think the present situation is, Eddie, a presidential campaign telethon? It has been calculated that fifty-five percent of the public can indeed be induced to allow such a preposterous fairy story to glide down their gullets. And while this is a good deal less than an optimum outcome, the spin doctors have been unable to concoct anything else that produces numbers even *that* sweet when cranked through the software."

"I can't believe I'm hearing this!" Franker groaned.

"Sure you can, Eddie," Coleman crooned. "You know as well as I do that no one ever lost an election by overestimating the gullibility of the American people. Or won one by overestimating their attention span. The presidential popularity rating will indeed take an immediate hit, seven and a half percentage points is the estimate, but by the time the folks signing off on this order are forced to face the electorate, it is estimated that only thirty-two percent of the rubes will even remember what happened, and only thirteen percent will take it into account when they step into the voting booth, sixty-three percent of whom would have voted for the opposition anyway. On the other hand, if this circus is allowed to continue to the point where Brazil retaliates economically, the rest of Latin America goes dingo, car trashing, gas-station burning, and freeway clogging gets to be a popular pastime among the economically and morally disadvantaged. . . . Well, the spreadsheets can't handle such horrendous imponderables. . . ."

"You'll never get away with this, Coleman," Carl snarled, sounding foolish to himself even as he said it.

"We won't? Well gee, Mendoza, if you got any holes to poke in this little scenario, I'd sure like to hear 'em."

"No one's gonna believe that the building was blown away by some bullshit electronic malfunction with all that itchy-fingered firepower out there," Carl said tentatively.

"Very good, Mendoza, you get a gold star for that one, seein' as how that's just what I told 'em. So why don't y'all go look out the window and observe the results of what *they* told *me*."

Horst Klingerman was first out of his chair, springing up, crossing the room in four big strides, staring out one window, dashing across the room, staring out the other, muttering "I do not understand . . . I do not understand. . . ."

By this time, Carl had reached the window facing the parking lot, and when he looked down, he didn't get it either.

The Hummer-mounted Gatling missile carousels, the SWAT teams, the robot minitank, the National Guard troops, were all gone. Nothing remained but the lines of police buses parked as crowd barricades around the periphery of the parking lot and a line of cops in blue inside them, armed with nothing more overtly sinister than standard-issue squad-car shotguns.

"What the fuck is this?" Kelly Jordan's voice asked behind him.

Carl shrugged without turning around. "Damned if I can figure it," he muttered. "We better ask the man. . . ."

"*Deniability* is what the spin doctors call it, folks," Coleman said when they had all trooped back within speakerphone pickup range.

"Bowin' gracefully to public opinion, we have withdrawn all offensive forces from the vicinity of KLAX, leaving only enough cops to assure that dumb rubberneckers don't get too close to this dangerous situation, and we are prepared to blather on till hell freezes over or the atmosphere turns entirely to carbon dioxide, whichever comes first, to bring about a peaceful conclusion to this hostage crisis. Having thus established our bona fides as wimpish liberal pussies, who is gonna believe *we* blew the building and not the crazed terrorist amateurs within, especially given the absence of survivors to contradict the press release?"

"And just *how* do you expect to blow up this building and make it look like an internal explosion?" Carl said, grasping at anything as he sunk back into his chair numbly.

"Oh, the ordnance boys are still engaged in an interservice pissin' contest over who gets to try out their favorite toys on that one! Fuel-air warhead delivered by over-the-horizon short-range ballistic missile? Or a supersonic cruise missile? Artillery guys claim they can do it a whole lot cheaper, if not quite so elegantly, with a howitzer from the Hollywood Hills. There's even spook-shop wizards claim they can detonate the actual Green Army Commando charges with some kind of focused electronic pulse-beam dingus, but that stuff is beyond me. They're still havin' a high old time arguin' about it, you want t'get your two cents in, Mendoza, I'll pass it along."

"I think I'm going to puke. . . ." Carl moaned. And then it hit him.

"Wait a minute, Coleman, aren't you forgetting something?"

"Am I?"

"The Agency is forbidden by law from operating inside the U.S., isn't it? This whole operation is illegal."

"Oh dearie me," Coleman drawled. "Then I guess we won't be able to take any credit or get our names in the papers, will we? Why . . . *why we'll have to keep the whole thing a secret!*"

"We'll blow the whistle on this whole stupid operation! We'll smear so much shit all over it you'll think . . . you'll think you fell into a pigpen, isn't that right, Franker?"

"Better believe it," Eddie Franker said.

"Sorry, guys, but I don't, and what's more, seems to me that's a pretty lame metaphor, Mendoza. Can't you come up with anything more colorful than that? Cornered the market on Ex-Lax? Corn*holed* a diarrhetic rhinoceros?"

"Very funny, Coleman, but you won't be laughing so hard when the whole slimy story comes out on StarNet!"

"I wouldn't if it did, but it won't, so I am."

"Que?"

"KLAX is off the air as of now. Well, wait a minute, let me amend that. You can keep pumpin' out all those crappy old movies an' stuff locally. In fact if you don't, we'll do it for you t'make it look good, but there will be no more live transmissions, an' you can kiss your uplink to the StarNet satellite good-bye. You try and use the dish, an' the circuitry will be reduced to corn pone and hominy grits, or chicharones en mole verde if you prefer a less Anglo metaphor, by the Star Wars Death Ray Laser we have already emplaced with a clear line of fire through the second O in the Hollywood sign."

"And how will you explain *that?*"

"What can you expect from a bunch of ignorant furriners messin' around with fancy high-tech American equipment?"

Horst Klingerman hadn't sat down or said anything since they had all returned from the window. He had stood there frowning intently at the speakerphone on Franker's desk like a batter in the on-deck circle trying to figure out the stuff of the knuckleballer on the mound making the batter ahead of him look like a monkey.

But now he looked like maybe he had a notion as he took a step forward into the batter's box to take *his* cuts at Alex Coleman.

"Do I understand you?" he said. "You are saying that you will permit no further live broadcasts? That if we attempt to use the satellite uplink, you will destroy the circuitry of the dish on the roof with a laser beam and blame it on our incompetence?"

"You got it, Horst, old buddy," Coleman said.

"If our access to the national airwaves is denied, I will detonate the charges with which this building is mined."

"That's your option," Coleman said in a casual cavalier tone of voice that Carl somehow found ultimately unsettling.

"You doubt my sincerity?"

"Not relevant."

"*Vas?*"

"Hasn't anything I've been saying penetrated your consciousness, Klingerman? Don't you get it? The scenario I've been ordered to follow calls for *us* to *fake* what *you're* threatening to do for real! You wanna make things a whole lot simpler and do the job for us, well shoot, go right ahead, it *would* resolve the pissing contest among the technical types, eliminate any lingering credibility problems, and save us a few bucks on the ammo bill."

"You are willing to allow a cloud of plutonium dust to poison vast areas of Los Angeles?"

"More than you are, good buddy, now ain't that the truth?"

"What . . . what . . . what do you mean?" Horst stammered.

"Well now, the head doctors in Langley have gone through your files with the proverbial fine-tooth program, modemed the results to the dirty number crunchers in the White House cleanroom, who have correlated it with the pattern of tea leaves in their cups, run it up to the spin doctors, who ran it through an I-Ching simulator program, and reached the same conclusion that anyone with his head not firmly implanted in his rectum could have come to in about thirty seconds."

"Vas?"

"Folks who are puttin' us all through this agro for the purpose of persuading people to do some hard leanin' on the various bastards that are chokin' our fair planet to death with puke and pollution are not going to release plutonium into the atmosphere themselves. It's a fake. The stuff don't exist. You're bluffing. We're calling."

"Chingada . . ." Carl muttered aloud.

The look on Klingerman's face said it all. Coleman couldn't see it, of course, but then, he didn't have to.

"And if you are wrong?" Horst said. "If tens of thousands of people die and hundreds of kilometers are contaminated for generations? Your government is really . . . is really prepared to risk taking the blame for such a catastrophe?"

"Who, *us?*" Coleman said. "Why should we? Why, we're as pure as the driven snow!"

"I do not—"

"*Your* plutonium, old buddy, your evil lunatic action, not ours! And after the government of the United States has bent over so far backwards to prevent you fuckers from doin' somethin' crazy that it's practically licked the dingleberries off its own asshole! Why . . . why . . . how were we to even know the stuff existed?"

"We will tell the public—" Horst stopped himself.

"That's right, Horst, you are off the air as of now," Coleman said. "We detect so much as a carrier beam and we fry your sat dish and microwave antenna. On the other hand . . ."

Coleman paused. "Now, you understand this ain't ol' Alex talkin'," he said in a tone of voice whose genuine uneasiness Carl found convincing. "I mean, I'm proud of my big ol' cast-iron stomach, but *some* victuals are a bit greasy for even me to swallow. But, well, there are certain reptilian life-forms who are of the opinion that you should be allowed, even encouraged, to threaten Los Angeles with your plutonium dustup. Then, whether the stuff is real or not, whether you use it or not, the Green Army Commandos become discredited monsters, the Brazilian coffee boycott collapses, and so much shit is smeared on the Save-the-Biosphere movement that the Great Unwashed would vote to nuke the whales."

Klingerman sank down onto the nearest chair. Kelly Jordan's

face turned into a death mask. Franker sat there behind his desk staring at nothing in particular. Carl knew just how they felt.

Like dead meat. Like amateurs up against professionals. Like a platoon of draftees fresh in country from Keokuk up against a division of NVA regulars, like the Sacramento Bees served up as a spring-training exercise for the Dodgers.

Nobody moved. Nobody spoke for a long loud silence.

10:48 A.M.

AND I LIKE TO think of myself as a cynical old pro! Eddie Franker thought numbly.

"That's all so *cold*," he finally managed to say.

"The greenhouse notwithstanding, Eddie," Alex Coleman said in a tone of voice that seemed strangely soft under the circumstances, "it's still a cold cruel world full of cold cruel people, or hadn't you noticed?"

"And you're lookin' to be the champ, is that it, Coleman?" Mendoza said bitterly.

"You got me wrong, Carl," Coleman said in that same regretful, almost tender, voice. "I'm not gonna weep a lotta crocodile tears an' go on about how I don't like this any more than you do, but that don't mean that I *approve* of this whole thing either."

"Then why—"

"Because I'm a professional agent of the Central Intelligence Agency and I've been ordered to implement this scenario."

"You vas only following orders, jawohl!" Eddie mimicked savagely in a thick mock-German accent, instantly regretting it when he saw the look on Horst Klingerman's face.

"You can sneer all you like, Eddie, but yeah, way I see it, my duty *is* to carry out the orders passed down the chain of command from the duly constituted legal authorities elected, in their infinite wisdom, by the American people, whether I like them or not."

"It's a dirty job, but someone has to do it, is that it, Coleman?" Eddie snapped angrily.

"It sure as shit is, and they fuckin' well do," Coleman told him.

"Including faking a terrorist bombing and killing all of us to protect the administration's instapoll ratings?"

There was a moment of silence on the other end of the phone. "I *do* gotta admit that there are aspects that kinda stick in my craw," Coleman said rather sourly.

"You seem to have delivered the lines they wrote for you with a certain conviction," Eddie muttered.

" 'Cause I want Horst and Kelly there to comprehend the bottom line," Coleman said in a voice suddenly transfused with much more energy. "You're up against *professionals,* kiddies, with the full weight of the United States government behind 'em, whose highest circles have made the cold, calculated, and admittedly disgusting decision that you *will* release your hostages and surrender, or everyone inside KLAX *will* die in a great big explosion that will be pinned on terrorist action. You surrender or everybody in there dies."

Horst Klingerman and Kelly Jordan stared at each other. The fear on her face was naked and open. His was as hard and unreadable as Eddie had yet seen it as he pulled a vial of pills out of his shirt pocket. Carl Mendoza sat there looking like death warmed over, but not very much.

Eddie knew how he felt. His limbs had gone cold and stiff, and all coherent thought seemed to have been frozen out of his mind.

No one spoke for long, long moments.

"It's over, Horst," Kelly Jordan finally said softly. "We have no choice."

"On the contrary, Kelly, we have a clear choice between two alternatives, one leading to defeat, and the other to victory," Horst said, thumbing open the vial, extracting a white pill, gulping it down dry.

"We can surrender, submit to a show trial, and spend long years, or perhaps the rest of our lives, in an American prison. Or we can prove our sincerity and inspire the peoples of the world to take direct action to save the planet by demonstrating our willingness to die so that the Earth might live."

"You . . . you can't be serious," Kelly stammered.

"*You* are the one who seems to lack seriousness, Kelly. You knew it was likely to come to this when we began this action."

"The fuck I did!"

"How did you expect this to end?" Horst demanded. "With the total capitulation of the United States government to the demands of the Green Army Commandos and a nice victory parade for us in Washington?"

Kelly regarded Horst with a look of horrified dawning comprehension. "You were *never* going to release the hostages and surrender after the referendum like you said," she said. "You planned this all along, didn't you?"

"Not in detail," Horst told her evenly. "But surely you realized that once we seized a television station by force we would be committed to holding it and using it to the maximum advantage until . . ."

"Until *what*?" Kelly demanded angrily.

Horst shrugged. "Until we were no longer able to do so," he said.

"And then we use the plutonium to negotiate a soft surrender!"

"Or force the authorities to reveal themselves for what they are!"

Kelly was up on her feet shouting. "For what *they* are! Haven't you been listening to the man? If we blow up this building, they'll use it to prove what monsters *we* were and discredit everything we've already accomplished! Our lives aside, all we've accomplished by communicating with a national audience on television for nearly a week will be wasted, and—"

"That's all this has ever been to you, isn't it, Kelly?" Horst snapped. "A chance to see yourself on television! *The Green Army Commando Show,* starring Kelly—"

"Holy shit!" Eddie shouted. "That's it! Horst, you're a genius!"

Eddie felt the synapses in his brain suddenly unfreezing like a TV dinner flashed to piping hotness in a microwave. "You still there, Coleman?"

"Would I have flipped channels on a soap like this?" Alex Coleman's voice said over the speakerphone.

"Look, Coleman, as far as you're concerned, the best outcome is a Green Army Commandos surrender, right, you're not just shining me on?"

"Hell's bells, Eddie, ain't that what I just spent all this time tryin' to bring about?"

"Is it?" Eddie said. "Is it *really*?"

"You are losing me, Eddie. . . ."

"I think I'm losing *myself* a little, give me a minute to collect my thoughts," Eddie said, taking a deep breath, and forcing his brain to slow down by act of will.

The Green Army Commando Show . . . surrender . . . the *real* best outcome for the government . . .

It had all come to him in a flash, like a mental picture of a finished architectural structure with all the elements already fitted together. But now he had to take it apart and present it to Coleman and to Klingerman and Jordan too in the right sequence. . . .

"I'll tell you, Alex," he said slowly, "it occurs to me that your bosses have good reason to prefer a nice big explosion that kills everyone in this building to a peaceful surrender."

"Say what?"

"After all, if everybody survives, that means there are fourteen people who know that the White House violated the law by putting the CIA in charge of a domestic operation, at least ten of whom will not exactly be feeling grateful during a long public trial."

A long silence on the other end of the phone.

"Aw come on, Eddie," Coleman finally said in a breezy dismissive tone that seemed to be trying a little too hard to be convincing, "you been readin' too many Machiavelli comic books. I mean, if we *do* pull it off without anybody gettin' hurt, they're gonna be too busy pinnin' hero medals on our chests to give a swamp-rat's ass about that kinda legal technicality."

"Maybe," Eddie said. "Or maybe they'd prefer to cover their tracks, discredit the Green Army Commandos, cool things with the Brazilians, and maybe even get the Seawater Referendum passed the next time around with one big ball of fire that neatly restores the status quo ante."

"You *really* think I'm that low?" Coleman said, and if the hurt in his voice wasn't genuine, it was a pretty perfect simulation.

"To tell you the truth, Alex, I don't really know you well enough to answer that, do I? But even if I give *you* the benefit of the doubt, you so sure all those spin doctors you spend so much time bad-mouthing calculate that you have a need to know *everything*?"

"She-*yit* . . ." Coleman moaned. He paused, then in another tone of voice: "Aw come on, Eddie, this is just a lotta paranoia. . . ."

"Maybe," Eddie told him. "Maybe I'm just doing what you did and laying out the worst-case scenario so you'll take the option I want you to take."

"Which is?" Coleman said more sharply.

"What if I can guarantee a hostage release and a surrender with no one opening their mouths about CIA involvement afterward?"

Horst eyed Eddie suspiciously. Something like hope began to glimmer in Kelly Jordan's eyes.

"How you think you gonna do that?" Coleman said.

"A *negotiated* surrender. A surrender with terms."

"Terms?"

"Nobody talks about the CIA. And as long as nobody does, nobody goes to prison."

"Be real, Eddie, we're talking about kidnapping, seizure of property, possession of automatic weapons and explosives, who knows what-all other menu of charges."

"The hostages refuse to testify for the prosecution. The station ownership refuses to press any charges. The White House machinery puts the case in the hands of a cooperative judge, the Justice Department allows the Green Army Commandos to plead to lesser charges, they get short terms which get suspended to a zillion hours of public service cleaning up the environment. The legal eagles can work it out."

"El stinko, Eddie, it'd smell like a boxcar of used kitty-litter."

"The other outcomes are any better?"

"Well . . . but wait a minute! I can see how the four of you would agree to shut up to save your own asses, but how can we trust a bunch of terrorists? And why the hell would the KLAX owners play ball?"

"Enlightened self-interest," Eddie said. "Horst gave me the idea."

Klingerman frowned. "I did?" he said.

"The Green Army Commando Show."

"I was hardly serious!"

"But I am," Eddie said. "We put together some kind of TV format giving the Green Army Commandos national exposure for their point of view, say something like the phone show we've already done for one hour a week. That's their end of the deal. They welsh on it by talking, the suspended sentences get revoked, and the show is canceled. StarNet distributes it, giving Robby Hildebrandt an interest in helping the White House doctor the spin on the suspended sentences. KLAX produces it for a piece of the action, giving the owners a good reason for playing ball, aside from saving their real estate."

"This is insane!" exclaimed Horst Klingerman.

"Far fucking out!" observed Kelly Jordan.

"More twists and turns than a spaghetti pot fulla night crawlers," Alex Coleman said thoughtfully. "This show-biz stuff is just too Byzantine for a poor ol' country boy used ta dealin' with nothin' more complicated than Latin American revolutionaries, Colombian drug barons, the KGB, an' the machinations of poor ol' Nguyen Cao Ky."

"At least kick it up your chain of command, Alex," Eddie told him. "If nothing else, how they react to it will give you a pretty good idea of whether I'm being totally paranoid or they never intended to let you talk everyone's way out of this peacefully in the first place." He paused for a beat. "Or don't *you* think you have a need to know, either?"

"Well, shoot, Eddie, I gotta admit that when you put it that way. . . ."

11:19 A.M.

''OUR OWN FOOKIN' TV show?" Nigel exclaimed. "We take over this bloody station and the fookin' Yank government gives us a *TV show* ta give it back?"

"Not the *government*," Kelly Jordan said, "it wouldn't be on Public Television, it'd be syndicated commercially by StarNet."

"You mean with fookin' *adverts* an' all?"

Kelly shrugged. "I guess maybe we could insist that they only be for ecologically sound products or something."

"Bloody *surreal*, innit?"

"Ain't capitalism bloody fookin' marvelous?"

Heather Blake exchanged a glance with Toby Inman, who rolled his eyes and gave her body language that said that he too felt that he had fallen down a peculiarly cynical rabbit hole out of the real world of machine guns, explosives, death threats, CIA agents and terrorists, and into that madly logical Wonderland called Show Business.

When Kelly had come bouncing down from Eddie's office by herself and laid out Eddie's scheme, the idea that anyone in the so-called real world on the other side of the screen would buy it had seemed as improbable to Heather as it did to the Green Army Commandos.

But on a show-business level it made perfect sense. Heather had no doubt Eddie Franker could sell just about anything called *The Green Army Commando Show* to StarNet, if only because Fox or NBC or CBS or ABC would surely gobble it up if *they* didn't.

After all, these six days had unintentionally been both pilot and massive launch campaign for just such a show, and the ratings had been terrific. A network programmer would need neither brilliance nor courage to pick up a show with all *that* behind it, especially when it was only a matter of talking heads and a budget of next to nothing.

Helga Mueller popped another pill. Amphetamine of some kind, no doubt. "What does Horst have to say about this madness?" she demanded harshly.

It suddenly occurred to Heather that she had no idea where any of their captors slept, or even *if* they slept at all. She had seen both Helga and Horst taking speed, and she had heard that amphetamine had been invented to keep pilots awake indefinitely if need be, and, come to think of it, by the old German Luftwaffe too.

A combat drug.

"Well, uh, Horst is a little skeptical . . ." Kelly admitted.

Helga grunted wordlessly, glanced at Ahmed. "A little skeptical?" he said dryly. "In my lifetime, I have witnessed the Syrians shelling PLO positions in Tripoli from the land while the Israelis bombarded them from the sea, but even for someone with my experience, this level of cynicism is impressive."

"Hey, lighten up, mate," Malcolm drawled. "Wuzzinit Karl

Marx who said capitalists would sell ya the bloody airtime ta call 'em motherfookers if they could make a few quid inna process? Or wuzzit Groucho?"

Ahmed did not react, but Helga clearly found the humor a good deal less than amusing.

With Jaro apparently in the control room and Hiroshi and Paulo apparently guarding the entrances, the Soldiers in the cafeteria were outnumbered by the Media Freaks.

That was how Heather had come to think of the division within the Green Army Commandos.

Warren, Jaro, Malcolm, and Nigel were a production crew, recruited by Horst and Helga to run the station when they took it over, and Ahmed, Paulo, and Hiroshi were more or less idealistically motivated mercenaries recruited to take it.

That the four Media Freaks had whatever it took to kill or die for whatever cause was not something Heather found at all credible. That Helga, Ahmed, and Hiroshi could and would, on the other hand, was entirely credible, seeing as they already had. Paulo Pereido was harder to figure, an admitted criminal who had killed a man once, but not really a hardened terrorist.

Nobody had written or blocked this scene, but this was just the way Heather would have shot it, with the Media Freaks at one end of the table clustered around Kelly Jordan, the outnumbered soldiers in the middle, and herself and Toby at the other end, with as many empty chairs between them and the terrorists as possible.

"Look, I know the idea takes a little getting used to," Kelly said. "But on the other hand, hey, so does the smell of napalm in the morning. . . ."

Nobody got the reference but Heather and Warren.

"Robert Duvall's famous line in *Apocalypse Now,* guys," he said. "Plays a crazy soldier like certain people I could mention. 'I love the smell of napalm in the morning. It smells like victory.' "

"Getting your own television show is your idea of victory, is that it, Kelly?" Helga snapped.

"Uh . . . no one said it would be *my* show. . . ."

"Oh, I see, then they plan to make Horst the star," Helga sneered. "Or perhaps they will ask *me,* yes? But they must be told I will refuse to work topless!"

"Hey, I think they can handle that, Helga," Warren drawled.

"Please!" Kelly shouted. "Hey, even Horst is willing to *consider* it at least, that's why he's up there in the station manager's office negotiating with—"

—the cafeteria door flipped open, and Eddie Franker and Carl Mendoza stepped inside, followed by Horst Klingerman.

Eddie had a thin little smile creasing his lips. Carl's face was no more readable than usual.

The psychic fatigue in Horst's body language, the weary disbelieving befuddlement in his bloodshot eyes, told Heather all that she needed to know about the inevitable results of the negotiations.

11:29 A.M.

"WELL?" TOBY INMAN SAID nervously. "Did they go for it?"

"They which?" Franker said with an air of bedazzlement. "It what?" But Toby found that impish gleam in his tired old eyes instantly reassuring.

"Well, Horst?" Kelly demanded.

Horst Klingerman shook his head slowly as he walked to the head of the table, where Kelly sat clocking him. He pulled a chair toward himself, grabbed the back of it with his left hand, leaned on it for support, but didn't sit down.

"This is an insane country," he muttered.

"Meaning bloody fookin' *what*, Horst?"

"The Central Intelligence Agency has provisionally agreed to allow us to an hour of live broadcast time for this . . . this *Green Army Commando Show* . . . provided an agreement can be finalized that meets their conditions."

"Conditions?"

"There may be no use of telephones. I may not appear. No illegal acts may be advocated. If any of these conditions are violated, the satellite dish will be destroyed."

"But what about the surrender deal, guy?"

"That is still under discussion."

"With who?"

"Apparently within the American government," Horst said, shaking his head. "And . . . and between the government and StarNet."

He moved around to the front of the chair he had been leaning on and seemed to almost collapse onto it.

"And . . . and . . ."

"*And?*"

"And it has been strongly suggested that we secure the services of an agent."

"*An agent!*" Toby exclaimed. Every last one of the Green Army Commandos looked like cartoon characters who had just been conked on the head with a baseball bat.

"*Coleman* made this suggestion?" Toby said.

"Arlene Berkowski," Eddie Franker said, seating himself beside Heather while Mendoza flopped down next to Toby. "Apparently after talking to Coleman. And then Alex called back to second the motion."

"Let me get this straight," Toby said. "StarNet *wants* to deal with an agent? *The CIA* told you to get an agent?"

Eddie shrugged. "Berkowski said the contract terms would be too complicated to negotiate with amateurs."

"That makes sense," Heather broke in. "Have you ever *seen* a syndication agreement?"

"But *Coleman*—"

"StarNet thinks he's White House staff," Eddie said. "The CIA involvement is supposed to stay secret, remember? We're . . . uh, authorized to tell the truth only to our agent, who will have an economic interest in keeping his mouth shut."

Eddie Franker shook his head. "You think about it, I suppose they've both got a point," Eddie said. "I mean, it's gotta be a five-cornered deal: the government, StarNet, KLAX, the Green Army Commandos, and the hostages. Every element is contingent on every other, and all the elements have to somehow be guaranteed by a credibly binding agreement."

He threw up his hands. "*I* certainly couldn't begin to negotiate anything like that," he said. "Any of *you* think you can?"

No one spoke. Horst fished out his pill vial, worried the cap off nervously with his thumb.

"Berkowski gave me a short list of the agents who've been sniffing after this situation through their end, just the reputable heavyweights, according to her . . . CMA . . . GAC . . . Shapiro-Lichtman . . . Leonard Isaacs Associates—"

"Lennie Isaacs?" Heather exclaimed. "You're *serious?"*

"You've heard of this guy?"

"Heard of him?" Heather said. "Are you kidding? He was a *studio head* who gave it up to open his own agency because he wanted *more power!* Studios and networks come to *him* with an element or two and *beg* him to put a package together."

"You're saying he's a heavyweight?" Toby said, feeling a heady heightening of his circulation.

"That's like saying that toward the end of his career, Orson Welles had gotten a little *chubby,"* Heather told him.

"You're saying we should go with Isaacs?" Eddie said.

"If we can *really* get him? For sure!"

"Well, then, okay, I guess I try and put a call through to Lennie Isaacs."

Throughout all this, their captors had been as quiet as any other set of civilians getting to eavesdrop on inside Hollywood chit-chat, and even Horst Klingerman had more or less sat there like a bump on a log.

But now he chewed down a pill and jerked his head sharply, as if forcing himself out of a trance.

"You are not in charge here, you are our prisoner!" he said angrily. *"I* make the decisions here!"

"You make the decisions, Horst?" Kelly Jordan snapped. "What about *we?"*

"Am I not the chairperson?"

"Isn't this a fookin' *collective?"* Nigel said.

"Fookin' A it is! We didn't join no bloody army!"

"Someone must command!" Helga insisted.

Horst and Kelly seemed to be ignoring all this, locked in what looked to Toby weirdly like a good old-fashioned grade-school staring contest. Then Kelly seemed to win it, or anyway Horst glanced down the table to suss out his support, which, as far as Toby could tell, consisted only of Helga and Ahmed.

Terrorist or not, Klingerman apparently still didn't lack the nose-counting acumen and political survival instinct of a southern small-town mayor dealing with a hostile majority on the local town council.

"You wish to vote on this?" he suggested in the voice of sweet reason. "Or perhaps elect another chairperson?"

"Hey, come on, Horst, you *are* the man," Kelly said in a conciliatory tone. "No one says you're not. But I think there *is* a consensus here that we at least *talk* to this guy. I mean, what harm can it do . . . ?"

Horst sighed, threw up his hands as if to say, oh no, please don't throw me in that old briar patch.

"Very well," he said. "This *is* a revolutionary collective."

He smiled not at all unlike that same species of small-town mayor in the act of gently outfoxing his good buddies in the courthouse.

"But since the question of leadership versus collective decision making *has* been raised, I propose that Kelly and I no longer conduct these negotiations with outside interests unilaterally," he said. "Warren, could you move the speakerphone in here so that everyone can take part?"

"Hey, no problem, Horst, you could do it yourself, there are plenty of jacks, all you gotta do is plug the sucker in."

"Are there any further objections? Or have we reached a collective consensus?"

Kelly Jordan eyed Klingerman warily as Horst in turn met the eyes of his constituents one by one. Warren nodded. So did Nigel. Malcolm even gave him a tentative thumbs-up. Helga locked eyes with him unsmilingly, and Ahmed didn't so much as blink.

Had this been Columbus, Toby thought, they probably would have all repaired to the nearest watering hole for a bit of bourbon and branch.

However, they would probably have stopped after the first drink, and certainly after the second. It had been a nice little piece of papering over.

But Toby had covered enough small-town politics to know that that was all that it had been.

12:05 P.M.

IT TOOK WARREN DAVIES no more than ten minutes to bring the office speakerphone down to the cafeteria, jack it in, and goose up the volume, but it took Eddie Franker almost as long to penetrate the layers of phone answerers, hold buttons, assistants, and canned music at Leonard Isaacs Associates before he finally got the Great Man on the line.

"Sorry for the delay, Mr. Franker," a rumbly, almost purring bass voice said, "but I was in a meeting."

And the check is in your mouth, and I won't come in the mail, Eddie thought sourly. There was something in that voice that grated on him, perhaps because it seemed so perfectly crafted to achieve exactly the opposite.

"Uh . . . I'm not exactly sure how we start this discussion, Mr. Isaacs," he said uncertainly.

"*Leonard,* please, Eddie, if I may, and the way we start is I bring all of you up to speed on the extent to which *I've* put myself in the picture. . . ."

Isaacs paused. "Can all the principals hear me?"

After much back-and-forth between Kelly and Horst, Malcolm and Hiroshi had been assigned to keep the entrances guarded, but all the other Green Army Commandos were indeed there.

The hostages' air mattresses had been removed from the center of the cafeteria and stacked against a far wall, a semicircle of chairs set up in the cleared area, and the speakerphone placed on the table facing it.

"All present and accounted for . . . *Leonard,*" Eddie said dryly, amused that Isaacs preferred the formal form of his informal first-name basis.

"Excellent," Isaacs said. "I've been following your coverage closely and reviewed the tape of what I've missed seeing live due to press of business. The bottom line is that Kelly Jordan and Toby Inman could be developed into major talk-show hosts. Heather Blake might successfully pursue a similar career, but after consulting with certain people at the Actor's Studio and studying her professional footage, I'm convinced that her potential would be better maximized by a carefully planned move into major motion pictures. I'm therefore prepared to offer representation to these three air personalities provided we are in basic accord on these career goals and strategies."

Heather emitted a wordless cry of joy quite similar to certain moans of orgasm, if Eddie's memory served him correctly. Toby Inman developed an apelike grin. Carl Mendoza gave no sign of displeasure at being left out of the deal.

Kelly Jordan seemed to be doing her best to contain her enthusiasm behind a poker-faced mask, but was not succeeding all that well.

Horst Klingerman was less than amused.

"I do not believe I am hearing this!" he shouted. "Talk shows! Movies! This is a life-and-death situation and you are babbling this Hollywood trivia at us!"

"Horst Klingerman, is it?" Isaacs said in that same smooth tone.

"Yes, it is Horst Klingerman, and if this is going to be the nature of the discussion, we might as well end it right now!"

"Don't worry, Horst, while I can't offer representation to the rest of you on a *career* basis, I *am* proposing an overall package which *will* include *all* of the Green Army Commandos and *all* of the hostages, and from which you will all profit handsomely."

"What on earth are you *talking about*?"

"I'm talking about two choice properties, the proposed *Green Army Commando Show* and a major motion picture."

"*A movie?*" said Eddie.

"Did you imagine that a true-life drama like this with massive national exposure and six excellent parts could *fail* to generate at least one major film?" Isaacs said. "The problem is that the story itself, being news, is in the public domain, and it will take your cooperation, and someone with my ingenuity, and, frankly, clout, to turn it into a protected and marketable property."

"What the fuck *are* you talking about, Isaacs?" Eddie shouted.

"We create a corporation through which you all own all the rights to your stories collectively. I act as its agent and sell the film rights for something like a million five, plus points, conceivably a piece of the gross. We retain maybe twenty-five percent of all subsidiary rights, including merchandising, which could prove unexpectedly lucrative. There might still be no legal impediment to some other company launching into a rival production without paying us anything. But I am sufficiently positioned to assure that any such sons of bitches would find it impossible to find financing, distribution, or above-the-line talent, and would find the craft unions highly uncooperative."

"Diabolical," Eddie said. "We all get to dip our wicks in this great big Hollywood honey pot. But aren't you forgetting an element, Leonard?"

"I don't think so, Eddie. I seldom do. Every sparrow."

"What about the fact that we've all got to get out of here in one piece first?"

"I was coming to that," Isaacs said. "May I be frank with you?"

"I'm sure we'd all find that refreshing."

"I contribute something like a mil a year to the best politicians money can buy. It makes me feel patriotic, done right it's deductible, and it buys me access. Also, I control a lot of major talent that is very useful for fund-raising. The bottom line is that when I tell these people I have a need to know something, they find it in our mutual interest to agree. So when I told the White House chief of staff I was considering placing myself in the picture, he was only too happy to cry on my shoulder about their PR and legal problems with the CIA involvement in this mess—"

"You . . . you . . . you know all that?" Eddie stammered.

"*Know it?* Not only do I know it, I've put together a sweetheart of a package to get everyone concerned out of it and at a handsome profit."

There was a hush in the room. All eyes seemed to be on the speakerphone, on the locus of Leonard Isaacs' invisible presence.

"The basic deal you set up was structured pretty cleverly for an amateur, Eddie, but it lacked a keystone element," Isaacs said. "That's the movie. You will all share in the proceeds through the corporation, which will own and control *all* rights to your stories. We write the corporate agreement so that anyone who opens their mouth to the press about the CIA is in breach and loses their piece of the whole juicy pie."

"Huh?" said Eddie. "What's the point of that?"

"To give you all a heavy economic self-interest in honoring an agreement to keep silent in return for a safe hostage release and suspended sentences for the Green Army Commandos. Which allows StarNet to pick up *The Green Army Commando Show* with the assurance that the hostess won't be in prison. Which gives the owners of KLAX an economic self-interest in not pressing charges, since they'll be the producer of record because an agent is unfortunately legally forbidden to produce a property he represents. But don't worry, what with packaging the film starring my own clients, the commissions on the various rights properties and talents, I'll get my fair share. What goes around, comes around."

"I'm sure you will, Leonard," Eddie muttered dazedly. "I'm sure it does."

Despite a certain visceral dislike for Isaacs, despite the total surreality of this bizarre show-business solution to the whole life-and-death problem, he did have to admire the beauty of the structure and acknowledge the lesson that Isaacs had just taught him, as if every man, woman, and child in the United States didn't really know it already.

In this day and age, as surely as water quenched fire and scissors cut paper, show business ranked news, and Hollywood ranked Washington.

"Now as to *The Green Army Commando Show,* there we have a few problems," Isaacs went on in the blithe and secure assumption that everything else was settled.

"Problems?" Kelly Jordan said.

Leonard Isaacs chuckled avuncularly, a sound like something off a sitcom laugh track. "Nothing that can't be handled," he said. "All the publicity means that StarNet will pick up just about anything we give them tonight as a pilot, and the ratings will hold up for about six weeks. But take it from me, what Eddie has proposed in the way of format will drop dead after that, which will seriously damage the movie which we won't be able to release for a minimum of fifteen months."

"You, I gather, have a better idea?" Eddie said dryly.

"For one thing, it's got to be thirty minutes, not an hour. That way we slot it for seven-thirty to eight as a lead-in to prime time, or, second choice, eleven-thirty to midnight as a late-news follow-on. Slot it into prime time as an hour show, and you might as well soak it in blood and drop it into the piranha tank."

Once again, despite himself, Eddie had to admit that Leonard Isaacs was bang on.

"Now have you given any thought as to just what we fill that half hour *with?*"

There was a long, loud, embarrassing silence.

"Well . . ." Kelly finally muttered, "I guess we'd do more or less what we've been doing all week. . . ."

"Wave machine guns at hostages and threaten to blow up buildings?" Isaacs snapped sarcastically.

If Kelly hadn't been black, she probably would have flushed beet-red. "I mean . . . you know, educate people, incite them to direct action. . . ."

"Of course," Isaacs said soothingly. "That's the *what*. I'm talking about the *how*."

"The how?"

"Look, people, less commercials, a thirty-minute slot means twenty-two minutes of program time. Now, to an extent you're right, Kelly. Each show could be devoted to promoting one new direct action the audience can take to help save life on Earth. Not stuff that will bring down the FCC or scare off sponsors, like burning gas stations and blocking freeways, but good, simple, legal stuff like your Brazilian coffee boycott. The first five minutes of the show is filled with reports on how previous actions are progressing, and the last is filled with proposing the next one."

"Hey, I like that!" Warren exclaimed. "You too can be a Green Army Commando out there in TV land!"

"Fookin' brilliant!"

Even Horst Klingerman seemed to be pondering the notion thoughtfully.

"That still leaves twelve minutes to fill with something, people," Isaacs said. "Any bright ideas?"

"How about what Eddie said, a phone-in show?" Kelly suggested.

"Forget it, Kelly, that's called *radio*. People kept watching heads talking to thin air while it was part of an ongoing news drama, but without that, most of the audience will tune out after the first three minutes and they won't tune in next week at all. Do I hear any other bright ideas?"

Dead silence.

"Think about it," Isaacs said, "that twelve minutes is supposed to keep people watching and make them tune in next week for more, and motivate them to carry out each show's suggested direct action. Isn't it obvious? Don't you get it?"

More silence.

"Celebrity interviews!" Leonard Isaacs proclaimed.

"Vas!" Horst Klingerman screamed, bolting out of his chair and taking a stride toward Eddie and the speakerphone as if he were going to slug the thing. "I am not really hearing this!"

Helga stood up a beat behind him. Even Kelly's eyes widened in astonishment. Eddie himself had trouble believing his ears.

"Celebrity interviews," the voice on the speakerphone babbled. "Major ones, real stars, not people trotting around the talk-show circuit to promote their latest movie or album. One per show."

"That is possibly the stupidest and most corrupt single thing I have yet heard in this cynical and degenerate country!" Horst screamed.

But nothing could faze Leonard Isaacs.

"On the contrary, Horst," he said blithely, "it's clever, it's idealistic, and it's good commercial television. Kelly will not interview these stars about their albums or shows or movies, she'll interview them about their *environmental concerns* in the context of that week's proposed direct action. She'll be *enlisting them in the Green Army Commandos*! She'll wear a green beret and put one on their heads too! With a logo, so we can market them, maybe T-shirts and warm-up jackets too, this is why I'm going to make a point of retaining a piece of the merchandising rights. Join your favorite stars in the Green Army Commandos!"

Horst staggered backwards toward his chair. "I think I am going to throw up," he muttered.

Leonard Isaacs' voice hardened, and for the first time, Eddie heard the steel in it, a hint of what this guy must have had to be to become what he had become.

"You're threatening to blow up buildings and kill people for the cause, and you're too pure to use the power of celebrities?" he snapped. "That's not being idealistic, that's just plain stupid. People tune in to watch major stars. They hang on their words. They listen to them. They long to *be* like them, so they emulate them. They're used to sell cars, and dog food, and deodorant, and political candidates, so why *not* the Green Army Commandos as a mass movement?"

"Sickening!" Helga snapped.

"Why?"

"These preening peacocks will say anything to secure free media exposure!"

"Wrong," Isaacs shot back. "Bullshit. Sure that's true of the usual run of talk-show rats, but people like that will never get bookings on *The Green Army Commando Show*. I can deliver first-magnitude people who need no further publicity for themselves or their projects, people who entirely shun the talk-show circuit. People who will do the show for one reason, and one reason only. . . ."

"Which is?" said Kelly.

"They believe in the cause of saving the planet as much as you do."

"Bloody fookin' bollocks!"

"What utter sophistry!"

"Is it?" Isaacs crooned softly. "Think about it. These are people who have already made more money than they can possibly spend in ten lifetimes. These are people who are bankable enough to exercise creative control over their own projects. I understand this class of people because I am one of them. I will make a great deal of money out of this situation because that is my habit, but I already have so much that I can't spend that I contribute about a mil a year to charities. They continue to make films and TV shows and albums because that is their creative outlet, I continue to represent them and structure packages because that is mine."

"What are you trying to say, Leonard?" Eddie asked unaggressively, almost beginning to *like* the guy for the first time.

"Simple. People like that don't do *anything* because they have to. They only do things because they *want* to. And why *shouldn't* they want to save the planet? They live on it too, don't they? They breathe the same air, they absorb the same ultraviolet, and all the money in the world can't buy you a lower CO-two count, an end to the drought, live coral reefs, or a cure for advanced malignant melanoma."

"Jeez, you know he's right!" Kelly Jordan exclaimed in a tone of surprised and reluctant self-discovery.

"But we can't use a celebrity interview on tonight's pilot," Eddie pointed out. "No more phone-ins on pain of having the guts lased out of the sat dish."

"No problem," Isaacs said, "I've already negotiated an agreement to allow us twelve minutes of full video-link through the StarNet transponder with the studio in my building, and you won't *believe* who I've lined up for the interview."

Somehow, Eddie thought, I doubt it.

At this point, if Leonard Isaacs promised to deliver Jesus Christ and the Twelve Apostles doing a medley of the Rolling Stones' golden oldies on electric guitars and angels' harps, he was prepared to believe it.

12:17 P.M.

"**ALLAN LAMONT!**" **LEONARD ISAACS** crowed.

"Allan Lamont!" Eddie Franker groaned.

"Allan Lamont," Kelly Jordan moaned.

"Allan Lamont!" Heather Blake exclaimed, not really able to believe it.

Allan Lamont was maybe the most reclusive figure in Hollywood. He hadn't appeared in public in three or four years, unless you wanted to count grainy still shots of a blimpopoid creature through very long lenses in the *Enquirer* and *Star*.

Allan Lamont had once been one of Hollywood's most bankable and expensive romantic leading men, and those whose opinions Heather respected said that the guy had the genuine acting talent to be the next Brando. *People* called him the next Gable. Major female stars threw themselves at his feet or points somewhat north, at least in the tabloids.

But Allan Lamont was gay. That in itself had never been a particularly significant handicap for major Hollywood leading men. However, Allan Lamont, for reasons that had never been made clear, had made vicious enemies in the gay community and had been outed in a truly horrendous manner.

First came the rumors in the tabloids, accompanied by the usual legal threats and denials. Then ambiguous paparazzi photos that could have meant anything. Then a couple of interviews with men who claimed to have been his lovers, followed by louder denials and more serious legal actions, raising the decibel level of the publicity—

At the height of which, copies of the notorious videotape were mailed anonymously to various legitimate and illegitimate outlets. Not even the sleaziest tabloids and only the slimiest public-access TV channels were willing to print or air the grossest bits, but the peripheral footage was more than enough, showing as it did Allan Lamont, dressed in fetish goods and dog collar, groveling at the booted feet of a platoon of rough-trade leather boys.

For more reasons that no one ever made clear, not even the gay community defended Allan Lamont as his career was sucked down the tubes, not that it would have mattered; the appallingly ludicrous and vivid image imprinted upon the popular consciousness made it impossible for him to be credibly cast in any serious role.

He visibly ballooned to Brando-like proportions before disappearing entirely from the public view. Rumor had it that he was undergoing major liposuction and plastic surgery and would some day reappear as another persona, but Heather put that one down to tabloid hyperbole. . . .

"Allan Lamont . . . ?" said Horst Klingerman. "Is this not the . . . movie star with . . . with the . . . who was . . . ?" Heather was amused to watch Horst actually blush with embarrassment.

"That's him," she said.

"But this is outrageous!" Horst shouted. "Ludicrous! Even *you* cannot be serious about this, Isaacs!"

"Can't I?" Leonard Isaacs said. "Do you know the man? I do. I was his agent. I still am. I'm modestly proud to say I stuck with him. Allan has gone through several kinds of hell, and instead of sympathy, all he ever gets is a horse laugh. Ask yourself this before you sneer at this masochistic leather-boy faggot laughingstock, Klingerman—if you were him, would *you* have the balls to expose yourself on TV for something you believed in?"

The unexpected level of passion in Leonard Isaacs' voice shocked Heather not at all unpleasantly, impressed her with its surprising intensity, convinced her of his sincerity.

"I'm not going to do any bullshit show-biz chitchat interview with an overweight has-been!" Kelly Jordan said.

"Of course you're not," Isaacs told her. "Allan will speak of nothing but his commitment to the Brazilian coffee boycott and this idea it's given him about doing something similar about the *American* rain forest. Not one word about Hollywood, his career, or the past, just Allan Lamont, human being, with the courage to face the camera again for something he believes in. They'll tune in to sneer, but they'll be surprised by this man's dignity. And so will you."

"You've got a hidden agenda here, don't you . . . Leonard?" Eddie Franker said. "You're trying to rehabilitate your client's marketability, aren't you?"

"There's something wrong with that?" Isaacs snapped. "Someone suffers for it? The world is made worse? Tell me how. Tell me who loses money. I don't have a *hidden* agenda, Eddie, I have a *synergetic* agenda, that's why I'm the best agent in town. In theory, every move an agent makes should somehow benefit *all* of his clients. Not really possible, of course, but as an ideal to move toward, not a bad moral compass."

No, it isn't, Heather thought. And whereas before she had merely counted herself fortunate indeed to be offered representation by an agent like Leonard Isaacs, now she felt *proud* to be added to this man's list of clients.

12:20 P.M.

CARL MENDOZA LISTENED TO all of this show-business bullshit with the growing feeling that he had been dropped down on another planet. Movies. TV shows. Leather faggot movie stars. Hollywood agents cutting deals no one could understand with the CIA and the White House.

It all seemed the way Nam had the first day off the plane in country, the first firefight, the way the World had seemed on his return, and the first start in the minors afterward, and the day he had finally faced the fact that, yeah, his arm was gone, he was through as a pitcher. . . .

But all those moments *had* been real, all those things really *had* happened, so, unlikely as it seemed, *this* was probably really happening too.

If there was anyone here he could sympathize with, it was poor fucking Klingerman and his sidekicks Helga, Paulo, and Ahmed. Nigel and Jaro were at least media people of a kind, and Kelly and Warren were Americans, which automatically made them kind of honorary Hollywood insiders. But two German revolutionaries, an Indian from the Amazon, and a Palestinian guerrilla dropped down in this cartoon—chingada!

"You cannot seriously expect us to go along with this," Klingerman said, his eyes darting around the room—at the speakerphone, at Kelly, at Helga, at Ahmed, at Paulo, at Nigel, Warren, and Jaro—as if uncertain as to who the *us* he was speaking for really was, or the *you* he was speaking to.

"Why not?" said the voice of the phantom Leonard Isaacs. "After all, Horst, as I've said to more than one suicidal client, if this move doesn't work out, you can always kill yourselves later."

"I wasn't talking to you!" Klingerman shouted.

"Then who the bloody fookin' hell *are* you talking to?"

Horst Klingerman stood up and rounded on the Green Army Commandos. "To all of you!" he said. "Don't you see this is a trick to divide us? To make a ludicrous mockery of everything we've accomplished! We cannot allow ourselves to be co-opted like this!"

"Come on, Horst, he's right," Kelly said, "what do we possibly have to lose?"

"Our dignity! Our self-respect! Our political credibility! Don't you see what these people are doing?"

"Bollocks!"

"*A celebrity interview television show?*" Helga shouted. "This is what we're fighting for according to you, Nigel?"

"Hey come on, Helga, it's *media access*!"

"As long as we agree to turn ourselves into a laughingstock!"

And then they were all on their feet shouting at each other. They weren't making any moves toward their weapons, but Carl did not at all like the smell of the developing situation.

"It is out of the question!" Horst shouted. "I will not permit this!"

"*Permit it?* Who the bloody hell sez we gotta ask your fookin' permission, Daddy?"

"Yeah, guy, this *is* a collective!"

"There are limits, Warren!"

"We should vote!"

"Yeah, let's vote!"

Helga, Ahmed, and Paulo were lining up with Horst against the rest of them, but only Helga seemed to really share his level of pop-eyed intensity.

"You want to vote?" Horst just about screamed. "Very well!"

He slipped his hand inside his vest, caressed the remote detonator switches, lowered his voice suddenly, and spoke in soft, calm tones, which, under the circumstances, were far scarier than the previous shouting.

"*This* is *my* vote," he said. "I would rather we all die right now than dishonor ourselves and our cause by permitting this action to end in such low farce."

Everyone froze for a long moment of dead silence.

"Hey, wait a minute, guy," Warren said, "don't do anything sudden, okay? Let's just talk about it. . . ."

"Very well," Horst said with glacial calmness. "We are talking about it. I am listening. Can you tell me one good reason why I should agree to this demeaning madness?"

"Well . . ." drawled Warren, "uh . . . at least we *do* get one last half hour of national airtime."

"In the form of an interview with a . . . a . . ."

Click.

Some kind of relay tripped in Carl Mendoza's brain. Maybe he was just a dumb old ballplayer without enough going for him to be offered representation by Mr. Hotshot Agent. But he *had* had his cuppa with the Agency, and he *did* have a certain insight into the thought processes of Alex Coleman and Company.

Maybe Leonard Isaacs did shovel so much money into political campaigns that he had the White House chief of staff in his pocket. Maybe he *was* capable of dribbling experienced spooks like the proverbial basketball.

Then again, maybe not.

Maybe *they* were dribbling *him*.

And maybe what seemed on the verge of happening now was what was *supposed* to happen.

And even if they weren't and it wasn't, Klingerman would certainly believe it.

Carl stood up. "Turn off the speakerphone, Eddie," he said loudly. "Tell our *agent* we'll get back to him."

Eddie froze. Horst whirled around to glare at Carl. Carl glared back. "Tell him to do it, Horst," he said. "We've got something to discuss in private."

"Do we?"

Carl nodded. "For sure," he said. He nodded again, this time in the direction of the phone. "And we have no idea who's listening in, now do we?"

Klingerman paused, nodded in the direction of Franker, slowly withdrew his hand from inside his vest, but kept it poised on the inner edge of the garment's closure.

Franker shrugged. "We'll get back to you later, Leonard," he said. And then the old buzzard's lips creased in a sardonic smile that Carl, in that moment, found rather endearing. "Right now, we gotta take a meeting."

"Look, I know you think you're desperate characters and all, but hey muchachos, we are dealing with *dangerous people!*" Carl began the moment Franker hung up on Isaacs. "We are dealing with an outfit which has proved itself perfectly capable of doing business with the smack barons of the Golden Triangle, and Manuel fuckin' Noriega, and the Medellin cartel, and better you don't know 'cause they'd snuff you if you did, all of who believed they were calling the shots at the time, and we got no way of knowing who's really using who to do what without a scorecard, which we don't have, 'cause here we are, holed up like Charlies inna tunnel for six goddamn days with no links to the outside but the phone and the tube, so I gotta tell you, we wanna come through this alive, or even not looking like dead dickheads, we better trust *none* of 'em, put our heads together, and buy ourselves some insurance. . . ."

It was by far the longest continuous speech Carl Mendoza had ever delivered in his life, and, in fact, as it emerged from him to his own enormous surprise, it reminded him of nothing so much as the gigantic and somehow terrifying shit that had emerged from his asshole in one long turd in a whorehouse crapper in Saigon after a twenty-four-hour pig-out upon returning from a long patrol full of famishment in the deep boonies.

Then, as now, he had been afraid to stop until he had gotten the whole thing out. Then, as now, he had not wanted to contemplate the final result before flushing it. Then, as now, he was unable to refrain from peeking anyway.

What he saw was that he had indeed captured the attention of every person in the room. What he sensed was that the psychic temperature had dropped a good ten degrees. What he knew was that this was now between himself and Horst Klingerman.

"What do you mean by insurance?" Klingerman said coolly, a fair indication that he had digested and understood the rest of it, had no real argument with it, was taking it as a given.

"If you just want all of us to go out in a great big fireball, then you might as well do it now and get it over with," Carl told him. "But if you want to at least take a shot at all of us getting out of here alive and nobody going to the joint like Isaacs claims he's negotiated with the Agency, or the White House, or whoever, movies, and money, and bullshit TV shows aside, the thing to do, tactically speaking, *is* to go ahead with tonight's dumb *Green Army Commando Show*."

"Why?" Klingerman said tonelessly.

"Because of what Warren said. Some interview with Allan Lamont seems about as stupid to me as it does to you. But that's not what counts. What counts is that it gets us that one last half hour of airtime."

"To do what?"

"To save our asses."

"How?" said Warren.

Carl shrugged. "Look, maybe all this is some Agency trick, or maybe it's all on the level, and Isaacs and Coleman and whoever really *have* cooked up a deal we all can . . . live with. We can't know which. But either way, isn't it in our best interests to have the whole thing made *public*? Why not go on the air, tell the world a deal is in the works, and challenge them to send some bigwig in here under promise of safe passage to nail it all down, *live on television*? How could they blow up the station and pin it on you after that? And how could they welsh on any promises they make in front of fifty million people?"

"Fook a bloody dook!"

"Genius, guy!"

Horst Klingerman locked eyes with Carl, his face slowly relaxing with comprehension as Carl sat down again and folded his arms across his chest. "I guess that's about all I've got to say," he said.

"More than enough," said Kelly Jordan. "Well, what about it, Horst, you got a better idea than *that*?"

Klingerman looked at her, at Helga, at Ahmed, at Paulo, and slowly sat down himself with an actual smile.

"No, I do not," he said. He nodded at Eddie Franker. "You may call our . . . agent back and tell him, as they say here in Hollywood, that . . . the show will go on."

He paused, his eyes narrowed. "But you tell him nothing else, yes. You say nothing about this conversation. Let it be a little surprise for him, yes."

Carl's sense of relief and satisfaction was suddenly shadowed by that twist to the smile, that secret something behind the eyes, that look of a pitcher who has somehow managed to load up the ball with Vaseline under the very nose of the umpire.

He didn't know how, he didn't know why, but Carl had a sudden sinking sensation in his gut that told him that Leonard Isaacs wasn't going to be the only one in for a little surprise from Horst Klingerman.

The guy was loading up some kind of trick pitch for the three-and-two count, and Carl had a feeling that when he finally threw it, it was going to cross *everyone* up, that not even his own catcher was going to like it.

7:30 P.M.

Onscreen:

A VERY CRUDELY DONE title card: THE GREEN ARMY COMMANDO SHOW, lettered on a piece of white cardboard with basic green Magic Marker.

Toby Inman's voice-over: "*The Green Army Commando Show*, with Kelly Jordan, and tonight's *very* special guest—Allan Lamont!"

A close-up on Toby Inman, eyeballing the camera earnestly, looking a little too slick, like an actor playing a TV announcer.

"But first, a word on just what this show is all about, and an announcement. As you all know by now, the Green Army Commandos have been in control of KLAX for six days, have been instrumental in defeating the California Seawater Referendum, have created the Brazilian coffee boycott, and . . . uh, certain other protest actions. Remarkably and responsibly, no one has yet been harmed by their actions, and as one of the hostages, I can testify that we have been treated humanely. So this show is an experiment and a . . . pilot to see if this . . . er, ah, terrorist takeover can be peacefully transformed into a mass movement to save our planet. The authorities have given us the go-ahead, and at the end of the program, stay tuned for the Green Army Commandos' exciting and positive response to *your* support and understanding. And now—here's Kelly Jordan!"

The camera holds on Toby Inman for an awkward extra beat as he sits there looking nervously glad that this little speech is over, then there is a cut to a close-up on Kelly Jordan.

She's still a terrorist in nattily tailored combat fatigues, but the explosive vest and the Uzi are gone, her Afro is meticulously combed, and the amateurish attempt at dramatic lighting somehow makes her look a bit like a Hollywood version of herself.

"*The Green Army Commando Show* is *your* show, the show that lets all of you out there join the battle to save life on Earth by enlisting in the Green Army Commandos and taking direct action yourselves!"

A rather nervous plastic smile appears on her face.

"Each week, we'll be reporting on the status of our struggle to save the biosphere, and each week a . . . prominent American will appear on *The Green Army Commando Show* to make *their* suggestion for *your* next direct action!"

She pauses, and somehow the smile changes, picks up a genuine twinkle.

"Now under normal circumstances, assuming we survive, and this show gets picked up, our guests will be here live in the studio, but due to the, ah, current situation, I'll be talking to Allan Lamont via satellite link. But . . . before we get to that, here's the latest report on the status of the Brazilian coffee boycott and the battle to save the Amazon rain forest. . . ."

She looks down at something off camera and begins to read openly as the camera pulls back into a wider angle, including the coffee table before her and a sheaf of wire-service printouts in her hand.

"According to the latest figures, coffee sales in general have dropped thirteen percent since the boycott began, with sales of identifiably Brazilian coffee down twenty-three percent, and one hundred percent Colombian rising twenty-seven percent. . . .

7:36 P.M.

". . . AND WHILE A GOVERNMENT spokesman in Brasilia denied that the authorities would ever surrender national sovereignty to terrorists or American pressure. . . ."

As Kelly Jordan read the wire reports, Toby Inman tracked Horst Klingerman as he paced back and forth behind the cameras like a caged panther. Toby couldn't quite put his finger on why, but something about the whole business just smelled wrong.

Eddie was in the control room with Warren and Jaro, and Nigel and Malcolm were on the cameras, but for whatever reason, Ahmed was holding Carl and Heather in the green room instead of the cafeteria, Helga was stationed outside the studio entrance, and Horst himself had appropriated the role of "Director."

He had let Warren pump the intro up on Toby's prompter, but he had refused to trust his extro to the technology.

"I may need to make changes depending on how the program proceeds, yes," he had insisted. "And this announcement is why we are proceeding with this stupid show in the first place!"

By that time, Klingerman was so ripped on speed that no one wanted to argue such a point, and so Horst had spent half an hour frantically lettering on pieces of cardboard with Magic Marker.

And there he paced, hand-made cue cards tucked under his left armpit, gun slung over his right shoulder, not calling camera angles, but clearly in total control of the set.

"And now, for tonight's guest Commando, the . . . uh, famous movie star Allan Lamont, making his first public appearance *anywhere* in over two years, to talk about trees and apples, yes, that's right, *trees and apples.* . . ."

7:42 P.M.

Onscreen:

A SPLIT-SCREEN SHOT. On the right, a close-up on Kelly Jordan on the KLAX talk-show set. On the left, in a somewhat longer head-and-shoulders shot against a blank blue background somewhere, Allan Lamont, holding a fat shiny red apple up to the camera as if about to launch into a paid commercial for the product.

Allan Lamont's face was obviously once conventionally handsome in a leading-man sort of way, but now the perfect features seem to have been etched more deeply by many miles of bad road. The skin hangs somewhat loosely on its gaunt musculature like a badly fitted mask, the lips are set in a kind of iron determination, and the dark eyes, deep in fatigued sockets, seem to be those of a much older man. Had Elvis managed to survive, dry out, and blow off the blubber, the effect might have been similar.

"This is an apple, Kelly," he says in a rich, carefully trained voice, roughened only slightly by the apparent wear and tear. "A nice juicy apple from the Pacific Northwest. They grow a lot of tasty apples up there—Delicious, Golden Delicious, Jonathans—and apples are an important part of the economy of Washington and Oregon."

"You, uh . . . sound like you, uh, know a lot about apples, er . . . Allan," Kelly Jordan says, looking rather uncertain and nervous.

Alan Lamont attempts a boyish grin in an apparent professional attempt to carry her, but it comes across a tad skeletal.

"Yes I do, Kelly," he says. "My parents still have an apple orchard outside Centralia, and that's where I grew up, so I know all about the apple business in Washington and Oregon. It's big business up there. But the lumber business is much bigger. And much, much, more destructive. And what it's destroying is the only rain forest in the continental United States. And that's why . . . I . . . I wanted to take this chance to say something about it tonight. I'm not here to talk about the past, or my career, or my next project. All I want to talk about is the future, the future of trees and apples."

"The, uh . . . future of trees and apples?"

"That's right, Kelly. Do you know much about our own Pacific Northwest rain forest?"

"Only that it's in danger of destruction from logging."

"It sure is," Allan Lamont says, "they've been fighting about it up there since before I was born. And I'm not as young as I look." He smiles, and the unintended effect is rather horrible.

"It's the only rain forest in the continental United States, and it's one of the few cool-climate rain forests in the world, and while it's much, much smaller than the one in Brazil that you're trying to save, Kelly, we've made just as big a mess of it as they have. We've clear-cut it, and we've divided the remaining old growth up into smaller and smaller isolated stands, tree *gardens* more than real habitats, and we've replaced a lot of that old-growth forest with pine tree farms."

Allan Lamont's eyes seemed to harden. If this isn't real passion, then he really *is* a superb actor.

"I've been thinking about the apple orchards I grew up on and the rain forest around them ever since this Brazilian coffee boycott began. And I think you, and me, and a lot of people out there, have been complete hypocrites about it."

"Hypocrites . . . ?" Kelly Jordan stammers. "About *what*?"

A full-screen close-up on Allan Lamont, addressing the camera like an off-screen character, playing to it shamelessly, a professional actor artfully portraying himself.

"Sure, I've stopped buying Brazilian coffee until the Brazilians act to save *their* rain forest, sure I know that compared to the Amazon basin, the destruction of *our* little rain forest wouldn't add much that was noticeable to the greenhouse. But on the other hand, who are *we* to push the Brazilians around so self-righteously when we won't even get our own act together in the Pacific Northwest?"

Back to the split-screen shot. On the right side of the screen, Kelly Jordan, still reacting rather uncertainly, content, if that is the word, to play foil for Allan Lamont, feeding him reaction lines to break up his monologue.

"Americans should set an example, even if it's a small one, to put moral pressure on the Brazilians?"

On the left half of the screen, a flash of cynicism shows through Allan Lamont's own righteous indignation. "Oh, the economic pressure we're putting on them is more than enough. Money speaks a lot louder than words or morality, Kelly, or haven't you noticed?"

Then, reacting to her reaction, and realizing the slip, much more earnestly. "But if Americans want their government to throw its weight around to save life on Earth, and I don't think there's any real choice because no one else *has* the weight to do it, then just maybe there'd be a lot fewer bricks thrown through the windows of our embassies when we do it if the American people prove to the world that Green Power begins at home."

"Green Power . . . yeah, I like that."

"You may use it as you wish, my dear, I relinquish all rights," Allan Lamont says dryly.

"Uh . . . you were saying?"

"I was saying that if we expect the Brazilians to sacrifice agricultural income to save *their* rain forest, then it's totally hypocritical for *us* not to sacrifice a certain amount of lumber exports to the Japanese. I'm saying there should be an end to all logging of old-growth rain forest in the Pacific Northwest. I'm saying all of the remaining old-growth groves should be contained in one single continuous national park, that the pine farms inside it be leveled, and that nothing be touched inside it till the forest has knit itself together again. And if it takes a century or two . . . well, then it takes a century or two."

"You're suggesting we take some kind of direct action against the logging industry up there?"

"Sort of, Kelly, but not exactly. . . ."

Cut to a close-up on Allan Lamont that fills the whole screen as he smiles a bit fatuously. "I'm sure what I'm going to suggest will outrage my parents," he says, and the smile acquires a certain sour tinge. "But then, I've long since become used to it, even if they haven't. What I'm suggesting to all you folks out there, what I'm suggesting to you, Kelly, is that while we're boycotting Brazilian coffee to force the Brazilians to save *their* rain forest, we should damn well be boycotting Washington and Oregon apples to force *us* to save *ours*."

He holds up the ripe red apple again. "Now as a native Washingtonian and the son of apple growers at that, I'm patriotically bound to believe that Pacific Northwest apples are the best there are. But there are a lot of growers in New York, for example, who would give me an argument, they grow more apples, and there's no rain forest there to be destroyed. Would it really be such a sacrifice to boycott Northwest apples until our only homegrown rain forest is protected? We can get along on McIntoshes from New York for a while as easy as we can get along on Colombian mountain-grown, now can't we?"

7:47 P.M.

"**. . . DON'T QUITE GET HOW** boycotting *apples* is gonna put the muscle on the *lumber* industry. . . ."

"What's needed is federal action to save our rain forest, Kelly. I admit that it's unfair to the apple growers, I can hear my father screaming at me right now, but how can you organize a boycott against *lumber*? Now a lot of apples don't have those nasty little stickers on them that get caught in your teeth if you forget to peel them off, but a lot of them *do,* and the growers up there have spent lots of money identifying *their* apples to the public. And people can talk to their supermarket managers about just not stocking Washington and Oregon apples unless they want to be boycotted too. It's just like the Brazilian boycott; the idea is to make the growers scream at Washington. After all, as I understand it, when they chop and burn Amazon rain forest, they put in *cattle,* not coffee trees. . . ."

While Kelly Jordan and Allan Lamont went on about apples and lumber, Toby Inman just sat there silently, trying to figure out why Klingerman wanted him on the set through the whole thing in the first place. Horst had made it clear that he was not to take part in the interview, his job was just to read the intro off the prompter and read those damned hand-lettered cue cards at the end. . . .

". . . but the lumber industry is a much bigger part of the economy up there than apples, isn't it? Why wouldn't *their* lobby shout down the apple growers?"

"Oh, they'd try. But what can they say? Better that poor little mom-and-pop apple growers go out of business than great big corporate monsters lose a little profit off the small part of their production that comes from the rain forest? Go back to eating Northwest apples, folks, so we can continue to sell ancient trees as throwaway chopsticks in Tokyo?"

. . . a set of cue cards that Horst was now rewriting, sitting on a folding chair behind the cameras with the cardboard slabs on his lap, the Magic Marker in his hand, the tip of his tongue stuck between his lips in concentration, and a predatory look about the eyes that sure made Toby wish he was going to get to see his lines before he was forced to read them. . . .

7:51 P.M.

Onscreen:

A **SPLIT-SCREEN SHOT,** Kelly Jordan on the right, Allan Lamont on the left. She looks a bit more confident now, as if she's been able to fuzz out where she is, what the situation is, the camera, and focus on the conversation. Or maybe just getting the idea that it's *her* show, not his. He seems to have grown a shade querulous, this is *his* baby, he's not being paid for this appearance, and he *is* the star here, isn't he? Isn't he?

"Well, Allan, I like the idea, but those poor apple growers like—"

"I don't see why you seem so concerned about my . . . the apple growers!"

"They're the ones who are going to get hurt!"

"This from someone holding hostages at gunpoint?" Allan Lamont snaps testily, his face contorted into something of a snarl. Then, catching himself, he smooths it out into a radiant plastic smile.

"Don't get me wrong, Kelly," he croons. "I think what you're doing is wonderful. I approve of it a hundred percent. It's what inspired me. It's what gave me the courage to go on this show and expose myself . . . expose myself . . . well, expose myself to a certain inevitable public ridicule. We Green Army Commandos must be brave, mustn't we? And sometimes, as you have so admirably demonstrated, that means we must have the courage to be quite ruthless. We're talking about saving the Earth, aren't we? Some of us are going to have to endure a little unjust pain, a subject upon which I have been forced to become something of an expert. And some of us are going to have to inflict it, as you have, now aren't we?"

"But we don't have to get off on it," Kelly Jordan shoots back. Allan Lamont's image freezes for a beat on his side of the screen, and Kelly Jordan's on hers. Via sat links and monitors, they seem to stare at each other, and a message passes between them, something complex, and when they unfreeze, he smiles a respectful smile at her, and the tension has evaporated.

"It was Ernest Hemingway, I believe, who said 'What's right is what you feel good after,' " Allan Lamont says silkily. "And I feel good about being given the opportunity to come on your show, Kelly, and present my proposal to the American people. And I think the American people will feel a lot better about inflicting a little necessary sacrifice on others if they set an example by accepting a little sacrifice themselves."

He smiles beatifically, he all but oozes benign certainty.

"And I'll tell you something, Kelly," he says. "I know those people up there, Kelly, I know those apple growers, I came from them long before I became an actor and a star. And I think that some day, those very apple growers will think about the rain forest that has been saved and the example all of us have set together to inspire the world, and they'll feel pretty damn good about playing *their* part in it too."

Allan Lamont's face fills the full screen in head-and-shoulders close-up as he holds up the shiny red apple one final time.

"And just think how much sweeter one of these beauties will

taste then," he says. "Think of how much more of them will be sold. For on that day, who could deny that these really *are* the best apples in the world?"

Cut to a full-screen close-up on Kelly Jordan, looking silently at something off camera for a long beat, her expression pensive, before she turns to face the camera.

"Well, that was really moving, Allan," she says, "and you've sure convinced me, and I think millions of people out there are gonna feel the same way. And I really want to thank you for being the very first guest on *The Green Army Commando Show*. And now it's up to *you* out there to take direct action! Okay, fellow Green Army Commandos, you've defeated the Seawater Referendum and you've shown the Brazilians that the conscience of the American people is ready to kick ass to save life on Earth! Now it's time to . . . to bring it all back home."

She groans in anticipation of her own next line.

"How's *them* apples, folks?"

It's an obvious extro line, and it would seem that's what she has intended, for she stares silently into the camera for several long confused and embarrassing beats.

Then she blinks, glances at something off camera, frowns, nods.

"Well that's the end of *The Green Army Commando Show* for tonight," she says, "except for the important and exciting news about . . . about the ongoing negotiations between the authorities and the Green Army Commandos aimed at . . . aimed at reaching a peaceful and just solution to the KLAX hostage crisis. . . . Toby? Toby?"

Cut to a close-up on Toby Inman, eyeing something slightly above and to the right of the camera owlishly.

"Uh . . . uh, thank you, Kelly."

He begins speaking, blinking and squinting, as if he's having trouble reading cue cards or can't quite believe what he's reading, or both.

"Throughout the KLAX hostage crisis, there have been . . . ongoing negotiations between . . . federal authorities and . . . Chairperson Horst Klingerman of the Green Army Commandos . . . aimed at . . . peaceful release of all hostages and . . . an honorable and productive cessation of the armed standoff between government forces and the Green Army Commando action group that serves the best interests of all parties and the peoples of the Earth."

Toby Inman pauses, squints, mutters something under his breath.

Faint male voice-over: "Read it!"

Toby Inman hesitates for a beat, then speaks in a flat singsong voice.

"As a gesture of goodwill, the Green Army Commandos have . . . have thus far honored the request of your government not to . . . not to reveal the nature of the explosive charges placed in this building in order to prevent a public panic. . . . *Jesus!*"

Faint male voice-over: "Continue!"

Toby Inman mops his brow, squints again, continues.

"But now that the Green Army Commandos and the federal authorities have reached broad agreement on a settlement of this crisis, it is now felt that further silence on this matter would be counterproductive. I am therefore authorized to tell you that . . . that . . . Jesus, Horst, this isn't—"

Male voice-over, faint with distance from the mike, but shouting: "*Read it,* Inman!"

Toby Inman has turned visibly pale. His voice loses all expression.

". . . that the explosive charges have been evenly salted with one kilo of finely divided plutonium."

He rolls his eyes, seems almost to be containing a frantic giggle at the next line.

"But there is no cause for panic. Since we will . . . will be the first to die if we are forced to detonate these charges, we can be trusted not to do so unless your government reneges on the tentative agreement that has already been reached. The Green Army Commandos now invite a representative of the government of the United States to come to KLAX under our guarantee of safe passage to finalize the details in full public view, live, on the air."

Toby Inman pauses, sighs in visible relief.

"We require that this agreement be concluded before the eyes of the American people and not in secret in order that the authorities not simply deny it ever existed once we are in their hands. You, the American people, must be our fair witness. And in order that reactionary elements of the bureaucracy not be able to use legal tricks to abrogate it in court later, we require that it be finalized and ratified before the world by the highest possible authority. . . ."

Another pause. Toby Inman's eyes practically pop out of his head. He looks this way and that, back at the camera, blinks, once, twice, thrice.

"We demand to speak directly and in person with . . . with the President of the United States. We . . . we challenge you, Mr. President, before the eyes of the world. Will you show your people the same courage you require of your minions? Your failure to do so will result in the destruction of this building and everything in it, and the release of a cloud of radioactive particles that will . . . that will kill thousands and contaminate this city for centuries. And . . ."

Toby Inman freezes, his lips tremble, as if he can't bring himself to read the next line. He starts at something off camera, a startlement of fear. He blinks, composes himself, recites it like a zombie's talking head.

"And all the world will know that all that innocent blood is on your cowardly hands."

DAY 7

8:30 A.M.

THE TELEPHONE FROM HELL blasted Eddie Franker into full head-throbbing nerve-jangling wakefulness, and he bolted upright in bed, reaching reflexively for the bedside receiver.

But it wasn't there, and he wasn't home safe in bed. He was sitting fully clothed on an air mattress in the KLAX cafeteria, and hostages and terrorists were stirring with various degrees of bleary indignation from their rudely interrupted sleep.

Helga and Warren, who had been awake and guarding the door, were moving across the room toward the horrible sound.

But Horst Klingerman had managed to wake up, bound off the floor, and make it to the speakerphone before they did, fumbling for a moment as he made the connection, as Eddie blinked himself to more or less full consciousness of where he was and what was happening.

As if anyone in here really knew what was happening anymore.

Certainly poor Inman hadn't known what was happening when Horst made him read that outrageous challenge to the President at gunpoint.

After it was over, Kelly and Horst had started to argue on the set, though Eddie didn't know what it was about at the time, since the mikes had been cut, and then the hostages had been hustled to the green room and held inside by Helga for the better part of three hours.

When they were finally trotted back to the cafeteria, it was obvious that the Green Army Commandos had spent those three hours having at each other over whatever.

The tables in front of the toilet doors had been shoved toward the walls to make room for six more air mattresses. Horst, Hiroshi, and Paulo sat at one, Kelly, Warren, Jaro, and Malcolm sat at the other, and the looks passing back and forth between the tables seemed a good deal less than fraternal.

Helga marched the hostages to their usual table in front of the vending machines, and when she joined Horst's crew, they all hunched together like a paranoid football huddle, jibbering and jabbering excitedly as they apparently brought her up to speed.

When the terrorists bedded down, the divide between them was maintained, and Eddie had the feeling that they were all sleeping in the cafeteria now mainly because each faction was reluctant to let the other out of its sight.

Just *what* the terrorists had been arguing about for three hours Eddie had no way of knowing, but now that he was wide awake, he remembered what Inman had told him.

Toby *had* at least heard the beginning of it, the set-to between Kelly and Horst on the set right after the show.

"What the fuck was that, Horst, a death wish?" he reported her having said. "You really think they're gonna hand us the President of the United States as a hostage?"

"Hostage?" Horst had said. "Who said anything about a hostage? I promised the President safe passage, did I not?"

"And the Green Army Commandos are an honorable organization. People believe in us. We keep our word."

"Why of course we do, Kelly," Horst had said.

But Toby had reported that Horst's smile had reminded him of an Okefenokee alligator sinking placidly to the bottom of the swamp with a pet poodle in its gullet.

8:32 A.M.

"*Vas?*"

The amplified voice of Alex Coleman filled the room.

"*Vas?* That's what *I'd* like to know, Klingerman! What's going on in there? Why'd you shut off the phones? What's with the double-cross on the plutonium? Where did you get this horseshit idea that Mr. Wonderful himself would be stupid enough to stick his neck in your bear trap? I mean, I gotta admit that sometimes it seems like he ain't hittin' on all cylinders, but this don't even require him to chew tobacco and spit brown at the same time!"

Carl Mendoza had to laugh. Coleman *did* have a way with words. He had such a way with words that he sometimes got so pleased with himself over it that he lost the count, like a second baseman makes a great stab of a liner with men on and one out, and then tosses the ball to the umpire thinking he's retired the side.

"I do not see why you are so upset, Mr. Coleman," Horst purred. "Have we not followed the arrangement negotiated between you and our . . . agent, Mr. Isaacs?"

"No, you have not," Coleman growled. "You've poked a stick in a nest of yellow jackets and don't bother to tell me you don't know it. We got the worst gridlock in the history of this gridlocked city! Five million people tryin' t'get their asses outa ground zero all at once and no one gettin' nowhere! Why did you do it, Klingerman? Why did you have to go ahead and create this goddamn plutonium panic?"

"But people were *told* there was no cause for panic," Horst said sweetly. "Why would we detonate the charges and kill ourselves? Your government does not intend to break its word on what has already been negotiated, does it? Perhaps the public believes that it may? But of course the moment your President announces that he intends to come here and finalize our arrangement, such fears will be revealed as foolish paranoia, will they not, and any public panic will quickly subside."

"You think you can blackmail the President of the United States into walking right into your hands!"

"Blackmail is such an unpleasant word, Mr. Coleman. I prefer to see it as a matter of trust. If we must trust our lives to the good faith of your government, is it not only fair that its leader trust his life to ours?"

"I'd like to know what you were smokin' when you got this idiot idea 'cause I wouldn't mind havin' the aid of a jay of the stuff myself under the current circumstances."

By now, everyone had shaken off their sleep, crawled off their air mattresses, and gathered in front of the speakerphone table, the factions eyeing each other suspiciously.

"I would have thought your masters would be pleased," Horst said. "Have I not offered your President what I believe his advisers call the 'perfect photo opportunity'?"

Carl couldn't see Coleman, but he could just about smell the smoke coming out of his ears. Carl was steaming pretty hard himself, but the object of *his* ire was one Carl Mendoza, who now realized what a dumb asshole mistake he had made sticking this particular cucaracha in Horst Klingerman's ear.

Carl knew, Coleman had to know, that if the President of the United States were fool enough to walk in here, Klingerman could never resist the temptation to take him hostage. The Green Army Commandos might be divided on such a tactic, but the remote detonators inside his vest made Klingerman a majority of one for terminal sanctions.

Horst couldn't seriously believe that the CIA couldn't figure out his intentions, and seemed to be baiting Coleman just for the hell of it.

"Oh, that's cute, that's really cute, Klingerman, you oughta send it in to your agent, maybe he can sell it to *Newsweek* for their Quotes of the Week section," Coleman said. He slowed down, his voice softened, he adopted a wheedling tack. "Come on, Horst, we're both big boys. You're not dumb enough to believe a demand like that can possibly be met."

"It was not my idea, Mr. Coleman," Horst said. "It was suggested by your former colleague, Mr. Mendoza."

Thanks a lot, buddy!

"Carl! Are you there, you son of a bitch? What in the Sam Hill is he talking about?"

All at once, Carl developed a razor-edged awareness of the subtle danger of the situation. Coleman was fishing for information, trying to confirm his obvious suspicion that Horst intended to take the ultimate hostage while fearful of putting any smart ideas in Klingerman's head in the unlikely event that Horst hadn't thought of it already. Carl only wished *he* had been so careful. Now he had to explain himself to Coleman in front of Klingerman without screwing up and setting off something even worse.

"I . . . uh . . . was able to defuse a . . . potential conflict situation by suggesting that public negotiations on TV would . . . make the contract ironclad," he said. Coleman should be able to figure that one out, if he hadn't already.

"Not such a dumb idea for an amateur," Coleman admitted sourly. "But why in hell did you have to suggest a starring role for the Big Enchilada?"

"Oh, that was my idea," Horst said. "The terms have already been negotiated, so why not offer the President himself the opportunity to take credit for resolving the crisis?"

"And if there's some little glitch in the fine print?"

"Will there be, Coleman?"

Horst was fishing too. The two of them were flicking lures in each other's faces like fly fishermen working the surface of a stream. Big shadowy shapes were swimming around down there, but none of them were biting.

"Look, Horst, I gotta tell you right now there is no way on Earth that the President of the United States walks into that building, and this comes from the Agency, and the FBI, and the Secret Service, and the Joint Chiefs of Everything, who for once have actually managed to agree on something."

"This is not your President's decision to make himself?"

"Buddy, if the President were crazy enough to walk in there, he'd be certifiable, an' they'd throw a net over him and drag him off to the filbert factory. It ain't gonna happen."

"Then the blood will be on his hands. That is *my* decision to make."

"Right, you'll smear yourselves all over the stratosphere, takin' innocent lambs with you, and *he'll* get pounded in th' polls for bein' a bloodthirsty pussy!"

"You think not? You think the . . . spin doctors, as you call them, can make it appear otherwise?"

"Well you wouldn't be around to find out, now would you, Horst ol' buddy?" Coleman said. "Come on, Klingerman, what are you *really* after?"

Horst Klingerman glanced at Helga. Carl did not like the knowing look that passed between them. He locked eyes with Kelly and smiled fatuously.

"Perhaps you had better have a talk with our agent," he said and punched out the connection.

"A damn good question, Horst, what *are* you really after?" Kelly Jordan demanded. "Don't you think we have a right to know?"

Malcolm and Nigel stood there on one side of her, glowering at Klingerman, and it dawned on Carl that these two punkers, at least, just might be up to a bit of bother to save their own skins, unlike Warren, whose reedy frame and laid-back body language did not exactly speak of combat readiness. Kelly herself was just a kid who probably had never even fired a piece.

Helga's pupils were dilated to the max; she looked as if she had already gobbled enough speed to be ready to bite the heads off live chickens. Ahmed seemed to have gone into a sort of prepatrol trance Carl knew all too well. Paulo was unreadable. Jaro and Hiroshi were doing guard duty. One was in it for the video footage and the other thought he was some kind of friggin' samurai.

You didn't need much of a scorecard to figure out who would come out on top if things got physical.

But Horst Klingerman wasn't pushing it, at least not yet.

"But you *do* know what I'm after, Kelly," he said with a smile. "Only what we've agreed upon by collective consensus. The American government must send a representative here to finalize the terms of our negotiated surrender in public."

"No one said anything about the President! They'll never agree to that, and you know it! You're trying to kill the whole arrangement, aren't you? It's a nonnegotiable demand designed to be rejected!"

Horst didn't raise his voice. "Nonnegotiable? Who said nonnegotiable?"

"You just told Coleman—"

Horst laughed. "Should I have told him that it was a bargaining position not meant to be taken seriously?" he said reasonably.

"That in the end, we would settle for a figure of lesser stature? Why, what would *our agent* say if I had done such a foolish thing, Kelly? Correct me if I am wrong, but I do not think that is the way deals are negotiated in your Hollywood."

9:11 A.M.

"ALLAN WAS QUITE PLEASED with the show," were Leonard Isaacs' first words when his secretary put him on the line. "He asks me to tell Kelly that he appreciates how tastefully and carefully she handled his . . . image problems."

"Terrific," Kelly Jordan said, "but how did the show itself go down?"

Heather had to smile despite the circumstances. For despite the circumstances, Kelly's tone of voice and her look of anxious anticipation were not all that unlike those of an actress waiting for her agent to cut the chitchat and get down to telling her the network reaction to her pilot.

"Well, the ratings were good, and StarNet is happy, and there's no real doubt we've got a go," Isaacs said. "Of course, you *are* going to need some work on not being overwhelmed by actors, they *do* tend to take over if you let them, it's supposed to be *your* show, after all, you're going to have to be more assertive and not let them hog the lines. But for a first try, it wasn't bad at all, Kelly. Sorry I couldn't send you the usual bouquet of roses."

Kelly sat there beaming at the speakerphone as if the flowers had indeed somehow arrived, with Malcolm, Nigel, and Warren standing behind her like a supporting cast, which, being three quarters of the crew of the show in question, they more or less were.

But, being below-the-line types, they were less bedazzled by the limelight than she was.

"But what about this bloody fookin' business about the President?" Nigel demanded.

"Yeah, has that thrown a fookin' spanner inna clockwork?"

The two cameramen eyed Horst Klingerman sourly.

Horst sat between Helga and Ahmed on the other side of the crescent of chairs they had once again pulled together in front of the speakerphone table in anticipation of a day spent living on the phone lines. Helga shot the cameramen a dirty look. Paulo, seated closest to the center, stared into space. Ahmed didn't react either.

Horst looked back at Nigel and Malcolm evenly, revealing nothing.

"I have to admit I'm unhappy with that," Isaacs said. "Things like that, you don't keep from your agent."

"Frankly, I didn't think it was any of your business, Isaacs," Horst told him.

"If it's *your* business, then ten percent of it is *my* business," Isaacs said evenly. "If you had told me what you were going to do, I could have put a writer on it, and believe me, you needed one. Those lines you gave poor Toby to read sounded like something out of *The Communist Manifesto*. And it would have been much more effective to have had *Kelly* read them; she's supposed to be the star, remember?"

"You're . . . you're not unhappy with the idea?" Kelly stammered.

"Only with the script, which was amateur night, and the direction, which was nonexistent."

"You don't think Horst made a mistake demanding the President?"

"Mistake!" Isaacs said. "It was a terrific piece of business! One of the problems with this package was that we needed an upbeat dramatic climax for the movie, and now we've got it!"

For the life of her, Heather could not tell whether Lennie Isaacs was really so narrowly focused on the Industry bottom line, or whether he was playing the part of a crass Hollywood cigar-chomper in order to control the situation, or whether both might not somehow be true, if there might not be Method in his madness.

Certainly he had them off balance.

"You . . . *like* the idea, Isaacs?" Horst stammered.

"It's brilliant, Horst, it's perfect," Isaacs crooned. "The President steps through a cordon of troops and walks across the parking lot all by himself, no Secret Service, he's met by you at the entrance, cut to the studio—"

"Are we talking about the real thing, or your movie?" Horst demanded.

"There's a difference?" Isaacs said.

Then, after a moment of reflection . . . "Well, yeah, in the film you'll all be wearing these Green Army Commando berets I've got people working on, and maybe when the President leads everyone out of the building, you put one on his head, and you could all salute each other or something, if you don't think that's a little too hokey. . . ."

"Are you *serious*?" Horst cried.

"Not completely," Leonard Isaacs said in quite another voice. "Are you? I sure hope not."

"What do you mean by that, Isaacs?"

"How shall I put this in terms you can understand?" Isaacs said silkily. "It's a great final scene, Horst, and a terrific cameo for someone. However, while I don't like admitting it, even Leonard Isaacs has his limits. So it pains me to say it at least my honest ten percent of what it pains you to hear it. I just can't get you the President, Horst. I have it on the ultimate authority that he's just plain unavailable. We're just going to have to be professional about it and come up with alternate casting."

Brilliant, Heather thought, absolutely brilliant! He's constructed this inner movie in which he plays the front office so he can warp Horst out of the role of angry terrorist and into the role of the talented but temperamental director demanding a star that will put *his* film way over budget!

"Alternate casting? What means alternate casting, Isaacs?"

"Let me put it this way, Horst. Once upon a time, certain economic powers in California wanted to elect themselves a governor. The script called for an All-American cowboy in a business suit who could flimflam the voters into allowing the needy to have their pockets picked in order to further enrich the greedy. A kind of hard sell, as you might imagine, requiring a major talent to play the sheriff. John Wayne was the perfect casting, but the Duke just wasn't available. So they did what had been done before in such circumstances and went for Ronald Reagan."

"The point of which is?"

"The point of which is, Ronnie might have been only second best, but they made it work anyway," Leonard Isaacs said. "And your final scene can work with less-than-ideal casting too, Horst. We don't *have* to have the President. It'll play all right with a lesser figure."

Horst Klingerman smiled, a smile that was entirely out of sync with the truculent tone of voice he used when he spoke.

"I will not settle for some official spokesman or sacrificial token!"

"And you think *I* would?" Isaacs shot back in a wounded tone that was probably about as genuine. "Don't worry, Horst, I won't let you down and accept some bit player. Maybe I can't get you the President, but I won't accept anything less than Cabinet rank for a role like this. The attorney general. The FBI director. A Supreme Court justice. We'll have to see who they make available and decide which way we want to go on it."

"Well . . . perhaps demanding the President *was* a bit unrealistic," Horst said in a tone of tentative sullen resignation, though his canary-eating smile never wavered. "You are sure you can get them to send a . . . a major government figure?"

Heather realized that Isaacs was not the only one who was capable of a little acting.

"Trust me," Isaacs told him. "They'll probably try to give us a list of loxes with instapoll ratings so lousy they're willing to try anything, but I'm in the catbird seat, don't worry. You keep playing Bad Cop insisting you'll settle for nothing less than the President, and I'll play Good Cop persuading you to reluctantly accept whatever we decide is second-best casting. You can handle that, can't you?"

"I believe I can manage it," Horst said dryly.

"Great. Now I'm gonna have to play some hardball, so you sit tight and don't expect to hear from me till after lunch. I've got a lot of calls to make. Ciao."

2:35 P.M.

WITH NOTHING ELSE TO do but wait for a callback from their agent, the Green Army Commandos had taken to whiling away the idle hours by arguing, while Eddie Franker and his fellow hostages whiled away *their* tense boredom trying to eavesdrop.

What Eddie had been able to hear was somewhat less than reassuring.

"Great performance, Horst," Kelly Jordan had drawled sarcastically as soon as Isaacs hung up.

"Why, what do you mean, Kelly, *you're* the star, isn't that what your agent said?" Klingerman said superciliously.

"You're *jealous*!"

"Why, of course not! It *is* your show, isn't it? I certainly could not handle the image problems of degenerate movie stars so . . . tastefully and carefully."

"You really *are* jealous!"

"Do you seriously imagine that *I* have any desire to be the star of a *television talk show*?" Klingerman shot back in a much harder tone of voice. "Has your sudden Hollywood stardom blinded you to the fact that some of us *really* do put saving life on Earth ahead of their own ego gratification?"

"Look who the fook's goin' on about bloody ego! The bloke that's demanding to have his fookin' picture took with the Prez a' Yankland on the telly!"

"I don't expect that to really happen," Horst said blithely.

"You don't?" said Warren.

"Of course not."

"Then why—"

"So that Isaacs can use the demand to get us an official important enough so that his word will be seen as binding on the government when it is given before the vast masses on television."

"You really intend to surrender, guy?" Warren hadn't sounded as if he found it credible, and neither had Eddie.

"Why, of course," Horst told him. "Assuming our demands are met, this is much the best outcome."

"It is?" Jordan had said, eyeing Klingerman dubiously.

"Such a television show *could* be a powerful weapon. It is the cause that counts, and if they are really so stupid as to hand us such a weapon, we should indeed take it and use it."

"Why don't I believe you?" Jordan had said.

"Perhaps because you are so obsessed with your own celebrity that you can no longer understand anything but careerism!" Horst had snapped.

On and on like that it had gone as the Green Army Commandos drifted toward the far end of the room, the voices diminishing into only occasional audibility as they sat down to wait it out and the confrontation guttered into poisonous growling and muttering.

". . . FBI director, maybe . . ."

". . . naive victim of co-option . . ."

". . . Bollocks—"

Eddie Franker was wound so tight he almost jumped out of his chair when the phone rang.

Across the room, Kelly and Nigel literally did, and about a beat and a half later, all of them were standing around in a mob in front of the speakerphone waiting for someone to step forward and punch in the call.

Kelly glanced at Horst, Horst glanced at Kelly, Helga eyed Warren, Warren clocked Horst, Nigel stared nervously at Ahmed, and within two rings, the factions were shuffling their feet and sorting themselves out.

Eddie, out of force of professional habit never a man to let a phone ring in his presence more than thrice, hit the button himself.

"Hold please for Leonard Isaacs," an irritably chirpy female voice said.

A maddening thirty seconds or so of a syrupy elevator-music orchestral version of "A Hard Day's Night" . . .

"Well, there's good news, and there's good news," Leonard Isaacs' voice said. "Which do you want to hear first?"

Nobody made a move to sit down. Nobody was amused.

"Get to the point, Isaacs," Horst Klingerman snapped, and for once everyone, both terrorist factions and the hostages too, seemed in total agreement.

"It's a done deal," Isaacs said. "We've got the whole package. StarNet picks up *The Green Army Commando Show*. Sierra Communications is producer of record and won't cooperate with any prosecution. I've been on the horn to my union connections, and your cameramen and production team are in, meaning we can give them work on the show."

"Bloody fookin' terrific," said Nigel. "But what about our littul copper problem?"

"I was getting to that," Isaacs said. "This independent judiciary stuff presents a few complications—"

"Complications?" Horst said.

"Relax, Horst, nothing that a little creative structuring hasn't been able to finesse. You'll all be charged with kidnapping and—"

"Fookin' hell!"

"That's a capital offense, ain't it?"

"It's a *Federal* offense," Leonard Isaacs' voice shouted over the tumult. "That's the whole point. The attorney general was so cute about it, I may offer him a job in my agency. Kidnapping is the most serious charge involved as long as no one gets killed, so it enables the White House to drop everything else, taking California out of the loop entirely. Meaning, you only get tried for kidnapping in a Federal court. Meaning that if you're convicted, the President can pardon you. Which he has promised to do. It's a wrap."

"And we are supposed to take their word of honor, I suppose?" Helga said.

"You really think I'm such an amateur?" Isaacs said. "*Of course* I've got it all on paper! Deal memos from StarNet and Sierra Communications. A letter of intent signed by the President."

"Something which has no legal force," Eddie found himself blurting a microsecond before regretting it.

"Of course not!" Isaacs shot back. "But a promise made by the President's representative before the largest national TV audience since the Kennedy assassination will have plenty of *political* force, better believe it. We're slotting it for seven-thirty tonight to maximize the national prime-time spread. StarNet is about to start dropping thirty-second promo spots every half hour. I've already got it on the wires."

Isaacs laughed. "CNN and the nets are having shit-fits," he said. "The announcement itself is a major news event, so they'd look like idiots if they didn't report it, but you can imagine how happy they are giving free promotion to something that's going to slaughter them in the Nielsens!"

"Do I have this right?" Kelly said slowly. "The President of the United States is going to publicly promise us pardons before there's even a trial? He can really do that?"

"Ford did it for Nixon and Bush did it for Weinberger, and those guys never even came to trial," Isaacs told her. "You probably will, and it'll be to our advantage, weeks and weeks of free hype for *The Green Army Commando Show*. But if you're sentenced to any actual jail time, he'll pardon you out of it. The trial judge will know that, and sentence accordingly, especially since it will be the expressed will of the American people."

"Huh?"

"Of course—"

"I don't—"

"Didn't I tell—"

"Tell us *what*, Isaacs?" Horst Klingerman shouted, his voice cutting through the confusion.

"I guess I hadn't gotten to it, had I?" Leonard Isaacs said. "As you might imagine, the White House would like their public relations ass covered on this separation-of-powers business. So some bright boy came up with the idea of running ongoing instapoll results as a crawl across the live coverage of the actual event. A television first! The people get to express their support for what the President's representative is promising in real time, *as he's doing it*!"

Eddie just couldn't help himself, he couldn't keep those old newshound reflexes from taking over at a time like this, maybe, in some perverse manner, *especially* at a time like this.

"But if the instapolls run *negative*?" he said.

"They won't," Isaacs said with cavalier confidence. "Believe me, their people have run this scenario through the computers against the demographic profiles over and over again, and as long as everyone follows the script, the worst run they have gives the deal a sixty-three percent approval rating. . . ."

"Very clever . . ." Eddie muttered, and then he made himself shut up.

For the question that his old reporter's instinct was prompting him to ask now was, *what if they don't?* What if Horst Klingerman makes new demands? What if he kidnaps the presidential representative?

This, of course, was a question nobody dared to ask, and besides, Eddie already knew the answer.

The instapoll crawl would display the public reaction to *that* in real time too. And the authorities could act accordingly without taking any more political responsibility for the results than Nero did counting the thumbs-up against the thumbs-down on the life of some poor son of a bitch in the Roman Coliseum.

It was hard to deny that in some perverted manner it was a kind of ultimate electronic democracy. Yet it was also somehow an ultimate abdication of moral responsibility on the part of government.

We were only following orders, was the whining excuse of Nazi henchmen. This was so much better, so much more sophisticated, so much more democratic. *We were only following the will of the people as expressed in the polls.* Hitler himself could have copped a plea with that one!

"It gave me an idea and I'd like to run it by you," Isaacs said. "Why not make it a continuing piece of business for *The Green Army Commando Show?* Ongoing instapolls during the interview, so the audience can see its own reaction to the proposed action of the week. It establishes participation, and two eight hundred numbers wouldn't be *that* hard on the budget—"

"Enough of this nonsense!" Horst Klingerman shouted. "Come to the point! *Who* have they proposed as their public representative?"

"You're gonna love this, Horst!"

"I will be the judge of that!"

"It took some doing," Leonard Isaacs said. "They kept throwing names at me, the FBI director, a minor Supreme Court justice, a couple of Cabinet officials want to run for the Senate, a couple of TV preachers, I must admit I was a little surprised as to how many people were *that* desperate for the media exposure. . . . But I kept telling them that my client insisted on the President himself, not one of these turkeys, and I kept knocking 'em down with it until they came up with what I was angling for in the first place."

"Which was?" Horst demanded angrily.

"I don't like to make promises to my clients I'm not sure I can keep, so I didn't mention what I was after because I didn't want to disappoint you if I couldn't pull it off," Isaacs said. "But I *did*. The President was unavailable, but I did get you second best. Mr. Number Two. The Vice-President of the United States himself."

"The Vice-President?" Horst said, not without a certain tawdry awe, and murmurs of surprise and bemused approval went through both factions of the Green Army Commandos.

Eddie Franker was a lot more impressed with the cleverness of the choice than with the office or the man himself.

Vice-presidents, in his experience, came in three basic models, or combinations thereof. A few, like Mondale, Bush, and Gore, were political professionals of some standing chosen as credible understudies. Others, like Quayle, Agnew, Nixon under Eisenhower, seemed to have been chosen as life insurance; I go, and *this bum* is what you get, folks! Mostly, though, they were ticket balancers intended to deliver key states or pieces of party machinery, like Truman, Garner, Lyndon Johnson, though if they did succeed, you never could tell.

The current incumbent was mostly a vice-president of the third kind. The senior senator from Texas, *very* senior, actually, pushing seventy when he was nominated if Eddie remembered correctly, had survived for three terms as a middle-of-the-road figure in a volatile swing state by avoiding strong stands on anything in particular, concentrating instead on polishing his oratory, making himself useful to those whose financial resources would later prove useful to his campaigns, and sinking his tendrils deep into the tender meat of the party machinery in Texas.

A good speaker and even better fund-raiser from a state the President needed, white-haired, dignified, uncontroversial, and clearly of an age that reassured the usual gaggle of wannabe presidential successors that the vice-presidency was his political gold watch rather than a position from which to maneuver upwards and onwards in the manner of Bush or Nixon, he was the perfect unexceptional and unexceptionable administration mouthpiece.

"He has the authority to conduct serious negotiations?" Horst asked naively.

Leonard Isaacs laughed. "He has about enough authority to go to the toilet without informing the White House staff, as long as his office doesn't issue a press release about it before they review the wording," he said. "But he *is* the number two elected official in the United States, and he *is* a professional who can deliver his lines with sincerity and conviction, and he *will* be working from a script we've already all agreed on, and for that matter, he looks a whole lot more presidential than the President himself."

"I suppose this person is acceptable," Horst Klingerman said sourly.

But there was a bright eagerness in his eyes that belied the grudging acceptance in his voice, a thin predatory smile, the merest ghost of a shit-eating grin, perhaps, but enough to give Eddie Franker the good old-fashioned willies.

I suppose this person is acceptable.

Oh, please, said Brer Rabbit, don't throw me into dat briar patch!

3:25 P.M.

IT WAS A DONE deal. Tonight it was all going to be over, he was going to be safely out of here.

But while Toby Inman's head told him that this was true, his gut could not quite believe it. His head told him that he had only been holed up in here for a week, a teeny tiny fraction of his life span, yet somehow this cafeteria, the broadcast studio, the green room, the toilet, had become his whole world, all that was real, and that other world out there had become something like memory's syndicated reruns.

It was almost as if he was somehow *reluctant* to leave the station now, scared of his imminent return to that other more complex world, and that crazy thought itself was more than a little frightening.

It's just the boredom, the tense boredom of waiting, Toby told himself. Or maybe Mendoza's paranoia is becoming catching.

The Green Army Commandos had switched guards again, Paulo and Nigel for Hiroshi and Jaro, apparently so Jaro, Warren, and Eddie could huddle together ironing out the technical details of downlinking the instapoll feed and pumping it up on the air feed while simultaneously uplinking the mix to StarNet, a subject that seemed to be of great interest to the three of them but that glazed Toby's eyes just to hear it.

Horst, Helga, Hiroshi, and Ahmed huddled at another table, whispering and muttering. Kelly and Malcolm sat at a third table, apparently killing time by eyeing the four of them suspiciously.

Which left Toby to sit there with Heather and Carl Mendoza, who kept sneaking paranoid looks over his shoulder at Klingerman's table, then measuring Toby with narrowed eyes for something Toby hoped was not a coffin.

Finally, Toby could take it no longer.

"What's with you, Carl?" he said.

"I've been thinking . . ." Mendoza muttered.

"So I've noticed."

Mendoza glanced at Heather, gave Toby yet another of those unsettling speculative looks, shrugged, turned the shrug into a move closer, hunching towards Toby.

"What I've been thinking, Inman," he said in a near whisper, "is maybe we better think about you and me taking a shot at Horst after all, if it comes down to it."

Heather's eyes widened.

"You *serious,* Carl?" Toby hissed. "I mean, like Isaacs said, it's a done deal, isn't it? The Vice-President walks in here, reads his lines like he's supposed to, and then he leads us all out—"

"Maybe, maybe not," Mendoza grunted. "Maybe Horst takes it into his head not to let it happen. Maybe they move in. Maybe he sticks his hand inside his vest—"

"That's an awful lot of maybes," Toby said.

"Maybe," Mendoza said, grinning sourly. "But if he *does* start making a move toward those remote detonators, whichever of us is near enough is gonna have to make *his* move. Either of us should be able to initiate the action on our own. We oughta have a signal—"

Heather shook her head. "Hey, come on, guys—"

"—either of us thinks he's about to go for his detonators, whoever's close enough goes for him! But in case we're *both* in range, the guy that decides to make the move gives a signal."

"Signal . . . ?"

"Yeah, like . . . like *pick your nose,* left nostril, think you can remember not to go in after any boogers otherwise, Inman?"

Heather's frown broke up into a giggle for just a moment, then she shook her head again. "Look, Carl—"

—and the phone began to ring.

The sudden loud sound froze every conversation.

Horst Klingerman bounded across the room and punched in the call before the third ring cycle had ended.

"Y'all still there?" said the voice of Alex Coleman. "I know that's a stupid question, folks, but I've been so hip deep in the pea-brained behavior of the high and the mighty today that I guess I just don't wanna feel left out."

"What do you want, Coleman?" Horst said harshly.

"That you, Horst old buddy?"

"You want to say something to me, Coleman, you say it, yes."

"Now there's no need to get testy with me, good buddy," Coleman said in sweet tones that seemed to groan with their load of sarcasm like a swamp cypress heavy with Spanish moss. "I just called to congratulate you."

"Congratulate me?" Horst said dubiously. The German's English might not be perfect, but Toby reckoned that even if he understood nothing but Swahili, the music of Coleman's words would have been enough to tell him that he was being shined on.

By this time, everyone in the cafeteria had formed up into a knot behind Horst in front of the speakerphone, except for Jaro and Warren, still too deep in tech talk to bother. And Carl Mendoza, who sat there still eyeing Toby appraisingly like the Wizened Old Trainer in some dumb boxing movie watching the Kid throwing leather amateurishly in some dim tank-town gym. For some reason, Toby found this freezing him in place too.

"Why sure, Horst, you must be feelin' right proud of yourself long about now, I reckon," Coleman went on in the same vein, "dribbling all these agents and spin doctors and bright boys and media wizards like a basketball, well shoot, that ain't bad for a good ol' boy from Deutschland. . . ."

"I have no idea what you are talking about," Horst said evenly, but Toby did not find it convincing in the least.

"Why sure you do," Coleman purred like a puma. "You got the hottest agent in Hollywood, a profession not previously noted for naive bumpkinism, believin' butter won't melt in your mouth, or so you think. You got the spin doctors up there on Pennsylvania Avenue whistlin' your version a' 'Dixie,' now ain'tcha? You got 'em all conspirin' t' drop the Vice-President of the United States right down your throat like happy hour at the alligator farm. Oh, you're a bright lad, good buddy, or so you think, you got 'em all fooled real good. . . ."

Coleman paused for a beat, and when he spoke again, all the goose grease was gone, and his voice was hard and sharp as Mr. Bad Cop. "But don't you get to thinking you're fooling *me*," he said.

"I have no idea what you are talking about, Coleman," Horst said, but there was a slight hint of a stammer in his voice.

"Well now, you go right ahead and play it that way if you want to," Coleman said, reverting to sweet sarcastic form. "Maybe it's for the best. Anyway, all I really wanna do is tell you a story. . . ."

"A story . . . ?"

"A *true* story, Klingerman, wouldn't that be as refreshin' under the circumstances as a nice cold mint julep on a hot July afternoon? Wouldn't y'all like to hear what *really* came down between your hot-shit Hollywood agent and those Beltway bozos?"

"Mr. Isaacs has already told us," Kelly Jordan said. Horst just stood there, not turning to look at her. Nobody moved.

"I'm sure he has," Coleman said. "I'll bet good ol' Lennie went on at considerable length about his Machiavellian efforts on your behalf, what a ball-bustin' brouhaha it was to convince the powers that be to serve up the Vice-President of the United States."

"It's not true?" Kelly blurted.

"Not the way I hear tell," Coleman said. "I wasn't there, but it was too juicy not t'come down the Company grapevine from those what were. Besides which, as the operational point man here, y'might say I had a need to know."

"Why . . . why are you telling us this?" Horst demanded.

"Ain't it obvious?" Coleman said. "I believe *you* have a need to know too."

"Know what, Coleman?"

"What the rules of engagement are," Coleman told him. "Which are that I am to close down this situation one way or another tonight. The Vice-President walks out of there as a hero with y'all, or I am ordered to rescue him from your clutches by force."

"Now who's not telling the truth, Coleman?" Klingerman snapped. "They would never—"

He caught himself short, suddenly aware that Kelly and Malcolm were staring at him in a most paranoid manner, that even Warren and Jaro had risen from their table and were making with the fish-eyed stares.

"You're counting on that, aren't you, Klingerman?" Coleman said. "Push came to shove, why, they'd never risk the life of the *Vice-President of the United States.*"

Horst clammed up. No matter what his intentions, Toby realized with a sinking feeling in his stomach, nothing he could say to that would serve them.

Coleman let them all sweat for a few silent beats. Then he laughed.

"It might amuse you to know that the professed wisdom among Isaacs, the spin doctors, the White House staff, the Large Lasagna, even the old gent from Texas himself it would seem, is more or less exactly the converse, namely that not even a desperado like yourself could possibly be so self-defeating as to screw up such a honey pot of a deal for all concerned for no good reason, why you'd have to be *crazy,* now wouldn't you. . . ."

Horst Klingerman just stood there silently without moving. But Toby could see a clenching of his jaws, a flush spreading up from his neck to the fair skin of his face.

"Of course those whose commission it is to deal with just such irrationality are of a different opinion," Coleman said. "The Secret Service, the FBI, the Agency, unanimously agreed that sending the Vice-President of the United States into a nest of terrorists on the blithe assumption that his survival was guaranteed by the political and economic logic of the situation was . . . was . . . *major assholery,* I believe is the technical term."

"This . . . this is your story, Coleman . . . ?" Horst finally managed to say.

Coleman laughed. "Oh, no, my little story is much more amusing, the foregoing being by way of *backgroundin'* y'all, as we say in the trade. Now the way I hear it, your agent Mr. Isaacs got the White House chief of staff on the horn and read him this long wish list of candidates for the starring role in your little drama. We'll get back to you, they say, after which, there was a lot of internal back-and-forth over the wisdom, or lack thereof, of sending in . . . *some poor schmuck* was apparently the chief of staff's term, to close this supposed sure-thing deal on television."

Coleman paused for a beat, like a well-rehearsed comedian. "Various scenarios were poked through the decision-making software. What came out the other end, like beets through a baby's backside, were two what they call *clades* of outcomes. If no one was sent in to play hero on the tube, any negative consequences, and no positive ones could be modeled, would redound to the administration's disadvantage in the polls. On the other hand, if someone *was* sent in, there were two possibilities, neither of which would have negative spin. The spokesman would emerge with the hostages, in which case the administration would have a live hero, or the Green Army Commandos would put on the black hats and snatch the sucker before the outraged eyes of the American people, in which case, yours truly would be ordered to play Rambo, and they would most likely have a dead one.''

"That's your idea of humor?" Franker said.

"Oh no," Coleman said in a much less supercilious tone of voice. "That's my idea of the kind of cynical behavior on the part of the shitheads that the American people, in their infinite wisdom, have put in charge, that makes my job disgusting. I was just getting to the punch line."

"Which is?" Toby blurted.

"They get back to Isaacs. Okay, the chief of staff says, this is the deal. The Vice-President is what you get, take it or leave it. The Vice-President? says Lennie. That lox? I dunno."

Coleman paused. Toby locked eyes with Carl Mendoza. Carl grimaced, shrugged almost imperceptibly.

"This comes straight from the President himself, says the chief of staff. It does? says your agent. Fuckin' A, says the chief of staff, or words to that effect. . . ."

Another pause. Toby could almost see the grin plastered across the featureless imaginary face of the man he had never met, never seen.

"What the fuck do I have a vice-president for? says our glorious Commander in Chief. Who else am I supposed to send to a funeral that just might turn out to be his own?''

6:11 P.M.

"You sure you really know how to mix this thing?" Eddie Franker said nervously as he watched the numbers crawl across the bottom of the control room's air-feed monitor like an instapoll from hell:

. . . For: 81.35% Against: 18.65% . . . For: 31.30% Against:

68.17% . . . For: 99.90% Against: 0.10% . . . For: 0.00% Against: 100.00% . . .

"Is easy," said Jaro, "feed from downlink transponder into mixing board, mix with camera feed, uplink to StarNet."

The picture on the air-feed monitor was simply a test shot of the empty newsroom set, and the number crawl across the bottom of the screen just some comedian on the other end of the sat link's idea of humor, a test of the circuitry and software, not real instapoll results.

Whatever *they* were.

Yes, the damn instapolls had long since proven their accuracy. But at least to Eddie's knowledge, no one had yet gone so far as to run a real-time instapoll over a breaking news story as it happened. He found it ghoulish, somehow, found it violating a deep journalistic principle he could not quite put a name to.

What comes next? Some poor suicidal bastard out on a window ledge somewhere, a priest trying to talk him down, the whole thing covered live, a real-time instapoll crawl across the screen of a monitor they set up for him? When 50.01 percent of the vox populi are in favor, over you go, kiddo?

Worse still, Eddie suddenly realized, only the necessity of maintaining their credibility as prediction against subsequent facts prevented nefarious whoevers from tweaking the numbers. And now, with the event and the instapoll reaction to it going out simultaneously in real time, cause and effect were totally bollixed, there *weren't* going to be any predictions as such and the facts weren't going to be subsequent, and under dire circumstances like these, with maybe the government itself mixing in. . . .

"Try it again, Nigel, and this time I want a pan onto the entrance, and a reverse zoom at the same time, like you're following a slow walk," Warren babbled into his headset.

One of the monitors displayed a long hand-held shot from a second-story window inside the building on the revamped deployment in the public parking lot facing the front entrance.

Sunset Boulevard had not only been closed to traffic and cleared of rubberneckers, all the parked cars had been removed along with the trash cans and dumpsters. A line of Hummers barricaded the street, parked tail-in toward the station, the large-caliber whatevers mounted on their truck beds pointed ominously inward and upward at the camera. The front parking lot itself had been cleared of all vehicles and turned into a free-fire zone for the line of Federal troops sweating unhappily at so-called ease about ten yards inboard of the Hummers. The buildings overlooking KLAX weren't in the shot, but Eddie found it hard to believe that they hadn't been cleared and loaded with Secret Service and Army snipers.

Without exterior sound, Eddie had no idea of whether military choppers were already overhead, but a quick flip through the competing channels had already told him that every station in town that had a helicopter had already deployed it for coverage, though from all the crappy telephoto shots, it seemed that the authorities had imposed a rather large no-fly zone around the station.

" 'Kay, guy, let's have it. . . ."

The camera slowly began a rather jerky reverse zoom as it panned more smoothly inward toward the building from the line of troops, as if following the phantom promenade of the Vice-President across the parking lot. By the time it reached the lower steps of the entrance, it was nearly vertical, and had the theoretical walker climbed them, the angle would have blocked the shot of his actual entry into the building.

"What do you think, Eddie?" Warren said.

Eddie shrugged. "I'm no director. . . ."

But by default, he *was* more or less the producer.

CNN, the networks, every local station, had mobile units as close as they could get to the KLAX building, but what with the security arrangements, and, Eddie suspected, government media-control policy, that wasn't very. The angle of this shot might lose the Vice-President's moment of entry, but at least KLAX, shooting from the inside out, would have a much closer shot than any of the opposition, constrained to shoot long telephoto shots from distant buildings and useless garbage from far-off choppers.

On the other hand, KLAX's coverage of events outside the building didn't figure to be exactly ideal either, since all they had were the two hand-helds brought into the building by the terrorists. Nigel, who more or less knew what he was doing, was on this one, while Ahmed substituted for him on the number two studio camera, where skill was a lot less critical.

"What do *you* think, Warren?" Eddie said.

Warren scratched at his head. "Well, it's either get this, or lose the whole shot, and put him inside to track them into the studio. . . ."

He shrugged. "Your call, guy," he said. "We just can't cover both without a fourth cameraman."

Which Horst Klingerman would not permit. It had been hard enough to get him to agree to this much. The original setup had put Nigel and Malcolm on the studio cameras, Horst and Kelly on the set with Toby and the Vice-President, leaving Paulo and Hiroshi to guard the building entrances and Helga and Ahmed to keep an eye on Carl and Heather in the green room and Toby in the studio.

Warren had been the one to ask for a third cameraman. "Hey, Horst, without it, all we get is talking heads on a newsroom set. Give me Ahmed, he can handle a studio camera, he's not terrific, but he'll do, and then I can move Malcolm or Nigel—"

"Out of the question!" Klingerman had insisted at first. "This will leave only Helga to guard all of the hostages, and she cannot be in two places at the same time!"

"Well, shit, then move Heather and Mendoza out of the green room and into the studio with you, I *gotta* have Ahmed."

"For what? To show pretty pictures of the Vice-President's arrival?"

"Well . . . uh, yeah . . . I mean . . ."

"This is not a television show!"

"Sure it is, guy, I mean, what if something *happens* when the helicopter lands—"

"Such as—"

"I dunno—"

It had all gone on in front of everyone in the cafeteria, and it had gotten pretty scary, with Horst and Helga getting hot under the collar about this being a serious direct action and not a TV show and Warren and Jaro going on about the coverage. Kelly had finally resolved it, if not exactly to Eddie's current satisfaction.

"Jeez, this is dumb, Horst! You and me and Helga and Malcolm and Ahmed will all be there in the studio! That's *five* of us to do the show and keep an eye on three hostages! What do you think you need, the Bundeswehr? And besides, you can always blow us all up if you think things are getting too dicey, now can't you?"

That had been a serious conversation stopper. Enough, anyway, to get Horst to allow Ahmed to replace Nigel as number two studio cameraman.

But there was no way he would free up one more Commando to provide second hand-held coverage, for that would have left Heather and Carl sitting there in the studio more or less unguarded. And when Eddie had suggested that maybe Heather could fill in, Horst had given him a stare that would've melted glass.

So this was it. Nigel running around with one hand-held like a maniac, and the second hand-held just sitting there invitingly in a corner of the studio without a free pair of hands to pick it up.

Eddie shrugged. "I guess we might as well go with this shot," he said. "At least this way, we get the chopper coming in, the walk across the tarmac, and no one else is gonna have any better. . . ."

He sighed. He might not be a real news director, but he had certainly been station manager for the tightwads who owned KLAX long enough to be resigned to the unfortunate technical realities of a shoestring operation!

He glanced at the air-feed monitor, with its shot of the empty newsroom set and the phony instapoll figures crawling across the bottom of it. He managed a little smile.

After all, whoever was watching what channel as the Vice-President landed and approached the building wasn't going to mean jack shit once he was inside. At that point they would all be reaching for their remotes out there in televisionland.

Because from that moment on, KLAX-TV was going to be on the inside looking out, and the competition was going be on the outside looking in.

6:51 P.M.

TOBY AND CARL SAT across the green room from each other trying to avoid obvious eye contact, at least while Helga was watching, while Heather Blake perched on the edge of her chair, wishing that she had never overheard that stupid business about nose-picking signals.

Or at least been able to say something coherent before Alex

Coleman's phone call had interrupted. Or hadn't been so distracted by Coleman's story that she had forgotten all about it until now.

If something *did* cause Horst Klingerman to try to blow them all up, there was admittedly nothing to be lost by trying to stop him.

But Heather didn't trust Toby *or* Carl to read Horst Klingerman correctly and act accordingly. Better me than either of them.

For Heather was pretty certain that *she* could not only read Horst, but that she could, well, *handle* him.

And while she understood her effect on the heterosexual male of the species far too well to discredit the sexual component, there was more to it than that. On some level she could not quite put into words, even to herself, she *understood* Horst Klingerman a lot better than Horst understood himself.

She had, well, *controlled* him with a few basic acting tricks and what probably had appeared to be a lot of courage. But courage had had little to do with it.

Maybe Horst Klingerman was capable of killing someone in a fight. Maybe he was capable of throwing those detonator switches and killing himself and everyone around him in a hot moment of passion.

But he couldn't fool Heather Blake. Horst Klingerman could not kill an unarmed innocent woman in cold blood. When push came to shove, she could, and he wouldn't.

If necessary, Heather would stake her life on that.

That wasn't courage. That was her considered professional judgment.

7:02 P.M.

THE GREEN ROOM DOOR opened, and Malcolm stuck his head inside. "All right, ducks, bring 'em on out," he called out to Helga, "it's gettin' t'be showtime!"

Helga stood up, gestured toward the door with her Uzi, and Carl Mendoza popped up off his chair, maybe a shade faster than he had intended, his nerves sizzling with adrenaline.

Heather got up a moment later, Inman followed, a little hesitantly, and Helga marched them across the hall to the newsroom studio, with Carl bouncing along on the balls of his feet in the lead like a relief pitcher who has finally gotten the sign from the manager after three innings of warming up in the bullpen.

That was what his body told him, but his mind knew that it was a frustrating illusion. No one was going to hand him the ball after the walk across the outfield to the mound. Instead, they were gonna sit him down in his warm-up jacket in the dugout to wait, and watch, and sweat, and hope he was just being paranoid.

Kelly Jordan was already seated in Carl's usual slot, looking pretty wired herself, her face mirrored in expanding and contracting perspectives on the monitor as Ahmed practiced camera angles. Malcolm was already behind the other camera, putting on his headset. Klingerman was nowhere to be seen.

Inman stepped around the desk, started to take his place in the center anchor position, but Helga waved him off with the barrel of her gun. "That's for the Vice-President," she said, "you sit next to Kelly."

Meaning, Carl realized, that the Vice-President was going to be positioned between Inman and Klingerman, shielding Horst from any sudden moves by Toby.

Shit!

Was that a clever move on the part of Klingerman? Carl wondered. Or am I just getting *really* paranoid?

As Helga marched Heather and himself toward the folding chairs near the rear of the studio, passing by the front of the newsdesk, Carl managed to pause for just a beat and make eye contact with Inman.

What he saw, or what he imagined he saw, was pretty cold comfort.

Toby Inman looked right back at him, but nobody seemed to be at home. Nobody but the old familiar KLAX-TV anchorman personality waiting to go on, bland Anglo good looks staring right through him into space.

No, Carl realized as he moved away from the set and glanced at the monitor.

Inman wasn't staring into space. Malcolm was using him to set up his camera, and KLAX-TV's prime-time anchorman, Toby Inman, was practicing his professional smile as he watched himself on television.

7:16 P.M.

THE MORE THINGS STAY the same, the more they change, things are more like they are now than they've ever been before, or however all that goes, Toby Inman thought inanely as he sat there as usual waiting to go on the air while the tech types adjusted their mikes and cameras.

Of course, the cameramen had machine-pistols slung over their shoulders, and so did the control-room crew, and his cohost, or cohostess, or whatever the hell to call her, not to mention Helga, who stood there in the back of the studio hovering over Carl and Heather like a carrion bird, over *his* weathergirl, *his* sportscaster, the guys that were supposed to be up here with him.

I am babbling to myself inside my own head, Toby realized. Is this what they mean by stage fright?

Ordinarily, at this point, while he served as a dummy for adjusting the cameras and the sound levels, he would be focusing himself by reviewing the script that was going to crawl across the teleprompter.

But tonight, folks, there would be no teleprompter crawl, Inman the Magnificent would be working without a net or a script.

Well, not exactly, Toby told himself. There *was* a script of sorts, worked out by the Vice-President's press secretary, and StarNet, and his brand-new agent Leonard Isaacs, and presented to him by Horst Klingerman, who had apparently signed off on it.

At 7:30 P.M., the Vice-President's helicopter would come down in the parking lot. Three minutes for him to descend, cross the concrete, and be met by Horst and Hiroshi at the front entrance. No mike, no dialogue, so Toby would have to narrate. Another three minutes to get him into the studio, unavoidable dead air, which would have to be filled by hand-held shots of the scene outside the station taken by Nigel and Toby's ad-libbed voice-over.

That's going to be the worst of it, Inman, Toby tried to tell himself. About six minutes of babble over the pictures that you're just going to have to wing.

After which, introduce the Vice-President, Horst, Kelly, then lean back and shut up.

Not really that difficult, is it, Inman? Toby thought, regarding his own image on the studio monitor. Your grandmother could handle that much without a script.

Toby took a deep slow breath and regarded his own video image on the monitor. He curled the muscles of the corners of his lips upward, and it smiled. He tightened the muscles of his brows and it frowned.

It's all right, that's *you* up there, the KLAX-TV Evening News, with *Toby Inman*! You control the horizontal. You control the vertical. He will jump when you say frog.

Or will he?

Toby found himself looking into the eyes of a stranger. This was the face in the shaving mirror, yes, but . . .

Perhaps it was just the lack of makeup, but the face up there seemed ten years older. Perhaps it was just a trick of the lighting, but it seemed to be looking back at him with a gleam in the pixels of its eyeballs, with an unsettling smirk of superiority, with a strange phosphor-dot life of its own.

7:30 P.M.

Onscreen:

STATION LOGO.
"KLAX-TV, Los Angeles!"

A close-in telephoto shot from a somewhat elevated angle on a continuous line of soldiers, enough to fill the screen from this angle. They're wearing fatigues and combat helmets, standing at ease with their M-16s slung.

Toby Inman's voice-over: "Good evening, ladies and gentlemen, this is Toby Inman, speaking to you from inside KLAX-TV, as

all of us, hostages and Green Army Commandos alike, await the
. . . uh, imminent arrival of the Vice-President of the United
States, who, uh, has been rushed here from Washington by military
jet, and should be, er, arriving from the airport by helicopter any
time now to negotiate our—wait a minute . . . I think . . ."

The soldiers don't move, but their eyes do look upward as the
camera reverse-zooms with jerky and dizzying rapidity into a much
wider shot across the empty parking lot on the cordon of soldiers
and the HMVs behind them, the upward angle of their Gatling
rocket-launcher carousels more or less matching the downward angle of the shot.

Just the empty parking lot for a couple of beats. Then two black
shapes drop into the shot from above.

Toby Inman's voice-over: "Yes, here come the helicopters, I
guess, but . . ."

Two helicopters descend onto the concrete of the parking lot
about halfway between the troops and the building and about
twenty-five yards apart.

They are painted in green-and-brown camouflage patterns. Machine guns protrude from the greenhouses below and forward of
the cockpits. Multiple rocket launchers and Gatling guns depend
from pylons attached to the slightly drooping stub-wings hung from
the fuselages. The rotors continue to turn slowly at idle speed.

Toby Inman's voice-over: "Those look like, uh, military choppers, uh, maybe some kind of escort . . . yes, here it comes, I
think. . . ."

Another helicopter descends to the parking lot behind and between the two gunships, a large single-rotor transport model,
painted blue and white and bearing the presidential seal on either
side of its fuselage. The engine powers down, the rotor slowly coming to a stop, while those of the gunships continue to whirl slowly
and regularly and somehow ominously like the wings of hovering
yellow jackets.

A hatch opens amidships in the left side of the fuselage, and a
built-in step-ramp flips down automatically into position. One,
two, three, four men in blue suits double-time down it, flank the
ramp, stand there in military at-ease position with no display of
weapons, while the line of troops well behind the helicopters unsling
their M-16s and bring them to port arms.

The camera zooms in on the open hatchway, but the angle is bad, and nothing is clearly visible until a man has cleared it and is walking slowly down the steps. He's tall, spare, wearing a light-gray suit that's almost pearlescent, a white shirt, a black western string tie. His hair is thick, earlobe length, dramatically snow-white.

Toby Inman's voice-over: "The Vice-President of the United States!"

The Vice-President descends, glances backward at the troops well behind the helicopters, says something to the Secret Service men, one of them says something back, the Vice-President nods, turns, begins walking toward the camera, between the two gunships, then past them. The camera zooms in, trying for a close-up, but the distance is too great to frame anything narrower than a head-to-waist shot for long beats.

Toby Inman's voice-over, somewhat hushed, like a sportscaster doing a golf match: "As per the agreement with the Green Army Commandos, the Vice-President is approaching the building alone, without his Secret Service escort. . . ."

The Vice-President continues to walk toward the camera, closer into the shot. His gait is even and steady, but slow and somewhat stiff-kneed, the gait of an old man in rather good shape. About halfway between the helicopters and the building entrance, the camera is finally able to frame a close-up, the high angle foreshortening the Vice-President's face. His nose is long and eagle-bridged but thin, the nostrils flaring. His brows are thick and dramatically white. His mouth is broad and thick-lipped, but the lips seem a bit artificially pursed. His skin is tanned, seamed with a fine webwork, like an old farmer who has spent his working life in the sun. His blue eyes look unknowingly straight into the camera but reveal no emotion.

As he continues to approach the building entrance, the camera slowly reverse-zooms to more or less match his pace, trying to hold the close-up, but as he nears the building, the high angle allows it to get nothing but the nose jutting out below the thick shock of white hair.

Toby Inman's voice-over: ". . . the Vice-President is nearing the entrance. . . ."

The camera is shooting almost straight down now, getting not much more than the top of the Vice-President's head as he mounts the stairs, then nothing at all but the ground as he climbs them out of the camera's ability to get the shot.

Toby Inman's voice-over: "Uh . . . we can't show you this, folks, but, uh, down there, the Vice-President is being met by Horst Klingerman, Chairperson of the Green Army Commandos. . . ."

The camera abruptly gives up on the empty shot, sweeps around uncertainly, settles on a shot on the lurking gunships, their rotors still thrumming, petrol fumes visible in the heat waves of their exhausts.

Toby Inman's voice-over: ". . . but stay tuned to KLAX, folks, because in a couple of minutes, we'll begin our *exclusive coverage* of the negotiations between the Green Army Commandos and the Vice-President of the United States, and *that* will be brought to you *only* by StarNet, live, from the studios of KLAX-TV, Los Angeles!"

7:35 P.M.

". . . UH, YES, AS YOU can . . . as I've already said, the, uh, security outside is . . . uh, very tight, those are HMV 'Hummer vehicles' you're seeing now, folks, and those things on the back of them pointed up at the station look like giant revolver barrels, they're, uh, some kind of rapid-fire multiple rocket launchers. . . ."

Where the fuck were Klingerman and the Vice-President? By the studio clock, Toby Inman could see that this had really been only a couple of minutes, but those two minutes had been the longest eternity of dead air that Toby had ever been called upon to fill.

While Nigel flashed shots of the choppers, the troops, the background of the Hollywood Hills almost visible through the smog, Toby had been forced to improvise a line of babble that sounded like gibberish even to him.

". . . now those helicopters, they look to me like Air Force types, why they've left their motors running, your guess is as good as mine . . . uh, maybe they're afraid they'll run their batteries down. . . ."

Why couldn't they have dropped a commercial in here to—

The studio door finally opened, and the Vice-President of the United States entered, followed at two paces behind by Horst Klingerman, with his Uzi pointed squarely at the pit of the old man's back.

"Well, uh, here's the Vice-President and Horst Klingerman now!" Toby exclaimed with a feeling of gratitude that almost emerged as a sigh of relief.

Toby clocked the Vice-President for silent beats as Horst marched him to the set. There was courage in the way he walked stonily and steadily with a machine gun aimed at his back. His blue eyes were watery and maybe a bit bloodshot, but his gaze seemed glacially calm under the circumstances. He didn't smile, but he didn't frown either. His face was a kind of official mask of authority. In the flesh, as on the tube, the Vice-President looked more impressively presidential than the President himself ever did.

Horst gestured with his gun, and the Vice-President slowly made his way behind the desk and into the long shot on the set as displayed on the monitor. Slowly, he took his seat to Toby's left, making eye contact with the camera professionally all the while. A beat later, Horst sat down to the Vice-President's left, placed his Uzi conspicuously on the desk top, and his right hand conspicuously atop the grip.

Now what? Toby thought nervously.

Glancing at the monitor, he saw his own face in close-up. Glancing at the control-booth window, he saw Eddie Franker waving frantically, then crawling his hand slowly across his chest.

Right! Yeah!

"Well, ladies and gentlemen, we're about to begin these negotiations, but before we do, KLAX-TV and StarNet have arranged for *you* to take part yourselves. We'll be displaying the instapoll results continuously, so that the participants will have the benefit of *your* opinion on . . . uh, what's going on. For, call eight hundred, six eight zero, one one one one. Against, call eight hundred, six eight zero, zero zero zero zero. It's as simple as that, and remember, the numbers are toll-free, so use them as often as you like."

Toby paused, tried to remember the tone of voice in which this was done, checked his face on the monitor, made it as dignified as he knew how.

"And now, to present the government's proposal to the Green

Army Commandos . . . ladies and gentlemen, uh, my fellow Americans . . . the Vice-President of the United States!"

The Vice-President half turned to favor Toby with a grave, serious, really impressively dignified little professional smile, the kind that had no doubt launched a thousand fund-raising speeches.

"Thank you . . . ah, Toby," he said in a rich gravelly baritone only lightly perfumed with a hint of Texas twang.

The bourbon on his breath, however, was almost enough to blow Toby away.

7:38 P.M.

Onscreen:

A CLOSE-UP ON THE Vice-President of the United States, his leathery face evenly tanned beneath the leonine mane of white hair, the thick white brows dramatically framing the blue eyes that look unwaveringly into the camera. He looks almost like a character actor cast in the part of himself.

"My fellow Americans. As you all know, this television station has been in the hands of a terr—of the Green Army Commandos for the past seven days. And as you all know, they have threatened to blow it up, killing themselves and their hostages, and releasing a cloud of plutonium dust into the atmosphere, or so at least it is claimed, if your government attempts to retake it by force."

His voice is mellifluous, sincere, his cadence deliberate, evenly paced, his demeanor grave but composed.

"Now of course, you would not want your government to condone illegal acts, however idealistically motivated, for this would undermine the principle of the rule of law upon which this great nation was founded. Those who break the law must be brought before a jury of their peers."

The first instapoll figures crawl across the bottom of the screen from left to right: For: 69.10% . . . Against: 30.90% . . .

The lines at the corners of the Vice-President's mouth curl upward slightly, the merest hint of a smile.

"On the other hand, neither the American people nor their elected representatives would wish innocent victims to perish in the name of absolute justice, for the right to life, liberty, and the pursuit of happiness is another sacred pillar of our democratic form of government."

Instapoll crawl: For: 67.84% . . . Against: 32.16% . . .

"And while the Green Army Commandos have indeed violated the law, they have not yet harmed their hostages, contaminated the city of Los Angeles, or destroyed private property, though they have threatened to do so. So under the circumstances, your government has wisely chosen patience and forbearance over . . . precipitous action to prevent the loss of life, the peaceful path of negotiation, rather than . . . recourse to military force. . . ."

Instapoll crawl: For: 53.33% . . . Against: 46.67% . . .

"Then too, these . . . uh . . . Green Army Commandos are neither Communists, ideological extremists, or narcoterrorists, and their demands thus far are . . . ah . . . more or less related to the concerns for the survival of the biosphere of this planet without which . . . without which . . . uh, which all thinking citizens share. . . ."

The Vice-President hesitates for a beat, looking solemnly into the camera, blinks once, twice, thrice, as if searching for a thread he has lost.

"So, after due consideration, and with regard for the lives of the hostages and the citizens of Los Angeles, private property, and the manifest desires of you, the American people, whose will we serve, as expressed in the instapolls, as well as . . . uh . . . indications of reasonableness on the part of the Green Army Commandos, we have agreed to conduct these open and public negotiations to see if we cannot reach a peaceful resolution of this hostage crisis acceptable to all concerned and to the American people. . . ."

Instapoll crawl: For: 72.12% . . . Against: 27.88% . . .

The Vice-President smiles slightly again, but this time it seems like a bit of a sickly smile, his lips have become somewhat unpleasantly overmoist, and the shooting lights have brought beads of sweat out on his lined forehead.

"Uh . . . press of matters of state has prevented the President from conducting these public negotiations himself, as he so . . . dearly wished to, but . . . but . . . they . . . he has given me a

detailed set of proposals . . . and fully authorized me to . . . con-
clude a binding agreement before the American people with . . .
with the full weight and majesty of the . . . ah, government of the
United States. . . ."

Instapoll crawl: For: 48.41% . . . Against: 51.59% . . .

The Vice-President stares sincerely into the camera for a silent
beat. For another. He glances nervously to the left, then to the
right, stares fixedly back at the camera.

Cut to a somewhat crookedly framed close-up on Toby Inman,
looking confused himself, in the process of turning back to face the
camera.

"Uh . . . thank you, Mr. Vice-President. Well, ah, before we
begin, would either of you like to make an opening statement?"

Cut to a full shot on the newsroom set as Toby Inman glances
to his right at Kelly Jordan, to his left past the Vice-President at
Horst Klingerman. Kelly looks at Horst questioningly, Horst looks
at Kelly perhaps a shade ironically.

"Ladies first," he says.

Cut back to the same badly framed close-up on Toby Inman.

"Kelly Jordan, Minister of Information of the Green Army
Commandos, and, uh, host of the forthcoming *Green Army Commando Show,* which StarNet will be bringing to you live, right here
from the studios of KLAX-TV Los Angeles, providing . . . after
. . . uh, Kelly?"

A much better framed close-up on Kelly Jordan, serious but
smiling, looking quite composed and rather professional as she plays
to the camera.

"Thank you, Toby. And thanks to all of *you* out there who have
defeated the California Seawater Referendum, supported the Brazilian coffee boycott and the Northwest apple boycott, made the, uh,
personal risks we've taken, ah, worthwhile, and made *The Green
Army Commando Show* possible. Hey, maybe *we're* the ones who've
shown *you* the power of your own direct action, but we couldn't
have done it without you, folks!"

She projects a certain species of subdued stellar humility. She
turns and beams a warm smile in the general direction of the Vice-
President.

"And thank *you,* Mr. Vice-President, for having the ball . . .
for coming here tonight," she says with fetching sincerity. "Only

people like us, who have put our own lives and liberty on the line to save life on Earth, can really appreciate the courage that you've shown in trusting *yours* to our word of honor. And we won't let you down. Hey, when all this is over, you've got an open invitation to appear on *The Green Army Commando Show*. Anytime you want!"

She pauses for no more than half a beat, as she turns back to the camera. "Toby?"

Instapoll crawl: For: 71.11% . . . Against: 28.89% . . .

A close-up on Toby Inman, properly framed this time.

"Horst?" he says, glancing in the direction of Horst Klingerman, nodding, turning back to face the camera.

"Horst Klingerman, Chairperson of the Green Army Commandos."

A close-up on Horst Klingerman, but a wider one, including the Uzi on the desk in front of him, his right hand resting on the grip. Klingerman looks directly into the camera, but he doesn't smile, and the rapidity of his blink rate is noticeable.

"Yes. I am not good at making speeches in English. I would not be a good television talk-show host. I am a man of direct action. So, yes, as a man of direct action, I can respect the American Vice-President for putting himself in physical danger, even if he is only doing what he has been ordered to do by others whose courage is another matter."

He shrugs, he moves his hand to the barrel of his gun, stroking it nervously.

Instapoll crawl: For: 41.30% . . . Against: 58.70% . . .

"But we are not here to talk about courage, yes?"

He turns to the right, toward the Vice-President, and as he does, there is a cut to a two-shot on Horst Klingerman and the Vice-President, the Vice-President facing the camera, then slowly turning to make eye contact with Klingerman.

"We are here to listen to a proposal by the government of the United States, and to give you our response. So you may proceed with your statement of your government's position."

The Vice-President's eyes narrow, his nostrils flare, he's apparently not much used to exercising forbearance in the face of such lèse majesté. He glares at Klingerman for a moment. Klingerman glares back. Slowly, Klingerman takes his hand off the gun barrel and folds his arms across his chest.

Instapoll crawl: For: 35.00% . . . Against: 65.00% . . .

The Vice-President blinks, turns to face the camera as it moves in for a close-up, looking fully the septuagenarian in this moment, his lips wet with spittle, obviously sweating, clearly unnerved by what he has seen in Horst Klingerman's eyes, but still too much the professional to let it leak into his voice or really publicly crack that image of presidential composure.

"Yes, well, the, uh, position of the United States government is, uh, quite clear. The Green Army Commandos must release their hostages unharmed, vacate these premises, and surrender to the duly constituted Federal authorities. That was our position on the first day of this, uh, situation, and that is our position now. . . ."

He forces a rather horrid false smile.

"After all, the only other possible alternatives would be the very bloodbath of destruction which I've, uh, come here to avoid, or, uh, some horrible domestic equivalent of the endless Iranian hostage crisis which destroyed the Carter administration, and which no government worthy of the name could indefinitely permit. . . ."

Instapoll crawl: For: 79.37% . . . Against: 20.63% . . .

Horst Klingerman's voice-over: "This insulting ultimatum is your government's official position—"

A quick clumsy cut to a two-shot on the Vice-President and Horst Klingerman. Klingerman's arms are no longer folded across his chest; he's got his right hand back on his gun, and he's glowering at the Vice-President.

"—*this* is your idea of *serious negotiation?*"

The Vice-President just sits there blinking, sweating, and staring at Klingerman for a beat.

"We *are* willing to stipulate terms," he finally says, "we are *not* talking about *unconditional* surrender."

"I do not accept the term *surrender* at all!" Klingerman snaps. "I only—"

Kelly Jordan's voice-over, quickly and loudly: "Let's just hear your terms, okay?"

A quick cut to a close-up on Kelly Jordan, looking rather exasperated. "That's what this is all supposed to be about, isn't it, Horst—?"

Horst Klingerman's voice-over, sarcastically: *"Is* it, Kelly?"

Instapoll crawl: For: 19.18% . . . Against: 80.82% . . .

Toby Inman's voice-over: *"Please!"*

A close-up on Toby Inman, his hands in front of his chest, palms up, in a shrug of dismay, his eyes rolling in exasperation for a beat. Then the anchorman seems to take over.

"Look, folks," he says, genially but with a this-is-*my*-show tone of authority, "we're not going to get anywhere if everybody starts talking at once! So, Kelly, Horst, will you just let the man speak?"

He flashes a pasty gallows-humor grin. "You can always fight among yourselves about it later," he says. "Mr. Vice-President . . . ?"

A close-up on the Vice-President, looking to the left.

"Uh . . . thank you, Toby," he says, turning to face the camera, his face sweaty and trembly, an unseemly crust of drying spittle at the corners of his wet lips.

"As I was about to say, Toby, I *am* authorized to offer terms on behalf of, uh, the United States government. As you know, this great nation of ours was founded on the sacred principle of . . . uh . . . separation of powers, the, ah . . . jury system . . . the . . . independence of the judiciary . . ."

Instapoll crawl: For: 39.51% . . . Against: 60.49% . . .

Horst Klingerman's voice-over, harshly: "This means *what?*"

Toby Inman's voice-over, loudly: "Please! Will you let the man finish, Horst!"

"Thank you, Toby," the Vice-President says once again, rather like a mantra, as if the standard acknowledgment of the standard anchorman allows him to function as if this were the standard talk show that he has done a thousand times. He stealthily cleans his lips with a quick flick of his tongue, his voice seems to firm, become, well, vice-presidential.

"What it means, Mr. Klingerman, for those unfamiliar with our form of government, is that not even the President of the United States has the power to overturn the verdict of a jury or direct the sentencing decision of a presiding judge—"

Horst Klingerman's voice-over: "Then what—"

Kelly Jordan's voice-over: "Oh, shut up, Horst!"

Toby Inman's voice-over, louder than either of them: "Shut up everyone who says shut up!"

That, at least, produces a beat of silence into which the Vice-President is able to smile, then speak.

"However," he says forcefully, "the most serious crimes you have committed violate *Federal* statutes, and the President *has* secured the agreement of the California authorities to drop any state or local charges and turn prosecution of this case over to the Justice Department. And while the President cannot direct the verdict of a jury or the sentence meted out by a judge after any guilty verdict, he *can* and *would be willing* to instruct his attorney general to recommend clemency. And the President of the United States *does* have the Constitutional power of pardon in Federal cases. Which he would agree beforehand to exercise if necessary to, uh, overturn any sentence that would, uh, violate the terms of this, uh, resolution to the crisis we are now, ah, attempting to negotiate."

Instapoll crawl: For: 51.23% . . . Against: 48.77% . . .

He pauses, looks this way and that, as if expecting a reaction.

But it doesn't come, and after a long beat, there is a cut to a long shot on the whole newsroom desk. The Vice-President looks at Horst, at Kelly, like a man at a tennis match. Horst glowers, perhaps in genuine confusion, Kelly eyes the Vice-President, then the camera, as if looking for something to read off a teleprompter that isn't there. Toby Inman, caught in the hotseat between Klingerman and the Vice-President, finally speaks.

"Can we have this in simple terms that we can all understand, Mr. Vice-President? You're saying that you, uh, that the President, uh . . . that you are authorized by the President to publicly state what, uh, maximum punishment he is willing to guarantee the Green Army Commandos in return for a peaceful release of the hostages and a voluntary surrender?"

The Vice-President starts, almost as if Toby Inman has kicked him off camera. "Isn't that what I said?" he says.

Instapoll crawl: For: 61.44% . . . Against: 38.56% . . .

"So . . . so what are you willing to guarantee?" Kelly Jordan says after another beat of silence, as if Inman has given her a nonverbal cue too.

A close-up on the Vice-President, smiling in evident relief, like a stage actor who, being forced to desperately ad-lib his way through a scene by having forgotten his lines, has finally been guided by a foil back into a recognizable part of the script.

"That is what these public negotiations are all about, Ms. Jordan," he says smoothly. "What form of sentence are you willing to accept?"

A close-up on Kelly Jordan, not smiling, but visibly relieved too. "All the public-service work you want to impose, but no jail time."

A close-up on the Vice-President. "We are prepared to offer maximum pro forma prison sentences of ten years, suspended in favor of five years' probation and two thousand hours of public-service work in the national parks and environmental cleanup."

A close-up on Kelly Jordan, smiling. "Yeah, I think we can handle that. . . ."

A close-up on the Vice-President, looking to the left. "Mr. Klingerman?"

A close-up on Horst Klingerman, smiling into the camera too. But there is an unsettling narrowness about his eyes, a certain sardonic gleam.

"Yes, speaking as Chairperson of the Green Army Commandos, I accept your terms for a negotiated . . . *settlement* . . ." he says.

Instapoll crawl: For: 79.99% . . . Against: 20.01% . . .

". . . provided you are willing to accept *ours*."

7:47 P.M.

"*YOUR TERMS?*" SAID THE Vice-President.

"*Our* terms?" said Kelly Jordan.

What the fuck? Toby Inman almost said, but he was professional enough not to. This was certainly not in the script!

Horst Klingerman continued to smile directly into the camera. On the monitor, his face was something of a blank mask, but his right hand, off camera, moved to the grip of his Uzi, his finger snaking into the trigger guard.

At the back of the studio, Helga, standing behind Carl and Heather, seemed to stiffen, become suddenly hyperalert.

Not in the script?

Whose script was it?

7:48 P.M.

Onscreen:

A CLOSE-UP ON Horst Klingerman, smiling like a fatuous shark.

"Yes, Mr. Vice-President, we accept your terms for a peaceful negotiated settlement. We are willing to release our hostages, place ourselves in official custody, face a public trial, and do the public-service work you require. So all you must do in return is publicly accept *our* terms, and everyone lives happily ever after. . . ."

A two-shot on Horst Klingerman and the Vice-President, emphasizing the Vice-President, who seems uncertain as to whether he's supposed to feel fear, confusion, or righteous outrage at what smells like some kind of impending double cross.

"Which are?" he mutters cautiously.

"Which are only three, and which are quite straightforward and simple . . ." Horst Klingerman says in a rather gross parody of the voice of sweet reason as the camera moves in for a close-up.

"The United States government must unilaterally declare a worldwide ban on the manufacture, distribution, and use of all ozone-destroying chemicals and impose a total economic embargo on nations which do not comply. The United States must ban the manufacture, sale, and ownership of all automobiles within its territory. The United States must order the immediate cessation of all logging and burning in the Amazon basin and dispatch a naval task force of sufficient size and strength to secure the Amazon River and enforce it."

A close-up on the Vice-President, his eyes wide, his mouth hanging open, flecks of drool depending from the corners of his lips.

"That's . . . that's . . . that's . . ."

Kelly Jordan's voice-over: "That's totally bugfuck, Horst!"

A full shot on the newsroom set. Horst Klingerman has both hands on his gun now. The Vice-President sits there utterly stunned. Toby Inman seems shrunken down in his anchor slot as if looking for a hole to drop down into. Kelly Jordan, furious, rises from her chair with her hands balled into fists.

Instapoll crawl: For: 19.45% . . . Against: 80.55% . . .

"That's not what we agreed on at all!" she shouts. "Those are ridiculous and impossible demands and you know it!"

7:50 P.M.

"**So it might seem** at the moment," Klingerman said, picking his piece up off the desk top. "Great things are not achieved easily or at once. . . ."

Chingada! thought Carl Mendoza. Here it comes! He picked at his left nostril, tried to lock eyes with Inman, picked at his nose again, but the son of a bitch was staring at the ceiling or something, and anyway, the Vice-President was between him and Klingerman, there was no way he was going to get to Horst before—

". . . but the Vice-President of the United States has so thoughtfully placed himself in our hands—"

Ahmed stepped away from his camera, yanked off his headset, unslung his Uzi—

Carl leapt to his feet, heard a crisp click behind him—

—turned to stare into the barrel of Helga's gun, about four inches from his nose—

7:51 P.M.

Onscreen:

"**—and we have plenty** of time."

A full shot on the newsroom set, as Horst Klingerman stands up, points his gun straight at the Vice-President's head. The Vice-President shrinks away from him. Toby Inman jumps up, bumps into his chair, staggers backward.

Kelly Jordan points her own weapon at Klingerman, then stares down at it in horror as if it's turned into a snake. Ahmed moves into the shot from the right, *his* Uzi held at belt height and aimed at Kelly's chest.

Instapoll crawl: For: 9.10% . . . Against: 90.90% . . .

"You . . . you . . . you . . . can't do this . . ." Kelly stammers.

"Of course we can," says Horst.

Malcolm dashes into the frame, his weapon pointed at Ahmed.

"We ain't gonna die for this fookin' bloody bullshit!"

The tableau freezes. Horst's Uzi aimed at the Vice-President, Kelly's at Horst, Ahmed's at Kelly, Malcolm's at Ahmed.

"Your choice, meine Kameraden," Horst says. "If you insist, we can all die for nothing right now."

And, holding the grip of his Uzi in his right hand, he flips open his vest with his left, revealing the remote detonators, the row of knife-switches—

7:52 P.M.

—AND RAN HIS FINGERS threateningly along them.

Everything seemed to be happening in slo-mo, like the inevitable climactic sequence in every crappy action movie that Heather Blake had ever seen. Only now, caught in the middle of just such a sequence herself, did Heather understand the truth of that hoary cinematic cliché, or rather the truth behind it that the cliché attempted, however inadequately, to portray.

Nothing was *really* happening in slo-mo; a blast of adrenaline was speeding up her time sense, just as shooting the scene with the camera running at double speed and then projecting it at the normal rate was one way of achieving the slow-motion effect in a film.

And just as a slow-motion sequence created that feeling of dreamy, graceful, liquid clarity that bad directors used as a substitute for true epiphany, so did this moment in real time seem to take place in some magical realm inside a moviola under Heather's control, as if what was happening was something she could edit frame by frame.

In freeze-frame, on the set, Kelly Jordan pointed her gun at Horst Klingerman, Ahmed at Kelly, Malcolm at Ahmed, and Horst, in the center of the shot as surely as if picked out by a spot, menaced the Vice-President with his own machine-pistol and everyone else with his hand on the detonator switches. Beside her, Carl Mendoza and Helga Mueller glared at each other, the barrel of her gun right in his face.

The shot was set up so that the only way it could unfreeze in any conventional movie would be in an explosion or a hail of bullets.

This, though, was real. This was not a movie.

Nevertheless, Heather Blake found herself perceiving it from the director's viewpoint, outside the shot.

And from that position, she *knew,* she knew more clearly, coldly, and dispassionately than she ever had known anything in her life, that she could act, literally *act,* as if it was.

Heather-the-director gave her instructions to Heather-the-actress, and Heather-the-actress was up out of her chair, across the room, and into the shot.

7:53 P.M.

Onscreen:

A STATIC FULL SHOT on the newsroom set as Heather Blake dashes into the frame from the left foreground, between Ahmed and Malcolm, right through their mutual lines of fire before they can even react, and reaches the newsroom desk just as the startled and dumbfounded Horst Klingerman begins to bring his Uzi around to bear on her chest.

As he does, she half turns so that the static unattended camera catches her in profile, her golden hair waving in the breeze of her motion, her arms thrown wide at her hips, her breasts arched up and out right at Klingerman, right at his gun, the perfect image of the All-American virginal self-sacrifice.

"Go ahead, shoot me, if that's what you want!" she cries. "Or blow us all up!"

"What the fook—"

"Horst—"

No one moves. Horst Klingerman stands there like a man caught with his pants down, trapped in the image of the evil menacing foil, his mouth moving for half a beat before anything comes out.

"What . . . what are you doing?"

"I'm saving your honor!" Heather declares. "I'm trying to save you from yourself!"

She puts so much ham into it that it seems deliberate, makes it such a groaner that the Vice-President's eyes roll upward, and even Horst Klingerman seems to wince.

"Sit down!" he finally manages to say.

But some elusive geometry has changed. Horst still has one hand on the remote detonators and the Uzi aimed straight at Heather with the other, but somehow he's no longer in control.

"I'm not going to do that, Horst," Heather Blake says very slowly and evenly. "I'm going to do something else instead. I'm going to do it slowly and carefully, but I *am* going to do it."

Kelly Jordan's Uzi droops, slips below the plane of its aim at Klingerman, Ahmed and Malcolm are no longer glaring at each other, no longer paying attention to each other's weapons. All eyes are on Heather Blake as she begins to move.

"I'm not going to hurt anyone or threaten anyone, and I'm not going to make any rapid or surprising moves," she says in a deliberately cadenced voice, "but you *will* have to kill me in cold blood in front of a hundred million people to stop me."

She slowly walks across the frame from left to right, her back to the camera now, across the front of the newsroom desk, her eyes locked on Horst Klingerman's as he tracks her motion like a cobra tracking the movement of its intended victim.

Or is it a mongoose?

From the look on Horst Klingerman's face, he doesn't look so sure either.

At the left of the frame, Kelly Jordan motions with her head in the direction of Malcolm, says something the microphones don't catch. Malcolm hesitates, then, weapon still in hand, backs toward the camera and out of the shot.

The camera moves in for a somewhat tighter shot, emphasizing Heather Blake as she walks around the end of the newsroom desk and behind it, Klingerman following her with the barrel of his Uzi, with his eyes, until she is behind the desk looking at the camera, and his back is turned to it as he tracks her.

Heather continues to move behind the desk, carefully and deliberately, from left to right until she is standing behind the Vice-President.

The camera slowly moves in for a shot framing just the three of them, the terrorist with the Uzi, the terrified and suddenly quite old-looking man in the gray suit, and the vision of blond midwestern All-American innocence, every father's daughter, every brother's sister, every red-blooded American boy's pinup fantasy sweetheart, as she smiles tremulously but bravely right at you and places both hands protectively on the shoulders of the Vice-President of the United States.

Instapoll crawl: For: 95.40% . . . Against: 4.60% . . .

"You gave your word of honor, Horst Klingerman," she says. "You promised this man safe passage before the world."

Heather Blake tugs on the shoulderpads of the Vice-President's suit. "Stand up, Mr. Vice-President," she says. "We're leaving."

7:55 P.M.

HEATHER STARED RIGHT INTO Horst Klingerman's eyes as the Vice-President slowly and shakily rose to his feet. Horst's machine-pistol was pointed right between her breasts, his lips were set in a conventional snarl of defiance, but those eyes told the story.

"This . . . this . . . this is just another acting trick," he muttered.

Heather nodded, almost imperceptibly, just for him.

Sure it is, and not a very subtle one, either, she told those eyes with her own. You know it, and I know it, and the audience out there knows it too. Beauty and the Beast, this one's called, you poor bastard, not the Cocteau or the Disney version, but King Kong and Fay Wray, and we all know how *that* one ends.

Of course, you could always kill me.

Sure you could.

For although she knew that this was playing as an act of incredible bravery, a feat of heroism that would endear her to the masses and leave 'em gasping, Heather felt no fear. This script put her in control.

Horst Klingerman was a real man, not a character she had been called upon to play against in some Method acting exercise, but the same basic technique was applicable.

Horst Klingerman was a character she had studied from the inside out, and she understood it well enough to play him too if she had to.

Horst might want to see himself as the big tough terrorist, but never as the villain; in his heart he believed his heart was pure. He might even have convinced himself that he could kill if he really believed it was in the cause of saving life on Earth, but that in itself made him a romantic.

And like all romantics, he was an idealist. Dress one up in terrorist gear, and what you've got is Sir Galahad in wolf's clothing.

And now he was finding out himself what Heather had already known.

He could not kill innocence in cold blood.

Outside of action movies, not that many people could.

And in this moment, that mutual knowledge was her weapon, and far more powerful than the one that he was holding.

The last line of *King Kong* said it all.

'Twas Beauty killed the Beast.

7:57 P.M.

Onscreen:

A THREE-SHOT ON Horst Klingerman, the Vice-President, and Heather Blake as Heather takes the Vice-President's hand, begins slowly backing across the frame to the left away from Klingerman, without taking her eyes off of him, pulling the Vice-President around the newsroom desk with her like a large reluctant dog on a leash. . . .

Klingerman stands there with his Uzi pointed at her chest. Then he begins to move with her uncertainly, keeping his distance as the camera tracks with the three of them. . . .

7:58 P.M.

EDDIE FRANKER COULD HARDLY believe what he was seeing. Still less could he fathom what kind of mojo Heather had on Horst Klingerman.

Was she *really* going to get away with this?

Eddie glanced away from the control-room window to clock the same scene on the air-feed monitor as shot by Malcolm's camera, then back at the set.

"For: 99.10% . . . Against: 0.90% . . ." the instapoll crawl said.

Eddie Franker's heart was as hypnotized as Horst Klingerman seemed to be, but his cynical newshound's instincts realized that if Heather *did* manage to exit the studio with the Vice-President, they were going to lose the shot.

And there was a hand-held just sitting there in the corner of the studio!

He turned, grabbed Jaro by the arm. "Get in there, and cover what you can with the hand-held!" he snapped. "Move your ass!"

"Stop right there!" he heard through one of the studio mikes. "This farce has gone far enough!"

Eddie whirled around, looked back out through the control-room window—

7:59 P.M.

HELGA MUELLER HAD TAKEN a long sidewise stride to the left and back, so as to clear Carl Mendoza. Carl whirled around to face the set, saw that she had taken dead aim at Heather Blake's head.

Kelly Jordan whipped up her weapon smartly, then found herself pointing it none too convincingly at Helga.

"If she doesn't lower her weapon at once, Ahmed, shoot her!"

Ahmed already had Kelly covered, but now he snapped to full hair-trigger alert.

"Don't do it, mate!" Malcolm shouted, stepping away from his camera and aiming his Uzi one-handed at Ahmed's gut.

It was a standoff about as stable as a bottle of nitro balancing on a pinpoint.

8:00 P.M.

Onscreen:

A THREE-SHOT ON Heather Blake, the Vice-President, and Horst Klingerman as Heather stops in the act of rounding the corner of the newsroom desk, looks to the left foreground—

Helga Mueller's voice-over: "If you take another step, I will shoot you."

8:01 P.M.

HEATHER STARTED TO MOVE, and Carl didn't even take the time to turn, instead he did just what Charley Bird had said he had done to a nonexistent woman with a gun back there in that nonexistent hooch in the jungle: he kicked hard backwards and to the side at where he estimated her crotch to be.

Maybe not as painful as the same blow to a soft set of balls, but good enough. Helga grunted, folded forward, and as Carl came around, he undercut her to the solar plexus with a short sharp punch, taking away her breath, turning her knees to rubber. She collapsed forward, let go of the Uzi, the strap slid from her shoulder, and the gun clattered to the floor as she fell.

As Carl bent to make his reflexive grab for the loose gun, he looked up and behind him and saw—

Kelly Jordan still had her weapon aimed at where Helga had

been, namely at him, though she didn't seem to have much of a notion of what to do with it, but Ahmed and Malcolm had him covered too, and they looked like they did.

Carl's mind moved as fast as his body had.

He stood up slowly with his hands in the air and a dumb smile on his face.

"Just thought you guys might like to have time to think about it before everybody blows everybody away," he said as he kicked the Uzi halfway across the floor.

8:02 P.M.

Onscreen:

A **FULL SHOT ON** Heather Blake, the Vice-President, and Horst Klingerman, a beat of living freeze-frame. Heather looks left, right, left at things off camera. The Vice-President's glazed eyes don't seem to be looking anywhere. Horst Klingerman's machine-pistol is still pointed at Heather, and his eyes are fixated on her as she turns to meet them, but his stare seems rather zombified too.

"I'm going to do this very slowly, and I'm going to tell you what I'm going to do first, every step of the way," Heather says, enunciating every syllable, as if speaking to a small, dim child.

"All I'm going to do now is turn around. . . ."

Slowly, deliberately, Heather Blake turns on her heel, turns her back to Klingerman, so that he stands there staring at the back of her head with his Uzi pointed at the small of her back.

Heather turns a three-quarter profile to the camera, plays to it as she speaks to Klingerman.

"Now what we're going to do is walk right out of here," she says. "And you're going to have to shoot me in the back in front of a hundred million people to stop us. You can't do that, can you, Horst? There's no reason to do it, is there? All you would do is dishonor your cause. You're too smart to do it. You're too good a man. I'd bet my life on it."

Horst Klingerman's lips tremble, his eyes blink rapidly, he

looks, in this moment, far more like a victim than a determined terrorist.

"And now I will," Heather Blake says. "And now I am. . . ."

And she takes a step forward, then another, dragging the Vice-President with her, his face tilted upward, his eyes screwed nearly closed.

Horst Klingerman stands there frozen like a bull fixed in place by the final capework flourish of a master matador. The camera tracks to the right with Heather Blake and the Vice-President as she lays one foot down after the other until Horst is entirely out of the shot and only she and the Vice-President remain in the frame as it moves with them toward the exit.

8:03 P.M.

THE VICE-PRESIDENT'S HAND in hers was doughy and trembling, and Heather could smell the sour perspiration of his fear. She should be afraid too, shouldn't she?

But Heather wasn't. Step by step by step, she moved toward the exit, with Jaro advancing backwards before her, getting the coverage as best he could with the hand-held camera. It was all like shooting a scene for a movie.

She had written her part, she had blocked the moves, she was directing it herself, a hundred million people were watching.

Like shooting a scene in a movie?

More like live theater.

You got it right all the way through the first time or you didn't. There would be no retakes.

See a movie, be a movie.

This was her moment—the last moment of her life, or the moment that would make her a star.

8:04 P.M.

Onscreen:

A HAND-HELD FULL shot on Heather Blake and the Vice-President as they walk hand in hand down a dull green corridor, the camerawork jiggly and jerky, the frame bouncing this way and that, as if the cameraman is tripping over things, stumbling against walls.

The Vice-President of the United States clumps along woodenly, like a poor old Frankenstein monster, like a terrified old man waiting to feel a hail of bullets in the back.

But Heather Blake is radiant. Her blond locks bouncing, she strides along confidently, moving like a star in a spotlight only she can see and calling it into being in the audience's mind's eye thereby. She plays to the camera, smiling determinedly, resolutely, bravely, the heroine of the movie promenading into the triumphant climax as the phantom theme music crescendos.

Instapoll crawl: For: 99.98% . . . Against: 0.02% . . .

She sweeps past a startled Hiroshi, sound of a door opening, and then, for a beat, the frame is washed out by a flare of white light.

It clears as the camera sweeps around into a shot on Heather Blake and the Vice-President of the United States from another angle, a full shot from the rear, shot through the doorway.

Heather and the Vice-President descend the short flight of stairs to the parking lot in a bright white spotlight that tracks with them as they parade across the tarmac. As they slowly recede into the distance, the angle widens, and the camera pans upward to reveal the source of the limelight:

About ten feet off the ground, the ominous black shape of a helicopter gunship glimmers and shines in the Hollywood twilight's last gleaming, floating backwards toward the line of troops at the parking lot's perimeter at a walking pace, at their walking pace, picking them out in a circle of light.

Heather Blake waves her hand at the soldiers before her as the camera, trying for a final close-up, zooms in on the back of her head. Then, via some cinematic sixth sense, some Hollywood magic, she seems to sense its attention.

Without stopping her forward progress, without leaving the limelight, she turns her head to face the camera and flashes it a perfect fade-out smile.

8:09 P.M.

Onscreen:

A **FULL SHOT ON** the KLAX newsroom set. Toby Inman slumps in the anchor seat, his eyes glazed, staring into space. To his right, Kelly Jordan sits with the butt of her Uzi propped on the desk top and the barrel in the air. Her expression is vacant. Horst Klingerman stands in front of the newsdesk, leaning on it with one hand, holding his weapon slackly with the other. His eyes are like fractured blue marbles.

Just this for a beat. And another. And another. And on and on for a full minute of dead air.

"Well, folks, uh, what is there to say . . . ?" Toby Inman finally manages to croak.

The camera moves in for a cruel close-up as he shrugs, moves his mouth, starts to say something, shrugs again.

"One picture is worth a thousand words, that's what they say," he babbles, "and what you've just seen, what we've all witnessed—*what?*"

He looks to the left of the frame, leans his head out of the shot for a moment or two, looks back into the camera with a worried look on his face.

"Well, uh, folks, I've just been informed that KLAX-TV weathergirl Heather Blake and the Vice-President of the United States are safe and sound, which is more than can be said for those of us still in here," he blathers frenetically. "And I've just been told that until, uh, further notice, or the, uh, final solution of the KLAX-TV hostage crisis, we, ah, will be off the air."

He smiles a truly ghastly death's-head grin.

"So, uh, I guess this is good-bye from Toby Inman, Carl Mendoza, and Heather . . . uh, everyone here at KLAX-TV Los Angeles. Or maybe just so long . . . I hope. . . ."

Cut to black.

To multicolored static on a dead TV screen.

DAY 8

7:03 A.M.

EDDIE FRANKER FOUND HIMSELF awake in the darkness yet again. Beside him, Toby Inman tossed fitfully on his air mattress, but Carl Mendoza, snoring lightly, slept like the proverbial brick.

How the hell does he do it? Eddie wondered. He himself had woken up so often he had lost count, and he doubted whether he had had forty-five consecutive minutes of sleep all night.

Peering across the cafeteria at the entrance, he could make out the shapes of Jaro and Hiroshi, guarding each other as much as their hostages by now, Eddie reckoned. No doubt the building guard shift was also split along the same fault line.

Not that you could say that the two sides weren't talking to each other!

Oh no, they had gone on till after one A.M., and since neither faction was about to let either the remaining hostages or the other faction out of their sight, it had all gone on in the cafeteria. Toby, Carl, and Eddie had been forced to endure it long past the point of bleary exhaustion, until finally the terrorists had hammered out their only agreement of the night—to turn down the lights, shut the fuck up, and try to get some sleep before it started all over again in the morning.

Which it would, Eddie knew for a dreadful certainty, rolling over, closing his eyes, and trying to escape from the inevitable one more time.

For nothing at all had been resolved.

And he really didn't see how anything could be.

After Heather cut Horst Klingerman's terrorist media nuts off in front of maybe a hundred million people, Eddie had half expected Horst to detonate the remote charges and end it all in a fit of rage.

After Carl had kicked Helga in the twat and socked her in the gut, Eddie had more than half expected her to pick herself off the floor, retrieve her gun, and blow him away.

Instead, Horst just stood there on the set like a Disneyland audio-animatronic robot with something broken inside. And Carl had leaned over and offered Helga his hand. She had given him this peculiar look, but she had taken it. And let him help her to her feet. And flipped him an ironic salute as she went to pick up her weapon.

Everybody had seemed to be in their own peculiar personal trance.

Horst, Kelly, and Toby staring stonily through an eternity of dead air. Malcolm shooting it in what seemed like the longest static shot in television history for want of anything better to do. Ahmed standing stupidly by the number two camera wondering if maybe there was something he should do with it.

And me and Warren and Jaro not even noticing that *this* was what was going out on the air.

The inevitable call from Alex Coleman had come as a relief.

"Just thought you'd want to know that your girl is safe and sound, Eddie," Coleman's voice said in about the gentlest tone Eddie had yet heard from that quarter.

"Thanks, Alex," Eddie said sincerely.

"I don't think I've ever seen anything ballsier in my life, and I have been witness to a couple three Silver Star performances and a Medal of Honor nomination or two."

"Now what?" Eddie muttered numbly. "Helicopter gunships and multiple rocket launchers?"

"Not with half the country with their eyeballs glued to the tube just waitin' for it to happen," Coleman told him. "The spin doctors have gone back to the drawing board happy campers. They got a heroine, and a happy ending, an' instapoll figures for the whole thing t'die for, and they're not about to rain on their own parade tonight. So the word is that any wetwork takes place later, way out of prime time, and well off screen."

"I don't follow you. . . ."

"We're shutting the show down now, Eddie," Coleman said, "we're jammin' your feed to the local transmission tower, and we have prevailed upon StarNet to terminate their downlinking of any KLAX uplinks. I'll give you time to announce it, but after that, you're off the air."

"But Klingerman will—"

"Ol' Horst didn't pull the chain just then, and my guess is he won't do it now either."

"Your fuckin' *guess*, Alex! It's our goddamn *asses*!"

"My *professional opinion*, Eddie. Herr Klingerman looks like some poor bastard sergeant just lost his whole platoon in an ambush and ain't in much shape to make any snap command decisions long about now. Or are you suggestin' I'd better take the opportunity to move in while he's still shell-shocked and hope for the best?"

Eddie had had no answer to that one, so he had screwed up his courage, slipped into the studio, and passed the word to Toby. And Coleman *had* been right, Klingerman had hardly reacted at all when the broadcast was shut down, let alone blown them all to kingdom come.

Malcolm and Ahmed marched Toby and Carl out of the studio, while Helga stayed behind, getting into something or other with Kelly and Horst.

With the studio mikes turned off, Eddie couldn't hear it, but he had a chance to watch it through the control-room window for a minute or so before a rather dazed Warren shooed him off to the cafeteria too.

Kelly had begun shouting something at Horst, and then Helga joined in, though from the body language of it, the two of them certainly didn't seem to be agreeing with each other either. Horst seemed to be getting it from both of them.

Nor, at least not while Eddie had still been around to watch it, did he seem to be giving much back. He just stood there in some kind of trance, absorbing the abuse, looking like . . .

What had Coleman called it, some poor bastard sergeant had lost his whole platoon in an ambush . . . ?

Not quite, as Eddie was to learn a bit later, when the three of them burst into the cafeteria still going at it.

"—should have known better than to listen to a café intellectual like you—"

"—asshole thing to do in the first place!"

"—we had *the Vice-President of the United States* in our hands, and we lost him because our great leader wasn't enough of a man to face down some blond—"

"What was I supposed to do, Helga?" Horst Klingerman whined. "I would have really had to shoot her to stop her."

"So? We would have still had a live Vice-President as our hostage! And our credibility as a direct-action force! Neither of which, you might notice, Horst, remain to us now!"

"Right, Helga, brilliant," Kelly snarled, "shoot an unarmed woman in the back in front of a hundred million people to maintain our credibility as crazed killers! And what about our popular support?"

"You mean your *television show*, Kelly?"

No, Horst Klingerman didn't seem like a sergeant who had lost his whole command in a firefight. More like a commander who had screwed up so badly he had lost the control and respect of his own surviving troops.

From recriminations, it had passed to what to do next, with Kelly and the Media Freaks insisting that they had no alternative but to release the remaining hostages and surrender, and the Soldiers, mostly Helga, insisting that since they still had three hostages and a building full of explosives, the tactical situation hadn't changed.

While those hostages themselves were constrained to listen, past the point of terror, past the point of boredom even, and well into the realm of exhausted stupefaction, where Eddie, at least, could think of nothing but his longing for darkness, silence, and sleep . . .

Which was eluding him once more now in the early-morning after, with the sounds of Toby tossing restlessly on the air mattress beside him, and Carl's snoring, and the rustling noises of others beginning to stir in the big darkened room.

Groaning, without raising his head, Eddie peered into the gloomy dimness.

The Green Army Commandos had divided up into two camps when they had finally bivouacked for the night. The Soldiers had set up their air mattresses to the left of the entrance and the Media Freaks to the right. Horst Klingerman had placed his mattress in between them, but further away from the wall, pointedly alone.

And when the guards had been posted, and the lights dimmed, and the rest of the terrorists had laid themselves down to try and get a few hours' sleep, Horst sat there cross-legged on his mattress staring into the darkness at God knew what until after Eddie had fallen asleep.

The first few times that Eddie had awoken, Horst had still been sitting there. At some point after that, he seemed to have finally laid down and at least tried to sleep.

But now Eddie could make out his form again, sitting there with the barrel of his weapon visible in outline, like some weird counter-Buddha, meditating on better-you-don't-ask while the sleeping forms stirred and moaned and tossed toward wakefulness around him.

Eddie shuddered, closed his eyes again, tried to go back to sleep, or at least pretend to go back to sleep, in no hurry for the dawn of this new day to arrive.

No hurry at all. And maybe only a fifty-fifty chance that he would live to see another.

8:21 A.M.

MAYBE IT WAS AN old survival reflex from Nam. Carl Mendoza woke up rested and alert on the morning of what might turn out to be the last day of his life from what at least in memory had been a solid and dreamless sleep.

Things were already stirring as he sat up. Nigel and Helga were replacing Jaro and Hiroshi on guard duty, but no one was quitting the cafeteria for someplace where they'd have a better shot at catching some Zs. Instead, Hiroshi flopped down on his mattress over on the left side of the cafeteria, and Jaro did likewise on the right, even as everyone else was waking up and turning on the lights and starting to make noise. Ahmed and Warren went to relieve the building guards, Paulo and Malcolm. A few minutes later, they returned to the cafeteria and flopped down on their mattresses too.

Experienced grunts coming off guard duty at a time like this might be longing for sleep, but while Carl had known guys so accomplished at the art of gorking off that they could actually come off duty guarding the perimeter of a forward artillery position and catch a few even with the guns launching outgoing, he could see why no one was about to quit the cafeteria now for a cozy silent somewhere.

Guard duty in a forward position if you insist, Sarge, but none of these people was now willing to let the others out of their sight except in such cases of obvious tactical necessity.

Inman was already awake and squatting on his mattress. Old Franker was groaning up into a seated position. Heather—

Shit.

Shit, Mendoza? Chingada, what a way to think!

But Carl couldn't help it. Sure he was glad that she was safely out of there. But he missed her. It had nothing to do with sex, and still less with the machismo of having a blond princess to feel protective about either.

Far from it.

It was Heather who had proven to have the brass balls in this outfit. It was Heather who had scooped up the live grenade and tossed it back into the jungle. It was Heather who had triggered his own ancient combat reflexes, or inspired his own act of heroism, as the news was no doubt putting it. It was Heather who had been his only real comrade-in-arms in this situation.

Except, in some really twisted way, for Helga Mueller. Had it been cleverness to hold out his hand to her, a piece of psychological judo, like kicking the piece across the floor instead of going for it? A reflex reaction? A genuine gesture of courtesy? All three?

Whatever. She was a cold speed-freak bitch who admitted to killing any number of people in what she considered the line of. Carl had no doubt in the hot moment, or now, upon considered reflection, that she would have blown Heather Blake away if he hadn't made his move, and done him too if the kick had missed.

He did not like Helga Mueller. He seriously doubted that Helga Mueller liked him, or for that matter, anyone else. And he had hurt her.

Carl doubted that anyone in here but the two of them could possibly understand what had passed between them when he held out his hand to the fallen foe and she took it—least of all, poor fucking Klingerman.

A gesture of courtesy? Yeah, but not the man–woman kind. Strictly professional. Because that's what she was. And that was why she didn't kill him afterward.

Carl wondered if anyone had overheard what Helga had grunted at him as he helped her to her feet after taking her out, whether anyone had noticed her saying something and wondered what it could have been, built some elaborate explanation for what she hadn't done out of it.

In reality, it had been simplicity itself.

"Excellent move," Helga Mueller had said, and to the two of them, that said it all, after which she had just saluted and walked away.

Heather, and Helga, and me, Carl thought sardonically. The blond bombshell, the Baader-Meinhof bitch, and the beat-up old ballplayer.

So much for fancy theories of all-male battlefield bonding.

"You sleep okay, Carl?" Inman blathered.

"The condemned man stacked a solid shitload of Zs," Carl muttered sourly, then instantly regretted it. Inman might lack a certain something that Heather had, but he really wasn't that bad a sort, and a crack like that was not exactly a morale builder.

"Sorry, Toby," he said, "I'm not at my best before my first cup."

"And you snore, too," Franker grunted, grinning wanly in a lame attempt at camaraderie.

"So I've been told by prettier people than you, Franker," Carl said in his own lame attempt at humor.

What the fuck, Mendoza, like it or not, this is the team you've been traded to, these guys are maybe who you're gonna finish out your last season with, so even if it *is* last place in the California League with ten games to go, leave us play out the string with a little class. Learn something from mean old Helga. Get professional.

Carl rose to his feet and did a toe-touching stretch. Inman rolled out and up but didn't bother. Franker clambered into a standing position with the first two fingers of his right hand clamped around a cigarette that wasn't there. The three of them staggered over to the table by the machines where the sack of crap sat, plunked themselves down, reached in, pulled out handfuls of trail mix, began slowly choking it down.

"What a last meal . . ." Franker moaned. "You could do better on death row in Mississippi."

"Fried eggs and ham with red-eye gravy," Inman said dreamily. "Buttered cornbread and a big scoop of grits."

"Disgusting," Carl muttered. "Right now, I'd settle for a couple of crappy donuts from the nearest Winchell's, 'long as they came with a double coffee."

"What do you think our chances *really* are now, Carl?" Inman muttered. "I mean. . . ."

Carl shrugged, grunted noncommittally, looked back over his shoulder. Horst Klingerman was pacing obsessively, weaving in and out among the empty mattresses in the center of the room, back and forth, in and out, over and over again.

It reminded Carl of a wolverine he had once seen in the L.A. Zoo.

From what Carl had heard, the wolverine was supposed to be the fiercest and most tenacious predator, pound for pound, to be found on the North American continent. A kind of overgrown badger with the disposition of a Nazi weasel on methedrene, the wolverine had been voted the creature most animals would least like to meet outside in the alley a million years running, a real bad-ass son of a bitch that not even a pit bull would care to fuck with.

They had caught themselves one of these vicious motherfuckers. They had put it in a little steel cage, with nothing but a zinc water cup and a trayful of dog food. The wolverine had paced its cell in an invariable figure-eight pattern, touch the wall, sip the water, touch the food tray, touch the wall, over, and over, and over, brain-burned by its captivity.

Klingerman, the terrorist wolverine, had been turned into a public pussy before the world by an unarmed girl, and in front of his own troops too, and was probably still trying to figure out how. He had isolated himself from Jordan and the Media Freaks when he made his move to snatch the Vice-President, and he had destroyed his authority with the bad-asses by wimping out when push came to kill.

Leaving him pacing in his invisible cage, snarling and sputtering to himself, and wondering how the hell he had gotten there, where the hell *there* was, just like that wolverine in the zoo.

Carl had felt sorry for the poor ugly little bugger, and a part of him had wanted to set it free. But that was only a very small part, for he knew all too well that anyone dumb enough to open the cage door on such a furious little hairball of frustrated nastiness would be rewarded by a crazed leap at the nearest throat, namely his own—

—the phone began to ring—

"Guess who?" Carl muttered sardonically.

Kelly, Helga, and Horst all raced to the speakerphone table, then stood there glaring at each other in three-way mutual distrust.

—ring—ring—ring—

Screw this, Carl thought, got up from his table, and ambled over.

"Any objections?" he muttered, looking right at Helga. "Don't you think we all have a need to know what's going on out there?"

Helga nodded. "This will no doubt be your CIA friend Coleman," she said.

"I never had any *friends* in the CIA," Carl told her.

Helga Mueller said nothing, but she did nod at the phone, and Carl punched in the call.

"Coleman here," Alex Coleman said dully. He sounded like a man who had been up all night, and probably was. "Can you hear me?"

Kelly, Helga, and Horst exchanged hostile glances, each daring the other to speak. Or not to speak.

"Mendoza here, Alex," Carl finally said. "They can all hear you, but they're having a little chain-of-command problem. . . ."

Helga scowled. Kelly started to say something, looked at her, then thought better of it. Horst commenced to acquire the old thousand-yard stare.

"Well listen up," Coleman said. "I have been up all night bullshittin' with the bullshitters, and somehow I don't think I'm gonna get my beauty rest today either, so I'm just gonna give you the quick an' nasty and see if I can't at least steal an hour or two before any more fertilizer feeds the fan. What I've worked out with the

powers that be is this: you release the hostages unharmed and surrender and we still honor the deal we made. That's the good
news. . . ."

An audible sigh issued from the phone speaker. A hollow feeling blossomed in Carl's gut, for he really believed that Alex Coleman was genuinely reluctant to say whatever he was going to say
next, which didn't seem likely to make it something that Carl was
going to be happy to hear.

By now, everybody had gathered round the speakerphone table
in neat little factions: Franker and Inman flanking Carl; Jaro, Malcolm, and Nigel behind Kelly; Hiroshi and Paulo with Helga. Only
Klingerman stood there alone in his body-space cage.

"The bad news is if you don't do it by seven P.M. tonight, my
orders are to move in."

"At the first sign of any approach to this building, we will
detonate all the charges," Helga said icily, "so it would be best not
to make us paranoid."

She rounded on Klingerman. "That is right, Horst, is it not?"
she snapped. "You are enough of a man to do it? Or perhaps you
would rather give me your remote detonators?"

Horst Klingerman almost seemed as if he was about to burst
into tears. He reached into a pocket, pulled out a pill, gobbled it
down.

"I am fully capable of direct action when it does not involve
cold-blooded murder, Helga!" he snapped at her. "As you will find
if you try to take my vest away from me! Perhaps you would like to
do it now? Perhaps you would like to get it over with?"

But instead of setting Helga off, that somehow seemed to reas-
sure her. "You are still the Chairperson, at least for the moment,
Horst," she said. "The last thing we need right now is an internal
coup."

"Then as the Chairperson, Coleman, I confirm what Helga has
told you," Horst babbled rapidly, "and I go further and tell you
that you are lying to us twice over. The authorities will honor no
agreements with us now! And you would gain nothing by attacking
this building! This is a bluff, Coleman, and we are calling it, that is
the correct idiom, is it not?"

"Like you called Heather's bluff, dickhead?" Coleman
snapped.

Horst went pale. Helga smirked.

"Look, I'm too bone-tired to endure further assholery," Coleman said. "You don't get it, do you? Unless you *do* release the hostages and surrender, my peerless leaders *want* you to blow up the building, they don't expect me to be able to effectuate an Entebbe, they'd be perfectly satisfied if I just set you off by trying, old buddy! Think about it! They're on record as havin' offered you a sweetheart of a deal. You're on public record as bein' nuts enough to refuse it in favor of some moron set of impossible demands no one even believes *you* can take seriously, and breaking your word by trying to kidnap the Vice-President too! And they got themselves a wonderful presidential photo op with a live superstar heroine to shine that ol' limelight on just as soon as the loose ends are tidied up. . . ."

"Loose ends . . . ?" Horst muttered.

"That's *you*, shithead. If you guys play ball, all well and good, but if you don't, tonight the curtain finally comes down on the KLAX Hostage Crisis when the crazed terrorists blow up the building, whether you do it yourselves, or I gotta fake it for y'all. There will unfortunately be no survivors."

"That's sick," Carl found himself saying. "That's a new level of cynical sleaze even for the Agency!"

"Hell's bells, Carl, it's not the *Agency* callin' this one," Coleman snapped peevishly. "It's those reptiles in the White House. You think I *like* it? You think I *want* to do it?"

"But you'll follow orders, won't you, Coleman?"

"I don't, they'll just find some other poor ol' boy who will."

"You'll never get away with it," Franker said. "We'll . . . we'll . . ." He spluttered out futilely.

"Right, Eddie," Coleman said softly, "you're off the air. If the building blows, all that the folks out there in televisionland are gonna see an' hear is a great big mother of a special-effects explosion in the dark, shot through the telephoto lenses of mobile units and news helicopters who as of now will not be allowed within five miles of the scene in the interests of their own safety."

"If you do not reestablish our satellite line with StarNet by noon," Horst shouted, "we will . . . we will—"

"Blow up the building?" Coleman said tiredly. "Well then, why don't you just do it right now, and let me get some sleep?"

Helga glared at Horst. Horst's eyes blinked rapidly. His right hand went to the closure of his explosive vest, the fingers worrying the fabric, but not yet slipping inside. . . .

"Horst!" Kelly shouted. She made a grab for his hand, Helga caught her arm, Carl moved forward, Hiroshi whipped around his Uzi, everything froze—

"Bloody fookin' hell, Horst, hold yer water, mate, we can always do ourselves in later!"

A shudder went through Horst Klingerman's body. He looked down at his own hand, twitched again, let it drop clear of his vest.

"What's goin' on there?" Coleman's voice shouted. "What just happened?"

"Just . . . just a little difference of opinion," Kelly Jordan said.

Helga snorted audibly.

"Look, folks," Coleman said plaintively, "I've been ordered to terminate contact after this, so this is my last chance to be the voice of sweet reason, which I much prefer to what I'm gonna be forced to perpetrate if I don't get through to you this time. . . ."

He paused, Carl could almost hear the intake of breath. "You got no reason not to surrender. You let those people go, nobody gets hurt, you don't do any jail time to speak of, you get yourselves this TV show, and from what I get from your cotton-pickin' agent, a ton of money from everything from movie rights to Green Army Commando berets. This is a fate worse than death? And don't kid yourself, that *is* the alternative, you let me throw you into that green velvet briar patch, or you are dead meat. Do I make myself clear?"

"Yeah, sure," Kelly Jordan said, "it's just a matter of—"

"You are pathetic, Coleman, you understand nothing!" Helga Mueller snapped. "Perhaps there are some of us who you can co-opt with money or television shows, but there are others here who will never be co-opted, and we are the ones with the will and experience to take direct action, whose commitment to the cause is that of serious revolutionaries, not bourgeois adventurers!"

"Who are you calling a bourgeois adventurer?" Klingerman snarled.

"Whoever acts like one. Whoever lacks the courage to take direct action to its logical conclusion."

"And that is me, I suppose?"

"Until you prove otherwise!"

"Enough of this, Helga!" Klingerman barked, whipping his gun off his shoulder. "There will be no more of this dissension in the face of the enemy! If you disagree, we are going to have to settle matters right now!"

It was almost as if he had fired his gun in the air. Everyone froze. Everyone shut up. Suddenly the wolverine was out of his cage. At least for the moment, Klingerman was back in command.

Was it Carl's imagination, or did Helga Mueller smile?

"Calm down, will you, Horst, I'm not your enemy," Coleman's voice said soothingly.

"Perhaps you are not," Horst said sharply, "but the people and the system you serve are the enemies of life on Earth. And Helga is right, you *do not* understand. . . ."

He turned, locked eyes with Helga Mueller as he spoke, speaking as much to her as to Coleman now, or so it seemed to Carl.

"You believe it was weakness that caused me to allow Heather Blake to walk out of here with your Vice-President. The moral weakness of a man who could not shoot an unarmed woman in the back when the tactical situation required it in the service of a higher cause."

He shrugged. "Perhaps you are right," he said, still staring Helga down. "I have been thinking about this. Perhaps there is some flaw in my character. Perhaps there is some instinct I lack. But it was also a matter of honor. The Green Army Commandos gave their word that the Vice-President would have safe passage. When Heather Blake reminded me of that, I could not dishonor the cause before the world by breaking that promise whether I could have killed her or not."

"I don't see what this has to—"

"We made another promise before the world, Coleman!" Horst shouted. He didn't quite break eye contact with Helga, but he did do a little half-turn so that he was talking simultaneously to her, Coleman, and the sullen circle of his troops.

"We promised that we would not surrender this station until your government placed an embargo on all nations producing ozone-destroying chemicals, banned automobiles on its territory, and sent a naval task force up the Amazon to save the rain forest—"

"Fer the love a' Sweet Jesus!" Coleman groaned. "Why don't you ask for the Second Coming while you're at it! You gotta *know* it can't happen!"

"We made a promise, and we will keep it! We will hold this television station and these hostages until our terms are met!"

"Haven't you heard a word I've been sayin', Klingerman? By seven o'clock tonight, *it will be over*. You'll end it, or I will."

"That is your option, Coleman," Horst Klingerman said.

Helga nodded.

A chill crawled up Carl's spine, the chill of utter conviction, as Horst slipped his hand inside his vest and began caressing the remote detonator switches like a monk doing his worry beads, challenged all of them with his eyes.

"Keeping our word of honor on what we will do if you try to exercise it is ours," he said.

"Hai . . ." Hiroshi grunted.

Klingerman smiled, an awful Buddhist sort of smile that loosened Carl's bowels. This was not the predatory grin of the escaped wolverine. This was something much worse.

"So you see, my conscience is clear, and my honor is clean, and if you force me to it, the act will be pure," Horst Klingerman said, his face still set in that horribly familiar mask. "Will you be able to say the same to yourself?"

Carl had seen such a smile, such a deadly Buddha mask, once before in Saigon. A monk, his saffron robes soaked in gasoline, had appeared out of nowhere and plunked himself down on the sidewalk not ten yards away from the café table where Carl had been sitting.

He had had the very same smile on his face as he struck the match.

10:21 A.M.

THE GREEN ARMY COMMANDOS sat there at their separate tables—Nigel, Malcolm, and Jaro with Kelly; Helga, Paulo, and Hiroshi with Horst—glaring at each other sullenly and silently. At least they've stopped talking without starting to shoot, Inman, Toby thought nervously, so be thankful for small miracles.

Heather might have called their factions the Media Freaks and the Soldiers, but as far as Toby was concerned, it was simply the sane and the crazy.

It was *sane* to want to live, and have a TV show, and lots of money, and be popular with the public, wasn't it? And it would be crazy to throw all that away and blow yourselves up because you promised in public you'd go ahead and do it if the United States government didn't get down on its knees and kiss your ass.

That was a difficult choice to make? In Toby's opinion, Kelly had said it all right after Coleman hung up.

"This is total assholery, Horst! Isaacs has got them to meet every reasonable demand we could make and some I didn't think possible! This shit about banning cars and sending naval task forces up the Amazon is bugfuck bananas, and you know it! They'll *never* do it! You *know* they'll never do it! What the hell for?"

"It is a matter of honor, of not being co-opted, of not being faced down, of calling their bluff!"

"I don't think that bloody bugger's bluffing, mate!"

"If the American government goes through with their threat, the blood will be on *their* hands, and the moral victory will be ours!"

"Fookin' hell, Helga, you're talking about *our* blood, now ain'tcha! An' our guts and brains plastered all over the fookin' landscape as well!"

"Are you so afraid to die?" Horst blurted. "Is there nothing at all you would give your life for?"

"You got a fookin' *hard-on* for it or somethin'?"

"My conscience is clear."

"Bloody fookin' marvelous!"

"They won't take the lives of innocent hostages to prove a point."

"No, Horst, *we* will, goddamn it, that's the way the world will see it—"

"Is that all you care about, Kelly, even when it comes to your own death? Not its true meaning, just how it will look on television?"

"Fuck!"

"Shit!"

"Coward!"

"Asshole!"

And so forth.

With every last one of them carrying an automatic weapon, it had been a miracle that the shouting match had wound down without gunplay.

The nature of the miracle, however, was something that Toby found a good deal less reassuring.

Throughout the whole thing, Horst Klingerman had not removed his right hand from the inside of his explosive vest, stroking those detonator switches like some pervert playing pocket pool inside his raincoat.

That was what had kept anyone from reaching for their weapon. That was the hole card, and Klingerman held it, and no one was about to provoke him into using it.

Not either faction of the Green Army Commandos, and mercifully not Carl Mendoza. If there was any moment when Mendoza was going to pick his nose and flash Toby his goddamn signal, that had figured to be it.

But Mendoza hadn't said a word or made a peep or flashed Toby any body language about the two of them jumping Klingerman since Horst had stuck his hand inside his vest. There the three of them sat, Eddie Franker, Mendoza, and himself, hunched over at the table by the vending machines, as far away from the confrontation as they could get, keeping their mouths shut and trying to pretend they were invisible.

The look on Carl's face every time he stole a glance in Horst Klingerman's direction said it all. Every time he looked at Klingerman, he seemed to be seeing some ghost out of his past.

Or worse, a ghost out of the future, namely his own.

11:19 A.M.

"PLEASE HOLD FOR LEONARD Isaacs," said the syncopated female voice over the speakerphone, and then it was replaced by a syrupy electronic organ version of "Born in the USA," a double dose of surreality as far as Eddie Franker was concerned.

Klingerman had punched in the call this time; the split between the terrorist factions might be deeper and wider than ever, but his hand on the remote detonator switches had put him back in charge of the situation, and no one was about to make any moves before he did or do anything sudden in his vicinity.

Helga, Hiroshi, and Paulo got up and stood behind him as the sardonic Muzak continued to play. Kelly walked slowly and carefully over to the phone table too, followed by Malcolm, Nigel, and Jaro. Eddie thought it prudent to stay as low-profile as possible, so the hostages didn't move from their table by the vending machines, where they could hear but not be heard, and hopefully not be noticed.

The idiot hold music went on for what seemed like a million years as Horst fingered his detonators, Helga stroked the sling of her Uzi, and Kelly Jordan shifted back and forth nervously on the balls of her feet.

"Sorry to keep you waiting," Leonard Isaacs' voice finally said. "I've been on the horn to StarNet and Washington and this guy Coleman who's directing their show out here, and I've finally got them to deal. . . ."

"Deal?" said Kelly.

"Hildebrandt was *really* pissed about this TV blackout, he started squeezing on his end, and I called in some markers on mine, and we finally got them to agree to a half hour of live national coverage tonight and to move their deadline up to eight to cover the national prime-time spread."

"Coverage of *what*?"

"The hostage release," Isaacs said. "What else? I've even got them to release one of the KLAX mobile units so we can get decent coverage, no offense, but that hand-held stuff was for shit."

"There will not be any hostage release, Isaacs," Horst said.

"Come on, of course there will, I've got it all arranged."

"We release no hostages until our terms are met!" Helga snapped.

"A total ban on automobiles within the United States, a naval task force—"

"Come on, come on, this is *your agent* you're talking to, I mean that's the kind of bullshit you throw at the *beginning* of the bargaining process—"

"We have made a public commitment! Our credibility must be restored! We have no honorable way of backing down!"

"Hey, no sweat, I've already got writers on it—"

"We are serious," said Horst.

"Dead serious," said Helga.

There was a long silence on the other end of the phone, and when Leonard Isaacs spoke again, his voice had dropped half an octave, and it seemed to Eddie that the breezy Hollywood razzmatazz was gone, that this was the real Leonard Isaacs speaking, assuming that such a personage actually existed.

"Look, I am a professional negotiator, and it is my considered professional opinion that the other side is not bullshitting. You release your hostages and surrender tonight, or they will keep you blacked out while they blow you away. That *is* the bottom line."

"I believe you, Mr. Isaacs," Kelly Jordan said.

"Me too," said Nigel.

"I may even believe you myself," said Horst, "or at least I believe that you believe what you are saying. But it is not relevant."

"Then what is?" Leonard Isaacs said very gently. "Talk to your agent. Tell me what you want me to get for you. That's what I'm here for."

"—to save—"

"—to get out of here alive—"

"—not to fookin'—"

"—none of your—"

They all started shouting at once.

"PEOPLE!" Leonard Isaacs' voice roared. "ONE AT A TIME!"

A beat of sudden silence, into which he spoke.

"Look, this is not the first time I've had to sort out differences of self-interest in the same package among my own clients, so let me handle it, okay, let's break this into modules we can deal with one by one. Kelly, you first. What do *you* want me to negotiate for you?"

"The deal you've already worked out for us, Mr. Isaacs. We release the hostages, walk out of here alive tonight, stay out of jail, and do *The Green Army Commando Show*."

"And how many of your . . . colleagues . . . agree with you?"

Nigel and Malcolm nodded enthusiastically. Jaro grunted his assent.

"Four. The cameramen and the production crew."

"Now, Horst, what is it you want me to negotiate for *you*?"

"You are serious?"

"You're the client. You tell me what you want, and my job is to try to get it for you."

Horst Klingerman stared at the speakerphone. He looked at Helga. Helga grimaced. Horst shrugged.

"I . . . I . . . do not understand . . ." he said.

Despite Eddie's visceral dislike for Leonard Isaacs and what he stood for, which as far as he could see was exactly nothing, he had to admire the way the agent was handling this situation. The son of a bitch was such a slick chameleon, such a *handler*, that Eddie allowed himself to hope that Isaacs *could* somehow talk their way out of it. Klingerman still had his hand inside his vest, but somehow something had shifted, somehow Isaacs had managed to take charge.

"Look, this is *Leonard Isaacs* you're talking to, so let's cut the crap. You can't tell *me* you seriously believe that the government of the United States is going to ban automobiles, slap an embargo on half the countries in the world, and invade Brazil to just keep you from killing three hostages and blowing up a piece of real estate which is probably overinsured anyway. Can you?"

Horst looked at Helga. Helga looked at Horst.

"Well?"

Kelly looked at the two of them. Nobody spoke.

"I'm waiting. . . ."

"A bloody fookin' good question!" Nigel finally said.

"Right," Isaacs said, "you can't seriously expect even Leonard

Isaacs to negotiate the end of the great American love affair with
the automobile and an invasion of Brazil in the next eight hours. So
come on, cut to the chase already, what's your *real* bottom line?"

Dead silence.

"You don't really know, do you? You haven't thought it
through."

"He's right, Horst," Kelly finally said.

"Now is the time for a bloody fookin' futile gesture, that's it,
innit, like the fookin' stupid IRA!"

"People, people, please!" Isaacs shouted. "Look, what we're
dealing with here is an *image* problem—"

"Enough of this Hollywood blather!" Helga shouted.

"Not enough at all!" Isaacs bellowed in a voice that Eddie
hadn't heard before.

It wasn't louder than Helga's, it wasn't a matter of shouting
her down, but there was something in it, some subsonic undertone
of command, that suddenly established yet another Leonard Isaacs
personality.

And if there *was* an inner Leonard Isaacs, Eddie was certain
that this had to be it. Because this was a voice that assumed its own
utter authority, the voice of the most powerful agent in Los Angeles, the voice of a man accustomed to intimidating studio heads and
White House staffs, and in no mood to take lip from mere terrorists.

The Voice, Eddie had heard it called once, in great big capital
letters.

"Now you listen to me, and you don't interrupt until I'm
quite finished," Isaacs went on in that preternatural voice of command. "You're in no position to pontificate about *Hollywood
blather*. You didn't take four people and a building hostage. You
took *television* hostage. It's been a media war, an instapoll war, a
ratings war, an *image* war, from the git-go. You want me to tell you
what you *really* want me to negotiate for you, Klingerman?"

"I am sure you are going to tell me. . . ."

"You want a way for this movie to end without you looking
like either a slavering monster or a prize schmuck."

A long moment of stunned silence.

"If you kill three innocent people in the act of some futile
gesture, your instapoll rating for whatever you think you'll be trying

to prove will be about that of Heinrich Himmler at a Hadassah meeting. If you wimp out and surrender after thumping your chest in front of a hundred million people like King Kong, you turn yourself and your cause into a public putz."

Isaacs paused for a beat. "You shot your mouth off about this car ban and Brazilian invasion stuff when you thought you would have the Vice-President in your hip pocket, but now that you don't, you're trapped in your own script with no way out."

Isaacs paused again, then spoke much more softly. "How am I doing, Horst? Any questions or comments?"

Horst Klingerman stared fixedly at the speakerphone. He didn't remove his hand from the inside of his vest, but it seemed to Eddie that Leonard Isaacs had him totally under his spell.

"You . . . you . . . are doing well, Isaacs," he stammered.

"Now would you like me to tell you what you really want?" Isaacs said seductively.

Horst's lips trembled, but nothing came out.

"You put on this TV show to mold public consciousness," Isaacs said. "And tonight is the last episode. And you've written yourself into a hole where it ends in either tragedy or farce. Horst Klingerman, crazed killer, or Horst Klingerman, pussy."

The quiet in the cafeteria was total. Nobody moved. It seemed to Eddie that he could count the dust motes moving in slow motion through the stuffy air.

"What you want is what we all want in our heart of hearts, to play the brave idealistic hero who inspires the multitudes. When we make the movie, you want them to walk out of the theaters afterward humming *your* tune. You want to be a legend. But that legend must not be hated, it must be admired. Emulated. Maybe even loved."

"Yes . . ." Horst muttered softly.

"*That's* what you want me to get for you, isn't it?" Isaacs crooned.

Klingerman nodded. It took him a beat to realize that the enormous presence of Leonard Isaacs was only a voice. "You can do this?" he said.

"I'll put some writers on it right away and get back to you this afternoon," Isaacs said.

"What!" Horst screamed. "You cannot be serious!"

"Don't you think there's been enough amateur night around here already?" Isaacs said.

"But—"

"I'm no writer, I'm an agent, Horst, I'm a deal maker. I identify the self-interest of my clients, I analyze the necessary elements, and then I structure a package. I can't act, I can't direct, and I can't write either, but then I don't have to, because I *am* the best there is at picking the winners among the people who *can*."

And somehow Leonard Isaacs had segued back into that other persona without Eddie really being able to identify where or when the transition had occurred, back into that somehow reassuring self-caricature he hid behind, the cartoon of the superagent that threatened no one.

And *this* guy had just finished saying he couldn't act!

"I'll get back to you when I've got something," that Leonard Isaacs said. "Trust me."

Even under the circumstances, Eddie almost cracked up at that one. Yet, he found that somehow he did.

3:49 P.M.

"CARL, YOU REALLY THINK we're going to get out of this alive?" Toby Inman found himself blurting for want of any better conversational gambit with which to break the latest long stretch of dead air.

Mendoza shrugged. "Why ask me?" he said.

"Because you know Coleman," Toby told him. "Because you've had experience with the CIA."

Carl smirked deprecatingly. "Just a cup of coffee, really, Toby," he said.

"But you've had combat experience."

"This ain't that. . . ."

"Do we really have to talk about this?" Eddie Franker groaned.

"Maybe we should talk about the Dodgers' pitching problems?" Toby snapped nervously. "Think the rain'll hurt the rhubarb?"

"There ain't been no rain for two months."

"No shit."

It had been going on like this ever since Leonard Isaacs' phone call. There they sat, with a strong possibility that these were their last few hours on Earth, and what were they doing?

Killing time with idle bullshit while . . . while they waited for their agent to call back.

Across the cafeteria, their captors didn't seem to be doing much better. Paulo and Jaro had relieved Warren and Ahmed as building-entrance guards. Ahmed had his weapon disassembled and was cleaning the thing. Beside him, Hiroshi seemed to have gone into some kind of trance. Warren had managed to doze off, Nigel was drumming his fingers to nonexistent music, and Malcolm appeared to be studying the cracks in the ceiling. Helga marched back and forth compulsively in front of the cafeteria entrance. Horst and Kelly both paced in circles in front of the speakerphone, staring at it as they moved, carefully avoiding eye contact with each other, making sure that their trajectories didn't intersect.

It was the same sort of atmosphere of endless boring tension that Toby remembered from hospital anterooms full of other fathers-to-be waiting nervously for their kids to be born, or, worse, like a dentist's waiting room in hell.

"You know," Toby said, trying to pump himself up, "I've got a feeling that Isaacs *is* going to talk us out of here somehow—"

"I know what you mean," Eddie Franker said. "The guy gives you the feeling that everyone else is sort of out of their depth—"

Toby practically jumped out of his seat when the phone rang.

So did Eddie and Carl. Helga, Horst, and Kelly raced to punch it in. Kelly won.

"Please hold for Leonard Isaacs. . . ."

About forty-five seconds of a lush orchestral version of "Billie Jean" . . .

"Well it hasn't been easy, let me tell you," Leonard Isaacs' voice said. "But we've got a package. Are you there, Horst?"

"I'm here, Isaacs . . . none of us have gone anywhere."

All the terrorists gathered in front of the speakerphone table. Toby got up, crossed the room, and stood right next to Kelly Jordan. Franker and Mendoza, he saw, were there beside him. None of the terrorists had made a move to stop them. None of them even seemed to notice the hostages were there.

"First of all, no hostage release, no TV coverage of whatever happens," Isaacs said. "They wouldn't budge on that, and frankly I didn't try to move them, because it wouldn't have been ethical conduct. I'd have a clear-cut conflict of interest negotiating anything that lets one of my clients in this package kill the others—"

"But this is only what was offered in the first place!" Horst whined in exactly the tone of voice of a client complaining to his agent.

Toby would have laughed if it weren't *his* life they were negotiating over like a cigar-chomping producer and a prima donna director.

"Hold your water, Horst, there's more. You've got to release the hostages, and you've got to let any of the Green Army Commandos who want to surrender walk out of the building too, that's your end—"

"This is *nothing*, Isaacs!" Klingerman shouted. "It's surrender!"

"Let . . . me . . . finish!" Isaacs shouted back in that eerily commanding voice he had used to shut Horst up before.

When silence was achieved, he switched right back into Hollywood agent-speak.

"As I was saying, Horst, that's what you gotta *give*. Now let me tell you what you get. We've got a half hour of prime time. It's got to open with the hostage release, but that's ten minutes max. The rest of it *is all yours*, Horst. A minimum twenty minutes of airtime and no commercials. A built-in audience of a hundred million people. We've got use of a mobile unit and a backup sat link. We can mike it. They'll even light it for us with the spots on those choppers! It's golden!"

"I . . . I do not understand . . ." Horst stammered.

"You don't understand?" Isaacs exclaimed. "You trade three live hostages and free passage out of there for the star of *The Green Army Commando Show* and her crew for *twenty uninterrupted minutes of national prime time*! With the whole world watching, I'm closing foreign coverage deals with BBC World Service, ZDF, CBC, Canal Plus, RAI Uno, and NHK right now, and maybe the Russians, if we're willing to swallow a ruble deal!"

"To . . . to . . . to do *what*?"

"Don't you get it, Horst? To do *anything you want*! I've gotten you *total creative control*!"

Toby could not believe his ears. Twenty minutes of worldwide prime-time exposure with a built-in rating like . . . the seventh game of the World Series . . . the Moon Landing. . . . To die for!

Certainly to get a piece of, old son! *Somebody*'s going to have to do the narration and the color, and there's only *one* experienced anchorman on the spot. . . .

Horst and Helga exchanged befuddled glances.

"Vas `. . . ?" Horst finally muttered. "Total creative control . . . ? This means what?"

"You want your message to *reach* people? You want *impact*? You want to move the world? Well, the whole world will be watching you for twenty full minutes, Horst. And in about eighteen months, you'll whack 'em *again* with a movie version featuring *your* twenty minutes as the climax, and a major star playing *you,* that will gross minimum three hundred million worldwide excluding video or I'll eat every last release print!"

Hiroshi and Ahmed exchanged dim uncomprehending glances. Kelly Jordan bounced up and down on the balls of her feet. Warren shook his head in wonderment. Nigel and Malcolm grinned like apes. Eddie Franker rolled his eyes toward the ceiling. Mendoza, strangely enough, looked as if he had just found a rat turd in his burrito. Toby began considering just when and how he could best point out that those twenty minutes needed a pro to anchor them.

Helga Mueller squinted at Klingerman.

Horst seemed to be finally getting the point.

"You mean . . . you are saying . . . I can repeat all our demands? The banning of American autos, the embargo against all nations producing ozone-destroying chemicals, the securing of the Amazon rain forest by an American naval task force . . . ? I can call for direct mass action? I can call on the American people to force their government to act?"

"You can call for the nuking of the whales or the resignation of the President or the repeal of the law of gravity! For twenty minutes, you are the proverbial eight-hundred-pound gorilla, Horst! You can say or do *anything* you want!"

"Anything?"

"Once those who want to leave have reached the police lines, *nothing you do* will allow them to pull the plug on the show. You could *drop your pants and expose yourself*, and they'd still have to air it, my lawyers have gotten that one engraved in stone!"

"But . . . but . . . I certainly do not wish to do that . . ." Horst mumbled. "So I repeat our demands . . . and then . . . and then . . . ? And then what happens . . . ?"

3:53 P.M.

''**You don't have any** hot ideas of your own . . . ?" Leonard Isaacs said, and it seemed to Eddie Franker that a certain furtiveness had leaked into his voice, an oily tinge of sleaze.

A moment or two of silence.

"Well, I *have* put some writers on it," Isaacs said in that same tone of voice. "And they've come up with three alternative climaxes. . . ."

Un-fucking-believable! Eddie thought.

"You can make your speech and surrender, I've got three different drafts of the dialogue, you want to hear them—"

"Out of the question!"

"Yeah, well to tell you the truth, they all *do* read pretty damn lame, so I guess we can agree to shitcan it."

Isaacs paused. "Version two is a lot more dramatic," he said. "You make your speech, and uh, they move in, you, ah, stand your ground heroically, and the whole thing ends in a firefight—"

"Jesus H. Christ!" Eddie groaned in appalled astonishment.

"Is there a hole somewhere for me to get sick in?" Carl muttered.

"—which is a nice action climax, and will look real good in the movie version, but makes the wrong thematic point."

"Thematic point . . . ?" Horst stammered.

"You're gonna use this golden opportunity to make some extreme demands, demands that will call for a lot of heavy-duty sacrifice, particularly on the part of the American people, right?"

"Yes, yes, but—"

"And you want to persuade that huge TV audience that those sacrifices *must* be made or life on Earth dies. And you want to make them lean on their government hard enough to get it done. Are you with me? Have I got it?"

"Yes! Yes!" Horst exclaimed excitedly. "That is it exactly! That was the ultimate purpose of this action! To inspire mass direct action! To start the Green Revolution in a manner that will make it ongoing and self-sustaining!"

"What can I tell you, Horst, not even Shakespeare could write dialogue with that impact, even if the speech was delivered by a major star, which, let's be frank, you ain't," Isaacs said. "You need a cinematic moment that makes you an instant legend. A moment of heroic self-sacrifice with visual impact. Like that Chinese kid stepping in front of the tank, like Davy Crockett fighting to the end at the Alamo, like Kirk Douglas in *Spartacus*—"

"Yes! Yes, Isaacs! You *do* understand! That is it exactly! It must be a moment of direct action! A deed, not another beerhall speech! Like the march into the Opera Platz in Leipzig! The first hammer blow against the Wall! Like the revolt of the Potemkin sailors! An act of genuine revolutionary courage in full sight of the world to ignite a real Green Revolution!"

Horst's eyes glowed a nuclear blue. Ahmed had a strange faraway look. Hiroshi's mouth was set in a line of grim determination, his head nodding slowly up and down.

To Eddie's surprise, even Helga Mueller seemed to have developed a certain limelight glow, even *she* seemed to be falling under Leonard Isaacs' Hollywood spell.

"Well, a shootout might be a satisfying action climax for braindead morons, but if you kill anyone you become the heavy and blow the whole thematic point," Isaacs said. "You can see *that*, can't you?"

Helga and Horst exchanged narrow glances.

"*Anyone* should be able to understand that!" Kelly said.

"Fookin' A!"

"Look, Horst, maybe you think you looked like a wimp when you couldn't pull that trigger," Kelly babbled a bit frenetically, "but hey, it made you look good, like a terrorist with a heart of gold. The audience is ready to be sympathetic to the next thing you say, but if you kill anyone afterward, you turn whatever you've said into shit."

"She's dead right, Horst," Isaacs said. "I had a lot of people on this, and none of them put it any better."

"Perhaps you are all right," Horst finally admitted. "But then—"

"Now I can't in all conscience tell you to do this, Horst, you understand," Isaacs oozed, his voice almost squirming. "I mean, I'm your agent, and I've gotten you these twenty minutes, and I've gotten you total creative control, and I've helped you understand what you want to accomplish with them, and I've put some really good writers on this, and this is the best they could come up with, and, professionally speaking, I believe it would work, but you understand this is *your* decision to make, I know this is going to sound a little extreme, but—"

"God in heaven, Isaacs, spit it out!"

"It all takes place at the main entrance. I've gotten approval for everything just in case you do want to go for this, the authorities will cooperate, you understand, I mean. . . ."

"Say it, will you!"

"The hostages emerge first, they walk down the steps, the camera holds on them until they reach the barricades, then Toby Inman turns around and narrates the rest of the sequence—"

—beside Eddie, Inman let out an enormous sigh—

"—then *you* emerge from the building into close-up, followed by the rest of the Green Army Commandos. You say some good-bye-to-the-troops words, then the Commandos who are surrendering walk out of the shot. All except Kelly, who stands beside you while you make the big speech. Then the two of you have a few lines, passing the torch of the Green Revolution over to her show, a final comradely good-bye. The camera follows Kelly offstage. The helicopter gunships lift off, pin you in their spotlights, kind of drift toward you, you have a final line or two. . . ."

Isaacs paused, whether for dramatic effect or because even he had trouble getting it out, Eddie could not tell, but he had an awful gut-churning flash-forward to what was inevitably coming.

"Well?" demanded Horst.

"And then you strike the heroic pose that becomes the sig-

nature image for the movie and the show and everything the
Green Army Commandos stand for, and then you blow yourself
up."

Although Eddie had sensed it coming the moment before, it
was like being bonged on the head by a mallet.

Everyone else, who apparently had not, froze in absolutely
dead stunned silence.

Everyone but Leonard Isaacs.

"I'm your agent, Horst, not your guru, not your shrink," he
said. "This is your decision to make. I'm not competent to advise
you any further. My job is to make the best deal possible for you
and explain your options. And those twenty golden minutes in exchange for a hostage release is the best deal you can get. You decide
what to do with them. I've gotten you the best writers in town, and
this is what they've come up with. You come up with anything you
like better, no blame, go with it."

Horst Klingerman's eyes blinked rapidly. Helga Mueller goggled at him. Ahmed's eyes narrowed, and, consciously or not, he
took two steps backwards away from them.

Hiroshi seemed dreamy and far away. "Mishima . . ." he
muttered. "Victory by seppuku . . . way of Bushido. . . ."

"I suppose you could look at it this way," Leonard Isaacs
blathered, "you refuse to surrender, and they storm the building
with *no* TV coverage, you take the blame for the bloodbath, and
you die anyway. . . ."

At least this way, you're still in show business! Eddie Franker
thought mordantly, but mercifully not even Leonard Isaacs was
Hollywood creature enough to drop *that* punch line.

But as Eddie scanned the faces of the terrorists—Kelly, Nigel,
Malcolm, and Warren, numb with disbelief; Helga and Horst already being sucked fatalistically into the inevitability of this dreadful
movie, Hiroshi already living in a samurai fantasy, Ahmed inching
away from this trio—he knew that Isaacs didn't have to.

At that moment, Eddie Franker knew he would live. Every
newshound's instinct told him so. Not only would he live, he would
make enough money on his share of this ghoulish film to tell his
bosses to take this job and shove it. And retire. Or take some zilch-
paying job on a newspaper in some little burg and enjoy his declin-
ing years as a grandfatherly city-room cynic.

He was going to make out. He was going to get out. He had even stopped smoking somewhere along the way.

But Eddie Franker's elated relief was soured by disgust. And anger. And a sympathy for his poor pathetic captors that had nothing to do with the so-called Stockholm Syndrome.

They'd need a new name for *this* one.

The Hollywood Syndrome was the only choice.

Still in show business?

These poor naive bastards had put themselves in it from day one, from the first day they had taken the media hostage. Or thought they had. They never really had a chance. And now they really had no choice.

Now, inevitably, it had all come full circle round.

The media held the terrorists hostage.

5:25 P.M.

CARL MENDOZA HAD CERTAINLY seen more than enough of his share of cynical shit in Nam and Guatemala. He had seen Agency deals with drug barons who sold smack to American troops. He had seen heroin shipped back to the States in dead bodies. He had seen a bit of the triangle trade in arms, coke, and drug money. Torture. Hooch-burning. Cold-blood assassination. Ear-taking. He had seen, and heard of, and done more than enough to want well out of it.

He was certainly no innocent.

But *this* was enough to make a cokehead Central American secret-police chief puke.

There beside him sat Toby fucking Inman, all but creaming in his jeans in anticipation of his glorious piece of the disgusting action, and there sat Eddie Franker, who at least had the grace to look properly nauseated.

And there across the room sat Horst, Helga, and Hiroshi, all by themselves, already long gone into that death trance that Carl knew all too well.

Carl didn't know much about this Bushido stuff, hara-kiri and swords in the gut and samurai movies, and all. He knew a little bit more about Vietnamese self-immolations, having seen it himself.

But he knew more than he had ever wanted to know about that look he saw on those three living corpses now. *That* he had seen all too often in Nam, *that* he had even tasted the edges of once or twice himself.

Sometimes a grunt got it into his head that his number was up. That there was a bullet out there with his tag on it and no way he could escape. Sometimes there was a mission you couldn't get out of where the chances of survival were slim and none. Sometimes you found yourself in a firefight against odds you knew were impossible.

There was a state some people got into in such circumstances. They knew they were going to die. They accepted it, or anyway psyched themselves into believing that they did. And they used it. It could make them incredibly strong. Incredibly brave, or incredibly crazy, as if there was any difference.

The Medal of Honor trance.

Carl could see quite clearly that Horst, Helga, and Hiroshi were entering that twilight zone now. In combat, you stayed as far away from people with that look as you could, muchacho. Unless, of course, you were *already* in deep dark shit and looking for a savior.

But this wasn't Nam, and this wasn't a combat situation.

These poor fuckers had been psyched into it.

Horst Klingerman would believe he was doing it to save the planet, Hiroshi in the name of honor, and Helga Mueller out of some kind of crazy revolutionary principle.

But these people weren't going to die to save the planet or the platoon or to win the war. They were going to die just because people who were smarter and more ruthless and a whole lot more cynical than they could ever be had mind-fucked them into believing they had to do it to look good on TV.

To look good on TV.

Carl couldn't see any other reason. To look good on TV. He remembered seeing a kid on a stretcher, with everything south of his belt blown to hamburger, mugging into some fucking TV camera and answering questions for the reporter until he died looking good on TV.

Carl just didn't get it, and he hoped he never would. He would rather grow old as what he was, a washed-up old ballplayer reading the scores with no burning desire to be anything else left to him, than be like any of these people who cared so much about looking good on TV.

That wasn't such a really bad thing to be, was it? Most of the kids he grew up with, most of the guys he knew in Nam, would be real happy to have a job like his.

He knew, as the only one in here who had seen this thing before, he really *should* go over there and take a shot at talking some sense to these assholes. But he knew he wouldn't. It had never worked in Nam. When people got that stare, they were dead already. They were death just waiting to happen. You wrote them off and you stood clear.

Then, just for the briefest of moments, Horst Klingerman caught Carl looking at him, and their eyes met.

And Carl knew then that there was a part of him that didn't really want to try. Not just because Klingerman's death would be buying him his own life but because of what he saw in Horst Klingerman's eyes.

The look was there, just as he had seen in Nam, the death stare, the sense that this man had accepted it as inevitable and was preparing to act it out in the jungle.

But it *wasn't* the look of that kid on the stretcher dying cooperatively for the camera; whatever all this was about for Horst Klingerman, it wasn't about looking good on television.

He had a reason for wanting to look good on television that he believed was good enough to die for. Carl had known people like that in Nam too, true-blue patriots fighting freedom's war against godless atheistic Communism, and of course he himself had interrogated VC prisoners often enough who had this very look in their eyes.

For a moment, he envied what he saw in Horst Klingerman's eyes a little. Those were hero's eyes. Crazy with purity. Stoned on glory.

Envy it?

Hell no!

Carl had certainly never wanted to turn into one of these

dickhead Perfect Warriors himself. He had never believed in anything with the crazy Azteca certainty it took to put that loco look in a man's eyes.

But at least for the duration of this brief eye contact with Horst Klingerman, he found himself able to admire someone who did.

8:01 P.M.

TOBY INMAN TOOK A deep breath, pushed the door open, and stepped out of the air-conditioned dimness of the building lobby and into a blinding white light, a blast-furnace heat, a choking smog. It was like stepping out of an elevator in the Beverly Center and finding yourself on Venus.

In the shock of it all, Toby was only dimly aware of Eddie Franker and Carl Mendoza slowly descending the steps behind him, of Malcolm backing down in front of them with the camera and mike. . . .

He had told himself he would be ready. He had rehearsed this moment over and over again inside his head. But nothing could have prepared him for *this*.

After eight days in an air-conditioned seventy degrees and constant 40 percent humidity, the heat, the desiccating chemical dryness of the naked Los Angeles smog, were devastating to his nasal passages, his lungs, his sinuses. It was like being plunged headfirst into a steaming pool of chlorine.

The spotlight that tracked him seared his tearing eyes with the continuous brilliance of a million flashbulbs going off at once. And continuing to explode. He could see nothing but the light and vague shapes behind.

Toby brushed his streaming eyes with the back of his hand. He took a deep breath of air that tasted like toasted laundry detergent. He stared blinking into the bright white light.

Welcome to the center ring of the media circus, Inman.

This is it, old son, this is what you've always wanted. Your chance to prove you're a little more than just another pretty talking head.

Choked by the smog, blinded by the light, enervated by the heat, Toby Inman forced his eyes wide open by an act of will, met the steely eye of the camera with a professional smile, and began to speak.

8:03 P.M.

Onscreen:

A SHAKY HAND-HELD head-and-shoulders shot on Toby Inman, walking toward the camera inside a bright circle of light, a spot moving with him that whites out the background, that makes him squint and blink like an owl caught by the sun.

"Uh . . . ladies and gentlemen, this is Toby Inman, here at KLAX-TV Los Angeles, and what a moment this is, as we are released from our long eight days of captivity. . . ."

Cut to a long telephoto shot from another angle on three figures walking across the KLAX parking lot toward the camera, Toby Inman tracked by the bright spotlight, two shadowy figures in the penumbra behind him.

Toby Inman's voice-over: "This is an incredible feeling, folks! This is the first time I've breathed the open air or seen the sky in eight days, and it doesn't seem quite real, it doesn't seem like this nightmare can really be over for me . . . for the three of us . . . for station manager Edward Franker, sportscaster Carl Mendoza, and myself. . . ."

The spotlight widens to include Mendoza and Franker. Carl Mendoza squints against the hard light, seems somewhat dazed. Eddie Franker is squinting too, but the curl of his lip gives it the look of narrow-eyed cynicism, an expression that would seem rather strange under these circumstances.

The three of them walk silently toward the camera for several beats, a fourth figure hovering on the edge of visibility outside the spotlight circle, then passing through the edge of it for a moment as it cuts across their paths from left to right, circles around behind them, a man in a black leather jacket with a Mohawk crest carrying a videocamera. . . .

Cut to a hand-held shot from behind Inman, Mendoza, and Franker, a fairly tight shot on just the three of them walking away from the camera in a circle of light. Although the camera doesn't move, the angle slowly widens as they recede from it, as they become smaller, and smaller, revealing the source of the light, a bright beam emanating from a shadowy shape in the right background, that solarizes the shot for a beat, whites it out.

The shot blurs as the camera moves rapidly and jerkily to the right, and when it clears, the source of the spotlight is out of the shot, and the camera is moving forward slowly as the three walking figures recede before it.

The camera moves forward faster and faster now until it catches up to the three walking men from behind, moves into the spotlight between Mendoza and Franker, shoots past Toby Inman's shoulder, simulating his viewpoint:

A line of troops, their automatic weapons at port arms. Behind them, half a dozen Hummers, their Gatling rocket carousels pointed toward the camera and upward, the shapes of soldiers vaguely visible on the truck beds. In the center of the line of Hummers, a KLAX-TV mobile-unit van, sat dish on the roof behind the cameraman, long shotgun mike aimed downward.

In front of the troops, just to the left of the center of the shot, stands a tall, heavyset, loose-boned man with an unruly shock of thick salt-and-pepper hair wearing khaki fatigues with no insignia and slackly holding a bullhorn.

Toby Inman's voice-over: "We're nearing the barricade now, we're only a few steps away from safety and freedom, from a peaceful end to our long ordeal. . . ."

Cut to a long shot from behind the line of standing soldiers and above them on Toby Inman, Carl Mendoza, and Edward Franker walking toward the camera in the spotlight, toward the civilian, as the man with the hand-held camera backs out of the spot and disappears into the darkness back toward the building.

The camera moves in closer as Inman, Mendoza, and Franker approach him, as the man with the bullhorn moves forward two steps to greet them.

"Coleman?" Toby Inman says.

The heavyset man in fatigues nods, holds out his hand. The camera moves in for a tighter shot on just the two of them as Toby Inman takes it, just the back of Coleman's head visible.

"This is Alex Coleman, ladies and gentlemen, the . . ." Toby Inman hesitates for a beat, seems to be looking toward Coleman for some kind of cue. ". . . the government crisis negotiator who has been instrumental in peacefully freeing us from captivity. On behalf of Edward Franker, Carl Mendoza, myself, and Heather Blake too, I want to thank you from the bottom of our hearts for all you've done, Alex."

"Uh . . . just doin' my job, ol' buddy," Coleman mutters uncomfortably, not turning to face the camera as he delivers the line.

Toby Inman drops Coleman's hand, takes a step backward. Edward Franker takes a step forward, shakes Coleman's hand briskly.

"Considering the alternative, I'm pleased to meet you, Alex," he says somewhat sardonically. He shrugs. "No, really," he says in another voice, "you did what you had to, and it was a real professional piece of work."

"Takes one to know one, Eddie, one old pro to another."

Edward Franker smirks, nods at something he sees on Coleman's face, gives way to Carl Mendoza.

Carl Mendoza smiles when he shakes Coleman's hand, but there is something forced about it, something hooded about his eyes, and this time it is Coleman who speaks first.

"Pleased t'finally meet you, Mendoza," he says.

"Yeah, Coleman, but strangely enough, I feel I've already known you a long, long time. . . ."

Alex Coleman's face is still hidden from the camera, but he hesitates for some reason as Mendoza gives him a deadpan stare.

"Kinda . . . *spooky,* ain't it, Fireball?" he finally says.

And now Mendoza cracks a real smile, he even laughs.

"Five by five, my man," he says, "five by five."

Toby Inman's voice-over, somewhat dramatically breathless: "I see there's activity now up at the building entrance!"

A hand-held shot from a low angle, up the steps of the main entrance on the doorway, where Horst Klingerman has emerged, blinking and squinting, into a bright white circle of light.

Toby Inman's voice-over, somewhat hushed, the color commentator behind the tee: "That's Horst Klingerman, Chairperson of the Green Army Commandos, ladies and gentlemen. . . ."

Horst stands there alone for a beat, his Uzi hanging from his left hand, his right hand inside his bulky vest.

Toby Inman's voice-over: "Inside that vest Horst Klingerman is wearing, in addition to powerful explosive charges, are remote detonator switches which allow him to set off even more powerful explosive devices positioned throughout the facilities of KLAX-TV. . . ."

Two more terrorists wearing explosive vests, a man and a woman, emerge from the building into the spotlight and flank Klingerman on the landing, a step behind him. The woman holds her Uzi at port arms. The man has his still slung over his right shoulder, grips the strap.

Toby Inman's voice-over: "Helga Mueller and Hiroshi Igaramu, two of the most militant of the Green Army Commandos. . . ."

Helga Mueller seems determined to glare down the spotlight. Hiroshi Igaramu seems to be using it as a meditative mandala. Klingerman blinks rapidly, clearing his eyes, narrows them against the cruel glare as the camera moves in for a close-up.

Toby Inman's voice-over: "Let's just listen to this now, I think Horst Klingerman is about to speak. . . ."

"I . . . I am not good at making speeches . . . in your language. But in my own language, the truth of it is that I had done little else but talk while the planet died around me until. . . . But now . . . but now the talking is over. The time has come to act. There is no choice. Each of us must find this moment for himself. Some people find the courage to do so and some do not. You do not know which you are until the moment arrives . . . until you look into . . ."

His voice is clear, but his cadence is becoming choppy and frenetic, and he frowns, as if realizing he's starting to babble.

"So . . . so now we see who the real Green Army Commandos are. Now the café philosophers and television personalities come to the parting of the ways with . . . with those whose dedication to the Green Revolution transcends egoistic narcissism. . . ."

The three terrorists standing in the doorway, but from another angle than the previous such shot, the perspective flattened, the colors somewhat washed—a full shot through a very long telephoto lens.

One by one, more terrorists emerge from the building to stand behind Helga Mueller and Hiroshi Igaramu, blinking in the spotlight, fanning out across the landing.

A thin reedy man with shoulder-length blond hair depending from a balding crown, bleering nerdishly through wire-rim glasses.

Toby Inman's voice-over: "Warren Davies, who has been in effect technical director of broadcast operations for KLAX during the Green Army Commando takeover. . . ."

A stockier man, well-built, straight black hair, high cheekbones, looking straight ahead expressionlessly.

Toby Inman's voice-over: "Jaro Olgar, his assistant. . . ."

A beefy-faced man in a black leather jacket festooned with chrome doodads, a crest of bright red spikes running down the center of his shaved head, scowling theatrically.

Toby Inman's voice-over: "Nigel Edwards, one of the Green Army Commando cameramen."

A moment's hesitation. No one else emerges from the building. Nigel Edwards motions with his hand, and another punker in black leather and chrome gear trots up the stairs and into the shot, this one carrying a videocamera.

Toby Inman's voice-over: "Malcolm Macklin, the other Green Army Commando cameraman."

Macklin moves into position beside Edwards, points his camera in the general direction of Horst Klingerman, but without looking into the viewfinder, using the camera's mike as an audio pickup.

For a few beats they all stand there in the spotlight, staring vacantly into the camera, for all the world like a small-town high-school senior class posing woodenly for their graduation picture.

Finally, Horst Klingerman turns to face them, his face hidden from the camera as he speaks.

"Warren, Jaro, Nigel, Malcolm . . . perhaps you are not . . . samurai of the Green Revolution, but yes, you are Green Army Commandos too, you were recruited to . . . to . . . present ourselves to . . . to . . . all you people out there, to . . . to do the technical work, yes, you have carried out your part of the mission successfully, and . . . and more cannot be asked of you, so . . . there is no blame if you leave. . . ."

Klingerman's face is hidden, Hiroshi Igaramu's is totally impassive, but Helga Mueller's contemptuous snarl is all too visible.

Warren Davies, Jaro Olgar, and Nigel Edwards unsling their weapons, lay them down on the landing. They wriggle out of their explosive vests and place them by their guns.

One by one, they troop past Horst Klingerman, Helga Mueller, and Hiroshi Igaramu, sliding past them and down the steps without making eye contact.

Hiroshi Igaramu shows no reaction, but Helga Mueller flips the whole group a sarcastic salute of contempt.

The last to leave is Malcolm Macklin, carrying the videocamera. He places the camera on the landing behind Klingerman, says something the camera mike doesn't pick up, detaches the microphone. Horst slings his weapon. Macklin hands the mike to Horst, walks down the stairs.

Only Klingerman, Igaramu, and Mueller remain in the shot now, Horst with his back still to the camera, looking into the doorway behind him, holding the hand-mike limply, as if it were a dead fish.

Just this for a couple of beats, and then two more terrorists emerge from the doorway side by side. One is short, stocky, coppery-skinned, with Indian features. The other is taller, leaner, black-haired, olive-skinned.

Toby Inman's voice-over: "That's Paulo Pereido and Ahmed Jihad, the last of the Green Army Commandos. Under the arrangement between the Green Army Commandos and the authorities, personally negotiated on the air before your eyes by the Vice-President of the United States, all the Commandos who wish to are allowed to surrender peacefully, but there's been some doubt about what Paulo and Ahmed will choose to do. . . ."

Paulo Pereido and Ahmed Jihad stand on the landing for several long beats. They look at Klingerman. Horst's face is still hidden, his emotions and expression unreadable by the camera, but one can guess them from Pereido's and Jihad's hesitant, hangdog looks as they break eye contact with him, look down for a beat.

Then they try to make eye contact with Hiroshi Igaramu, but he acts as if they were not there. Or as if he isn't.

When they look at Helga Mueller, it turns into a grim-faced staring contest for a few more beats.

Then Ahmed Jihad shrugs, unslings his weapon, drops it on the landing, slips out of his explosive vest, tosses it aside. Helga snarls something the mike in Klingerman's hand doesn't pick up. Jihad says something back. Helga looks away. Paulo Pereido drops his gun, wriggles out of his vest.

Horst Klingerman turns to face the camera as Ahmed Jihad and Paulo Pereido lope rather slump-shouldered down the stairs and out of the shot. The camera moves in for a medium close-up on Klingerman as he raises the microphone somewhat awkwardly to his mouth. His expression is grim but composed, shaken perhaps, but seemingly devoid of anger.

"Our . . . our . . . our comrades having chosen to surrender under terms offered by the government of the United States. . . . This . . . this leaves only Hiroshi Igaramu, Helga Mueller, and myself to . . . to . . . to complete our mission. . . ."

Klingerman starts at something behind him, half turns as the camera pulls back hastily to reveal a young black woman in sharply tailored fatigues and vest, stepping out of the shadowy doorway and into the bright white circle.

Toby Inman's voice-over: "That's Kelly Jordan, of course, folks, the Green Army Commando's Minister of Information, and the star of the forthcoming *Green Army Commando Show,* which StarNet will be bringing you at seven-thirty every Thursday night, ten-thirty in the East, right here on KLAX-TV. . . ."

Kelly Jordan looks like a TV star and moves like one. Her short Afro is carefully combed, her uniform unwrinkled. She moves gracefully, almost in slo-mo, as she goes to Klingerman's side, her right hand on the strap of her slung Uzi somehow turning it into a prop, her eyes conveying the impression that she is gazing sincerely and intently at Horst and the camera at the same time.

"So, Kelly . . ."

They stand there awkwardly for a long silent moment, looking into each other's eyes, Horst holding the microphone between them.

"So, Horst, I just want you to know that I admire what you're doing," Kelly Jordan says. "I've learned a lot from you. And I want the folks out there to know that . . . that . . ."

Her voice breaks with what seems like genuine emotion.

". . . that every week when I'm out there doing what little I can to save life on Earth, when I'm sitting out there talking to all those people, I'll be remembering the example you set for us all, for me, for all our fellow Green Army Commandos of the spirit, and for the peoples of the Earth. . . ."

"That is very touching, Kelly," Klingerman snaps. "Really it is."

"Hey, Horst—"

"No, really, Kelly," Horst Klingerman says in a much softer voice. "We are who we are. We fight how we can. We do what we must."

Kelly Jordan reaches up, brushes the back of her left hand across her eyes, wiping away tears, perhaps. Or perhaps it is choreographed, a deliberate dramatic gesture.

"I'll stay with you a little longer then," she says, and she takes a full step to the rear, into the background, as the camera moves in tighter for a head-and-shoulders shot on Horst Klingerman, centered in the spotlight, with Kelly Jordan's somewhat shadowed face floating behind his left shoulder, staring resolutely ahead into the camera like the proud little wife of the candidate.

It all almost looks as if they're being moved around by a director, but Horst Klingerman's line doesn't seem to come from the same script as he glances backward and snaps it off at her.

"You could stay till the very end if you had the courage, Kelly!"

"I would if I could, Horst. . . ."

"But you can't, of course. The show must go on, as they say here in Hollywood."

Horst Klingerman turns to face the camera again, the microphone held a bit too close to his mouth, his voice a bit harsh and fuzzy.

"Perhaps this is not such a bad thing. When we took direct action to seize this television station, all we hoped for was to hold it long enough to begin the Green Revolution. We knew we couldn't liberate it permanently. And yet, now, in some strange way, in some small way, perhaps we have. . . . This Green Army Commando television show, it must be a good thing, yes, it will reach the masses, and so will the stupid movie they will make of us, the

T-shirts, yes, the berets, the cheap plastic toys, the chewing gum.
. . . Maybe even these endless souvenir items are good things too,
they will remind people of what they are about to see, and it must
be better for children to play at being Green Army Commandos
than at being soldiers and hunters and cowboys killing Indians, yes,
even if it *is* all trivialized to make money for the same people who
make the automobiles and the nuclear power plants and chop down
the rain forests. . . ."

He sighs, he shrugs, he mops sweat from his brow with the
back of the hand holding the microphone.

"I have learned much of such things these past days, I have
learned more than I want to know. . . . And . . . and I would
hope that you have learned things too. Things that will not be forgotten. Things you must not be permitted to forget. . . ."

He pauses, frowns, visibly struggling to find the words.

"You are not bad people, but you are committing a crime
greater than anything dreamed of by Hitler or Stalin. They merely
sought to exterminate whole peoples. You are killing life on Earth
itself. And you cannot claim not to know it. You are told this all the
time on television, so you know it must be true. Now there will be a
Green Army Commando television show, and a Green Army Commando movie, and Green Army Commando toys and videogames,
all designed to make money by tricking you and your children into
believing that by buying them you become 'honorary Green Army
Commandos' and your conscience is clean. . . ."

The camera moves in for a slightly tighter close-up on Horst
Klingerman as he lowers the microphone slightly, clarifying his
voice, probably without knowing what he is doing, and for the first
time there is naked anger in his eyes.

"But this is bullshit, that is the word you Americans have for it,
is it not?" he says. "As long as your country has the power to save
this planet and fails to use it, your conscience can never be clean.
You will be nothing but bullshit Green Army Commandos watching bullshit television and buying bullshit products until the whole
world chokes to death on the revolting results!"

The camera pulls back as if stunned by this into a wider shot,
Horst Klingerman centered in the spotlight and flanked by Helga
Mueller and Hiroshi Igaramu, with Kelly Jordan's shadowy face
floating behind his left shoulder like some kind of video ghost.

"Someone must show you the way," Klingerman shouts. "Someone must awaken your conscience! Someone must choose death over surrender!"

Then, as if realizing he has begun to rave, Klingerman seems to calm himself by act of will, lower his voice, soften its tone somewhat, and, as if in acknowledgment of this, the camera moves back into a close-up.

"There are only three of us," he says in a flat cold voice. "But we will not surrender to your government. We will prove that this is not a movie. We will show you what is real."

The camera pulls back into a two-shot on Horst Klingerman and Kelly Jordan as he turns to face her.

Toby Inman's voice-over, very hushed indeed, as if narrating a twenty-foot putt for the title: "Horst Klingerman has threatened to use his remote detonator switches to destroy the KLAX building and everyone who chooses to remain by it, folks, and it looks as if we're about to see whether he's actually going to go through with it. . . ."

Kelly Jordan steps forward, lays a hand on his shoulder. "Horst. . . ."

Horst Klingerman does not pull away from her touch, but his body language still seems to distance him from her.

"Horst, this is nuts, man, this is crazy, this is—"

"This is a necessary action, Kelly," he says in a steady voice. "In years to come, you will understand this." He forces a rather bizarre sickly smile. "And of course, it will be excellent publicity for *The Green Army Commando Show*."

The line seems to wound her, she winces. "Horst, please—"

Klingerman touches her cheek rather gently with his free hand. He lowers the microphone to waist level, says something it doesn't pick up.

Kelly Jordan kisses him on the cheek, begins to walk down the stairs and out of the shot.

But the camera begins to pan with her, and the spotlight tracks with her too as she descends the stairs and strides slowly across the darkness of the parking lot toward it, pulling back gradually as it does so that she becomes a tiny figure in silhouette crossing a black void, a moth caught in the circle of limelight.

A black screen for half a beat. Then the spotlight pins Horst

Klingerman in a medium shot, Hiroshi Igaramu and Helga Mueller just visible beside him.

Klingerman's face is beatific, and somehow terrifying for it.

"We repeat our demands. The United States must embargo all nations producing ozone-destroying chemicals. The United States must ban all automobiles. The United States must dispatch a naval task force to the Amazon River to protect the rain forest. These are our terms for leaving this building. Your government must meet them, or take it by force."

The camera begins to inch back almost imperceptibly.

"As for the plutonium in the explosives, the truth, of course, is that there is not any, and it wouldn't matter if there was," Klingerman says. "We will not detonate the main charges. We will sacrifice no one's life but our own. But that we will do at the first movement forward of government forces."

Horst Klingerman seems to almost smile.

"Thus the act will be pure," he says. "Your government will kill us to recoup private property rather than agree to do what we all know is right. And we will die to save life on Earth. And you will now watch what is done in your name."

Now the camera has pulled back into a full shot on Horst Klingerman, Helga Mueller, and Hiroshi Igaramu, standing on the top of the steps in the darkness, illumined by the spotlight.

Horst Klingerman slips his hand inside his vest.

"Our conscience is clean, our final act is pure," he says, his smile serene, his eyes radiant. "Will you be able to say the same?"

The camera reverse-zooms abruptly into a full shot on the entrance of the building from across the entire expanse of the parking lot, centered on three tiny figures in a circle of light at the top of the stairs, three tiny figures in the everlasting darkness, as—

—a thrumming, drumming, whirring thunder, as two darkly ominous shapes arise into the foreground of the shot, the beam of light pinning the terrorists rising from the one on the right as they do, two ponderous helicopter gunships lifting off the concrete, their rockets and Gatling guns hanging heavily from their curving stub-wing pylons like overripe fruit from the branches of groaning trees, as they drone forward like monstrous metal wasps at less than the pace of a walking man—

Toby Inman's voice-over: "You're really seeing this, people, this is happening as you watch it, only here on KLAX-TV—"

The camera zooms in suddenly on Horst Klingerman, Hiroshi Igaramu, Helga Mueller, framed in the bright white spotlight as its angle rises, illumining their faces like a fast-motion sunrise.

Helga and Hiroshi cross their weapons on their chests. Horst Klingerman blinks, rolls his eyes upward, looks back into the camera.

A flare in the lens, a trick of perspective, a random moment of confluence between the angle of the moving spotlight and the camera eye, halos his face in a blast of brilliant white light as he stands there, the centerpiece of a perfect movie poster, a moment that will live forever in cinematic legend, a golden piece of random special effects that no budget could buy, though no doubt many will try.

A blast of light.

A roar of thunder that rolls into silence.

Toby Inman's voice-over: "Dramatic end to hostage crisis! Green Army Commandos die in fiery blast! More pictures at eleven . . . right here, on . . . on KLAX-TV, roll a goddamn commercial, will you!"

Fade to black.

ABOUT THE AUTHOR

NORMAN SPINRAD is the internationally acclaimed author of sixteen novels including *Bug Jack Barron, The Iron Dream, Little Heroes,* and *Russian Spring* that have been translated into more than a dozen languages. He is also the author of numerous short stories and screenplays, is a political commentator, literary critic, and an occasional songwriter. Spinrad currently resides in Paris.